Night Flying

TAB
PRACTICAL
FLYING SERIES

Night Flying

Richard F. Haines
& Courtney Flatau

**Foreword by John K. Lauber, member,
National Transportation Safety Board**

TAB Books
Division of McGraw-Hill, Inc.
New York   San Francisco   Washington, D.C.   Auckland   Bogotá
Caracas   Lisbon   London   Madrid   Mexico City   Milan
Montreal   New Delhi   San Juan   Singapore
Sydney   Tokyo   Toronto

FIRST EDITION
THIRD PRINTING

© 1992 by **TAB Books**.
TAB Books is a division of McGraw-Hill, Inc.

Library of Congress Cataloging-in-Publication Data

Haines, Richard F., 1937-
    Night flying / by Richard F. Haines and Courtney Flatau.
        p.   cm.
    Includes index.
    ISBN 0-8306-3780-X   ISBN 0-8306-3773-7 (pbk.)
    1. Night flying. I. Flatau, Courtney. II. Title.
TL711.N5H35   1992
629.132′5214—dc20   92-11303
                                              CIP

Acquisitions Editor: Jeff Worsinger
Director of Production: Katherine G. Brown
Book Design: Jacklyn J. Boone   PFS
Cover photo: Thompson Photography, Baltimore, Md.   4098

Contents

Foreword

I will never forget my first night flight. I was just learning to fly, the location was a small grass strip in northwestern Ohio, and the aircraft was a mighty 65 horsepower Aeronca 7AC Champ. Although it wasn't really night, it had gotten dark enough that street lights and house lights were on, and most automobile drivers had switched on their headlights. The weather was crystal-clear, and even from pattern altitude, I could see for what seemed like forever. I thought it was a scene of incredible beauty, and at some point during that flight, what had been deep infatuation with airplanes and the magic of flight was transformed into true love.

Even now, more than 30 years later, when I'm in an airplane at night as either a passenger or a pilot, I often think back to that wonderful experience.

Flying at night is different. Piloting at night is different. This book is about those differences. But it is also about fundamental issues that affect every flight and every pilot, day or night. The chapters on human factors contain useful and important information for all pilots, including those unfortunate ones whose experience is limited to daytime flying. It is well known that human error is the largest single cause of incidents and accidents in aviation. A good understanding of some of the fundamental principles, and limitations, of human performance should be a part of every pilot's arsenal.

Similarly, much of the information contained in the chapters on flight procedures and techniques applies to flight in general, not just night flight, and also should be required knowledge for all pilots. Being a safe pilot requires much more than good piloting skills. Understanding the machinery and mechanics of flight is important, but of equal importance is an understanding of the flyer. This book is about both flight and the flyer, and should go a long way towards making good pilots safe pilots, day or night.

JOHN K. LAUBER
Member
National Transportation Safety Board
Washington, D.C.

Acknowledgments

This book could not have been prepared without the published work of many gifted and dedicated researchers who have provided a wealth of knowledge in the field of human factors and also of those pilots who have shared their valuable experiences in articles and books that deal with night flight. We are also very grateful to Arthur M. Olsen and William B. Sasnett, Jr. for their expert editorial assistance; to Delores M. Kelley for her faithful and dedicated technical and secretarial support; to Cynthia L. Haines for her valuable typing skills; and to James M. Rachetto for outstanding analytical and technical support in a variety of areas presented here. We are also indebted to Jeff Worsinger, aviation acquisitions editor of TAB Books, a division of McGraw-Hill, Inc., for patiently waiting for years for completion of this book. Finally, we are deeply indebted to David A. Faust, graphic artist and computer-manipulator extraordinaire who converted our simple concept sketches into obviously superior and much clearer renderings.

In addition, the following professionals in government, academic, and private enterprises have given generous and unselfish assistance. Even though their talents and knowledge are in heavy demand, these leading authorities in their respective fields gave us uncountable hours of their time. We indeed are indebted to each one.

Malcolm M. Cohen, Ph.D., Chief, Neurosciences Branch
Ames Research Center-NASA, Moffett Field, California.

William E. Collins, Ph.D., Acting Director
Civil Aeromedical Institute, FAA, Oklahoma City, Oklahoma.

ACKNOWLEDGMENTS

Major Penny M. Giovanetti, USAF, Chief, Aeromedical Services,
Victorville, California

R. Curtis Graeber, Ph.D., Boeing Airplane Company,
Seattle, Washington

James L. Harris, Manager, Aeromedical Education Branch, FAA Aeronautical Center, Civil Aeromedical Institute
Oklahoma City, Oklahoma

Sandra G. Hart, Chief, Rotorcraft Human Factors Research Branch,
Ames Research Center-NASA,
Moffett Field, California

A. Howard Hasbrook, expert in aviation crash injury research, survival studies, and crash safety design,
Prescott, Arizona

Phyllis Kayton, Ph.D., Investigator,
National Transportation Safety Board, Washington, D.C.

Conrad L. Kraft, Ph.D., Engineering Psychologist,
Bellevue, Washington

John K. Lauber, Ph.D.
National Transportation Safety Board, Washington, D.C.

Hershel W. Leibowitz, Ph.D., Evan Pugh Professor of Psychology,
The Pennsylvania State University, University Park, Pennsylvania

Saul M. Luria, Ph.D., Naval Submarine Medical Research Laboratory
Naval Submarine Base New London, Groton, Connecticut

Henry W. Mertins, Ph.D., Supervisor of Workload and Performance Section,
FAA Civil Aeromedical Institute, Oklahoma City, Oklahoma

Merrill M. Mitler, Ph.D., Senior Staff Scientist
Sleep Disorders Center, Scripps Medical Clinic, Inc.
La Jolla, California

Stanley R. Mohler, M.D., Professor and Vice Chairman, Director of Aerospace Medicine, Wright State University School of Medicine,
Dayton, Ohio

Captain William Price, United Air Lines
Redwood City, California

Loren Rosenthal, Manager, Project Office
Aviation Safety Reporting System, Battelle Institute
Mountain View, California

Donald E. Schein, Supervisor, Information Management Section
FAA Aviation Standards National Field Office
Oklahoma City, Oklahoma

James B. Sheehy, Ph.D., Vision Laboratory
Naval Air Development Center, USN
Warminister, Pennsylvania

Thomas J. Tredici, M.D., School of Optometry, USAF
School of Aerospace Medicine, Brooks AFB, Texas

Daniel J. Weintraub, Ph.D., Human Performance Center
University of Michigan, Ann Arbor, Michigan

Laurence R. Young, Ph.D., Professor of Aeronautics and Astronautics, Director of
Man-Vehicle Laboratory,
Massachusetts Institute of Technology, Cambridge, Massachusetts

Introduction

The purpose of this book is to save lives through the dissemination of the information relative to the most advanced night flying techniques and supporting scientific data. Hopefully, as one of many benefits of studying this book, the readers will become familiar with the common reasons why some pilots create their own emergency situations during what should be routine night flights.

This text offers something for all pilots—students through professionals. Although professional pilots already might be aware of many subjects contained in this text, they might not know much about the latest findings in human factors research. Studies in human factors deal with how people perceive, process, and control complex systems. The perceptual basis of many night visual illusions is described here as are circadian desynchronization, simple in-flight muscular exercises, and many other topics special to night flying. All readers will learn some professional secrets and other bits of pilot wisdom.

Until now, there has not been adequate information relative to the major aspects of night flight readily available in one definitive source. During the course of conducting research for this text hundreds of reports, scientific research papers, and aviation handbooks were reviewed. In none of these works was there a significant treatment of the practical issue of flying at night. Obviously, several important subject areas needed additional research and amplification.

This book should have a shelf-life of many years because it presents principles and laws that are not likely to change but that are inherently applicable to night flying. One fact that has been overlooked too often is that piloting an aircraft at night is much more demanding than piloting an aircraft during the day. Almost every aspect of piloting activity becomes more difficult and complex with reduced lighting during the nighttime hours. Consider, for example, cockpit references, takeoffs, navigation, landings, coping with emergencies, and gauging the position and speeds of other air traffic. There is little argument that the safety factor for some operations is reduced significantly during periods of darkness and anyone who pilots an aircraft at night must exercise more caution than during normal day VFR flight.

The authors of this book have varied and different backgrounds. As a result, the objective of this work has been approached by working in synergistic unison from three different perspectives: pilot, engineer, and research scientist.

During the early years through present day, night flying has been slow in developing. This is partly due to the lack of the necessity and desire for nighttime flying and the relatively slow development of nighttime-related technology during aviation's infancy. Today, it is due to the lack of a thorough understanding and implementation of the latest in human factors research. Indeed, the area of human factors research concerning nighttime flying activities is just now coming to the forefront of aviation research.

Some might argue that aviation has come a very long way since the early years. Gone are the days when pilots crossed the United States by navigating using the stars, road maps, bon fires, and airway beacons, then landing with the use of car headlights or smudge pots illuminating the runway. In many respects, nocturnal piloting activities have developed considerably.

The greatest advances in night flying during previous years have been technological in nature; however, today's advances not only incorporate the latest technology but are also incorporating the latest in human factors research. This is evident in modern cockpit design, instrumentation, and piloting procedures.

Unfortunately, mankind has not developed as rapidly as has his hardware. Over the course of millions of years the human body has become primarily adapted for daytime activity. Consider, for example, sleep-wake cycles and the structure of the human eye, neither of which have changed for the past 10,000 years. Today's nighttime aviation problems concern not only aviation hardware but also the human factor. Without any doubt the human factor is the most difficult aspect of all nighttime flying activities to contend with.

Until now, nighttime human factors research from the scientific community has not been distributed to the aviation community in a form that lends itself to rapid pilot adaptation. This book is primarily intended to help bridge that broad gap between the pilot and the aircraft.

Federal Aviation Regulations (FARs) play an important part in night flying. Those regulations applicable to night flying are presented in the appendix.

This book presents a vast array of valuable information that is related to night flying. Its primary objective is to lay out these human factors in a way that can be put to practical use.

If incident and accident rates should fall as a result of this book, our grandest expectations will have been met.

RICHARD F. HAINES
COURTNEY L. FLATAU

1
Overview

THE WIDELY HELD MISCONCEPTION THAT FLYING AT NIGHT IS LITTLE different than flying during the day is not only false, it is dangerous. Every pilot who intends to fly at night safely should read carefully and take positive action to implement the many suggestions that are given.

THE HUMAN FACTOR

Figure 1-1 portrays the three primary subjects that are presented in this book: pilot, airplane, and nighttime. It is the ubiquitous human factor that links all three, much like the invisible lines that the mind seems to extend from corner to corner to corner in this illustration. Exactly what is the human factor?

Human factors include all of the subtle and obvious capabilities and limitations of human beings. Human factors engineering is the application of this detailed knowledge gained from such fields as perception, physiology, cognition, psychology, and other fields of behavioral science to the optimization of the operator-machine interface, normal and abnormal operational procedures, training, and maintenance. Its two primary goals are to improve the effectiveness of the system being operated and promote the well-being of the operator.

The human factors of night flying have been largely overlooked to date in aviation books. *Night Flying* attempts to correct this deficiency. The human factor must take into account the many differences between day and nighttime flying in planning and conducting a flight. It does so through the careful integration of both past aviation experience and up-to-date scientific knowledge. The human factor is the essential link

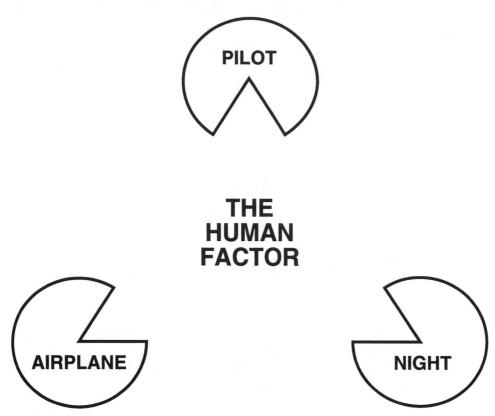

Fig. 1-1. *The human factor.*

between the pilot and his or her airplane and the aviation human factors specialist seeks to improve all aspects of flight safety in the air and on the ground. Finally, the human factor, applied through human factors engineering theory and practice in the laboratory and shop, also links the airplane with the night sky. It does so through knowledge of how one affects the other, not in a purely aerodynamic sense but from the standpoint of how a pilot actually handles the airplane at night. Performance margins are slightly different at night and the pilot must somehow take these differences into account.

EARLY YEARS

Nighttime aviation was slow in its development compared to other areas of aviation during the early years. The first powered aircraft night flight took place several years after the Wright brothers first flight. Even after numerous night flights had been completed successfully, night flying was generally thought to be impractical and was employed primarily as a means for emergency missions until approximately 1920. This prevailing attitude maintained by the early aviators was promoted by the fact that their flying machines were primitive in design, not designed for nighttime operations, and quite unreliable (it was a very good flight if an aviator did not have a mishap even during a daylight flight). Additionally, ground lighted landmarks were sparse, and very few aerodromes had any lighting aids that would facilitate safe landings.

Runway lighting generally consisted of the use of the headlights of cars, torches, and smudge pots. The night navigational references primarily consisted of city lights, bon fires, the stars when they could be seen, and very few light beacons until the government established a lighted network of airways. (Pilots had no maps designed exclusively for aerial navigation.)

The federal government did much to foster night flight during the 1920s when a transcontinental airway system was established using an airway beacon network consisting of blinkers and beacons equally spaced three miles apart. The early aviators were then able to determine their location and the distance to their next checkpoint with reasonable accuracy. With the advent of this new navigational development coupled with basic runway lighting and dramatically improved aircraft reliability, in less than one decade, pilot fatalities per mile decreased by a factor of more than 20 times. Still, much development was needed to increase the practicality of nighttime piloting activities during aviation's early years.

Some of aviation's great pioneers set sterling examples for others to follow. Charles Lindbergh was one man who regularly demonstrated how consistently safe takeoffs, landing, and other night operations could be executed. Jimmy Doolittle also encouraged the public, the government, and the aviation community to fly during the night with his great accomplishments, such as his record setting flight on September 4, 1922. In a De Havilland DH-4, with the aid of little more than Rand McNally road maps, aviator Doolittle piloted his aircraft from Pablo Beach, Florida, to Rockwell Field in San Diego, California, in a total time of 22 hours and 30 minutes. Even though milestones were continually passed, wide-scale fear and ignorance of flying after dark prevailed for decades after the first night flight.

ONE BASIC TRUTH

Upon initial mental review, one would think that piloting an aircraft during nighttime hours would not be much different from daylight operations; however, nighttime piloting activity is not as simple as climbing in and going. When a pilot is at the controls of an airplane during hours of darkness, a radically different set of parameters come into play.

Most pilots with any flying experience intuitively know night flying holds more risk than comparable daytime flying. Such basic concerns as accidentally running into bad weather, experiencing electrical failure, visual navigation, and engine failure are obviously more hazardous during hours of darkness.

Obviously, every pilot must be more aware of his or her own aeronautical strengths and limitations. In knowing those limitations, more caution must be exercised and much more attention given to every detail in the preflight preparation and planning stages of flight.

Nighttime flying activities can further be divided into two categories: night-dark operations and night-moonlight bright operations. The significance? Most accidents occur during dark, moonless nights. A pilot is several times more likely to have an accident on a dark night as compared to a bright night. These facts provide quite illuminating evidence that night flying is at least an intermediate step toward instrument flying. When the moon illuminates the terrain, flying an airplane at night is, in many respects, similar to daytime flying; however, when there is a new moon, an overcast sky, or a seemingly starless night, a pilot must refer to the aircraft instrument panel. Some type of attitude reference becomes necessary when encountering a pitch black environment.

There is much yet to be learned about nighttime flight operations. Not surprisingly, accidents are not unique among the low-time general aviation pilots, but are also not uncommon among high-time military and airline pilots.

Such psychological and physiological factors as night vision, visual incapacitation, circadian rhythms, microsleep, short-term memory loss, and subtle incapacitation have led to a much more sophisticated set of nighttime cockpit procedures, in some respects, vastly different from those procedures used for daytime VFR flight.

The basic truth about piloting an airplane during the night is that flying an airplane during periods of darkness is more complex than the normal demands of piloting an airplane during periods of daylight. Some additional skills are required for nighttime flying.

LACK OF KNOWLEDGE CAN BREED
A NIGHTMARE OF CONSEQUENCES

A pilot once said "I like to fly late at night because there is hardly any traffic. . . not much going on. . . I just climb out, level her out, kick back and enjoy the night."

Many pilots have been equipped with that perspective of night flying and, as a result, all too often have encountered some unpleasant surprises. Lack of knowledge certainly can falsely elevate a pilot's level of self-confidence that can contribute to complacency. Too often pilots launch off without proper preflight preparation or pilot proficiency. The result? Some pilots have become totally disoriented over their home airport! Other pilots have experienced vertigo on cloudy and dark nights when low visibility or ceilings obscure the horizon. Still other pilots have encountered problems on clear bright moonlight nights when ground lighting and the stars seem to blend together, making the natural horizon very difficult or impossible to discern. And, of course, many pilots have perished. The results of complacency, inexperience, and lack of proficiency are as varied as the pilots who fly during nighttime hours.

DARKNESS CAN AMPLIFY PILOT DEFICIENCIES

The body doesn't function at peak efficiency during nighttime hours. Many of the body's senses seem dull at night in comparison to daytime hours. Consider the following: The human body has developed over aeons with a sleep-wake cycle that is primarily suited for daytime activity.

The human anatomy is also designed to function during the daylight hours. The eye is an excellent example of this fact. As discussed in chapter 4, pilots can see much better during the day versus the night. As a result, the pilot's physical condition might have a more pronounced effect at night than during the daytime. Pilot procedures often take longer to accomplish at night as compared to day and simple mistakes can be made more easily and regularly.

Today, research scientists are discovering that there is much more to night flying than was initially thought decades ago. Their conclusion is that the darkness does amplify pilot deficiencies.

COMMONLY OVERLOOKED ASPECTS

An airplane's utility increases with nighttime operations. It is impractical and unrealistic to restrict flying activity to daylight operations. Night flying becomes a necessity during those months when there are fewer daylight hours and in order to complete a trip in a single day, flying typically begins during the predawn hours and concludes the trip after sunset.

Night flying is an excellent introduction to instrument flying because darkness, naturally, demands more reliance on aircraft instrumentation. Instructional flying at night offers the student an opportunity to work with the air traffic control (ATC) system in a more friendly environment. The ATC facilities are generally not as busy and, as a result, training flights are more apt to receive better and less hasty handling.

Accidents most often result from a series of mistakes and not a single error. The conclusion that should be derived? The night pilot of tomorrow must be better equipped to meet all of the challenges he or she faces in the cockpit through better flight training and a more thorough understanding of all of the variables relating to the human factor in night flying.

The simplest of procedures when executed during periods of darkness can become troublesome. If anything should go awry, even something that would be inconsequential during daytime piloting, an acceleration of several nasty and potentially disastrous consequences can happen. For example, if a pilot should accidentally drop a chart on the floor of the cockpit during a daylight operation it is generally not too difficult to glance down to see where the chart fell, reach for the chart and then resume normal exterior and interior scan; however, at night, this simple daylight exercise might become far more difficult.

With generally poor cockpit lighting, and because the human eye is not as efficient in a dark environment, the chart becomes more difficult to see and more time is spent looking for the chart. After the chart has been retrieved more time is needed first to refocus the eyes on the instrument panel and outside visual references and second to mentally process the new data regarding the situation of the aircraft. If the pilot is lucky, he or she will not experience vertigo or spatial disorientation during this time.

It is easy to understand that low workloads during the day can become high workloads at night for any one of a number of reasons. A pilot who is quite proficient in daylight flying might become overwhelmed at night during what should be a low workload procedure. Lack of proficiency in nighttime flying can contribute to the magnitude of difficulty of a certain cockpit task, which in turn can contribute to information overload. There is also the possibility that some pilots will deny that a problem even exists at night, perhaps due to the fact that there is less visual information with which to confirm the existence of the problem.

Tomorrow's night flight training will be much more thorough as compared to yesterday's. Not only will future flight training deal with the old basics of takeoffs, approaches, and landings, but there will be much more time and emphasis given to dealing with the human factor aspects of nocturnal aviation. Such areas of training as information management, cockpit resource management, and nighttime physiology will become more pronounced as further research becomes available.

Because the human body will not noticeably change or evolve in the near future, much of the research and resulting design carried out in the years ahead will center around the human limitations that are encountered during night flight. Human factors research will continue to contribute further to the safety of night flight. New aircraft systems, lighting systems, cockpit layout design, and nighttime piloting procedures will come about through new discoveries as a result of this relatively young frontier of research. It is hoped that this book will help foster this necessary and important trend.

MOST REWARDING FLYING

Night flying can be a wonderful experience. The beauty of a full moon shining down on a layer of clouds is a spectacular sight for any pilot who views it from the cockpit of an airplane flying high above that layer of clouds. To see lightning suddenly illuminate the inside of a cumulonimbus cloud in the distance or just to see the reflected moonlight on rivers, lakes, and streams can be an exhilarating experience. The lights of large cities are also exciting for any pilot, no matter how experienced that pilot might be or how often those cities lights might be seen. Every night flight provides new visual feasts of nature's works of art.

The air is generally much smoother at night than during the day, especially during the hot summer months. Depending upon the geographic area, there is usually much less traffic resulting in fewer delays in the metro areas, and fuel savings. The airplane performs better in the cooler night air. During periods of good visibility, cities, airports, highways, and other lighted landmarks can be seen at far greater distances than during daylight hours. Indeed, it is very easy for experienced pilots to become quite relaxed in the cockpit at night.

Flying at night need not be risky if the pilot is qualified and the airplane is airworthy for its intended mission. With adequate knowledge, preparation, proficiency, and respect for the task at hand, night flying can be a safe and pleasurable experience.

PART 1

Night flying:
The human factor

2
Pilot health can affect flight safety

GOOD PILOT HEALTH IS THE BYPRODUCT OF UNDERSTANDING HOW TO BE healthy. Numerous signs signal when the body is getting out of shape and, just as the experienced pilot knows when an airplane is running rough, he should also recognize the telltale signs of reduced medical airworthiness.

IMPORTANCE OF GOOD GENERAL HEALTH

Are you medically airworthy? This relatively new concept has introduced us to the importance of being as fully trained to be aware of the physiological factors of safe flight as we are trained for piloting and decision-making skills. The term *medical airworthiness* has been defined as "any condition of flight that affects a pilot's ability to fly safely. It's any factor that could either incapacitate a pilot or, at the very least, erode his skills and judgment, even if only for a brief moment." (Reinhart 1989). A night pilot's medical fitness to fly is far more than just being healthy. It relates to his judgment skills, his experience level and self-confidence, and a myriad of other factors that are discussed later. The assumption is often made that if the pilot feels all right and has a currently valid medical certificate, he must be safe for flying. This is not necessarily so.

The night pilot should be in as good general health as possible in order to cope with all of the situations he might confront during night flying. The following factors are important at any time one flies, however at night they become even more important.

Paragraph 1422 of the Airman's Certificate of the Federal Aviation Act of 1958 specifically states that you are "physically able to perform the duties pertaining to, the position for which the airman certificate is sought." A subsequent court decision in Day vs. the National Transportation Safety Board (NTSB) (1969; CA5) 414 F2d 950 ruled that the statement "is physically able" must be interpreted to mean "is free from significant physical risks." It is the pilot's responsibility to ensure that one is free from significant physical risks. The night pilot must be in good overall health; some should be interested in an audio tape program titled "Flying Fit," which contains useful tips on how to prepare for a Federal Aviation Administration (FAA) flight physical, exercises performed in the cockpit, and other useful information. (EN 2-1)

The following factors are symptoms that can indicate health is changing, be on the lookout for them:

- Sleeping problems
- Chronic fatigue
- Gastric disturbances
- Shortness of breath
- Appetite changes
- Vision changes
- Reduced eye-hand coordination or muscle tremor
- High blood pressure
- Body weight change (more than 10 percent when not dieting)

AGE RELATED BODY CHANGES

It is important to accept the fact that age brings with it many body changes that can influence performance during night flying. Yet in spite of these changes it is also known that experience, motivation, and wisdom can either mask or totally overcome some of them. Among the most important changes for the pilot are those that affect eyesight, visual perception, hearing, neuromuscular coordination, and thinking capability.

"On the average, visual functions of older workers differ significantly from those of younger workers," according to a report published by the National Research Council's Working Group on Aging Workers and Visual Impairment (Anon 1987). The more significant visual changes related to night flying are discussed in this chapter. The researchers go on to point out that about 25 million Americans are 65 and older, a figure that will double in 25 years.

Some night pilots might not be aware of the fact that as one gets older, the body changes in many subtle ways. Some of these changes are more significant than are others and can lead to reduced capability to cope with normal situations and some stressors that occur in the cockpit. TABLE 2-1 presents an abbreviated list of such age-related changes.

Despite this list of bodily and sensory changes that occur with increasing age, it is important to realize that "the past experiences that older people are able to draw on in the performance of certain tasks may overcome certain age defects in visual function.

Table 2-1. Age related body changes.

Pupil size decreases. At age 20 the pilot's pupillary area in the dark is about 10 times greater than when 50 years old*.

Range of eye focus is reduced in increasing amounts after age 30 (Simonelli, 1983).

The resting eye focus distance recedes along with the far point of vision beginning at about 40 years of age (Simonelli, 1983).

Visual acuity is reduced, typically in middle age. This impairs the ability to discriminate fine detail.

Color discrimination becomes more difficult (particularly telling blues from greens in dim illumination).

It takes longer to read under dim illumination conditions.

It is more difficult, and sometimes painful, to adapt to darker areas in the visual field from brighter areas. This is illustrated in FIG. 2-2 (adapted from Birren and Shock, 1950).

It takes longer to process visual information in general.

Sensitivity to glare increases to the extent that stray light from very bright light sources at night obscure vision.

Sleep becomes progressively disturbed in middle age. One experiences less restfulness with spontaneous leg movements and changes in breathing pattern.

Duration of sleep tends to decrease as shown in FIG. 2-1.

Ability to adapt readily to time zone passage in airplanes tends to decrease.

Auditory sensitivity is lost with advancing age with the higher frequencies being lost first (from 3500 to 8000 Hz). Airplane radios are more likely to operate at frequencies less than 3500 Hz, so these hearing losses are not particularly dangerous.

One becomes increasingly prone to certain diseases, such as arteriosclerosis, hypertension, and diabetes, all of which have visual consequences. (Anon 1987, 5).

One becomes fatigued sooner following the same amount of exertion.

* This progressive change in area significantly reduces the amount of light that can reach the retinal carpet of light-receptive nerve endings. The light adapted eye of a 20-year-old receives about six times more light than that of an 80-year-old while in the dark adapted state (chapter 4), the 20-year-old receives about 10 times more light. It is as though older persons are wearing medium density sun glasses in bright light and extremely dark glasses in very dim light.

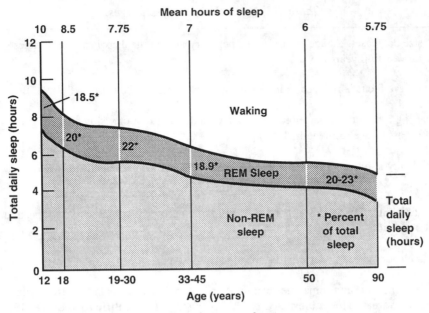

Fig. 2-1. *Sleep requirements as a function of age.* Copyright 1990 by the AAAS

Practice is the principal agent creating important skill differences between experienced and inexperienced workers. And the expertise that comes with practice is certainly among the older worker's strong suits." (Anon 1987).

Figure 2-1 shows changes in total amounts of rapid eye movement (REM) and nonrapid eye movement (NREM) sleep and percentage of sleep as a function of age (adapted from Roffwarg Muzio and Dement 1966, *Science*, 152, Pp. 604-619, Copyright 1990 by the AAAS).

Presbyopia (old eyes) refers to a loss of the range of the eye's lens focus, which usually requires wearing glasses. Age profile analyses of airline pilots shows that there will continue to be a large and permanent block of pilots in the age bracket that is affected by presbyopia, a basic fact that must be recognized by everyone seriously involved in air transport operations.

Figure 2-2 shows that older pilots take longer to achieve a given level of visual sensitivity in a dark environment. The vertical axis is presented in units of brightness where each tick mark represents a factor of 10 different from the adjacent marks. Notice that the top and bottom curves are separated by almost a factor of 10. Also note that the entire process requires as long as 25 to 30 minutes in darkness. The top one-third of each curved line represents the change in light sensitivity of the cone receptors that are sensitive to colors, while the lower two-thirds represents the change in sensitivity of the rod receptors that are sensitive to shades of gray.

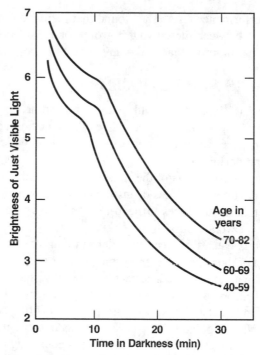

Fig. 2-2. *Rate of change of visual sensitivity over time as a function of age.*

ALLERGIES, MEDICATIONS, AND MOTION SICKNESS

If the pilot has any allergies for which he or she takes prescribed or nonprescribed medications, it is important to understand the possible side effects. One might experience drowsiness, sleepiness, or loss of the ability to concentrate. It is always a good idea to read the fine print on the label of the pill container before taking any drug, particularly the section labelled "contraindications." These are various adverse symptoms that might occur in some people as a result of taking the drug.

A variety of medications are available to reduce or prevent the symptoms of motion sickness, primarily nausea and *emesis* (vomiting). Scopolamine and dextroamphetamine are two such drugs. Scopolamine is associated with drowsiness, amnesia, fatigue, and memory impairment, also, some people experience restlessness or delirium; however, in normal (clinical) dosages, it is primarily a depressant for the central nervous system. This drug has been given together with dextroamphetamine (known as *scop- dex*) to help cope with motion sickness and space sickness associated with microgravity. Research by Schmedtje and coworkers (1988) administered 0.5 mg each of these two drugs to eight volunteer subjects in a double blind manner so that no one knew whether they were taking the placebo or the actual drug. They also administered a battery of performance tests. They found that there were no significant differences in performance between these two test groups on any of the performance tests. In short, this combination prophylactic therapy appears to be safe.

SLEEP DISORDERS AND DIFFICULTIES

One of the specific signs of ill health is that of sleeping disorders in which one either does not sleep long enough or sleeps irregularly during an eight-hour period. Sleep disorders can have many different causes, each of which can contribute to impaired night flying performance.

Disturbed sleep. Disruptions of the timing of sleep and wakefulness can result either in excessive daytime sleepiness or insomnia. Weitzman, Kripke, and Goldmacher (1970) found that disturbances to sleep result if one's sleep is shifted to a new time of day, which is several hours from its usual time.

There are various causes of sleep disorders in man and it is important to have some understanding of them. Persistent insomnia and/or excessive daytime sleepiness should be discussed with an aeromedical examiner because such symptoms might hide actual pathological problems. A report by the Advisory Group for Aerospace Research and Development (AGARD) on sleep and wakefulness for flight medical officers written by Nicholson and Stone (1987) points out that up to one-half to two-thirds of those people with chronic insomnia have no underlying psychiatric or personality disorders (depression). Some might be taking hypnotics (sleep-inducing drugs) or might be abusing alcohol.

Personal coping with new or stressful work, a change in surroundings, or nutritional changes can lead to disturbed sleep. Unfortunately, many aircrew face these circumstances as a part of daily life.

Both the amount and quality of sleep each day are important to the pilot. It has been found that sleep following a night shift usually contains less midsleep stage brain activity and also less rapid eye movement (REM) sleep and that the older the pilot gets, the less adequate (both physiologically and socially) he or she is in adjusting to a new work-rest cycle.

Transmeridian flights. For present purposes, a discussion of night transmeridian flights is important in regard to its effects on disturbing sleep patterns, the quality and quantity of sleep, desynchronization of one's biological rhythms, and various other secondary effects. For instance, in those pilots who fly from one continent to another, most complain of loss of appetite, tiredness, a general feeling of a loss of well-being, and of not being in tip-top condition. The effectiveness of the coping skills of these pilots plays an important role in permitting them to continue carrying out all required flight duties, day or night.

Body rhythm desynchronization can also lead to performance decrements at certain times of each 24-hour period; sleep difficulties ensue from the need to synchronize body rhythms to the new time zone.

Narcolepsy is a medical term that stands for excessive daytime sleep. It typically occurs between the ages of 15 and 25 years with some cases extending well into the 50s. Only one or two persons per thousand show evidence of narcolepsy. Associated with these sleep-related problems is sleep paralysis, *cataplexy* (a sudden loss of muscle tone), *hypnagogic hallucinations* (disturbed nighttime sleep with awakenings), and body movements. Narcolepsy often produces short periods (typically 10-15 minutes) of daytime sleep that can lead to dangerous situations in the cockpit.

Sleep apnoea refers to a temporary cessation of breathing and occurs most often in overweight males between the ages of 40 and 60 years. Most are heavy snorers. *Restless leg syndrome* occurs periodically (typically every 20 to 40 seconds during sleep) with episodes lasting from five minutes to two hours. Such limb twitches usually only disturb sleep.

Another rather rare sleeping condition is known as *parasomnia*. It can be characterized by sleep terrors, sleep drunkenness, and sleepwalking. They often occur during an arousal from a certain period of one's sleep (so-called *slow brain-wave* sleep).

FATIGUE

Normally, the human body functions as a coordinated unit so that when you are fatigued, there is seldom a single symptom. Fatigue is more often described as a constellation of feelings derived from the pilot's physiological and psychological systems.

Two basic types of fatigue are *acute* and *chronic*. Acute fatigue is the more mild of the two and usually results from inadequate rest and sleep, too much physical activity, disturbed physiological rhythms, prolonged and intense mental activity, or a combination of these factors. Chronic fatigue refers to the situation in which one feels tired and utterly worn out most or all of the time. This is not normal and if one feels this way it might be a warning sign that general health is changing or that you are not coping effectively with unconscious pressures.

Chronic fatigue often develops with acute fatigue if it is not relieved adequately. It should not be permitted to go on day to day. Chronic fatigue typically lasts into the leisure time of the day and might last through the sleep period so that one feels tired out upon going to work the next morning. Pilots who take off experiencing either kind of fatigue are at risk.

TABLE 2-2 presents some of the general symptoms of fatigue that night pilots should be on the lookout for before they go flying at night.

In considering the health and efficiency of flight personnel, McFarland (1953) devoted chapter 7 of a book to the operational aspects of fatigue and it remains as one of the most complete discussions of this complex subject for aviators. In his summary, he points out that fatigue is nonspecific in origin and very obscure in nature. The nervous system is subject to fatigue only under severe conditions of lack of oxygen or low blood sugar level.

A U.S. Army report by Duncan, Sanders, and Kimball (1980) presents a list of contributing factors to fatigue while flying. While some of these factors are more related to military missions, most are generic to all kinds of flying and should be

Table 2-2. Symptoms of fatigue.

Objective Symptoms (obvious to others)
    Absentmindedness
    Decreased startle response
    Degraded motor skills (inaccurate radio frequency tuning)
    Intolerance and irritability
    Mental confusion and fearfulness
    Overcriticalness
    Reduced short-term memory
    Reduced alertness (manifested by sloppy flying or a tendency to be easily distracted)
    Reduced level of initiative, lack of interest and drive
    Resentment toward others
    Significantly increased reaction time
    Stuttering (usually infrequent)
    Social withdrawal
    Tenseness and tremor
    Worried and anxious

Subjective Symptoms (only noticed by the fatigued pilot)
    Appetite loss
    Attentional narrowing or focussing
    Attentional fixation (halting or fragmented instrument scan)
    Breathing difficulties, palpitation, chest pain
    Burning urination
    Constipation
    Degraded visual perception
    Diarrhea
    Distractible
    Exhaustion (physical)
    Expanded tolerance limits (willingness to settle for less)
    Feelings of depression (often associated with unmotivated worries)
    Headaches
    Impaired mental judgment and decision-making
    Muscular aches and pains
    Visual impairment (blurred vision, double vision)

watched for, particularly at night. They are presented in TABLE 2-3 with those that pertain to night flying given first.

It is probably because the concept of fatigue is so difficult to measure, and even to define, that the National Transportation Safety Board does not classify it as an accident cause but more often only as a contributing factor. Because it is so insidious, fatigue can compromise a pilot's normally adequate capabilities so that he might not be able to meet the demands of even routine flight duties. Until fatigue can be mea-

Table 2-3. Selected factors contributing to fatigue.

Night flight (and night formation flight)
Lack of daily rest during daytime hours
Lack of sleep at night
Disruption of normal sleep/wake cycle due to irregular working hours
Limited visibility
Inadequate sleep and rest facilities
High number of takeoffs and landings
Airplane vibration and noise
Excessive radio "traffic"
Additional duties unrelated to flying
Instrument flying
Long or infrequent standby periods
Mental overload requiring high levels of alertness and information processing
Seat discomfort
Temperature variations
Bad weather, high winds, turbulence
Instrument pilot to student pilot ratio
Poor student pilot proficiency
Insufficient study and presentation time

(Partially adapted from Duncan, Sanders, and Kimball 1980).

sured accurately and counteracted in other ways, the risk it poses must be reduced by preventive measures. As John Lauber of the NTSB has written, "One of the most perplexing problems our accident investigators face is how to determine what role, if any, fatigue played in a specific accident. Unlike metal fatigue, human fatigue generally leaves no telltale signs, and we can only infer its presence from circumstantial evidence." (Lauber and Kayten 1988)

A review of 20,000 Aviation Safety Reporting System (ASRS) reports by Lyman and Orlady (1981) found that there is a small but significant number of cases showing fatigue-related performance decrements in those people engaged in aviation-related tasks. These performance decrements are thought to be related to awareness and attention loss due to disturbed sleep, in addition to long flight duty periods and a large number of flight segments.

In a study conducted by the National Institute for Occupational Safety and Health, two researchers tested workers' performance at a repetitive keyboard data entry task throughout a 12-hour day, five-day workweek followed by two days off. This work schedule is known as the *compressed workweek*. The typing work occupied just over 10 hours a day; testing continued for two weeks. This study found that performance declined steadily. The data "suggest that long workdays reduced motivation to perform carefully," remarked the researchers.

Flying at night has been listed as a contributor to pilot fatigue, according to a 1978 Air Line Pilots Association report. Other contributors included long hours, multiple landings, bad weather, delays, and time zone crossings. A U.S. Army survey of instructor pilots and student pilots found that nighttime tactics was the most fatiguing of six phases of training that were evaluated (Duncan, Sanders, and Kimball 1980), while daytime tactics was the least fatiguing. This was despite the fact that these pilots flew an average of 7.7 hours at night and 8.1 hours during the day per 24 hour period. When fatigue combines with nighttime, when one is more likely to be tired and ready for sleep, they can multiply in their end result.

As Golbey (1988a) correctly pointed out, "A pilot may manifest the symptoms of fatigue and not even feel tired." Generally, by the time fatigue is severe enough to be recognized, the pilot no longer is capable of recognition; he suffers from "an increased unawareness of performance deficiency," according to Richard Reinhart, an expert in aerospace medicine.

"There are clearly some serious deficiencies in our understanding and application of knowledge about sleep, circadian factors, and fatigue as they affect human operator performance in transportation systems—or for that matter, in any technologically complex system," according to Lauber and Kayten (1988). "The insidious nature of fatigue and its cumulative effect on flight safety require that . . . pilots work in an environment in which avoidable fatigue is minimized." (Golbey 1988a) The night pilot must try to find effective means of doing this.

GASTRIC DISTURBANCES

It is normal to have an upset stomach from time to time and to expect the feelings to go away in a day or so upon eating and drinking a balanced diet. And temporary stomach upset might be calmed with antacid tablets. But if one experiences gastric upset that lasts for a week or more it might point to a developing ulcer or other potentially serious physical problem. Unusual body pains are nature's way of saying that something is wrong. If these stomach pains persist, don't fly at all, particularly at night.

SHORTNESS OF BREATH AND RAPID BREATHING

Another sign of a general change in health is prolonged shortness of breath and rapid breathing when the pilot hasn't been exercising. While such symptoms might be no more than a temporary sign of anxiety at night, they might indicate a more serious change in health. The pilot should tell a physician about these symptoms.

CHANGES IN APPETITE AND BODY WEIGHT

As some people age, they tend to eat less food, while others tend to eat more, and these changes are often related to one's level of physical activity and metabolism. But when appetite or weight change suddenly without any apparent cause, it should make the pilot suspicious that a change of health might be taking place. Such changes are probably not as immediately critical to night flying as are other health symptoms. Nevertheless, the wise pilot will not overlook these changes.

OTHER HEALTH CHANGES

A pilot's health is one of his most precious assets. Because health undergirds almost everything else one does in life it makes sense to stay keenly aware of what constitutes one's good health and to take note as soon as possible when and if it changes.

ADEQUATE SLEEP AND EXERCISE

Day and night rhythms. Man experiences a repetitive and fairly regular sleep/wakefulness alternation that is synchronized primarily by the day-night cycles associated with the earth's rotation on its axis. Various *circadian* (circa, about; dia, one day) rhythm effects related to general aspects of performance are discussed elsewhere in this chapter. It is primarily the daily light-dark (day-night) cycle that acts to reset our biological activities once each cycle. Two cues in particular that are associated with these environmental events are light and temperature, both of which act to synchronize or *entrain* man's work schedules and sleep periods. Laboratory research has found that light is the single most powerful stimulus to human alertness. From the standpoint of flight at night, it should become obvious that humans are adapted to sleeping at night and when they must stay awake in order to fly at night there is a conflict. Humans are naturally less alert at night and might try to compensate by returning to the (normal) sleep state.

Of course social activities like work, meals, leisure, and the start and end of sleep also combine to reset our naturally oscillating biological rhythms.

If man is unable to adapt to a sudden shift of these external synchronizers he might experience a short-term desynchronosis of his circadian rhythm with that of his environment. Of course, flying across many time zones is one way of shifting them. Such relatively rapid biological phase shifting can lead to increased social conflict with others, impaired communications, impaired ease of going to sleep, reduced job accomplishment, and more.

Sleep loss can result in a rather wide variety of symptoms as shown in TABLE 2-4.

Table 2-4. Sleep loss and fatigue symptoms.

Reduced	Increased
short-term memory	fatigue
attention span	sleepiness
cooperativeness	irritability, anxiety, tension
susceptibility to criticism	tendency to insomnia
judgment capability	susceptibility to errors
	reaction time during decision-making
	development of certain sleep disorders

Night pilots should stay alert for the presence of any of them and take immediate action to reduce them.

There is an important difference between a single night of flying activity versus flying many consecutive nights. The key to understanding this difference lies in understanding the cumulative effects of sleep loss that can occur. Long haul trips extending two days or more in the same direction around the earth are often associated with difficulties sleeping. Another problem that is experienced is that the pilot can fall asleep for relatively long periods of time without realizing it. A pilot might not sleep as deeply and wakes up more easily at the slightest sound.

Some pilots have found that if they can't get to sleep, they just quit trying. This seems to help them overcome the mental anguish of lying there awake. Sometimes they soon fall asleep after giving up.

Maintaining a fixed rhythm. It should go without saying that man needs a relatively fixed schedule of sleep each 24 hours. If the night pilot takes off after a period of time during which he or she has had little or no sleep, or has slept irregularly, their awareness, perception, coordination, mental capacities, and other capabilities will be affected. This section briefly discusses these important subjects.

Fatigue results from insufficient rest, which can occur for many reasons. McAdams of the NTSB cited some reasons for getting insufficient rest in an article published in 1978: business events, personal problems (marital, alcohol, drug abuse), physical and mental disability that has been hidden or disguised, financial concern, and others.

There is research evidence to suggest that people who are accustomed to seven or eight hours of sleep each night have great difficulty in reducing their average sleep to five hours or less even when it is done gradually. If the pilot tries to reduce the total amount of sleep gradually, he or she can experience changes in mood, performance, and sleep parameters. (Johnson and McLeod 1973)

Acute (large) alterations in the amount of sleep the pilot gets leads to various performance decrements that are of importance to the night pilot, such as loss of the ability to detect visual targets or signals, significant decrement in vigilance, calculational tasks, and detrimental changes in subjective mood (Price and Holley 1982).

Sleep loss and task performance. It is known that most human task performance varies over the course of the 24-hour day. Performance has been found to rise during the daytime to a peak or plateau between noon and 11 p.m. and falls to a minimum between 3 a.m. and 6 a.m. Figure 2-3 (adapted from Klein et al., 1976) shows this effect for three different kinds of tasks carried out by 14 experienced military pilots in an F-104G flight training simulator. These data are from separate 24-minute flights where the pilot had to maintain 300 mph flying a circular pattern of 25 miles radius at 2,500 feet altitude with a 200 mph wind component that changed unexpectedly through 360 degrees two times per flight. The mean flight deviation refers to the change in performance from the 24-hour mean deviation from preset flight parameters. The smooth solid line (passing through open circles) represents the mean of the

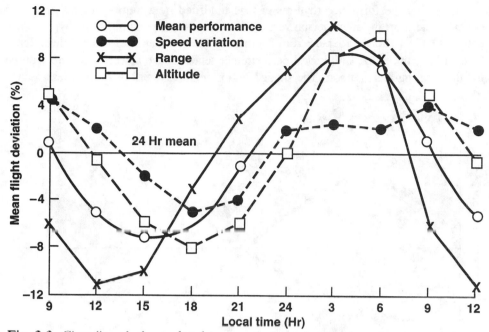

Fig. 2-3. *Circadian rhythms related to several of simulator flight tasks.* Klein, Aerospace Medical Association, 1976

three performance measures. Note that the bottom part of the graph represents best performance.

Neural processes that are thought to control sleep and alertness produce sleepiness and a reduced capability to function during the early morning hours from about 2 to about 7, and to a smaller degree from about 2 to 5 in the afternoon. Golbey (1988b) states in an article on this subject in AOPA *Pilot* magazine that performance errors in the airline cockpit tend to peak between 2 a.m. and 4 a.m. As might be expected, these effects are increased by sleep deprivation or disruption. He goes on to remark that, "inadequate sleep, even as little as one or two hours less than usual, can greatly exaggerate the tendency for error during the time zones of vulnerability. Moreover, sleep loss combined with periods of stress, such as is faced by working groups before production deadlines or launch deadlines, can lead to personality change and irrational behavior." (Golbey 1988b, 98)

If man stays awake "the phase of the rhythm tends to drift toward later hours and during the first night awake the range of oscillation is smaller." (Golbey 1988b, 26)

As sleep deprivation continues, the entire task performance curve will tend to drop toward worse performance. Such sleep loss seems to influence both uncertainty about the task's accomplishment and the response that is required.

Circadian performance rhythms can be modified by a number of factors. First consider the morning-alert person versus the evening-alert person. As the hypothetical data of FIG. 2-4 shows (adapted from Klein et al. 1976), peak performance level tends to shift later in the day and lowest performance tends to also shift later in the evening for the evening-alert person. The shaded region indicates periods of darkness.

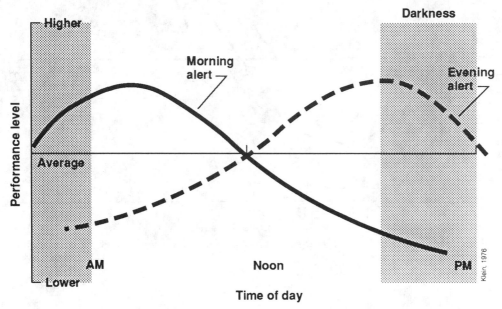

Fig. 2-4. *Hypothetical performance levels during the 24-hour period for the evening-alert and morning-alert person.*

Note the later maxima and minima of performance level. The range of oscillation is more likely to be lower. But what is likely to happen if the pilot cannot sleep? Figure 2-5 shows such hypothetical relationships suggested by Klein et al. (1976) related to normally rested and sleep deprived individuals.

Motivation is fundamentally the difference between what a pilot is capable of doing versus what he or she is willing to do. Clearly, motivation plays an important role in influencing one's performance level during each 24-hour period, as shown in FIG. 2-6. These data suggest that poorly motivated individuals will not only tend to show lower overall task performance scores than will people possessing higher motivation, but also that the size of the overall oscillation is likely to be less. There is evidence to show that performance errors will also tend to increase as motivation decreases. There are external sources of positive and negative motivation (the flight instructor's comments) and internal sources of positive motivation (the desire to obtain a private pilot license) and negative motivation (fatigue, sleepiness, poor health).

What triggers sleep and what makes it regular? Physical activity, in general, and regularly performed exercise, in particular, can also modify performance capabil-

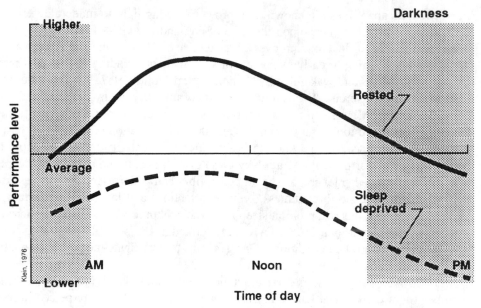

Fig. 2-5. *Hypothetical performance levels for rested and sleep-deprived individuals.*

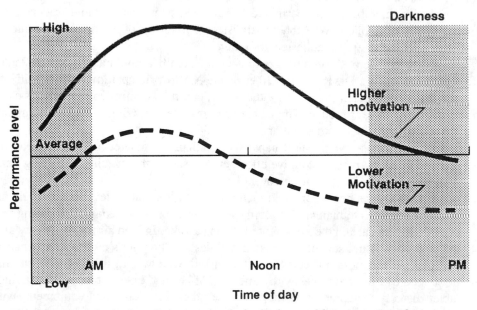

Fig. 2-6. *Hypothetical performance levels for higher and lower motivated persons.*

ities. Mental capabilities are known to improve following light to moderate exercise; however, this effect depends upon the time of day and the kind of task that is being done. Eye-hand coordination improves after exercise in the morning and afternoon but not in the late evening or early morning hours. In their outstanding review of what is known about sleep and wakefulness, Nicholson and Stone (1987, 28) point out that light to moderate exercise "tends to impair tests of memory at any time of the day."

Microsleep. Microsleep refers to periods of dozing off for periods lasting from a fraction of a second to several seconds. While the exact function of microsleep is still not understood, it is possible that the brain's electrical activity might somehow be reset or adjusted for normal operation by these brief lapses into the realm of sleep.

An overly tired pilot might slip imperceptibly into microsleep and these brief periods might produce forgetfulness, reduced attention, and lapses in performance. Federal air regulations still prohibit sleeping in the cockpit on U.S. airlines; however, a recently completed joint NASA/FAA study looked at the possible benefit of doing just this under controlled conditions. One goal was to investigate the possible benefits of permitting naps that are preplanned.

NASA Ames investigators carried out an in-flight study involving 10 B747 three-member flight crews from United and Northwest Airlines. Half were placed (at random) into the experimental group that was permitted to sleep, while the other half made up the control group that could not sleep. The investigators found that pilots who are allowed to sleep during the cruise segment of a flight are significantly more alert during the landing segment when their vigilance and workload requirements increase. Brain wave activity, vigilance and sustained attention, and general activity level were monitored and observations were made by investigators riding in the cockpit. The test flight crew members were permitted to rest for as long as 40 minutes during each flight and these pilots were able to fall asleep 93 percent of the time, when allowed. Their average sleep period lasted 25 minutes.

Performance of the control group declined significantly in alertness at the end of their final leg. As Dr. R. Curtis Graeber, the NASA principal investigator said, "We now have direct scientific evidence that short, carefully controlled rest periods can act as a 'safety valve' to reduce fatigue and improve alertness during the most important phases of flight such as descent and landing."

It appears that taking short naps of more than 15 minutes and less than an hour seem to offer the most restorative effect. It also seems that waking a sleeping person with some care might add to the overall benefit.

Finally, it has been found that increasing the illumination level is the single most effective stimulus to maintaining alertness. Turning up the cockpit lights during trans-oceanic flights can aid the tired pilot in staying awake. In high air traffic density areas, this approach is not suitable because it will destroy the pilot's night vision sensitivity and make it far more difficult to see out of the windows. In this instance, the night pilot should drink beverages with caffeine (coffee, tea, colas), take a sleep-reducing tablet (usually containing caffeine), and use other techniques and equipment, within legal limits, discussed in chapter 7.

ADEQUATE AND CORRECT NUTRITION

Carbohydrates. The body needs energy to sustain life processes (heartbeat, respiration, muscle tone and activity, maintain body temperature and carry on muscular activity) and this energy is found in the heat that is also known as *calories* (EN 2-2) produced as a result of eating food and drinking certain beverages. Among the various kinds of chemical compounds that we eat to produce this energy is one called carbohydrate. Carbohydrates come in various forms such as *glucose*, which is transported and used in the body and animal starch, or *glycogen*, which is the stored form of energy. Carbohydrates are made by plants through the process known as photosynthesis: sug-in his diet. Recommended daily dietary considerations are presented in TABLE 2-5.

A balanced diet always includes carbohydrates; simple sugars are derived from the digestive tract during the product of carbohydrate digestion. If the night pilot is feeling tired and listless it might be because he has not included enough carbohydrates in his diet. Recommended daily dietary requirements for men and women of various ages and weights are presented elsewhere in this chapter.

Proteins. Our muscles and other soft tissues are made up primarily of proteins. Digestion changes the foods containing proteins (meat, milk, cheese, fish, poultry, eggs) into *amino acids*, which are considered to be the building blocks of tissue because they recombine after passing through the intestinal wall to form the typical proteins of body tissue. Proteins are mainly needed for contributing to the generation of blood and muscle tissue, immune bodies, hemoglobin, and certain hormones. Some type of protein should be included in all three meals each day. By varying which type of protein is eaten during a 24-hour period, one helps the body counterbalance the various beneficial effects of them all.

Sugar. "It's been a long day and you're tired. Your dinner consists of a quick hamburger, and then it's off to bed because you have an early departure tomorrow. The next morning you get to the airport a little late—no time for your usual breakfast. In exchange for your dollar, the vending machine dispenses a candy bar and a cup of coffee, and the hunger pangs subside. A few hours later, enroute with a full load of passengers, you feel light-headed and a little shaky, with the beginning of a dull headache. You just don't feel right, but you must press on." (Reinhart 1989) This is a common scenario that many commercial pilots have experienced, but probably did not understand. Was the problem insufficient sleep, too much coffee, growing personal stress, or *hypoglycemia*? This last possibility is poorly understood by most people. It isn't a disease at all, but a perfectly normal response of one's metabolic processes that convert food into energy.

Hypoglycemia means low blood sugar level. If it is too high it is called *hyperglycemia*. Glucose is a chemical in the blood that converts carbohydrates from food into energy with the aid of the hormone insulin. Insufficient glucose can produce weakness, palpitations, faintness, sweating, muscle tremors, and nervousness. Indeed, variations of both glucose and oxygen in the bloodstream have clear effects on the central nervous system. The symptoms of hypoglycemia can vary from person to person and are unpredictable during different working environments. And, while such symptoms can be caused by other medical problems, hypoglycemia is most likely the primary reason for their occurrence in otherwise healthy pilots. If too much insulin is generated for the amount of food digested, the glucose level will drop (hypoglycemia). McFarland and Evans (1939) found that visual sensitivity to the dark is significantly impaired at altitudes as low as 6,000 to 7,000 feet in normal pilots, an effect that is the result of the reduced oxygen pressure present. They also noted that if one's blood sugar level was lowered by injecting insulin intravenously the eye's light sensitivity also decreased by almost a factor of 10. Ingesting either glucose or breathing 100 percent oxygen quickly counteracted this symptom.

Eating foods containing refined sugar and other highly refined starches (common to most junk food) causes these sugars to be converted to glucose so fast that one's blood sugar level also rises at an abnormally fast rate. When one's physiological self-adjustment system senses this sudden increase, it commands the pancreas to release insulin that acts to regulate the energy transformation (metabolism) of the carbohydrates. What results is that too much insulin enters the bloodstream. This causes the glucose level to be even lower than before one ate the snack. This is known as the *rebound effect*.

Reactive hypoglycemia refers to the various physiological effects listed above that occur from two to four hours after the food has been eaten. For instance, if a pilot eats a sweet pastry and coffee with sugar before takeoff in the morning, the initial blood sugar dose will be reached in about 20 minutes or so. One's system might rebound, however, only two or three hours later to far below safe levels. The physiological reaction can lead to subtle or partial incapacitation.

Insulin can be prevented from release by not eating breakfast (or other meals), but this isn't wise either because of the stress it can place on the body's biochemical (metabolic) systems. It is better to substitute fruit or unsweetened fruit juice because they do not stimulate the formation of insulin in the pancreas to such a great degree as does sugar. And, because proteins are converted so much more slowly than is glucose, a small snack of protein will help stabilize glucose levels. Finally, eating many small snacks throughout the day is better than eating a few large meals.

Pilots who experience repeated symptoms of hypoglycemia should have a medical checkup right away for other potential problems such as diabetes, pancreatic tumors, and the like.

What should pilots do to help avoid hypoglycemic symptoms? First, eat food that contains slowly metabolized nutrients (avoid empty calories such as sweets or some fast foods). Eat a balanced diet of fats and proteins that take longer to convert into energy. Additionally, eating more frequently but smaller amounts will produce the same desired effects. Second, stay physically fit. Such overall fitness will help tolerate the metabolic swings that accompany those unavoidable changes in eating patterns. Finally, plan ahead and either set enough time aside to get a balanced breakfast or take along the right snacks. Remember that food we eat takes time to be digested and metabolized and eat well ahead of the time you think you will need that added alertness and stability, such as during your final approach and landing.

In summary, everyone has heard of the sugar high. Some people think that a sugar high makes one more aware of things going on around them. Even if this is true, sugar can have many other potentially dangerous side effects. But what about an elevated blood sugar level?

Diabetes is a disease that is associated with an abnormally high blood sugar level (hyperglycemia). In this condition, there isn't enough insulin available to metabolize the food in one's digestive tract or the glucose in the blood. The raised glucose level is also found in the urine and such chemical findings are another symptom of diabetes. Diabetes mellitus, as it is called, is serious because of its many serious side effects. If the pilot begins to experience an abnormal hunger or thirst, loss of weight, excessive flow of sugary urine, weakness and itchy skin, a physical checkup is called for right away. Uncontrolled diabetes can lead to an elevated predisposition to infections, arteriosclerosis, neuritis, cataract development, and blindness. A simple blood test is done to determine blood sugar level.

Alcoholic beverages. Alcoholic beverages are consumed for many reasons, not the least of which is to help people relax. Sometimes pilots might think that they need to relax before they go flying. If they do drink and then fly, they are asking for many different kinds of problems. There is an old saying: "Eight hours between the bottle and the throttle." This saying is misleading and potentially dangerous, as shall be seen.

The subject of drinking alcoholic beverages before or during flight is basically related to the subject of *hypoxia* (inadequate oxygen). Flying at night in particular, the pilot can experience symptoms of hypoxia at altitudes as low as 5,000 feet. Its symptoms are sometimes difficult to identify without special high-altitude-chamber training, such as is given by the Air Force. Most pilots have never really experienced these symptoms, although they have heard the term and even read something about it during ground school. So how does alcohol play a role here?

Consumption of alcohol reduces the body's tolerance to oxygen deprivation. Even after eight hours of abstinence from drinking alcohol there is no guarantee that all of its effects have left one's system. And if one should have a hangover, its effects can be magnified by flying at higher than usual altitudes.

In addition, alcohol is a depressant. Night pilots cannot afford to cope with psychological depression at the same time they might be coping with other stressors. Alcohol should not be ingested fewer than at least 10 or more hours before flying if one is going to fly at night and then only in smaller than usual quantities. Even in very minute amounts, alcohol will significantly impair one's mental functioning by slowing down one's decision-making abilities, one's motor coordination, one's alertness to unexpected events inside and outside the cockpit, and one's overall judgment ability in stressing situations.

Stimulating drugs (caffeine, nicotine, amphetamines, methylphenidate, pemoline, and others). Caffeine is a drug that disrupts sleep and enhances performance during the day. Coffee, tea, or soda are the main sources of this drug today and are consumed before, during and after night flights as much for social and taste reasons as for its physiological arousal functions. Recent laboratory research has found that caffeine reliably increases daytime alertness in sleepy young males with no diminished efficacy over 2 consecutive days of drug administration. (Lipschutz et al. 1988).

Taken in moderation, caffeine as a stimulant presents no problems. According to a recent article in *Approach Magazine*, one can of soda that contains 32 mg of caffeine can significantly improve visual reaction time, auditory vigilance, and choice reaction time in persons who normally drink 1-4 cups of coffee per day. More importantly, abstaining from caffeine for even one-half day before a night flight and then drinking caffeine only before the most critical phases of the flight should help improve performance. Caffeine requires about 1.5 hours to reach its full strength in the bloodstream, so it makes little sense to drink it well before the flight or just before the critical phase of a night flight.

Caffeine actually enters brain cells via the bloodstream and then unlocks other chemicals that do the stimulating. Too much caffeine can lead to the depletion of too much of the brain's chemicals that might be needed during a critical phase of flight, such as landing. In addition, there is a dose intake limit, in that the more caffeine one ingests, the less it will stimulate. To maintain the same level of stimulation one must drink more and more coffee.

Caffeine can lead to psychological lows between cups and night pilots do not need such lows to add to an already overloaded list of potential problems in the cockpit.

Synthetic amphetamines (also known by the name *benzedrine*) act to drive the body because most are very similar to the hormones adrenaline and ephedrine in both chemical structure and physiological function. They are often taken to stay awake beyond the normal waking period when the body seeks sleep. Benzedrine is also used in treatment of mental depression and as an inhalant to give symptomatic relief in head colds and allergic nasal congestion by shrinking the nasal membranes.

Pilots experiencing sleep disorders such as central nervous system hypersomnia or narcolepsy should immediately consult with their aeromedical examiner. These conditions can be very dangerous during flight. Specialists in sleep disorders often administer various stimulant drugs (*dextroamphetamine*, *methylphenidate*, and *pemoline*) for symptomatic relief, however, these drugs can make it harder to go to sleep, can disturb sleep, and increase one's ability to stay awake.

Depressant, tranquilizing drugs (alcohol, benzedrine, dimenhydrinate). Because one is already naturally predisposed to sleep at night, one should not contribute to this effect by taking sedatives. Alcohol has a depressant effect on the body despite the common misconception that one is invigorated by it. The synthetic amphetamine known as benzedrine is a common depressant that some take to calm down. Likewise, various air sickness drugs might produce drowsiness or upset stomach.

Other Drugs (antihistamines and diet pills). Many people take antihistamines for symptomatic relief from hay fever and other upper respiratory tract allergy symptoms. These compounds act neurologically to inhibit the action of histamine, which causes the most severe effects of allergic reactions. Many products offer temporary relief of nasal and sinus congestion associated with the common cold, itching and watering eyes, sneezing, and runny nose. Some products can cause drowsiness in some people and, if taken in larger doses, nervousness, dizziness, or sleeplessness. The night pilot should always read the fine print, particularly contraindications.

Americans seem to be overly weight conscious. Many people take drug compounds that reduce appetite for food; these drugs are called *anorexic* drugs and they are often closely related to their stimulating drug cousins. Taken in small, periodic doses, diet pills should not pose a particular problem for the night pilot. A hot cup of coffee will probably do more good, however, during that long night flight.

Fast foods. Most fast foods in America are high in salt, fats (cholesterol-related), and sugar, and low in protein, vitamins, minerals, and moderate in carbohydrates, all relative to a balanced nutritional diet. While such meals might be convenient in terms of how long it takes to order and eat, they are not known for providing a balanced diet. From the standpoint of flying at night, how do such fast foods stack up? Several matters must be considered. First, the length of the night flight. Because the process of food digestion takes from 30 minutes to several hours, a quick night flight lasting 15 minutes or so would be over before one felt the effects of the fast food. But for longer flights, one should plan ahead and eat a balanced diet that is high in protein and carbohydrates with only moderate sugar and fat content. Second, how frequently one eats fast foods is an important consideration.

If the night pilot eats fast foods only infrequently, his body can tolerate the biochemical swings that might be produced by them. In effect, the other food he eats will fill in the nutritional gaps that might be produced by the occasional fast foods; however, a constant diet of such foods might lead to a gradual change in one's body health that might contribute to more serious problems.

Food poisoning. Many of us have experienced food poisoning and have suffered the stomach and intestinal pains, vomiting, headache, dizziness, double vision, and other highly unpleasant symptoms that followed quickly (sometimes within minutes). Many people have been amazed at how rapidly the symptoms appeared. The natural response of the body's digestive system is to get rid of the offending food as fast as possible. For foods still in the stomach, this means vomiting (emesis). For foods that might already have passed into the intestinal tract the response is diarrhea and urination.

If the night pilot should experience food poisoning in flight, and is by himself he is in serious difficulties. He will have to cope with controlling his airplane while going through the various unpleasant symptoms discussed above. Severe food poisoning can even lead some people to forsake life itself and make completely wrong decisions such as crashing the airplane. What should be done?

1. Trim the airplane for straight and level flight so that it will almost fly itself. Do not attempt to land (unless a field is within 1-2 minutes from one's present location).

2. Radio flight service with your problem, present position, and request a may-day situation.
3. Do not worry about vomiting in the cabin. It can be cleaned up later.
4. Try to ride the early symptoms out. Use air sickness bags if they are available because this will help control the stench of the vomit. (Most food poisoning symptoms will clear up as soon as the offending food is expelled from the stomach. If one has eaten a food that produces an allergic reaction (certain shell fish) don't expect the symptoms to go away for several days. If you know that you are allergic to the kind of food you just ate, don't go flying at all, or if you are already in the air, land as soon as possible.)
5. If possible, open an outside air vent to improve the volume of fresh air and help remove the stench.
6. Fly the airplane, continually monitoring altitude, airspeed, attitude, and position. It is imperative that the pilot knows where he or she is at all times.

If the pilot is in the far more fortunate situation of having a copilot, then turn the flight over and provide assistance only to the extent possible. For instance, if one is experiencing double vision while being sick, do not offer to monitor altitude or airspeed for the other pilot. It would be more appropriate to radio the ground for assistance.

Recommended daily dietary considerations. While the health conscious night pilot will want to consult detailed books on nutrition and diet, TABLE 2-5 lists the four basic food groups and provides examples in each group.

Table 2-5. The four basic food groups and suggested specific foods.

Milk group....... milk (whole, skim, evaporated, dry, buttermilk), yogurt, pudding cups, ice cream, milkshakes, cheese (cottage, cream, string cheese, cheddar, natural or processed)

Meat group....... beef, beef jerky, lamb, pork, liver, heart, poultry, eggs, fish, shellfish. Alternate protein foods include dry peas, beans, lentils, nuts, peanut butter

Vegetable and Fruit group...... All types of vegetables and fruits, fruit roll, apple-sauce cup, yogurt-covered raisins

Bread and Cereal group..... Breads, cooked cereals, dry cereal, crackers of all kinds, cookies, snack mixes, flour, grits, macaroni, spaghetti, noodles, rice, rolled oats, rice cakes, bagels, and other baked foods

RESPIRATORY AWARENESS

Hypoxia means low oxygen. Each breath we take includes about 70 percent nitrogen and 30 percent oxygen; however, the lungs extract the oxygen and transfer it to the red blood cells during the act of *respiration*. But because this transfer process depends on a pressure difference between the air (lung) and the fluid (blood) systems, ambient cockpit air pressure becomes an important consideration.

Because air pressure is greater at the surface of the earth than it is at higher altitudes, the lungs have more difficulty in forcing the available oxygen into the blood when one is in an unpressurized cockpit at higher altitudes. Use of supplemental oxygen improves this situation by increasing the percentage of oxygen in the air one breathes.

What are some of the major symptoms of hypoxia? They are listed in TABLE 2-6. Remember that the primary problem with hypoxia is how imperceptible it is at the onset. Even a slow cabin pressure change could go undetected and lead to hypoxia.

Table 2-6. Some of the major symptoms of hypoxia.

Psychological or Mental Effects

Subtle euphoria (feeling of well-being)
Mental confusion and impaired judgment
Abnormal, strangely unsettled feelings
Headache and eye strain
Feeling of general fatigue and/or irritability

Visual Effects

Decreased visual acuity
Reduced ability to focus the eyes (particularly at night)

Balance and Equilibrium Effects

Decreased tolerance to spatial disorientation
Dizziness or vertigo
Reduced capability to regain normal flight attitude following an upset

Other Effects

Loss of consciousness
Slowed reaction time

The night pilot must remain aware of these symptoms at all times, cross check cabin pressure, and keep an eye on the behavior of the other crewmembers looking for the above symptoms.

Use of supplemental oxygen. Because the brain requires oxygen to perform its many functions at all times, it doesn't matter whether one is flying during the day or night. The same basic principles apply. It is important to understand what happens when one experiences a low air pressure situation without supplemental oxygen. The typical array of symptoms that occur after the onset of exposure to 25,000 feet altitude without oxygen include loss of peripheral vision (*tunnel vision*), dizziness, buzzing in the ears, and a hot flash. Some pilots will also seem to become confused and unable to think straight. These symptoms can develop in under a minute in less well conditioned individuals and in several minutes for those who are in excellent physical condition. If a smoker, obese, or out of physical condition, a pilot should breath oxygen at all altitudes at night.

When flying at night, some pilots set between 5,000 and 7,500 feet as the altitude to use supplemental oxygen in order to help improve their visual acuity.

At exposure to an altitude of 18,000 feet without oxygen, the typical anoxia symptoms take many minutes to develop. As vision begins to constrict, other visual details might seem to become dimmer. While sweating and an audible buzzing might occur, they will be of less intensity and slower onset. One's mental reasoning capability might also be affected to varying degrees. In fact, anoxia is an insidious problem in flight because its symptoms can develop so slowly and imperceptibly.

Upon donning the oxygen mask, one recovers fairly rapidly with only slight and inconsequential after-effects that can remain for hours.

Influence of physical exercise. Performance of physical exercises in the cabin during night flying has many physiological effects that are too complex to discuss here. Briefly, muscular exercise increases body metabolism (producing an overall heat production that can approach 20 times normal); lung oxygenation (up to 20 times the normal amount of oxygen); heart output that causes blood flow to increase through the lung tissue (*capillaries*); blood flow through the muscles that are being exercised and accompanying nervous system reflexes to increase arterial blood pressure; and water loss through the lungs and the skin, particularly in very hot environments. Another effect of light to moderate exercise is to help the pilot remain more alert.

Mental alertness during night flight is very important so that anything that will maintain alertness should be considered. Because exercise relieves muscular cramps and soreness during long flights and adds stimulating hormones into the blood stream, exercise should be considered by the night pilot. These exercises should be planned so that they don't interfere with control of the airplane, don't lead to distraction of attention from ongoing flight duties, don't narrow situational awareness of what is happening outside the airplane, and don't affect all of the major muscle systems of the body. Nine such carefully planned exercises that meet these objectives are presented in chapter 11.

Hyperventilation and breathing control. Hyperventilation simply means breathing too fast. It can result in a feeling of light headedness and dizziness that can be mistaken for hypoxia. When the pilot flying is in doubt about whether or not he or she is hyperventilating, assume that such feelings are due to hypoxia and take immediate action. Almost every symptom of hypoxia will disappear when one starts breathing oxygen. It is best to begin breathing oxygen and/or descend to a lower altitude immediately. It might be hyperventilation if the problems will not go away after administering oxygen. In this case, have the pilot breathe into a paper bag for several minutes, which simply increases the amount of carbon dioxide in the air that is breathed.

Carbon monoxide. Recall that each breath of air one takes fills the lungs with oxygen and the other gases within the atmosphere; the oxygen is transferred within the lungs to a protein component of blood called *hemoglobin*. After combining with hemoglobin, CO becomes carboxyhemoglobin. Hemoglobin attracts carbon monoxide (CO) several hundred times more strongly than it attracts oxygen and, when each hemoglobin molecule is filled with carbon monoxide, there is no room left for oxygen to attach. Subsequent effects on thinking, muscular coordination, vision, and other performance capabilities are many and varied.

Because there are few suitably inexpensive, compact, light weight, and reliable gas monitoring and alarm systems yet available to warn the pilot of CO in the cabin, education of its physiological and sensory symptoms is essential. (*See* FIG. 7-15 and FIG. 7-16 in chapter 7.) Carbon monoxide is considered to be the most abundant air pollutant in the lower atmosphere, particularly in high density urban areas in America. Many night pilots are at increased risk of CO effects even before they take off. Beard and Grandstaff (1970) found that judgments of temporal intervals and visual discrimination were degraded at blood saturation levels of CO from 4 to 5 percent and that vigilance is degraded first. A CO blood saturation level of only 2 to 4 percent will reduce the pilot's vigilance. At 20 percent saturation, one experiences headaches and shortness of breath during mild to moderate exertion. From 20 to 40 percent saturation, one will experience sleepiness, nausea, and blurred vision. Incapacitation typically occurs at about 45 percent blood saturation of CO. Unfortunately, the weakness and dizziness that occurs might be the only premonitory warnings before coma sets in.

The susceptibility to CO poisoning increases with altitude if the pilot is not wearing an oxygen mask or is not within a pressurized aircraft. This is simply because at higher altitudes the air pressure within the unpressurized cabin is reduced, which makes it even harder for the lungs to extract oxygen from the air.

Tobacco smoke contains CO along with numerous other byproducts of combustion. Cigarette smoke will increase carboxyhemoglobin levels to 5 to 8 percent in smokers and to 1 to 3 percent in urban nonsmokers. The night pilot should not smoke in flight because of the various performance decrements that are associated with CO. In addition, nonsmokers in a closed aircraft cabin are forced to inhale secondhand smoke and can also incur performance decrements because of it; the pilot should not permit passengers to smoke because the pilot will be influenced by the CO, not to mention the irritating effects of the smoke, coping with hot ashes, and the odor that remains after the tobacco is extinguished.

Carbon monoxide might enter the cabin through minute cracks in the heat exchanger shroud or the heater itself. Sometimes air backdrafts might bring some of the engine's exhaust gases into the cabin.

Symptoms of CO poisoning include (at a low CO concentration stage) feelings of drowsiness and sluggishness, warmth, tightness across the forehead, headache, throbbing temples, ringing in the ears, tingling finger tips; (at an intermediate CO concentration stage) dizziness, general muscular weakness, blurred vision, severe headache, visual dimming; and (at a high CO concentration stage) loss of muscular strength, vomiting, coma, convulsions, reduced heart and breathing rate, and eventually death.

If one is in doubt whether any of these symptoms might be due to CO poisoning, assume that it is, and take immediate action. Open a window for more fresh air, shut off the cabin heater, take four or five deep-slow breaths of pure outside air (but do not hyperventilate), avoid smoking, breath 100 percent oxygen (if available), and concentrate on keeping the airplane under control at all times. If possible, land at the first opportunity to make sure that all physiological effects of the CO are completely gone. Continue the night flight only after all of the above symptoms have passed.

OTHER CONSIDERATIONS

Coping with a full bladder at night. The pilot had several cups of coffee hours before takeoff and now began to feel a painful and growing urgency to go to the bathroom; he was all alone in the darkened cockpit of an airplane. Such situations are common and can produce various untoward effects. Many important flying tasks can be overlooked so that the situation might compound into an incident or an accident. It doesn't take long to learn to take care of this situation before taking off, first by not drinking so much coffee and second by relieving oneself just before getting into the cockpit.

The physical sensations from a full bladder can distract the pilot from his or her ongoing tasks. And as he or she worries about what can be done to relieve the pressure, an important item of the checklist might be forgotten.

Keeping warm in a cold cockpit. Pilots who fly at high altitudes in the wintertime should dress warmly. Colder temperatures aloft might be more than the airplane's heater can handle. And if the lone pilot flying at night must cope with the cold in addition to the other possible stressors, a potentially dangerous situation could develop. Carry a blanket that can be wrapped around your legs, if needed.

Subtle incapacitation. In general, this term refers to loss of a normal level of human involvement in the piloting task. It should be obvious why such a loss would be so serious at night, particularly in a two-man cockpit. If there is a second pilot present, it is very difficult for him to detect that the pilot has changed his responsiveness in any obvious way, particularly during long and monotonous flights with a pilot who is normally not communicative anyway.

Most aviation medical specialists today accept two general categories of subtle incapacitation (SI), and obvious incapacitation (OI). SI or partial incapacitation occurs when the pilot inconspicuously slips into a dysfunctional condition without any obvious symptoms or warning. He might appear to be fully functional, but is really disengaged from all responsibilities. He might look awake and alert, his hands on the wheel, his eyes looking intently ahead, but he has entered a state of paralysis or coma.

He might even be conscious, but not able to think. Of course, when SI is not detected and the flight continues into a critical phase of flight, such as descent or approach to landing, the airplane could exceed its flight performance envelope or hit the ground before another crewmember realizes that a problem exists.

Obvious incapacitation refers to a physiological state that might accompany a stroke, massive heart attack, food poisoning, kidney stones, sudden diarrhea, vomiting, neuromuscular paralysis, airborne particles entering the eyes, or a number of other causes. The pilot suddenly collapses or becomes otherwise incapacitated without any warning. If he should slump forward, he can seriously interfere with the second pilot's manual control ability. Certainly, OI is easier to detect than is SI. As Manningham (1989) suggests, several causes of pilot incapacitation are somewhat controllable: hypoglycemia, low blood sugar, which is discussed elsewhere in this chapter; decreased mental functioning caused by tumors or aneurysms, which is an abnormal, and dangerous blood vessel dilation with ballooning and subsequent rupture of the vessel wall; and extreme dizziness or vertigo, most commonly due to infections within the balance organ in the middle ear. Don't fly if you have a cold or the flu.

In 1970, United Airlines carried out a simulated study of both SI and OI using a DC-8 simulator with two-man crews and also in a B-737 type airplane. One of the crewmembers was coached in advance to feint total collapse (OI) at an unexpected point during an approach to landing below 1,700 feet agl. The others present had no knowledge of what was to occur. They found that the others present were so startled by this precipitous collapse that this often hindered their situational awareness and subsequent control of the airplane. Fortunately, there were no crashes.

During the SI portion of the Douglas test, it was found that after the captain ceased functioning during an instrument approach inside the outer marker, 25 percent of the flights crashed. It took 90 seconds on the average to detect that something was wrong with the captain as compared with 10 seconds to detect that the primary radio navigation display had failed or five seconds for failure of the horizontal situation indicator (HSI) display (by the pilot making a nondirectional beacon (NDB) approach). These findings have helped alert the aviation community to the seriousness of both SI and OI. But what can two-pilot flight crews do at night to help detect SI in one of them?

First, a regular conversational mode, reciprocal challenge pattern can be conducted between the captain and first officer throughout a night flight. Such challenges can take the form of asking flight-related questions that require a precise answer or that call for logical thought processes. These challenges should be reciprocal in the sense that each crewmember should assume the responsibility of challenging the other. They should not be argumentative or meant to question the authority of the captain. Cockpit resource management concepts being taught today often incorporate such techniques.

Second, in the darkened cockpit it might be necessary to periodically turn the intensity of the cockpit lights up briefly and unexpectedly while watching the response of the other crewmembers. If a person is incapacitated he or she will probably not respond. Likewise, a temporary artificial change of some instrument's readout that can be seen by the crewmember suspected of being incapacitated might also provide sufficient evidence to take other direct action. Such sudden and infrequent illumination should evoke some obvious response from the others present. If no such response is noted, there might be cause to take more obvious action to verify that another person is not incapacitated.

In summary, while both subtle and obvious pilot incapacitation occur very infrequently, it is so potentially dangerous that flight crews should always be on their guard against this situation. At night, the behavioral patterns of someone who is incapacitated might go unnoticed far longer than they would during the day, particularly when flying on autopilot on long and uneventful legs. A mutually agreed upon challenge technique (initiated by the captain) and carried out periodically and in good humor by all of the flight crewmembers can help detect such physiological states without producing serious morale or discipline problems.

Colds and influenza. Pilots must be aware of the fact that the common cold and influenza can be extremely dangerous during night flight. First consider the wide range of symptoms that are experienced: eyes that feel tired, achy, and burning, eyes that tear, eyes that are more sensitive to light, tinnitus (ringing in the ears), impaired hearing (under some circumstances), blocked eustachian tubes that connect the middle ear with the outer ear canal, sore joints, headache, impaired thinking and performance, lengthened reaction time, and other problems. Second, consider the possible side-effects of the medications the pilot might be taking for these illnesses; added to these symptoms they could add up to a far more dangerous situation at night.

3
Psychological condition affects flight safety

JUST AS THE NIGHT PILOT MUST BE IN GOOD PHYSICAL HEALTH, HE OR SHE should also be in excellent psychological condition in order to be mentally alert and emotionally stable. Every pilot should know himself or herself very well, recognizing subtle as well as obvious psychological traits and reaction patterns to the many stressors that are found in the cockpit. This chapter offers a specially designed preflight personal night flight checklist that should be used before every night flight.

KNOWING YOURSELF AND YOUR LIMITS

The psychological state of the pilot before and during night flight can play a significant role in how safely he or she flies. The first subject that is discussed here is that of coping with stressors.

Personal Limits of Coping with Stressors. Everyone has their own personal limits in their ability to cope effectively with the stressors of life. The wise pilot will attempt to find out what these particular stressors are as well as what his or her personal limits of coping with them are. For example, if the pilot gets angry quickly over little frustrations, what are the possible consequences of this when flying at night when a chart is accidently dropped on the floor and after the flashlight that had been carefully placed on the adjacent seat is also missing? Can relatively innocuous events such as these add up to distract the night pilot so much that he or she cannot keep the airplane under complete and continuous control?

The pages to follow discuss a wide array of potential problems associated with night flying as well as many practical solutions to them. While most of these solutions center on the individual pilot there is another approach that involves a two-person flight crew. Because a two-person crew will significantly lessen the impact of many of the problems associated with night flying it is strongly recommended that every night instrument flight rules (IFR) flight have two qualified pilots aboard. Two pilots can cope with in-flight stressors more effectively than can one pilot if by no other means than division of tasks between them.

Recognizing Your Psychological Traits. Everyone possesses a certain array of psychological traits (EN 3-1). One pilot might be more introverted than extraverted and more emotional than stable. There are various other traits that are thought to fall between these two basic axes as is shown in FIG. 3-1. It is less likely that one can be

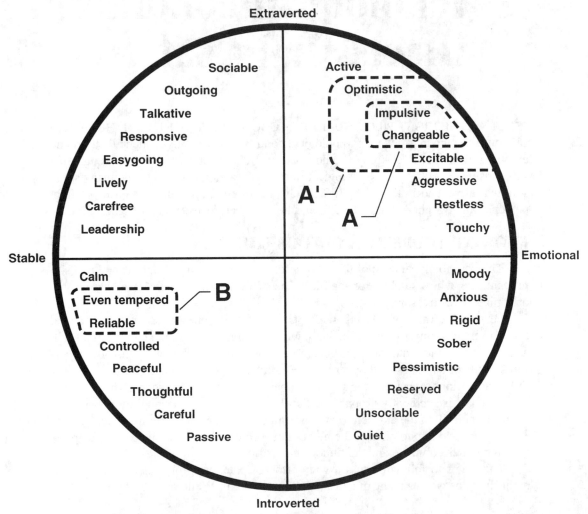

Fig. 3-1. *Dimensions of personality.* Eysenck and Rachman, 1965

precisely stable or emotional (exactly on the horizontal axis) or extraverted or introverted (the vertical axis). It is more likely that an extraverted but stable person, for instance, is going to be sociable, outgoing, and talkative or that an introverted-emotional person will exhibit traits of being reserved, pessimistic, unsociable, and/or quiet. This particular psychological model was proposed by Eysenck and Rachman (1965), who suggested that there are a small number of basic dimensions of personality that act to unify and direct one's behavior. What does this have to do with the night pilot?

The night pilot should know something about this concept to help him or her understand why they might behave the way they do. For example, suppose that the night pilot knows beforehand that he or she is an extraverted-emotional type personality (group A) on the basis of having taken a psychological profile test (EN 3-2). There is reason to believe that during a period of flight-related stress or fatigue this individual might not respond in the same way as a person who is an introverted-stable type (group B). The extraverted-emotional person might show impulsive and changeable behavior that is tied to other related personality traits, such as optimism and excitability (group A'). This person might sincerely believe that everything will turn out all right no matter what action is taken; thus, he or she might be tempted to take more risks while trying to cope with the stressful situation.

And if two or all three flight crew persons in the same commercial cockpit are of the introverted-stable category (group B), what might happen during an in-flight incident that calls for clear leadership and a talkative, outgoing, take-charge personality? Certainly this type of reasoning applies as much to daytime as to nighttime flight. But the darkened cockpit might possibly mask behavior related to these common personality types. Application of cockpit resource management (CRM) concepts is clearly called for here as is a greater awareness by pilots and management alike of the importance of careful selection and matching of personality types in the cockpit.

This personality model should not be used mechanistically. It is offered only to illustrate the potential importance of considering basic personality types and how they might assist or inhibit the timely and effective conduct of cockpit duties.

PERSONAL NIGHT FLIGHT CHECKLIST

This section presents a personal night flight checklist (TABLE 3-1). As with any checklist, it is only as useful as the pilot will allow it to be. And, even when the night pilot is trying to be perfectly honest, he or she might possess certain personality traits that will lead them to overlook and/or deny other actual personal characteristics. Some pilots might not even be aware of their actual physiological or psychological state. It is recommended that a second person present on the ground or in the airplane cabin administer this checklist before takeoff if possible, perhaps a chief pilot, flight instructor, or another crewmember. In this way, most of the answers given are more likely to be accurate reflections of the pilot's actual state of being or at least will be based upon an objective observation. A second person might also be able to exert

Table 3-1. Preflight personal night flight checklist.

		Score

1. How many hours did you sleep last night? _____

If under 4 hours	score 10
If 4.1 - 5 hours	score 8
If 5.1 - 6 hours	score 6
If 6.1 - 7 hours	score 5
If 7.1 - 8 hours	score 4
more than 8 hours	score 0

2. What was the quality of your sleep within the past 2 days? _____

Not at all (for any reason)	score 10
Fitfully (in/out of sleep)	score 8
Only moderately well	score 5
Very sound and deep	score 0

3. How regular has your sleep been within the past week? _____

Highly irregular	score 10
Moderately irregular	score 8
Plus/minus one hour each night	score 4
Same number of hours each night	score 0

4. How long have you been awake (the day before your night flight)? _____

If over 24	score 10
If 20 - 24	score 8
If 16 - 20	score 6
If 14 - 16	score 4
If under 14	score 0

5. Present level of mental alertness _____

Very low, groggy	score 4
Normal	score 2
Very high	score 0

6. Are you in a hurry right now? _____

Yes, very much	score 4
Yes, but only a little	score 2
No	score 0

7. Do you feel in a state of mental overload right now? _____

Yes, very much	score 4
Yes, but only a little	score 2
No	score 0

Table 3-1. Continued

			Score
8. Are you angry about anything now?			_____
Yes, very much	score	8	
Yes, but only a little	score	6	
No	score	0	
9. Are you afraid of anything right now?			_____
Yes, very much	score	4	
Yes, but only a little	score	2	
No	score	0	
10. If "yes," identify what you are afraid of: (If "no," skip to next question.)			_____
I have no idea at all	score	2	
Reason is irrational	score	2	
Reason is very reasonable	score	0	
11. Are you afraid while flying?			_____
Yes, all the time	score	6	
Yes, but only occasionally and with good reason	score	4	
No, never	score	0	

Total score = _____

Night flying scoring categories:

If your total score is from 46 to 72, it is better not to fly.
If your total score is from 18 to 45, you may be at increased risk to fly at night.
If your total score is under 17, you are probably in good shape.

proper influence on the impaired night pilot to prevent him or her from flying if it appears that there might be some danger in doing so. It could save a life.

As you read this personal checklist, assume that you are completing a flight plan for a night flight. You would be wise not to take off at night if you don't meet the guideline scores given here. Remember that it isn't any single item or any exact numeric score that could disqualify the pilot but a constellation of symptoms that could combine during the flight with disastrous consequences.

This checklist is nonempirical and tentative; it should be considered only as providing a set of a general guidelines to watch for. Each item has been found to relate in one way or another to critical night flight capabilities.

It is recommended that the pilot make a copy of the personal night flight checklist given here (TABLE 3-1) and use it prior to each flight. Your answers could indicate that you are not fit to fly. Your margin of acceptable response might be so close to the edge of breakdown that some unexpected event in flight could push you over.

SUBTLE DECREMENTS IN RESPONSE CAPABILITY

If an in-flight emergency is developing at the same time the pilot's capability to take timely and effective action is not sufficient to meet the demands, a performance decrement exists. It is somewhat similar to being "behind the power curve" in power-management terms. Other slowly changing and subtle human reactions related to poor self-awareness can cause pilots not to accept the presence of an emergency situation. One antidote for this kind of problem is to take an instructor pilot along on a night checkride if there is any possibility that the pilot might be overrating his or her performance capabilities. Another solution is to have a second pilot on board for the entire flight.

There are other sometimes subtle yet dangerous physiological and psychological changes that can occur during long night flights. These changes can gradually reduce a pilot's capability to respond to unexpected events. Figure 3-2 is a hypothetical diagram of this situation. Time in flight is shown on the horizontal axis and the pilot's capability to respond to unexpected events from low to high is plotted on the vertical axis. Four different flight conditions ranging from normal at the top to accident imminent at the bottom are shown by different shading levels across the graph. For the first third of this hypothetical flight the pilot's capabilities (from point A to B) remain in the safe zone lying above the "Normal Human Capabilities" cross-hatched bar.

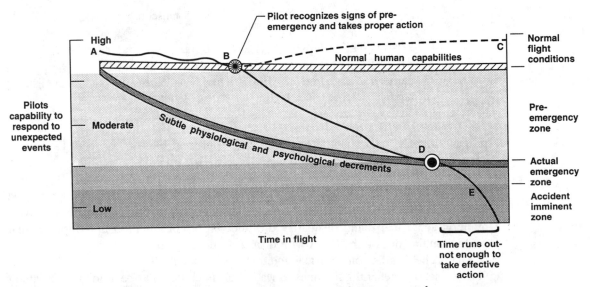

Fig. 3-2. *Theoretical changes in pilot's capability to respond to unexpected events.*

Nevertheless, subtle time and stressor-related decrements are taking place within the pilot's physiological and psychological systems. These decrements are represented by the slowly descending thick dark bar. At point B, the pilot notices an event that requires his or her active involvement; if it is performed successfully, the flight will continue safely as is shown by the dashed line from B to C. But if the pilot is overly fatigued, poorly trained, lacks motivation, is disoriented or is experiencing vertigo, is slightly anoxic, is overly stressed or is otherwise subtly incapacitated, the resulting capability curve might well be like the curve shown extending from B to D. This curve is still within the "pre-emergency zone" but at point D the pilot is on the edge of entering the actual emergency zone where time (altitude, fuel, or airspeed) might be running out.

The primary issue here is whether or not the pilot will be able to discriminate not only his or her critical situation but also his or her own personal state. Most physiological and psychological performance decrements change so slowly that one might not be able to tell how close they have brought one to an imminent accident or incident zone. Ideally one's normal capabilities should remain high enough to sustain normal flight conditions at night. The performance curves of FIGS. 2-4 through 2-6 also apply such that the time in flight axis of FIG. 3-2 must take into account local time and each pilot's personal 24-hour rhythms.

It should also be realized that each pilot and flight situation is different because of age, physical condition, level of experience, departure time, amount of sleep, and the like. Each pilot and situation will have a slightly different shape in comparison with FIG. 3-2. Nevertheless, this curve is generally representative.

"No amount of training can entirely compensate for inexperience," says Dr. John K. Lauber of the National Transportation Safety Board. He is correct. For a certain undefined period of time after one's training is over (whether it is training for a new airplane or a new position in the cockpit), there occurs a process of "skill consolidation." During this period newly learned knowledge and skills are integrated with past knowledge and skills into one's long-term memory where they should remain available for a very long time. Nonetheless, performance will tend to be somewhat slower and more deliberate during this period of consolidation as the pilot attempts to verify the accuracy of each step of the new integration. He or she might make more "blunder" type errors. Lauber suggests that it is important to enact some sort of operating and scheduling restrictions to "prevent the pairing of neophytes in routine flight operations," (Lauber 1989). His suggestion is particularly apt at night when it is harder to see the obvious control input blunders that are made. Flight experience is as important as stick handling.

DEVELOPING AND MAINTAINING SITUATIONAL AWARENESS

Situational awareness refers to one's ability to remain aware of everything that is happening at the same time and to integrate that sense of awareness into what one is doing at the moment. A highly developed situational awareness contributes to a pilot's ability to cope effectively with the unexpected and to maintain a balanced sense of well-being that is so important to staying calm under pressure.

Situational awareness is partly the result of training and experience and partly genetic. It is the training and experience that we are concerned with here because there is nothing we can do about our hereditary background. What training techniques can be used to develop the innate capabilities one might have to expand one's situational awareness?

Vision and attention scanning exercise. To exercise your visual attention sense sit in a comfortable upright chair in a well-lit room and stare steadily straight ahead at something. Now scan your attention or awareness in a clockwise direction around this point of visual fixation. Do this around the full 360 degrees slowly and near the point of fixation. Ask yourself what you can really see and identify. Now move your attention about halfway out to the edge of your field of view and scan in a CCW direction a full 360 degrees always trying to identify objects. Note shapes, colors, writing, and the like. To make sure that your mental scans were accurate, take a very brief look over at the object or detail and then look back again rapidly at the original point of fixation. You will be surprised at how you will improve over time in your ability to perceive peripheral visual details.

Listening exercise. To exercise your hearing sense, find a moderately quiet place and sit or lie down. Close your eyes and listen to all of the sounds present. Keep track of the total number of different sounds. The more the better. Now open your eyes and repeat this simple exercise. You might note that you haven't heard as many sounds as before when your eyes were closed. Repeat these two listening exercises until keeping your eyes open doesn't interfere with your listening ability.

Muscular exercise. The following muscular exercise is not meant to increase strength but rather to develop a new awareness of your various muscles. Lie down on a soft mattress or couch and place your hands beside you, palms up. Breathe slowly and evenly; inhale a little more slowly than you exhale. Now think only about your ankles and feet. As you inhale try to tighten all of these muscles as much as you can. Hold your breath and muscles tight for a second or two and then exhale, totally relaxing these muscles. Repeat this for two more breaths and then move up to your knees. As you take a breath in, concentrate on all of your muscles from your knees down. Hold your breath for two seconds and then forcibly breathe out, simultaneously relaxing all of these muscles. Repeat this for two more breaths before moving up to your waist. As you systematically move up your body you will slowly get in touch with many muscles. In fact, you will find this exercise very relaxing so that you might feel a slight tingling, which is normal. This entire muscular relaxation exercise should not take longer than about 20 minutes and is well worth it.

Cognitive exercise. The final exercise can help you improve your overall situational awareness of your mind. Here you must practice thinking about how you think. For example, try an arithmetic problem that begins with the number 20. Think of how many ways separate numbers can add up to this number (a) when you can only add two numbers: $1 + 19$, $4 + 16$, $8 + 12$. Now think of how many ways three separate numbers can be used: 1 + 1 + 18, 5 + 5 + 10, 6 + 4 + 10, and the like. Do this with your eyes closed at first until the task becomes almost habitual, then open your eyes and continue. As you do this, notice what might happen. Are you easily distracted? Do you suddenly stop calculating? These are sure signs that you need to concentrate only on the mathematical task. The objective is to be able to perform such "thinking" tasks as well with your eyes and ears working as when they do not.

Integration. Now put all of these exercises together at the same time. The objective is to be able to expand your sensory and cognitive awareness of everything around you, somewhat like a kung fu expert can do. As if a sixth sense, you will be much better prepared to both detect developing problems in flight and also take effective action. Your disciplined mind will know what courses of action are open to you. You will also gain added self-confidence about your coping skills in many different difficult situations.

STRESS AND STRESSORS

A stressor is anything that leads to a physical stress response. More specifically, stressors can be as subtle as getting insufficient sleep over a period of days due to gastric indigestion, disharmony in one's home or physical illness. A stress response is what happens within the mind and the body due to imposition of a stressor. According to Hans Selye, a leading authority on the subject, it comprises all of the nonspecific bodily responses to any kind of demand placed upon it. Each pilot will probably experience stress in a different way because each is influenced by unique past experiences, perceptions, values, needs, and culture.

Remember that stress is not necessarily bad. Actually, the night pilot should have some type of positive stress to help him or her perform efficiently. Personal excitement and anticipation of a night flight are both subtle positive stressors.

Most aviation books that discuss stressors talk about various environmental stressors such as extreme temperature, loud noise, vibration, and other things that can produce stress, particularly at night. And, indeed, it is during the nighttime approach and landing following a long, dark flight when the effects of many different cabin stressors can compound within the pilot to produce extreme fatigue and mental pressure when he or she can least afford these problems. Another large category of stressors arises from within each pilot. This category is a combination of the pilot's sociopsychological circumstances and personal makeup. This array of responses should also be of concern to the night pilot. They are often subtle and so are important in maintaining effective cockpit communications and crew cooperation. Courses on cockpit resource management usually discuss them. And what about CRM in this regard?

An FAA advisory circular states that between 60 and 80 percent of air carrier incidents and accidents have been caused, at least in part, by a failure of the flight crew to make use of readily available resources. Indeed, most of the problems encountered by flight crews have very little to do with the more technical aspects of operating a multicrewmember airplane but tend to be associated with poor group decision making, ineffective communication, inadequate leadership, and generally poor management. These kinds of problems can be less visible in the dark cockpit at night. Whether they are the cause or the result of in-flight stress remains to be seen. (EN 3-3)

Finally, the concept of arousal refers to the general state of awareness and responsiveness at any moment. The subject of arousal is explored in the last section of this chapter. See page 53.

Symptoms of personal stress. TABLE 3-2 presents an abbreviated list of some indications that one is experiencing stress. These symptoms may be subdivided into three different categories: physical or environmental stress, cognitive stress, and emotional or affective stress that is often unpredictable in intensity or duration. The last type can be the most deadly because it might be masked by the pilot's own extraverted personality discussed earlier.

Table 3-2. Symptoms of stress.

Anger (uncontrolled, spontaneous, or nonfocused)
Finding fault in the cabin
Lack of courtesy in the cabin
Shouting at air traffic control
Prolonged attentional narrowing
Being in a hurry without a reason
Social isolation from others
Confusion in receiving clearances
Calling for the wrong check list
Excessively distractible
Overly irritable
Mentally preoccupied
Forgetful (short-term or long-term)
Flight manual not updated
Overlooking a power setting requirement
Subtle erosion of self-confidence
Unwarranted over self-confidence
Drinking alcohol or taking drugs
Upset stomach
Irregular bowel movements
Very tight or sore muscles (gripping the wheel)
Headache
Eye strain and poor vision

These indications of personal stress usually build up slowly and subtly while at other times they can build up quickly, as during a panic attack. A condition of mental overload can occur during night flying as the pilot begins to realize that he has not planned adequately for the unexpected. Suddenly he finds that he is overwhelmed with things that must be carried out. Where should he begin? What things must take immediate top priority? Can some cockpit activities be put off until later? Why can't those personal problems back home be put out of mind for the time being? The end result of such emotional and mental overload can make you as unairworthy as an overloaded airplane because you were crammed with too much cargo. If the night pilot permits any aspect of the preflight work environment to come between him and his professionalism in flight, the results can be disastrous.

Night pilots who are at all concerned about personal stress should read a book entitled *Managing Pilot Stress* by Dr. Michael Thomas, a psychotherapist and commercial pilot. Dr. Thomas maintains that all pilots experience stress at one time or another and it can lead to potentially dangerous circumstances. He states that "the typical pilot personality" is often "a self-sufficient, achievement-oriented individual (who) . . . sometimes lacks the introspection, insight and emotional resources to admit when stress may be affecting performance." (Thomas 1990)

Another helpful suggestion is to follow the so-called 3-W approach: where, why, what. Try to find out where the stressors actually come from, why they affect the pilot the way they do, and what can be done about them. Sometimes professional counselling will be called for (EN 3-4), particularly when the pilot is not aware of his or her own stress responses but discovers that other people are aware of the responses. In this situation, the pilot might be deluding himself or herself in an attempt to keep from admitting that there is a problem. In short, the night pilot should be personally dedicated to stress reduction in any and all ways as preventative medicine.

Stressors. Stressors literally fill our waking environment. Indeed, they are a part of what motivates us to do what we do as we react. It should be remembered that stressors are neither good nor bad. When a stressor is present in small to moderate amounts, humans tend to work better. Stressors help keep the pilot more alert.

A sample list of some common stressors is given in TABLE 3-3 simply to illustrate the very broad range and subtlety they comprise.

Many of today's aircraft are very advanced and incorporate computer-based technology that can alert, inform, control, advise, warn, display, and organize massive amounts of information. To some pilots this advanced technology can become a source of in-flight stress. Pilots can be intimidated by its complexity and overloaded by all of the available information. New aviation displays and controls that require advanced training, a disciplined mind, and proper judgment about when and how to use it best can intimidate some pilots; some of these pilots might not use this equipment at all rather than have to face the fact that they are not as intellectually capable as they first thought. Other pilots might use such equipment incorrectly because they haven't taken the time necessary to learn about all of its intricacies.

Fear of flying and nonfocused apprehension. The so-called sweaty palms and white-knuckles syndrome is well known but seldom admitted. Nighttime often masks these visible symptoms from others in the cockpit; the pilot affected should simply face up to these fears and seek professional assistance, perhaps through a fear of flying clinic. (EN 3-5)

Table 3-3. Stressors.

Preflight

Morning alarm clock alarm (loud/unexpected)
Third cup of coffee in the morning (drugs in general)
Chain smoking
Missing the commuter train
Tripping on a child's toy leaving the house
Arguing with spouse
Traffic delays
Running out of gas in the car
Cutting yourself shaving
Upset stomach
Sore or tired muscles
Tiredness and fatigue

In-flight

Long, slow cross-country flight
Flight spanning daylight to darkness hours
Noticing that the gas tank is very low
Fear of flying and general (unfocused) apprehension
Packing the wrong flight charts
Sudden loud noise or prolonged repetitive noise
Unexpected minor flight-related events
Change in ambient air pressure and hypoxia
Vibration
Excessive eating
Low humidity
Gaseous irritants in the lungs (ozone, nitrous dioxide)
Prolonged physical inactivity
Cold cockpit
Hot cockpit
Smoking in flight

Another emotional response that some pilots experience is known as automatic rough. It usually occurs at night when the pilot is about to cross open water or mountainous regions with no place to land nearby. Both experienced and inexperienced pilots might confront the imaginary automatic rough if they are under stress; they begin to imagine that they hear a strange noise or feel a slight vibration. Their imagination can fill in the darkness with all sorts of unreal problems; the pilot's emotional response can lead to panic, fear, and immobilizing apprehension. What can be done to cope with the automatic rough syndrome?

• Be fully informed about all functional and procedural aspects of one's aircraft.

- Become as proficient as possible in all of the flying skills that night flying calls for.

- Apply balanced judgment about any new sounds, vibrations, or other sensations that are noticed. Remember that when dealing with an emergency one's emotions must be overcome by logic.

- Remember that automatic rough borders on pure emotion. If the airplane has been running fine up to this point in the flight there is a very good chance that it is continuing to do so regardless of what type of terrain one is flying over. It is also wise to cross-check other sources of information to ensure that the new vibration or noise isn't an actual problem. If it is a real emergency the pilot will know it.

- Ambient air pressure change is also a stressor found on all commercial flights because the cabin must be pressurized to about 7,000 feet equivalent altitude for flight at an actual altitude of 40,000 feet (or 6,000 feet inside equivalent altitude for an actual flight altitude of 31,000 feet). Older people will feel tired when they must physiologically adjust to even a 5,000 foot change in altitude where the oxygen pressure in the lungs drops to about 79 percent versus 100 percent at sea level. One might experience an early sign of *tachycardia*, which is increased heart rate. Breathing rate will also tend to increase and an acid-base balance shift of the blood occurs. Together, these body responses can lead to stress. These problems are most acute for smokers because smoking raises the effective physiological equivalent altitude from 2,000 to 3,000 feet above normal cabin altitude.

- A cold cabin and flying at night very often go together. One can lose critical dexterity of any extremity over time. Stored body heat is lost through the skin and shivering begins. If one wears gloves or a bulky coat, and the like, to stay warm at night, not only will one have more difficulty setting switches but one might accidently bump some control while taking these clothes off in flight. Make sure the cabin heater works well during your preflight warm-up check. Then wear a light sweater and wool pants and socks, if necessary.

    It is suggested that the cabin air temperature index be set at not more than 80 °F (wet bulb temperature) and not less than 65 °F. And if one must fly in excessively cold conditions for prolonged periods of time, consider buying electrically heated gloves and socks.

- Lowered cabin humidity can also be a stressor. Values of from 10 to 15 percent cabin humidity are common in commercial airplanes. This can lead to drying of the eyes, nose bleeds, and dry throat. Prolonged flights at high altitude while also drinking alcohol and or large amounts of coffee (with its diuretic effect) will lead to blood concentration as one starts to become dehydrated. Blocked ears and resultant pain also adds to one's stress level.

- Gaseous lung irritants and toxicants as are found in smog and aircraft engine exhaust fumes can also become contributors to pilot stress at night. They can cause coughing, tearing, excessive blinking, distraction, and other problems that can interact with current flight tasks. Of course if they are present in too great a concentration, they can also have toxic effects.

- Noise in the cabin has both physiological and psychological effects. The primary physiological concern about noise is its long-term effect on hearing. A gradual hearing loss sometimes occurs that can interfere with cockpit and ground communications. Noise can also contribute to overall fatigue and stress during night flights. While some pilots think of engine and other flight-related noises as comforting at night, their ever-present constancy can become a source of annoyance and stress, particularly during departure and landing. These two phases of flight require the most attention, skill, and concentration, yet the loud and constant noises of the engine and other sounds can be physically draining, amplifying the other effects of night flight.

  Commercial airplane cockpits might contain in-flight noise levels ranging from 75 to 100 decibels or more. Potential ear damage is variously defined as occurring at above 100 decibels. The generally accepted standard for maximum sound pressure (noise) without protection is 92 decibels (for frequencies from 150 to 300 Hz) and 85 decibels for all octave bands between 300 to 10,000 Hz.

  Part of the stress response to noise comes from other unexpected consequences that loud noises can produce, such as interference with hearing, irreversible hearing loss (especially at levels above 140 decibels), and general fatigue.

- While it sounds absurd at first, inactivity in flight can also become a stressor. Who has not felt some pain or muscular cramping in the lower extremities when sitting still in poorly fitting seats for hours on end? Use of isometric leg, torso, arm, and neck muscle exercises helps keep the blood from pooling in the lower legs and feet; this helps one to relax more.

- Analyses of accident reports and statistics have shown that it isn't the unexpected opening of an airplane door in flight that leads to problems as much as what the pilot decides to do next. Restrain the strong urge to take immediate action if time permits, otherwise the response might worsen the situation. When unanticipated events occur in flight think through all of the possible causes of the event and then mentally explore the consequences of each behavior you might take, while you continue to fly the airplane.

- It is vitally important to consider both the timing and duration of duty periods with sleep periods to avoid undue sleep disturbance and support the ability to sustain vigilance. In general, performance tends to rise during the first hours of work and then fall to its initial level by about the seventh hour. Then performance continues to fall until the 12th to 16th hour of work when it levels off as shown in FIG. 3-3.

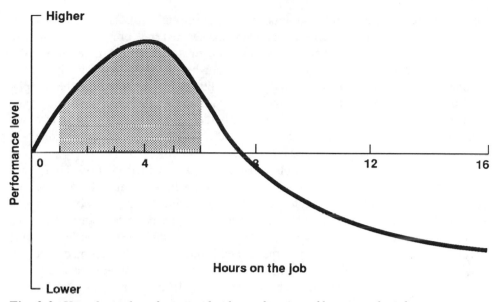

Fig. 3-3. *Hypothetical performance level as a function of hours on the job.*

If possible, flight duty scheduling should take this general performance curve into account by planning night flying during the shaded period when the pilot is most capable of sustaining higher performance. That is, because performance improves during daylight hours and decreases at night, reaching its minimum around 0500 local time, this performance curve should be superimposed upon the curves of FIG. 2-3 in order to arrange work to avoid low levels of performance related to the end of a prolonged duty period.

Another approach to stress management is to find ways to get away from the stressor(s). If the morning rush hour drives a pilot crazy, he or she should leave home earlier. If a pilot becomes stressed out because he or she is a person that has to anticipate every problem of life, he should see a counselor or at least read some books on stress reduction. The pilot should ask why something (or someone) is so bothersome. Is the pilot sweating the small stuff? Try the calming exercise that involves taking a slow deep breath while thinking "my body is calm...the source of the stress is really far away from me right now." This can offer the night pilot a minute's worth of relaxation exactly when it is needed. And if the pilot finds him or herself becoming increasingly tense, frightened, or panicked before or during flight, perhaps it is time to get a thorough physical checkup. One's body might be trying to say something important.

COMPLACENCY

Some pilots, particularly those with more flight experience, face a particularly insidious peril at night. It comes in a variety of different disguises ranging from boredom to overconfidence, from carelessness to a false sense of contentment. It is the attitude of complacency, sometimes defined as a contented state of mind, regardless of the actual circumstances. These pilots have problems dealing with otherwise trivial situations such as a slight banked attitude at night when the wings are actually level or an unusually high nose-up pitch attitude at low altitude. For some reason, the complacent pilot is more reluctant to cross-check the various instrument panel displays and compare them with the external scene. Certainly many years of successful night flying experience can breed an attitude that nothing can go wrong and if it does, one will have no difficulty in coping with the problem.

The complacent attitude probably is based upon a combination of self-confidence and confidence in the integrity of the airplane being flown. This attitude probably springs from many years of trouble-free experience flying it. There is nothing wrong with being self-confident, yet the pilot might reason that because nothing has gone wrong before, nothing can go wrong now. Particularly after he or she has become highly proficient in flying a new airplane and little new is being learned, one can become overly complacent. The earlier signs of stress are missed and everything seems to be routine. There seems to be more reason to let down the guard, to slack off on some cockpit procedures, or to overlook those little things that once seemed so important.

The complacent pilot is setting himself or herself up for an incident or an accident. What kinds of things can be done? Here are several. First, accept the fact that the pilot is not superhuman but subject to all the frailties of mankind, including complacency. Second, carry out a thorough and vigorous program of proficiency checks in simulators and in flight to help reinforce those repetitive habits that keep the airplane in the air. Third, develop a high standard of perfection in all areas of flying (preflight, in-flight, postflight). Fourth, keep an eye out for the subtle symptoms of complacency in other pilots and gently tell them of your observations. And fifth, the correct attitude to develop should be that of cautious optimism where every decision and manual control made at night is made after thinking through its consequences.

Of course, if two pilots are present, it should be more difficult to become overly complacent, particularly if each pilot takes responsibility for monitoring the general behavior of the other. A two-pilot flight crew cannot be overemphasized in this situation.

Carry out critical self-appraisal, particularly at night when it is easier to be lulled into a sense of well-being by the darkness and the natural tendency to doze off. Remember, the airplane doesn't know what time it is.

DENIAL

Another subtle but dangerous way of thinking that the night pilot should be aware of is denial: "Nothing is out there that will hurt me." Somewhat akin to complacency, denial is an unconscious psychological tendency in some people to distort reality in a way that leads them to act, feel, and think that "nothing will happen to me, I'm perfectly safe." While everyone uses denial at one time or another, an overreliance on it can lead to problems, especially while flying at night. In confronting a problem at night in the cockpit, the pilot in denial might become unexpectedly angry or hostile, for example, which can further interfere with carrying out effective rational behavior. Anger and hostility might signal an unhealthy denial response.

Another common form of denial is to set the wrong goals for oneself. If the inexperienced pilot with very little night experience assumes that night flying is the same as daytime flying, this is simple denial of reality that he or she might use as an excuse to launch at night. This excessive ego problem can be deadly.

As a primitive defense mechanism against anxiety, denial might arise as a result of an unwarranted and excessive trust in one's own abilities, or in the reliability of the aircraft. In effect, it is easier to deny a problem than to face it. Many documented accounts exist of pilots who were flying an aircraft low on fuel but simply continued on into the night rather than immediately seeking a suitable landing field. Similarly, there are pilots (probably in denial) who will not take account of a strong headwind in their calculations or planning and suffer the consequences.

Everyone (including the night pilot) and everything (including the aircraft) has limitations. Simply denying them will only compound the problem when and if it occurs.

AROUSAL

The level of arousal is also an important consideration for the night pilot because he or she is flying during a period when the natural bodily reactions are beginning to shut down to go to sleep. As is shown in FIG. 3-4, humans perform best at an intermediate level of arousal with performance decrements occurring when arousal either increases or decreases. Researchers have also discovered that level of performance also varies by the nature of the task that must be carried out as shown here. It might also be noted that this general upside down U-shaped curve, known as the Yerkes-Dodson law after its two originators (1908), predicts that the maximum arousal level should be higher as task difficulty increases (from A to B on the horizontal axis), regardless of the level of performance that is achieved. Of course, the length of time that the pilot can maintain this very high level of performance will likely be shorter for the more complex task than for the simpler task. Any pilot who has flown a back-course ILS or other complex approach procedure will probably realize this fact. The night pilot should study this figure carefully.

The continuous curves shown in FIG. 3-4 might imply that performance only changes smoothly and continuously. But note that the horizontal axis of this graph is not time but arousal level. The experienced pilot will quickly recognize the fact that one can be at a low arousal level one moment and at an extremely high arousal level the next, particularly during an emergency. His or her performance can change from low to lower without passing through the higher performance stage first. Likewise, level of performance might stay at the same magnitude even though level of arousal

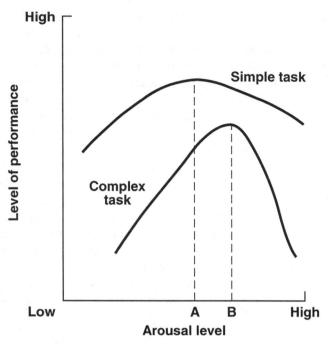

Fig. 3-4. *Level of arousal affects level of performance.*

changes. One lesson to be learned from this figure is to try to remain at a moderate arousal level whenever possible.

Everyone knows what workload is. In simple terms, it is the combined level of intellectual, physical, and psychological effort a person makes at any given moment to carry out a given task or tasks. It is also common knowledge that there are large variations in workload during any flight. Proper task load management between two pilots in the cockpit can be another effective means of leveling out workload. While there might be some small added workload associated with communications and coordination between the two pilots in order to coordinate these shared duties, in the end it is time well spent.

The night pilot might also find FIG. 3-5 of interest because it suggests that his or her performance level will decrease differently depending upon level of workload and skill level. One pilot (A) will find a gradually declining performance capability as workload increases simply because he or she does not possess a particularly high level of skills that are required. In one sense, skill level provides a cap on how high performance can go. At the opposite extreme is another individual (D) who can maintain a high performance level over a wide range of workloads; however, at some point (often during high skill tasks), his or her performance drops dramatically. This drop might not be as dramatic for other persons (B or C). These curves may be thought of as a variation on the Yerkes-Dodson law just discussed.

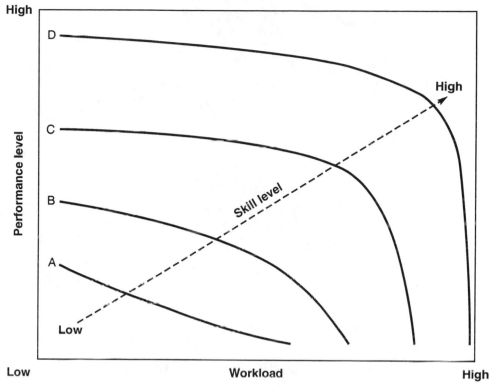

Fig. 3-5. *Hypothesized relationship between skill, workload, and performance.* Tole, 1982

4
Vision at night

A PILOT'S VISION IS HIS MOST IMPORTANT SENSE AND FLYING AT NIGHT will place the eyes in an environment for which they are only partially suited. It is important to have a fundamental understanding of how we see during the daylight hours, the gradually darkening twilight hours, and the pitch darkness of night. Armed with such understandings, the night pilot can use his or her eyesight more effectively and can carry out all required preflight, in-flight, and postflight duties better.

HOW THE VISUAL SYSTEM WORKS

Fundamentals of light behavior.

While we will not discuss the physics of how light is produced, it is important to know that light travels in straight lines from its source and only the light that enters the pupil of the eye is perceived. Whether or not a light source is bright enough to be seen at all is a tremendously important question that we will cover later. Suffice it to say that if the emitted or reflected light possesses wavelengths that fall within the visible spectrum and are of sufficient intensity (or luminance) the viewer will be able to perceive its presence as light.

A ray of light will be discussed here as if it were a thin and round but straight pencil. The eraser end will be the light source and the point the tip of the ray. Figure 4-1 illustrates three different optical principles.

Part A of FIG. 4-1, illustrates the refraction (bending) of light. It occurs when a light ray strikes a transparent medium like a parallel pane of plastic (or glass pane) of

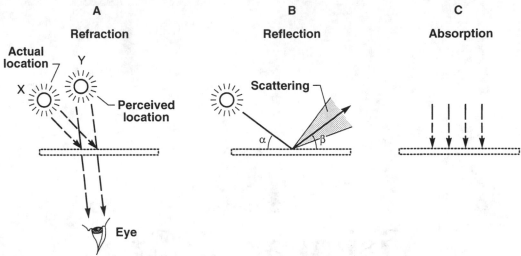

Fig. 4-1. *Basic optical principles.*

an airplane's windshield at an angle. The light ray slows down so that it bends approximately as shown. It emerges at a different angle than it first entered. Anyone who has stuck a pencil into a glass of water at an angle has seen this interesting effect when looking through the side of the glass. A ray that enters the transparent pane at a 90 degree angle will not be refracted under ordinary circumstances. Refraction is of concern to the night pilot because of the optical rule that states that a light source actually located at X will be perceived as being located not necessarily at its true location but along the direction that the ray enters the eye, at Y. For the optics pertaining to most windshields, the angular size of this refractive effect is so small as to be practically insignificant.

Light reflection and scattering are illustrated in part B; reflection is the process where all (or most) of the pencil ray is turned back toward the same side of the reflecting surface as the light source. Also illustrated is the well-known optical law that the angle of incidence (alpha) equals the angle of reflectance (beta). If the surface is not mirrorlike but matte or diffusely reflecting, the reflected pencil ray will be scattered as is shown by the conical shaded area. Smooth but diffusely reflecting metal airplane skin reflects light in many different directions making the airplane somewhat more visible from a variety of viewing locations. The night pilot should realize that even a clear pane of plastic or glass (not optically coated) will act as a partial mirror when it is lighter on one side than on the other. This is why, at night when it is darker outside the cockpit than inside, the pilot will see light sources inside the cabin being reflected off the inner surface of the windows.

Part C in FIG. 4-1 illustrates absorption. Here part or all of the pencil ray of light is captured at the surface or inside the opaque material so that none of it is reflected or refracted. A very small but measurable amount of light is absorbed in all transparent materials, which explains why windshields and other airplane windows become heated in sunlight. Aviator sunglasses absorb a small percentage of sunlight and cause the world to appear dimmer than otherwise. They also will absorb most of the harmful ultraviolet rays of the sun.

Optics of the human eyeball, retinal image formation

A simple understanding of how an image is formed at the carpet of neural receptors, known as *rods and cones* of the retina that line the inside surface of the eyeball, is essential for appreciating many other facts covered elsewhere in this chapter. The human eye works somewhat similarly to a camera because each possesses a focusing lens, an iris aperture, and an image capturing mechanism. Figure 4-2 shows a vertical section drawing of the human eyeball.

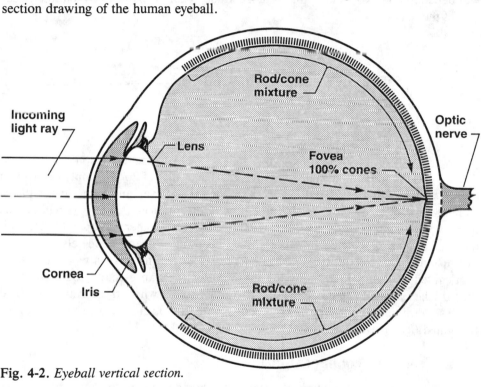

Fig. 4-2. *Eyeball vertical section.*

The incoming light ray (from the left) first passes through the transparent corneal cell layers and then through a semiviscous fluid that fills the front part of the eye between the cornea and the lens. The colored iris then contracts or expands to admit an optimal amount of light energy, depending upon existing illumination levels. In dim visual environments, the pupillary opening opens to about 8 mm diameter in the young person. In very bright environments it will close to about 2 or 3 mm diameter to protect the delicate retinal tissue. The lens is actually a semiviscous onion-like structure that can become thinner or fatter under the influence of thin hair-like connections to surrounding muscle tissue. Under relaxed muscle conditions, the lens is fattest, which will refract the incoming light ray by the greatest amount. Best optical focus is achieved when all of the rays come to a common focal point at the fovea. The fovea is populated only by long thin light transducers called cones that are sensitive to different wavelengths (*hues*). The proportion of cone to rod cells decreases with increasing distance from the fovea in all directions. This explains why humans cannot perceive colored lights or surfaces in the far periphery of the visual field, which is covered elsewhere in this chapter.

Everyone is aware of the term 20/20 vision. It is a concept that is both valuable and easy to understand with the aid of FIG. 4-3. Here we see that the visual angle (α) will depend upon two factors, the distance to the detail of interest (D) and the linear size of the detail (E).

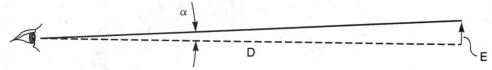

Fig. 4-3. *The concept of visual angle.*

Acuity refers to the sharpness of detail one can see and, of course, this will depend upon E and D in the above figure. A visual acuity of 20/20 simply means that a pilot standing 20 feet from the wall chart containing black and white letters of the alphabet, for instance, will be able to correctly discriminate details as small as one minute of visual angle. An acuity of 20/40 means that another pilot would discriminate one minute of angle detail on a chart 20 feet away where someone else with normal distance acuity could stand 40 feet away and see it. This person would be called nearsighted (*myopic*). Likewise, a person with 20/10 distance acuity could correctly identify the eye chart detail of one minute of arc at 20 feet where the normal eye would need to move up to 10 feet away. The person with 20/10 acuity would be considered farsighted (*hyperopic*). And so 20/20 indicates normal visual acuity.

Eye focus (accommodation)

Eye focus (visual accommodation) occurs automatically by changing the shape of the lens within the eyeball. This reflexive process occurs rapidly whenever the object one is looking at moves toward or away from the eyes. To understand this dynamic process it is important to first understand how the eye focuses images. This process is shown in FIG. 4-4 for three different focus situations. Part A (distance vision) shows that the incoming light rays from another airplane a long distance away (optically speaking this need be only 50 or 100 feet) are parallel with one another as they enter the eyeball. In the normal eye, they all come to a single focus at the *fovea*, located at the inside back of the eyeball. This normal condition is called *emmetropia* and the night pilot will not notice any significant difference in the way things look as they do

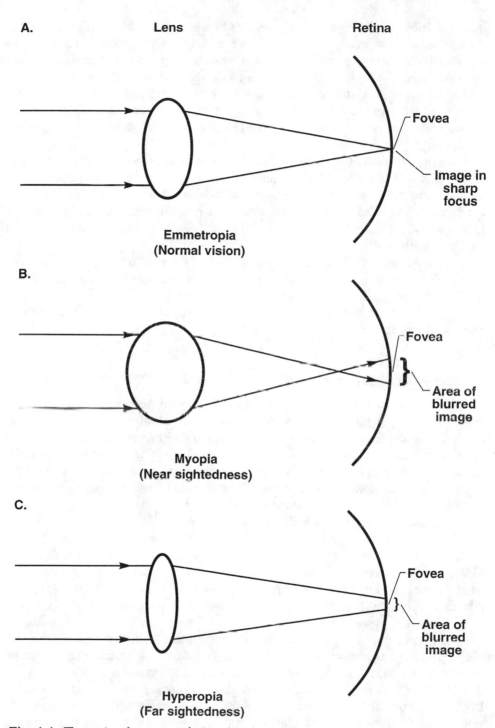

Fig. 4-4. *Three visual accommodation situations.*

during daytime. If this object being viewed is brought nearer to the eyes the shape of the lens bulges and bends the light rays more to keep a sharply focused image.

Part B shows the optical situation that exists for a person with nearsightedness (*myopia*). Here the rays of light come to a focus well in front of the retina and travel farther, ever expanding in size. What is seen is a blurred image of the distant target. Of course, the problem lies in the basic shape of the lens. As the object is brought nearer, a point is reached when the lens must change shape (accommodate) in order to maintain a sharply focused image.

The optical situation for a viewer who is farsighted (hyperopic) is diagrammed in Part C of this figure. Here, the incoming pencil of light rays comes to a focus well beyond the retinal plane so that what falls upon the fovea is also out of focus. Again, as the distant object is brought nearer the eyes, the lens must accommodate by changing its shape, but not as much as in nearsightedness because the ray is already focused well beyond the retina.

Of course, adding prescriptive lenses in front of the eyes in Part B or C can bend the pencil rays appropriately so that they come to a correct focus at the retina without requiring the lens to bulge or flatten as much as otherwise.

If the night pilot should experience a temporary blurring, just blink once or twice and it will probably clear up.

Empty field myopia

When flying at night (or in fog or cloud), the sky might appear totally dark and might also merge with the dark ground. When one is looking outside in such situations, the natural tendency of the eyes is to come to a resting focus distance of about three to four feet away. This process is called *empty field myopia* or *empty sky myopia*. In darkness or completely smooth textureless dim viewing conditions, it might be referred to as the *dark focus response*. Because empty field myopia is an unconsciously controlled reflex and cannot be sensed directly, pilots might be focused at about the distance of the windshield and not even know it.

Several problems can arise because of the eye's dark focus response. One of them is that the external visual world will seem slightly smaller than it does if the eyes are focused at the correct (far) distance; thus, objects on the ground might appear somewhat more distant and closer to the horizon than they really are. This might lead the pilot to perceive the glide slope angle to be slightly shallower and earth surface details higher than they actually are, leading the pilot to reduce the final approach descent rate and land long. If the eyes are myopic, distant airplanes with very dim lights might not be perceived as soon as otherwise (or at all) because their retinal image might be so blurred that there is insufficient light energy to elicit a visual response.

This condition can be overcome by constantly changing one's eye scan position. Look back and forth between the inside of the cockpit (at instruments) and then outside (at clearly obvious ground lights). If you have to look at the wing tips, turn the head slowly and deliberately, particularly if you are not flying straight and level. Turning the head quickly during a banked turn can produce disorientation and sometimes an illusion known as the *coriolis effect*. Never stare for more than 15 or 20 seconds into the darkness to help reduce effects of a dark focus response.

The head up display (HUD), which is specifically designed to help the pilot maintain an eye focus at or near optical infinity during an approach to landing (and also superimpose instrument information directly over the outside scene) actually is less than effective in doing this. Research by Iavecchia, Iavecchia, and Roscoe (1988) measured the eye's natural focus response when observers looked through the clear optics of a HUD's optical system while focusing a long distance away from them. They viewed either a natural background scene or read off numbers displayed on a manmade scoreboard panel 182 meters away. After determining the eye's stable focus distance with the HUD off, it was turned on. They found that the observers' focus shifted quickly in the direction of myopia; for nine of the 10 observers, their final focus distance averaged 2 meters from an average starting focus distance of about four meters. Importantly, each observer's focus response was closely related to their own individual dark focus distance. This visual response should become a part of a pilot's standard visual exam.

Accommodative speed

It is known that it takes slightly longer for the lens of the eye to change focus when it is changing focus from a near starting point, such as the instrument panel, to far away optical infinity, such as the distant runway (Weintraub, Haines, and Randle 1985). The whole accommodative process is very complex and requires about 0.2 to 0.8 second. Older people tend to take somewhat longer to reach full accommodation than younger people according to laboratory research findings. There is reason to believe that middle aged or older pilots might require as long as three or more seconds to accommodate from the instrument panel to outside scene. Because this line of sight transition is made many times during an approach, these eye focus delays can add up.

Of course, when one looks from inside to outside the cockpit, a shift of the line of sight occurs along with a change in accommodation. Because it is usually necessary to make the head-up and head-down transition many times during an approach, the night pilot should have a better idea of what is involved. Not only is it a good idea to have a fairly detailed understanding of this process, but this understanding might help him optimize this entire process by becoming more consistent each time it occurs. The four parts of FIG. 4-5 attempt to illustrate the approximate visual appearance of a commercial turbojet airplane's cockpit and corresponding outside scene during a head-up transition.

Part 1 shows the appearance of the airplane's instrument panel with the line of sight centered on the artificial horizon. Once the decision has been made to look up and the pilot's eyes start to rotate upward, the retinal image will be blurred in the vertical direction something like that shown in part 2. In part 3, the line of sight has now

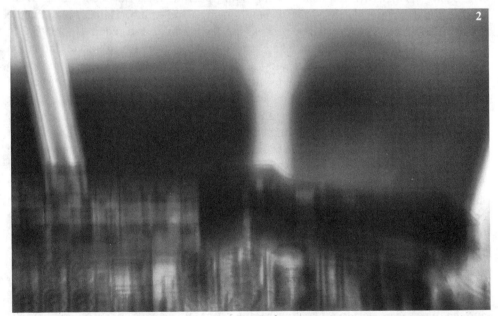

Fig. 4-5. *The effects of various states of visual accommodation and lines of sight during an approach to landing.*

Fig. 4-5. *Continued*

reached the runway out ahead of the airplane. Still, little useful information is available because while the vertical image blur is now gone from the retina, the distant runway is still blurred because the eye has not yet accommodated to its distance. Part 4 illustrates the situation where the runway is now in focus while the windshield posts and top of the glare shield are now somewhat out of focus. Of course, these illustrations are only photographic representations; they attempt to illustrate the well known depth of field optical focus effect where details located at two different distances cannot both be in focus simultaneously if the diameter of the aperture is too large. The eyeball operates in somewhat the same way as these photographs at any instant.

Of course there is more involved in a successful head-up transition than the change in line of sight and visual accommodation that occurs. The pilot must also mentally evaluate all of the available visual information and this evaluation must be performed correctly and as rapidly as possible. Such mental evaluations include a determination of whether: (1) the airplane's current location and (horizontal and vertical) approach velocity relative to the runway touchdown point are correct, (2) whether the pilot has correctly identified the runway surface, ground lights, and other detail, or has misperceived them, (3) whether there is any indication of crosswind or shear effects, and (4) in general, whether everything looks correct (in-the-slot) or whether there is something that is not quite right.

Laboratory research has shown that these complex processes can take more than four seconds during each transition for some approach conditions. Very confusing illusory conditions might take even longer. Another two seconds are required to transition back inside the cockpit. During low visibility approaches, keep the needles centered, and stabilize the airplane's heading, vertical rate, airspeed, and power. Finally, do not look outside for more than a few seconds at or near decision height, and when looking outside, look only for information that confirms the instrument information. If anything contradicts the instrument information, execute an immediate missed approach procedure.

Monocular and binocular visual fields

Everyone knows that we can't see behind us. Our eyesight is confined to a rather wide cone with its apex at each pupil. The unshaded part of the left side of FIG. 4-6 shows the angular size and shape of the right eye's field of view with the fovea at the center. Humans can see about 60 degrees above the line of sight where the eyebrows block vision. The nose blocks the lower left portion of the field at about 60 degrees arc from the fovea as well. It is important to note that one can see well beyond 90 degrees arc from the line of sight to the right side in the right eye (actually as far as 110 degrees in some people). The unshaded part of the right side of this figure shows the binocular field of view because the field of one eye overlaps the field of the other.

But how large are these visual cones when projected into the real world? In order to make the answer to this question as useful as possible to the night pilot, a line drawing of the outermost contour of FIG. 4-6 for the binocular field of view limits for a normal person have been superimposed over a cockpit photograph that presents a 360

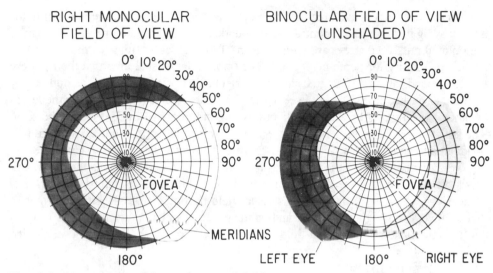

RIGHT MONOCULAR
FIELD OF VIEW

BINOCULAR FIELD OF VIEW
(UNSHADED)

Fig. 4-6. *Monocular and binocular visual fields.*

degree panoramic view of a commercial turbojet airplane cockpit. This photo (provided by the FAA) has been taken with a binocular camera with lenses located at the pilot's *reference eye position* (REP). This photograph is made up of a composite of many individual vertical photographic strips, each five degrees arc wide. The lighter shadows seen beside each window post represent what is visually obstructed by the post by each eye. Figure 4-7 presents this illustration.

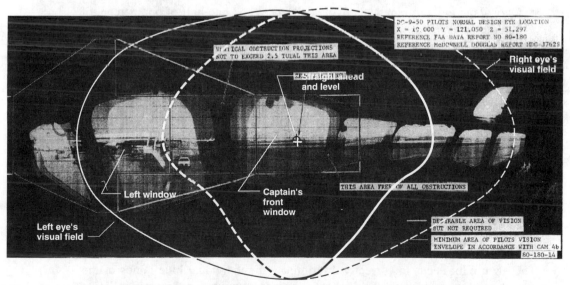

Fig. 4-7. *Normal binocular visual field superimposed over a 360-degree wide cockpit photograph.*

67

The (binocular) visual area that both eyes can see at the same time lies within the heavier weight white-lined, central-most bounded region. It encompasses an angular region of about 100 degrees arc wide total and 130 degrees arc high within which one has the possibility for depth perception. The (monocular) visual area that the right eye can see extends about 110 degrees arc to the right side of straight ahead, as outlined by the thinner dashed line. The left eye's visual field extends an equal amount to the left as is shown. If a light is located outside of this largest horizontal oval, it cannot be seen. The only way it will be seen is to look in its approximate direction so that its image falls inside this boundary. This calls for a systematic eye scan as described in chapter 8.

What happens at night is that the windshield posts and other details that are readily visible here (during the day) become far less visible as seen against the dark sky outside. The peripheral part of one's visual field becomes more sensitive to light so that even very dim lights in the air and on the ground can be detected with ease. Conversely, the portion of the visual field lying near the line of sight loses light sensitivity.

Color perception

The subject of how we see color is vast and complex, so much so that even vision experts cannot agree on very much more than the most basic processes. The night pilot really only needs to understand a few general principles about color perception, which are summarized here:

- When the visual system is adapted to darkness it becomes effectively colorblind to reflected surface colors that are of low brightness. This is obvious if one tries to read a colored sectional chart under dim cabin lighting. And with increasing age more light is needed to correctly see these same colors.

- Only about eight to nine percent of adult males and one-half of one percent of adult females in the population are color deficient in one way or another. Color vision is included in every class of aeromedical license exam mainly for this reason because there are some flying tasks that call for the correct perception of colors.

- The most common color defect is an insensitivity for perceiving greens and reds. If one's red sensitive retinal receptors (cones) do not function it is called *protanopia* and if one's green sensitive receptors do not function it is known as *deuteranopia*. An even less frequent color deficiency is blue weakness.

- Color perception results from the cone receptors in the retina and they are most dense at the fovea, where the image of something looked at directly falls. The density of cones decreases farther and farther from the fovea into the periphery, which explains why people cannot see any colors at all in the peripheral visual field as is discussed next.

The night pilot needs to correctly discriminate the individual blue lamps of the taxiway, the green runway threshold lights, and red runway end identifier lights beyond which one cannot go (*see* chapter 9), the red and green airplane navigation lights located on the right and left wing tips, respectively (*see* chapter 9), and the variation of the visual approach slope indicator (VASI) ranging from red/pink (indicating too low), to red/white (indicating on proper approach slope), to pink/white (indicating just above the approach slope), to white/white (indicating too high).

Color sensitive areas of the retina

The monocular visual field diagram shown in FIG. 4-8 was generated in the following way. First the eyes were dark adapted by sitting in a completely dark room for over an hour. Second, a small white probe light was slowly brought from outside the visual field into the field along many different radials. When its presence was just noticed, that position was plotted on a polar coordinate graph paper and produced the heavy, irregular, solid line that separates the clear from the shaded area. The clear area is the normal monocular (right eye) visual field. Third, a small, round, colored light is then used in the same way to locate the limit of sensitivity to that color. The result of many such trials is shown in FIG. 4-8.

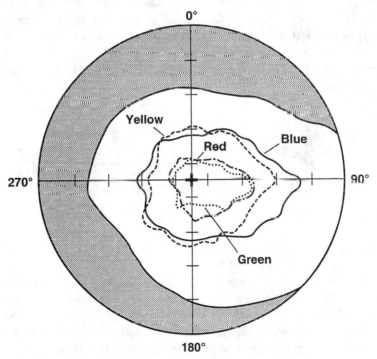

Fig. 4-8. *Color sensitive fields in the right eye.*

The center of this illustration (dark cross) represents the point at which one is looking. Each tick mark on the horizontal and vertical axis represents 20 degrees arc. Notice that the red and green sensitive area is smallest, extending only about 10 to 12 degrees on the nasal side and 35 degrees on the opposite (temporal) side. The yellow-green sensitive area of the retina is significantly larger, but still does not extend all the way out to the edge of the visual field. Of course when both eyes are open (and do not possess color deficiency), the color sensitive areas of the left eye overlap with those shown in FIG. 4-8 producing a symmetrical mirror image overlay of color sensitive cone receptors, which acts to increase the total color sensitive areas.

The intensity of the colored lights also plays an important role in that the brighter the light is, the larger will be the retinal areas that are sensitive to color.

In summary, to perceive colored lights, one must look at them almost directly. If the pilot should detect a flashing white light in the far periphery, it is wise to take a quick look over at it directly to ensure that it isn't actually colored.

The physiological blind spot

Many people do not know that inside each eye is an oval shaped area of blindness. If an object is imaged within this region it will not be seen. This is called the *blind spot*. It may be appreciated by following the simple steps of FIG. 4-9. Hold the drawing at eye level and in good light about eight inches away from both eyes. Slowly bring it directly toward your eyes while looking steadily at the center of the small X on the right side with your left eye only. As you place attention on the small airplane, notice what happens. By shifting your gaze slightly to one of the numbers near the X, you will temporarily see parts of the airplane reappear. Now stare at the airplane with your right eye and watch the X disappear.

Fig. 4-9. *Blind spot identification exercise.*

The blind spot is present at all times and under all kinds of illumination because it is a physiological feature of the retina. Because the blind spot in each eye is offset to the opposite side of the fovea from each other, what is invisible to one eye is seen by the other eye. Figure 4-10 presents the approximate size, shape, and location of the physiological blind spot in the left eye relative to the fovea (where the line of sight is imaged). Also shown is an overlay of perceived imagery as would be seen by the pilot at altitude. Note that nothing can be seen inside the circular blind spot.

Another kind of blind spot occurs after dark when the eyes are adjusted to the darkness. This *central blind spot* is far more important to the night pilot.

Because the retina photochemically adjusts itself to the ambient illumination level over an extremely wide range and because some of the neural receptors possess different light range sensitivity, the eyes become functionally blind within a central region of

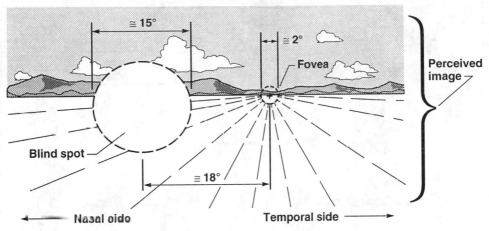

Fig. 4-10. *Physiological blind spot effect of the left eye at altitude.*

about 4 degrees arc diameter centered on the line of sight (LOS) known as the *fovea*. Figure 4-11 illustrates this effect. The upper drawing shows five aircraft during the day. After dark, when the visual system is fully adapted and the pilot is looking at the center aircraft, the pilot might not be able to see the airplane unless it has a white taillight on it.

This visual effect is why the night pilot should visually scan the outside world rather than stare steadily at just one spot. By visually scanning back and forth, he or she is more likely to spot the small dim lights of an oncoming airplane that might otherwise remain invisible inside his central blind spot. Remember that it only occurs after the eyes have been adapted to darkness and the other object does not have emitting light sources.

Prescriptive lenses

If your pilot certificate shows that you need to wear eyeglasses, then you should wear them although the FAA does not require you to wear reading glasses while flying. Nevertheless, it is prudent to do so anyway for your own good. Pilots fool themselves when they try to just get by their vision exams without having to wear eyeglasses because several visual capabilities can deteriorate in flight and make objects more blurred than otherwise. At night, eyeglasses function in exactly the same way as they do during daylight hours. Their function is merely to keep things in sharp visual focus at all times, but in a dark environment the pupil enlarges, which reduces the *depth of focus* of the eye. Depth of focus is the range of distances from the eye within which an object can be moved and still remain in focus.

With the increasing use of cathode ray instrument panel displays, pilot's vision must be capable of reading airspeed, altitude, and other flight information that is in numeric form, rather than in the form of a needle pointing in some direction on a round gauge. It is in such situations that pilots who wear prescriptive lenses should wear them in flight.

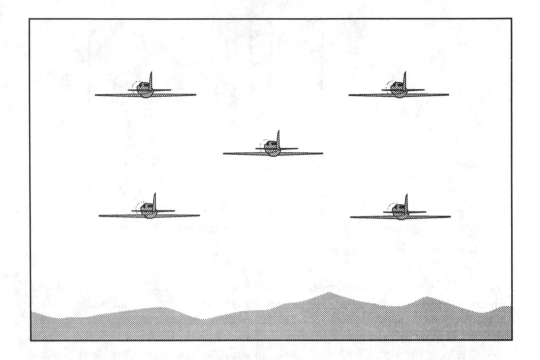

Fig. 4-11. *Central blind spot at night, assuming that the eye is adapted to the dark.*

Many pilots order eyeglasses for daytime flight that are tinted in order to reduce glare. Unless the amount of tint is very low a set of clear eyeglasses should be available for flying at night. Even a medium density gray tint can significantly reduce the visual range at which one can see an oncoming airplane at night.

Never wear sunglasses at night while flying.

Nearsightedness correction

Nearsightedness (myopia) is the condition where one can see things most sharply (without eyeglasses) when they are near the eyes. The myopic night pilot must wear prescriptive lenses that permit the eye to see objects clearly, although they are far away. Generally, the stronger the required optical correction is, the greater will be the optical distortion they will produce in the far visual periphery. In effect, the pilot will have tunnel vision to some degree. This will necessitate greater head movements to scan outside the cockpit completely. It is like trying to see around you while looking through a narrow cardboard tube. These optical corrections will also tend to increase the glare effect around bright lights.

Presbyopia correction

Almost everyone experiences aging of the eye (*presbyopia*) over time. Usually, by the time one reaches the age of 40, one cannot focus at very near distances. The older one gets, the farther one must hold the flight chart or checklist in order to focus on it. This progressive loss of near vision is so predictable that an eye doctor can measure the near point of focus and tell you your age usually within a year or two.

For a great majority of pilots over the age of 45, near vision will not be 20/20 without optical correction. And if one tries to get by without wearing these glasses, he will not only risk headache and muscular aches, but his vision might deteriorate further at night when he is fatigued or when he is experiencing even partial hypoxia at altitudes as low as 5,000 feet. The dim cockpit also adds to the difficulty in seeing without one's normal eyeglasses.

Because pilots must be able to see things clearly that are far away and also inside the cockpit, bifocal (two focal distances) lenses make this possible. The night pilot should request the optician to place the *break point* (the line separating the two different lenses) somewhat higher than would normally be used for daily wear. When looking straight forward out of the front windshield, the pilot should be able to see the break point line approximately superimposed over the near edge of the glare shield approximately as is shown in FIG. 4-12.

Farsightedness correction

Pilots who cannot focus at near distances (say less than 36 inches) require optical correction to bring their accommodation into reading distance, from 10 to 18 inches. This condition is known as farsightedness or hyperopia. The night pilot might need

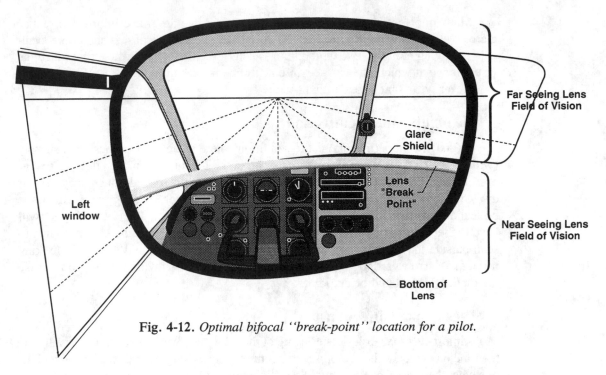

Fig. 4-12. *Optimal bifocal "break-point" location for a pilot.*

prescriptive lenses for this condition if the instrument panel is not in focus in the dark and if the pilot experiences eyestrain, tearing, blurred vision, and headaches when focusing there. If in doubt about whether eyeglasses are needed, see a vision care specialist. Make certain to tell them that the glasses will be used for piloting. Also tell the specialist exactly where different information is located in the field of view and its distance. Of course, this also applies to ordering corrections for nearsightedness.

Grey or color-tinted prescriptive lenses are not recommended for the night pilot, particularly if he or she is middle aged or older; the visual system gradually loses some of its sensitivity to light with increasing age.

Trifocal lenses

Some pilots wear eyeglasses with three separate distance corrections, *trifocals*. Figure 4-13 is a drawing of a standard trifocal that has the lens for seeing near details located at the bottom area of the lens. The intermediate distance lens is in the middle and the distance lens is at the top. Some older age commercial and corporate pilots order trifocal lenses with the nearest corrective lens located at the top because they need to be able to focus on displays and switches located just above their heads within 8 inches or less of their eyes. The central area of the lens is used for viewing at optical infinity (outside of the cockpit). The lower intermediate distance correction is for seeing the instrument panel located (typically) 28 to 34 inches away. Note that there are two break points.

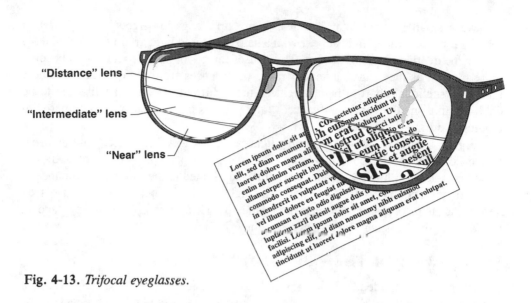

"Distance" lens —

"Intermediate" lens —

"Near" lens —

Fig. 4-13. *Trifocal eyeglasses.*

ANATOMY OF THE HUMAN EYEBALL

The eyeball is an almost spherical semirigid structure that is suspended within the eye socket of the skull on six eye muscles. When the muscles that are located on the opposite sides of the eyeball contract and relax in a coordinated manner, the eyeball rotates in its socket. The nervous control of these binocularly coordinated eye tracking movements is elegantly precise and acts to keep the image from a distant object focused upon the fovea of each eye. If these eye muscles do not function correctly one might experience *double vision* (*diplopia*), which might be corrected by surgery in extreme cases or by wearing specially designed eyeglasses that have prismatic (line of sight deviation) correction.

The inside of the eyeball is filled with transparent fluid that is being continually circulated in and out of the eyes to cleanse and nourish the tissue of the retinal (and other) tissue. If the outflow of this fluid is impeded, the pressure can build up inside the eyeball (*glaucoma*) and can result in serious visual loss or complete blindness. Loss of peripheral vision is a sign of early glaucoma and the night pilot should have an eye check immediately if he suspects such a problem. Glaucoma is not associated with any aches or pains, unfortunately. As a ray of light enters the pupil of the eye and travels back to the fovea, this ray is scattered slightly over other areas of the retina and is perceived at night as veiling glare.

Referring to FIG. 4-2, it should be noted that the pupillary area will enlarge in dark visual environments, which will: (1) lead to more light scatter from bright lights (including those on the instrument panel), (2) increase the amount of dazzling glare that will, in turn, decrease one's visual discriminability over much of the visual field,

(3) cause small colored lights, such as wing tip navigation lights, to appear less sharply focused (some might appear with a halo of colored light around them), and (4) reduce the depth of focus of the eye. This causes images of things looked at to become more blurred as they travel a smaller range of distances from the eye. For instance, reading a sectional chart at night might be more difficult because it will need to be held within a smaller range of distances (and perhaps more steadily) as compared to reading it during the daytime.

Figure 4-2 also shows that incoming light rays come to a focus exactly at the fovea, which contains special cone receptors. Cones support perception of color and very good visual acuity; however, cones are somewhat limited in the range of luminance to which they respond. Figure 4-15 shows this light sensitivity curve. As we have seen above, the shape of the lens changes automatically to keep a sharply focused image on the fovea even as distant objects approach the eye.

PHYSIOLOGY OF THE VISUAL SYSTEM

Eyes need an adequate blood supply and ample oxygen. The retinal tissue requires more oxygen per minute than any other tissue in the body. This fact seems obvious to pilots who pull high g loads and who begin to lose peripheral visual sensitivity. During the day this *peripheral gray-out*, as it is called, is quite obvious but at night it is much more difficult to notice. Fortunately, private and commercial pilots do not experience these high g acceleration loads. Chapter 2 discussed the importance of getting enough oxygen to the brain.

In general, there is almost no apparent visual effect of changing air pressure other than those associated with reduced oxygen supply. That is, air pressure is not as critical a factor as is the amount of oxygen that is supplied to the body.

The visual system automatically adjusts itself to an extraordinarily wide range of ambient brightness levels by means of a process known as *adaptation*. It is important to have an understanding of this process and what the eye can and cannot do. The normal, healthy, human visual system can dynamically adjust itself over a range of 1 to 10 billion or almost 100 decibels of brightness (EN 4-1). At the lower end, the visual system cannot perceive luminous energy less than about $10^{-5.5}$ log millilamberts (ml). [One ml is approximately equivalent to 10 meter candles or to about 1 foot candle.] This point is labelled A in FIG. 4-14, which depicts the full range of illumination in nature.

Across the top of this illustration is a schematic depiction of what kinds of visual receptors are involved over this range of brightnesses. There are rod receptors at the left and cone receptors on the right and a mixture of both in the middle. Night vision (also called *scotopic vision*) extends from the dark-adapted rod receptor threshold (labelled A) to the cone receptor threshold after dark adaptation (labelled B). Twilight vision is also known as *mesopic (middle) vision* and extends from the cone threshold for about three more log units to the point where virtually all of the vision is mediated by cone receptors (labelled C). Day vision (also called *photophic vision*) extends from this point for another 4.5 to 5 log units to the point where extreme visual pain is felt.

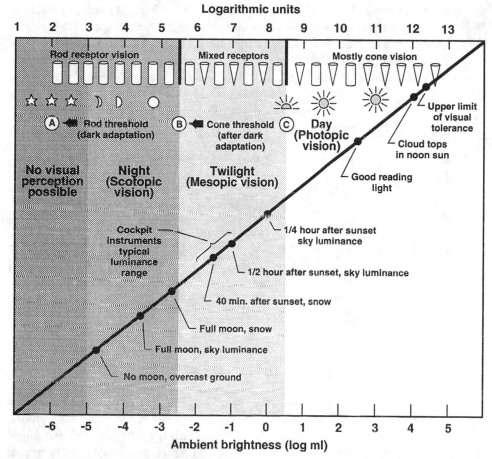

Fig. 4-14. *Full range of brightness levels in nature.*

Above this level, damage is done to the delicate nervous tissue due to the very high energies that are present in the bright light. The night pilot need not be concerned about the day vision portion of this figure except for the transition known as dark-adaptation.

Once the eye is fully dark-adapted (two hours or more in total darkness), the visual system will decrease in sensitivity by a factor of 1/5000th of its former sensitivity after being in bright light for only a few minutes. In short, the cones change in sensitivity far faster than the rods.

As one becomes older, the visual system loses some of its sensitivity to light. In effect, the older pilot will require more light in order to see the level of detail that the younger pilot can see with ease. How great a change is this? Figure 2-2 shows that almost one full log unit (factor of 10) of light sensitivity is lost between the ages of 40 and 80. Translated to FIG. 4-14, this is approximately equivalent to shifting points A and B to the right almost one logarithmic unit's distance.

Figure 4-15 shows both the actual measured rate of change of outdoor brightness (solid line) and the rate at which the visual receptors of the eye change in sensitivity to light as a function of local time of day (adapted from Beebe-Center, Carmichael, and Mead 1944). It is clear that the visual system gains in sensitivity somewhat faster than required to maintain a sensitivity equivalent to changing ambient brightness.

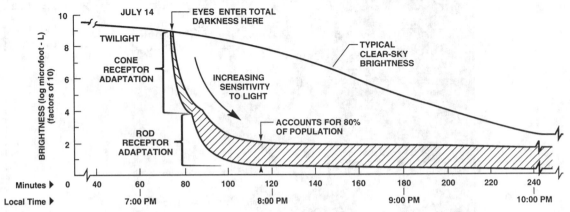

Fig. 4-15. *Outdoor brightness and visual sensitivity changes before, during, and after sunset.*
Beebe-Center, 1944

VISUAL PERCEPTION

Perception is generally defined as the end result of many complex nervous system activities that accept incoming sensory information, combine them with our memory, make new and creative associations, and then establish the potential for taking new action. Visual perception concentrates mainly on the visual aspects of these steps but is influenced by man's balance organs, stomach awareness, skin sensations, joint and muscle sensors, gastro-intestinal tract, and a host of other sources of information.

In order to more fully understand visual perception, one must know something about how man's visual system functions under both static (relatively unchanging) and dynamic (moving) conditions. Each is discussed from the standpoint of the night aviator.

Static phenomena

There is really very little that is truly static in life because life is characterized by motion of various kinds. Nevertheless, it is useful to think of some of the geometric aspects of our world as being static.

When a pilot climbs into a cockpit and sits very still the airplane's structure may be considered to be static and fixed, a rigid unit. Visually speaking, it is the presence of this rigid cockpit surrounding the pilot that plays an important role in helping him or her to become a semifixed part of the airplane. From a perceptual standpoint, the pilot should perceive him- or herself to be a component of the vehicle. Changes in the airplane's location and attitude in the sky are the pilot's as well. Visually static cockpit structure helps the pilot make correct manual control inputs by providing him or her with a relatively stable (visual) basis for judging what needs to be done next relative to an otherwise constantly changing external visual world.

Figures 4-16 and 4-17 try to illustrate the rather dramatic visual effects that occur when one simply rolls one's head in the cockpit relative to the instrument panel's glare shield. Hold the illustration normally upright and look at FIG. 4-16 very briefly. What is the current airplane roll attitude and pitch attitude? Do the same with FIG. 4-17. Take note of the sense of uncertainty that is felt at first; while the horizon has not rolled, it is still difficult to take a quick glance at the horizon and correctly interpret

Fig. 4-16. *Cockpit scene with head rolled clockwise 25 degrees.*

Fig. 4-17. *Cockpit scene with head rolled counter-clockwise 25 degrees.*

what the present situation is in each figure. Now look at each figure while tilting your head to the left 25 degrees.

    The cockpit design eyepoint and seat adjustment. The design eyepoint (DEP) is the location of the pilot's eyes in the cockpit that permits optimal internal and external visibility. This position has been carefully preplanned by the airplane designers and the night pilot should know where it is and how to locate his body and head correctly, particularly at night. Some texts will refer to the "cockpit cutoff" angle, while others will refer to the "over-the-nose" angle; both refer to the vertical angle below the horizontal to the point that is blocked by the nose of the aircraft or other structure.

80

This angle determines the slant range to the ground the pilot can see ahead of the airplane as is discussed below.

First consider FIG. 4-18, which shows an airplane on final approach at altitude h and a nose-up pitch angle of β as measured from the horizontal. The nominal glide-slope angle θ is usually about three degrees arc. In this example, the runway is obscured by fog, rain, or other precipitation so that all the pilot can see on the ground ahead of him is a short visible segment (H) that is shaded in FIG. 4-18. This visible segment sweeps along ahead of the airplane. It is limited at the farthest end by the fog and at the nearest by the physical structure of the airplane, usually the top surface of the instrument panel's glare shield. Angle alpha is the "over-the-nose" vertical visual angle from the horizontal.

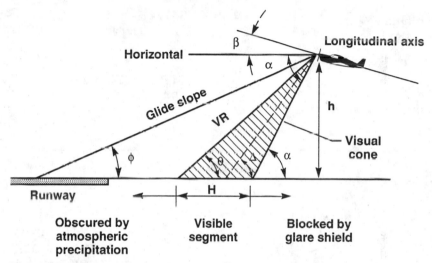

Fig. 4-18. *Diagram relating a cockpit's design eye point geometry.*

It should be clear that if the pilot adjusts the seat so that his or her eyes are higher than the DEP, angle alpha will increase (as long as the pitch attitude and the altitude of the airplane does not change). Figure 4-19 shows these geometric relations. Of course, the eyes move within a three-dimensional volume such that both vertical and forward-aft movement will influence the size of angle alpha. Even a small vertical movement of the eyes of several centimeters or so (at a constant horizontal distance from the eyes to the cockpit structure) can result in a large change in the distance to the nearest visible ground point (D). Figure 4-20 shows different values of D for four typical flare heights for a Boeing model 727 type airplane. Note that sitting somewhat higher than the DEP during low visibility conditions will increase the horizontal length of the visible segment. This can provide a little more valuable runway alignment (and other) guidance information.

Why are these factors important to the night pilot? One reason is that if one is making a low visibility approach at night it is particularly important to be able to see

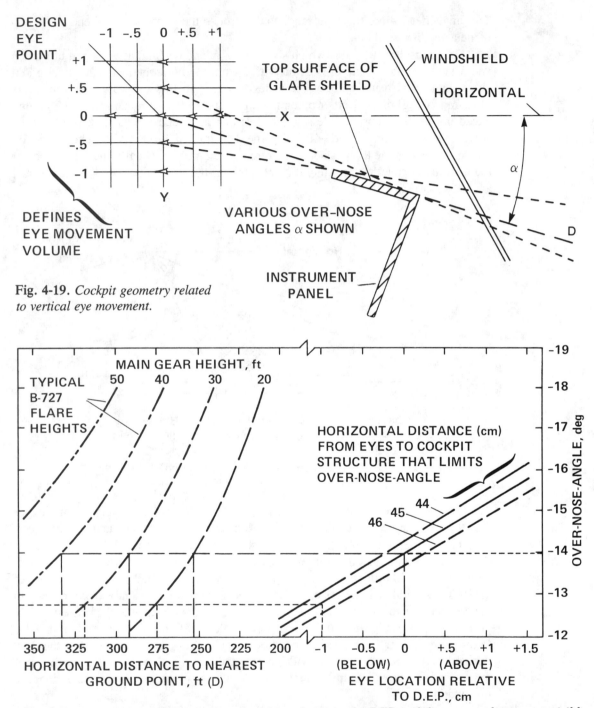

Fig. 4-19. *Cockpit geometry related to vertical eye movement.*

Fig. 4-20. *The relationship between eye location relative to the DEP and distance to the nearest visible ground detail for various main landing gear heights and other factors.*

as much of the available ground segment as possible. This is achieved by sitting with the eyes at the DEP. Do not stretch or slump vertically during the final approach. Do not lean forward or back as this will also affect the over-the-nose angle, and realize that the ground lights associated with the runway will not appear as early as they will if visual range is greater. Also try not to change the airplane's pitch attitude during the approach since pitching up will cut off even more of the visible ground segment than otherwise.

How should the pilot adjust the seat so that he is sitting at the proper DEP? There are two general approaches. The first involves the use of a special alignment device that is looked at during vertical seat adjustments. Figure 4-21 shows one such device that is used in commercial airplanes and is mounted on the middle window post. When the eyes are in the proper position, the nearer dark ball should be seen centered on the farther white ball.

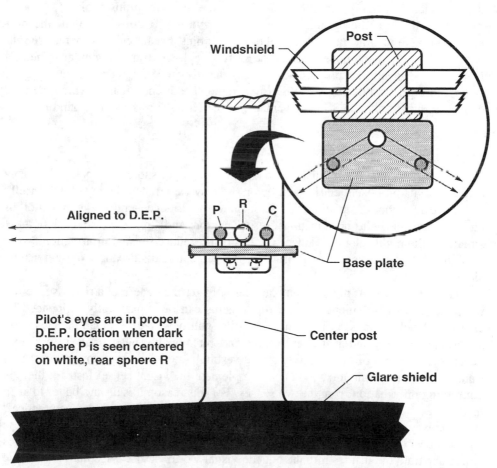

Fig. 4-21. *A vertical and horizontal seat adjustment sighting device.*

The second approach to adjusting the seat height at night is to (1) tighten the seat belt somewhat tighter than normal, which should pull the body down into the seat somewhat more than otherwise, and (2) adjust the seat so that the eyes can just see over the top of the forward sloping portion of the glare shield. Many private airplane manufacturers design the top surface of the glare shield to point to the DEP.

Also, remember that most people tend to slump down into the seat over time. This lowers the eye position by as much as two inches or more.

When sitting at the DEP a useful rule of thumb for most single engine aircraft is that slant range to the nearest point on the ground seen just above the nose of the aircraft will be about one mile for each 1,000 feet of altitude.

Establishing a stable visual frame of reference during final approach. The above discussion provided several important reasons for keeping the head in a stable position during the approach and landing phase of flight at night. But this is also important in order to help reduce the possibility of vertigo developing and some motion-related visual illusions that are discussed elsewhere in this book.

Importance of being able to see cockpit window frames. At night, the pilot should be able to dim the cockpit lights to the point that he can just barely see the windshield outline and upper edge of the glare shield. Contrary to popular opinion it is not a good idea to keep the cockpit totally dark because these cockpit outlines are very helpful in establishing a stable visual frame of reference against which the pilot can discriminate pitch and roll movements of the airplane relative to ground lights.

Dynamic phenomena

The night pilot should think about the important yet subtle role played by many different dynamic visual cues which he or she may experience. Here we will briefly introduce a number of situations that can negatively influence a pilot's judgment of his current status in flight: head motions, disorientation, and airsickness. In each of these situations the night pilot is also faced with greatly reduced visual information that is available during the day to compensate for the perceptual disturbances these dynamic situations create.

Head motions. At night, when one does not have the benefit of a rich visual environment, one's assessment of one's flight status can be significantly influenced by excessive head motions. Usually the night pilot will feel that his situation is less safe and secure during and just after rolling and pitching his head. This is probably because of the loss of the relatively stable vestibular sense organ information that is transmitted to the brain to support and complement the visual sense. Instead, there is conflicting information from the two senses. For this reason it is always better to keep the head as motionless as possible and rotate it as smoothly and as slowly as practical.

The way things look outside the cockpit changes continually during flight. These changes become apparent mainly because of the presence of cockpit window frames which separate the inside from the outside visual world as discussed above. Because the night pilot sits so close to these window frames and makes body and head motions voluntarily, he knows unconsciously that any apparent motion of the window frames relative to the outside environment is most likely the result of his motions. All other motions are imputed to be the result of airplane motion through the sky. Herein lies a source of problems for the night pilot.

In contrast, during daytime flight, pilots have many different kinds of dynamic visual cues for judging altitude, attitude, location, and even airspeed to some extent. It is very hard to define which of this vast array of information is really used at any particular moment. There are external scene visual cues and intra-cockpit visual information, there are sounds and vibrations. There are even air temperature and pressure cues that are unconsciously integrated together with everything else to yield an impression of one's present flight condition. Because vision is the primary sense and visual cues provide by far the great majority of airplane guidance and control information, any changes to our vision or the appearance of the external scene will have a disproportionately large impact on a pilot's safety. During nighttime flight the nature of the visual cues that are available changes dramatically.

Disorientation. This term is defined in many different ways but the core concept is that of loss of one's ability to maintain an accurate spatial orientation or reference. A subsequent section of this chapter presents a discussion of various kinds of disorientation.

In his now classic paper "Visual judgments in motion," Calvert (1954) states, "The most important features of the visual field are, first, the plane of the ground, because it gives the observer the horizon, and, second, the objects of known size on its surface, because they give him a scale of size and distance . . . (these two sources of information) . . . form a visual reference frame to which all our judgments are subconsciously related, and if we cannot establish this relationship we become disoriented and frightened." This explains one reason why some pilots feel more uncertain of themselves when flying at night because the horizon is either very difficult or totally impossible to see.

Disorientation can lead to very unpleasant symptoms of airsickness and extreme dizziness known as *vertigo*.

Airsickness. While everyone knows what airsickness is, no one knows what really causes it. But when its early symptoms begin to appear (sweating, buzz in the ears, inability to focus the eyes or to look at some object without wavering, double vision), the pilot is likely to have a sense of dread and fear. These feelings are actually powerful warnings to take immediate action to cope with these symptoms. Yet, just as airsickness requires some time to develop, it also requires some time to diminish after the originating causes are removed, if they can be removed at all.

The single IFR pilot is at most risk during these conditions and he should immediately stabilize the airplane in straight and level flight and turn on the autopilot if one is available. If an autopilot isn't available the pilot should (a) avoid all head motions, (b) look slowly and deliberately back and forth between the artificial horizon, airspeed, and altimeter, (c) open an air vent to introduce cool, fresh air (which will also reduce the odors of vomit), and (d) make no rapid or large control inputs that aren't required to counteract wind effects. If the pilot must vomit he or she shouldn't worry about using a paper bag (unless he has one immediately at hand). If he has to search all over for a bag his head motions will exacerbate the air sickness problem. It is only possible to clean up the cabin later if one is alive to do it. Here, once again, is another argument in favor of having two pilots aboard every night flight.

Reaction time. Everyone knows how important it is to be able to respond as fast as possible to an emergency situation. *Reaction time* (RT) refers to this response duration. Pilots who are mentally alert, in good physical condition, possess normal eyesight, and are motivated to react quickly will be able to respond in about a third of a second to the unexpected onset of a light signal or an auditory tone. Far longer RT values have been found for subjects who are tired, who are not certain about what kind of response they should make (a single button press versus two different button presses), who are sleep deprived, or who might be looking in the wrong direction when the alerting signal comes on.

When the eye is dark-adapted the visual system responds with different RT values depending upon where in the field of view the light is located. This is illustrated in FIG. 4-22 (from Haines 1977), which is a set of RT values from many dark-adapted test subjects superimposed upon a wide angle jet cockpit photograph. The vertical, dashed, curved line represents an imaginary vertical line passing through the pilot's straight-ahead point. The horizontal, dashed curved line with tick marks represents an imaginary horizon line as seen from the pilot's eyepoint. The smallest solid white line butterfly region labelled 270 msec shows the region within which a small white test light can be placed in the dark and, when it is turned on unexpectedly, will produce an average RT of 0.27 second. It can be seen that the farther away from the line of sight (fovea) the test light is imaged, the longer RT will be on the average. Reaction time at the fovea is about 0.26 second under these test conditions and can only be expected to lengthen in the actual cockpit.

Perception of advanced cockpit displays. Each new aircraft model that is designed seems to incorporate more and more advanced technology. As safety is enhanced by the addition of this technology, so is the perceived complexity of operation and the potential for information overload. Highly advanced cockpit systems can even become intimidating to those who cannot or will not study diligently to understand them fully. Two quite different aspects of perception of such advanced cockpit displays are considered here. First, that of the sensory perception of these cockpits in the sense of reacting rapidly and correctly to the information that is displayed, and second, the pilot's psychological reactions to them, particularly at night.

In order to illustrate several points with regard to the sensory perception problems that are associated with highly advanced cockpits at night, FIG. 4-23 shows an advanced cockpit that is operated at Ames Research Center by the Aerospace Human Factors Research Division. Here the cockpit structure has been illuminated for purposes of photography.

Situated in front of each pilot is a computerized workstation complete with touch-sensitive screens, multifunction color cathode ray tubes (CRT), voice warnings and

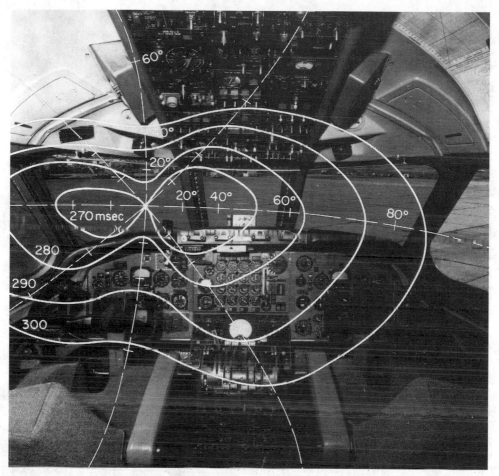

Fig. 4-22. *Distribution of average reaction time to onset of a small white light in the dark.*

annunciations of subsystem status, side-arm controllers (in place of the control wheel), more intelligent autopilot, and other advanced features that are being evaluated for research purposes.

Figure 4-23 shows the five large-format (9″ wide × 12″ high) color CRT displays spanning the entire instrument panel. At night, these slightly curved glass faceplates can reflect ambient light from behind the pilot into the eyes. Small areas of veiling glare can appear and partially mask the information that is displayed. Also, at night the different levels of sensitivity to light that exists across the retina will cause displays located on either side of the one being viewed to appear somewhat brighter. This should not be a particular problem, however. What can be far more of a problem is the sensation of flicker than might be seen in the peripheral visual field of these CRT that are driven at refresh rates under 60 per second or so. In fact, the far visual periphery can discriminate a pulsating white light at rates down to about 45 per second.

Fig. 4-23. *Advanced research cockpit simulator at Ames Research Center.*

The information that is displayed on any of the five CRTs shown in FIG. 4-23 can be rerouted to any other display in the event that one fails. While this capability makes sense from the standpoint of information redundancy, it might lead to possible positional confusion. If the captain has always found aircraft attitude information on the CRT directly ahead and now it is on the next adjacent display, one might ask how will the inside-to-outside-to-inside eye scan be affected and whether during a low-visibility, high-workload approach, pitch and roll attitude will be influenced?

With regard to the second type of perception of a cockpit containing highly advanced technology, the flight crew should begin to view themselves more as system managers and tactical decision makers than as real-time controllers of an airplane. Needless to say, younger and older pilots view this new role with some suspicion and anxiety. At night particularly, when everything is lit up like a Christmas tree, the massive amount of raw and processed information can be more than intimidating. It can swamp the pilot completely unless it: (1) is carefully designed to be matched to each pilot's mental and physical workload capability during different phases of flight, (2) is carefully designed to complement the human visual system's capabilities and limitations, and (3) is designed to make up for other deficiencies in the system operator (pilot) that can occur during unanticipated emergencies such as panic, immobilizing fear, or other untoward response.

If the automation employed in the advanced cockpit is so transparent that the pilot cannot trace its basic logic paths, there is the very real possibility that he or she will not be capable of taking effective diagnostic or remedial action when it fails. The pilot should also understand all of the backout procedures of an automated flight system and must be given override authority.

VISUAL ILLUSIONS

A visual illusion is a perception of something that is different from its normal appearance. Illusions are a commonplace experience in life so there is little reason to discuss them, except that several in particular can adversely affect one's night flying judgments. Harris, a vision researcher and long-time student of illusions, has made a valuable observation concerning visual illusions (1977). He states, "the term visual illusion represents an unfortunate choice of vocabulary (because it) seems to incite an air of magic . . . or to hallucinate elaborate imagery which has no physical basis in reality. The vast majority of false perceptions are not magical in nature. They are logical interpretations by the observer of what he actually saw. They are explainable and predictable on the basis of sound engineering concepts." And so the night pilot should become as aware as possible about the true nature of night visual illusions so that he can cope with them most effectively. The interested reader should also read Gillingham and Wolfe (1986) and Pitts (1969) for more information on this intriguing subject. For present purposes we will consider two basic kinds of illusions, those that occur under static conditions where the pilot's visual world doesn't appear to be moving and others that occur under dynamic conditions of head movement, eyeball rotation, and flight.

Static illusions

Static illusions occur when the pilot isn't moving relative to his visual environment. If he sits perfectly still, the cockpit of his airplane will not appear to move while the outside scene might appear to move. It is this differential movement in his field of view that can produce some interesting, if dangerous, visual illusions.

There are many static illusions that can occur at night or in dusk illumination conditions. Some of them are listed in TABLE 4-1.

Runway length/width illusion. Solid objects such as a runway possess certain outline shapes and sizes that depend upon the position and distance from which they are viewed. For instance, the surface of a runway might appear long and narrow or shorter and fatter than normal depending upon where one is in altitude and distance from it. Pilots often unconsciously rely on their mental image of a runway's outline that they have seen in the past to judge their distance and glide slope angle relative to a

Table 4-1.
Static visual illusions at night.

Runway length/width illusion
Foreshortening illusion
Sloped runway illusion
Vertical position illusion
Fog and rain-produced illusions
After-image illusion
False horizon illusion
Ganzfeld depth loss illusion
Size-distance illusion
Foreground occlusion illusion
Reversible perspective illusion
Up-sloped lighted city illusion

desired touchdown point on its surface. Herein lies a powerful potential illusory situation, particularly at night when many other surrounding objects of known size and shape are not visible to provide supporting information. The illusion arises because what is seen differs from what one expects to see.

Figure 4-24 is a diagram of this illusion based upon the work of Mertens and Lewis (1982). In each of the four examples, the runway length is 8,000 feet long and the eye's vantage point is the same, yet situation A appears as if one is lower and nearer to the intended touchdown point and situation D appears as if one is higher and farther away. In short, the more flight experience one has making approaches to a fixed runway length to width ratio, the more one becomes adapted to its resultant shape as the standard against which one estimates one's position on a given glide slope. Change the runway's dimensions and the resultant standard changes, which then very likely systematically influences one's estimate of one's position on the existing glide slope.

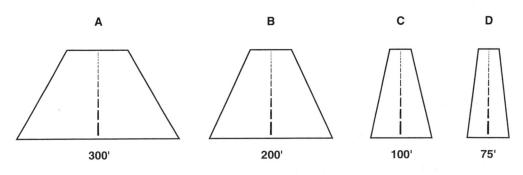

RUNWAY WIDTH (ft.)

Fig. 4-24. *Runway length-to-width illusion.*

As Mertens and Lewis (1982) point out, "Both anecdotal reports from pilots and theories of visual cues would predict lower approaches to narrow or long runways than to wide or short runways." These researchers conducted a series of VFR flight simulator studies on this subject where the length and width of the *computer generated image* (CGI) runway could be varied at will. They found that providing their subject pilots with prior knowledge of the runway's geometric size had no effect on their flight performance or judgments. They also found that making practice approaches to a narrow runway led to their making steeper approaches to wider runways. In addition, approaches made to longer runways tended to lead to shallower approach angles. The authors concluded their summary: "These findings add to the quantitative evidence of danger in night visual approaches due to visual illusions and large variability in the visual perception of approach angle." (Ibid., pg. 1)

Foreshortening illusion. One variation of the foreshortening illusion refers to the situation where the true, objective shape of an object or terrain feature seems to be more elliptical or shortened when it is viewed from a distance. Figure 4-25 is an illustration of this illusion where the same runway is seen from an identical glide path angle, but at different distances.

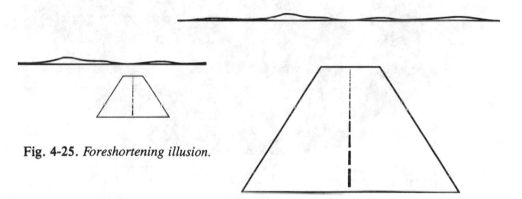

Fig. 4-25. *Foreshortening illusion.*

A variation of this illusion is that of the *downhill illusion*. It is produced by a number of converging lines of ground details that are sometimes used as approach alignment aids. For instance, long lines of trees or hedges are sometimes placed parallel to and on each side of the runway. One explanation for this illusion is that these converging lines in the horizontal plane provide a similar perception as do parallel lines in a plane that slopes downhill to the level threshold. Figure 4-26 illustrates this effect, which also occurs at night when there are long rows of lights all converging to a common point at the horizon.

Sloped runway illusions. If the ground under the runway is not gravitationally level (the runway is sloped), the resulting visual cues can influence a pilot's judgment of his or her height above the touchdown point, and how he or she flies the approach. Because the terrain located around the runway is usually on the same plane as the run-

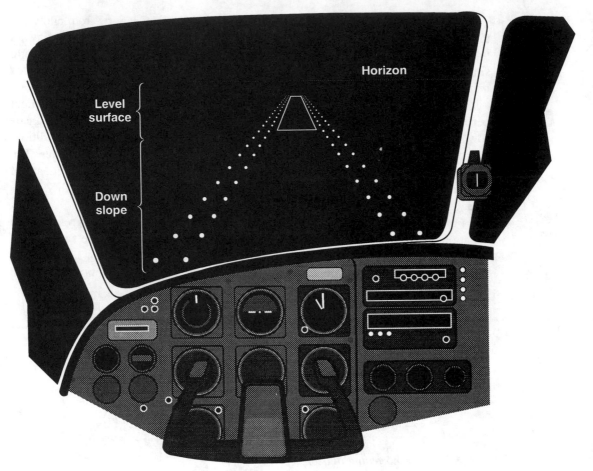

Fig. 4-26. *Downhill illusion.*

way, the approach-related visual information obtained from the ground will reinforce that from the runway.

For approaches that are made to runways where the runway descends to the far end of the runway, a down slope (part A of FIG. 4-27), the pilot will tend to fly a shallower approach (shown by the thin solid line flight path) than he would if the terrain were level. Angle X is the runway's down-slope angle from the horizontal, say two degrees. Angle Z is a three degree glideslope angle relative to the runway's sloped surface. The solid line oriented at angle Y above the horizontal (say four degrees) represents the shallower flight path that night pilots will tend to fly until reaching a point where the runway appears as it usually does from the normal glide path angle of three degrees. This illusory condition often leads to an overshoot of the desired touchdown point.

If the approach terrain slopes upward to the far end of the runway (part C of FIG. 4-27), the pilot will be more inclined to fly a steeper approach (shown by the thin solid

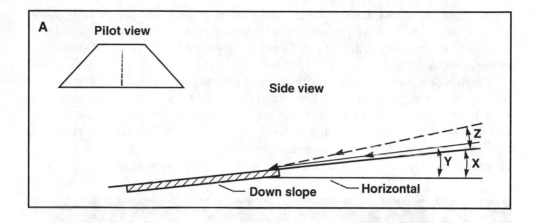

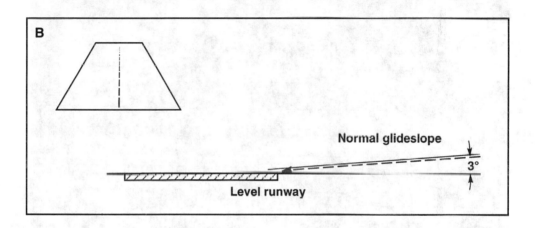

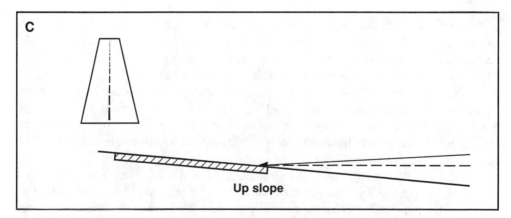

Fig. 4-27. *Appearance of a runway at different slopes with side view diagrams.*

line) for reasons similar but opposite to those just discussed. The pilot who is influenced by this illusory condition will be likely to land short of the desired touchdown point because his glide path will seem to be too high. Part B of FIG. 4-27 shows the level runway situation.

Vertical position illusion. In general, this illusion refers to the fact that lighted objects or terrain features are perceived erroneously because of the presence of wrongly interpreted real world information. For example, lighted features that are farther away from the pilot tend to appear higher on the horizon. This effect is shown in FIG. 4-28, which is a computer-generated nighttime approach scene. Notice how the far end of the runway appears to rise up out of the invisible ground plane.

Fig. 4-28. *Simulator night approach scene illustrating the vertical position illusion.*

Several other illusions can be considered as a combination of the vertical position illusion and the false horizon illusion; they can occur when the horizon is not visible and when the airplane is at a relatively low altitude as during a takeoff or an approach. Figure 4-29 shows an airplane seen from behind with a light on the ground a small distance ahead and to one side of it. The pilot must look at a downward angle in order to see the light relative to his wings. As long as the wings and pitch attitude are kept level, everything will be fine; however, this might cause the pilot to perceive his or her line of sight to the ground light to be more level (nearer the horizontal) than it actually is, which could cause a pitch-up control input.

In the following two figures, the airplane is again at a relatively low altitude. In FIG. 4-30, the pilot has allowed an imperceptibly small left wing down bank angle to occur so that the airplane is banking away from the light. Remember that the horizon is invisible so that there is almost no visual information available from the real world

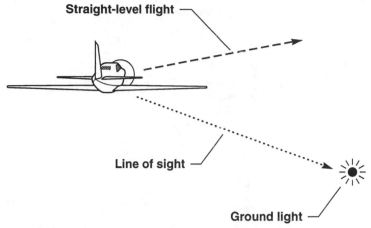

Straight-level flight

Line of sight

Ground light

Fig. 4-29. *Low altitude level flight pitch-up illusion.*
Reprinted with permission of Macmillan Publishing Company, from The Proficient Pilot, Revised Edition by Barry Schiff. Copyright ©1985 by Barry Schiff.

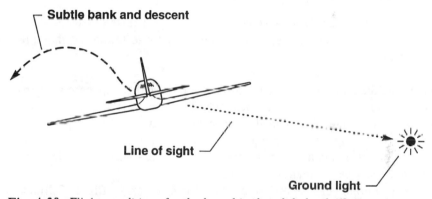

Subtle bank and descent

Line of sight

Ground light

Fig. 4-30. *Flight conditions for the low altitude subtle bank illusion.*
Reprinted with permission of Macmillan Publishing Company, from The Proficient Pilot, Revised Edition by Barry Schiff. Copyright ©1985 by Barry Schiff

to tell him that he is too low because he still thinks he is looking down on the light when he is actually banking more and more toward the ground. Only his artificial horizon will inform him of this small but dangerous bank angle.

Finally, in FIG. 4-31, we see the conditions that can lead to the *safe slide* illusion. Here the pilot inadvertently banks to the side on which the light is located. He or she notices that the light does not seem to be as far down below his wing as before and he thinks that his airplane and the light are at the same altitude, that is, he is very near the ground. Usually his immediate response is to gain altitude; at least this illusion produces a somewhat safer condition of flight.

Fog and rain-produced illusions. The combination of darkness and atmospheric precipitation can lead to several dangerous illusions. One of them is related to a condition of so-called *aerial perspective* where pilots can be deceived by the presence of fog

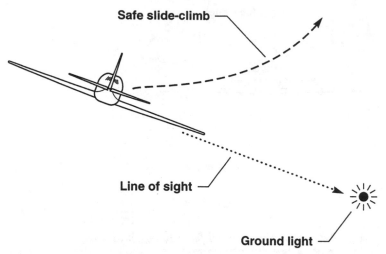

Fig. 4-31. *Flight conditions for the low altitude safe slide climb illusion.* Reprinted with permission of Macmillan Publishing Company, from The Proficient Pilot, Revised Edition by Barry Schiff. Copyright ©1985 by Barry Schiff.

or haze through which they must view the runway. The fog reduces the apparent brightness of the runway lights, which leads the pilot to think that they are farther away than they actually are.

Heavy rain on the windshield can also bend, diffuse, and fragment the rays of light entering the pilot's eyes from the ground and make them appear to originate from locations different from their true locations. This condition usually makes the pilot think that he is too high. Rain can also cause the runway to appear larger in size than it would appear in clear air, which would make the pilot believe he is closer than he is. Of course, heavy rain can also cause the horizon to disappear from view and a false horizon to appear closer than the actual horizon.

In their comprehensive review of spatial orientation in flight, Gillingham and Wolfe (1986) remark that a pilot can "have the illusion of banking to the right . . . if the runway lights are brighter on the right side of the runway than they are on the left." Of course, the opposite is also true.

During an approach made through thin fog or haze conditions, the vertical visibility to the ground is better than is the forward visibility toward the runway. This causes the brightness of the runway edge and centerline lights to reduce with distance. An illusion is sometimes produced where the airplane seems to have pitched up. Pilots might make an incorrect nose down corrective response under such conditions.

In clear air conditions at night, pilots might be more likely to descend short of the runway because lighted areas will tend to appear closer than they are. This is readily demonstrated by asking the tower to change runway intensity during a long, straight-in approach. Pilots will tend to fly steeper approach angles when the lights have higher intensity and shallower approach angles when the lights have less intensity.

What can the pilot do to counteract these illusions that distort the glide path angle one way or another? The first suggestion is to cross-check your altitude, airspeed, and vertical rate more frequently than you would otherwise. If your vertical sink rate is larger than you expect for your normal airspeed, that could indicate an unusually steep descent angle (or stronger tail wind). In general, it is wise to make more frequent transitions inside-outside than during the daytime. Secondly, it is wise to avoid excessively long and continuously descending straight-in approaches at night when flying over unlighted terrain. Two- or three-mile long approaches should be the limit at night, if possible. Third, maintain a safe altitude until you are in the near vicinity of the airport and then descend only when you are in the traffic pattern.

After-image illusion. If one looks at an intense light source at night, it can leave a visual afterimage. An example is the familiar bright yellow flash-bulb effect one sees remaining in the visual field for many seconds after having a strobe light go off unexpectedly. This after-image can create an unpleasant illusion that the visual world is more stable than it actually is. If the retinal afterimage seems too steady in position one is more inclined to interpret the entire visual world to also be steady. One could be undergoing severe attitude changes without being as aware of them as one would otherwise without the presence of the afterimage.

False horizon illusion. A common confusion that pilots can make on clear, dark nights over sparsely populated areas is the false horizon illusion. Even for relatively low flight altitudes, the horizon is not visible but it is thought to be in a position it isn't. One form of this illusion can occur when lights on the ground seem to merge continuously with stars on a clear night (FIG. 4-32). This further obliterates the location of the actual horizon. More than one pilot has placed his airplane in an unusual attitude in order to keep some ground lights above him, having mistaken them for stars. Which of these two illustrations is more likely to depict the actual horizon more clearly?

Another variation of this illusion can occur when one or more lights are seen beyond the runway and at a higher elevation. If it is dark between the runway and these lights, the pilot might erroneously believe that they are on the horizon. The unprepared pilot will think he is on the correct glide path but might be below it.

A useful technique the pilot can use in such missing or false horizon situations as these is to mentally extend the edge lights of the runway to their intersection point. This point will lie on the local horizon. Lights seen above this distant imaginary line must lie on elevated terrain.

Gillingham and Wolfe (1986) remarked about the potentially disorienting effects of the northern lights and aerial flares because of their false cues of verticality in one's peripheral vision. For instance, flares might not fall vertically downward but at an angle due to wind. Rapidly moving northern lights can also lead pilots to experience a visually produced perception of abnormal self-motion—in a direction that is different from one's actual direction of flight. At best it can confuse the pilot and at worst it can severely disorient the night pilot. One good remedy is to look at your instruments most or all of the time in the presence of such outside visual conditions.

Ganzfeld depth loss illusion. This illusion occurs during both day and night flights over snow fields, plains, water, or any other featureless smooth terrain. *Ganzfeld* is a German word for an evenly smooth, featureless visual scene. Because the

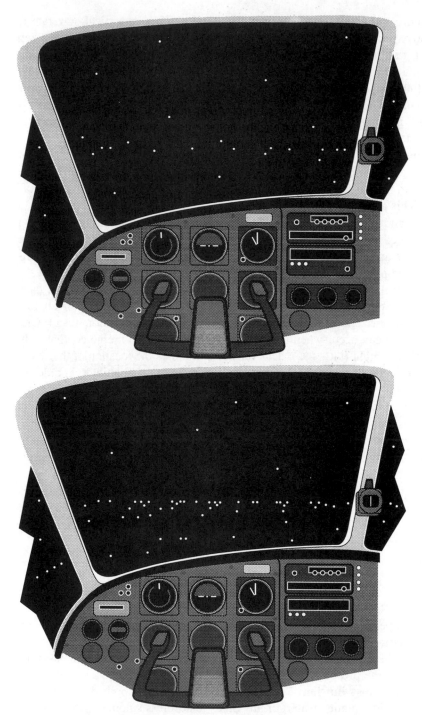

Fig. 4-32. *Missing horizon illusion.*

eyes have little or no details with which to judge distance, depth discrimination is reduced to varying degrees. Navy pilots flying antisubmarine patrols over the ocean often experience this illusion and need to refer to the altimeter more often.

At night, everything that is not illuminated by some light source such as the moon or artificial light sources, becomes a large and continuous Ganzfeld to the eye. Bodies of water merge with land. Heavily forested land merges invisibly with sandy beaches and deserts so that what was obvious on a colored sectional chart is now less than useless from the air.

Size-distance illusion. This illusion takes the form of small contractions and expansions in the apparent size of a light source or lighted object that is receding or approaching the observer. It occurs most often when the pilot is staring steadily at the light or object. At night, this effect is more likely to be due to light intensity changes than a change in the distance or apparent size of the other light source. Because our tendency is to look directly at something (in order to clearly identify it), our eye fixations are usually long enough for this illusion to develop.

Foreground occlusion illusion. Both experienced and inexperienced night pilots have noticed how lights on the ground can suddenly disappear. If the moon is present, one might see by its illumination on a cloud and realize that it was a cloud that lay between the airplane and the ground for a period of time. Yet during dark night flight with no moonlight available to help us understand what is happening, the nature of such foreground occlusions is not as apparent. Flying in hilly and mountainous terrain can produce occlusion illusions where a foreground hill can lie invisibly between the eyes and runway farther away. Figure 4-33 illustrates this effect. In A, the pilot sees foreground details such as roads, trees, buildings, and the like, because he has a continuous line of sight to a point x well short of the runway (A′); however, if these foreground lights and details suddenly disappear and are replaced by darkness as in B, the pilot should climb immediately or the situation shown in B′ might occur. A safer course of action is to continue flying level while keeping the runway and some foreground detail in sight. Don't begin the descent until it is obvious that there are no hidden hills lurking just under the wheels. The foreground occlusion illusion also can cause mental confusion, particularly if the pilot is unfamiliar with the local terrain. It also can distract the pilot from performing other cockpit cross-checks.

Reversible perspective illusion. Under some conditions it can be difficult to tell whether another airplane is traveling toward or away from the viewer at twilight; this is the reversible perspective illusion. As illustrated in FIG. 4-34, an airplane might be approaching when it is actually receding, a situation that isn't dangerous; however, the opposite might also be the case. In the instance that the other airplane has no navigation lights on, there might be neither sufficient details available with which to deduce the other airplane's orientation in the dark sky nor sufficient rate of change information in its overall visual angle to discriminate whether it is becoming larger or smaller. As is the case with a number of illusions, the central part of the retina known as the fovea is being called on to perform discriminations for which it was never designed.

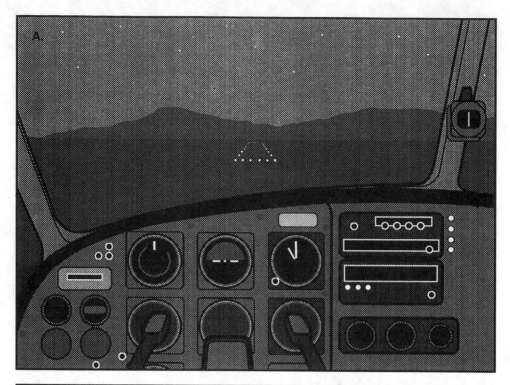

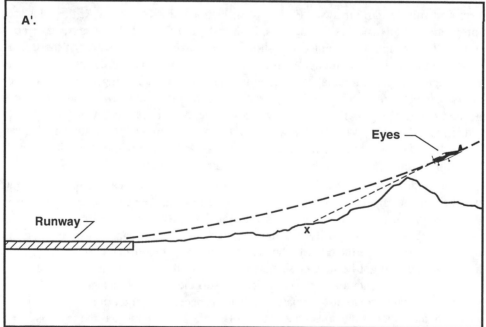

Fig. 4-33. *Foreground occlusion illusion.*

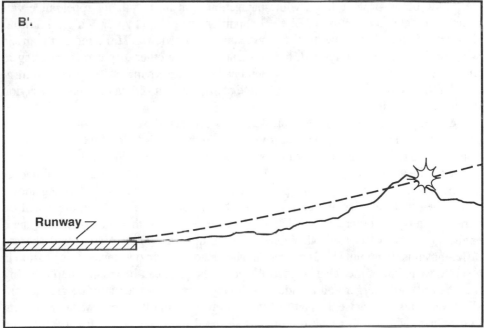

Fig. 4-33. *Continued*

Fig. 4-34. *Reversible perspective illusion.*

If the other airplane has a white navigation light in its tail, its appearance will clearly indicate its direction of flight. In addition, its red and green wing-tip navigation lights will also indicate its direction relative to the viewer. If the red or the green wing-tip light is seen along with the white taillight, the other airplane is traveling in the same direction as the viewer. Remember the useful saying, "Red, right, returning. " If the red light is seen on the right side of the green, it is traveling in the direction of the viewer's airplane.

Up-sloped lighted city illusion. The basis for this illusion is the intersection of two flat ground planes that intersect somewhere in the pilot's field of view. This situation can lead to ambiguity as to which of the two planes is level. Figure 4-35 shows this illusion. The top drawing shows the pilot's perspective view of the runway in the foreground with a city situated on an up-sloping hill beyond it. The bottom drawing shows a side view with an airplane on the approach path on the right. Often there will be parallel roads and other ground details on the level terrain that will share the same vanishing point (VP1). But other details on the upward sloping terrain will share a different vanishing point (VP2) nearer the visible horizon. In one sense, this illusion is a subtle variation of the false horizon illusion. The pilot can be tricked into thinking that the angularly larger and broader up-sloping terrain must actually be gravitationally level. This will cause the plane of the runway to seem tilted downward away from him or her, which will cause the pilot to descend more steeply to try to reach the apparently downward sloped runway.

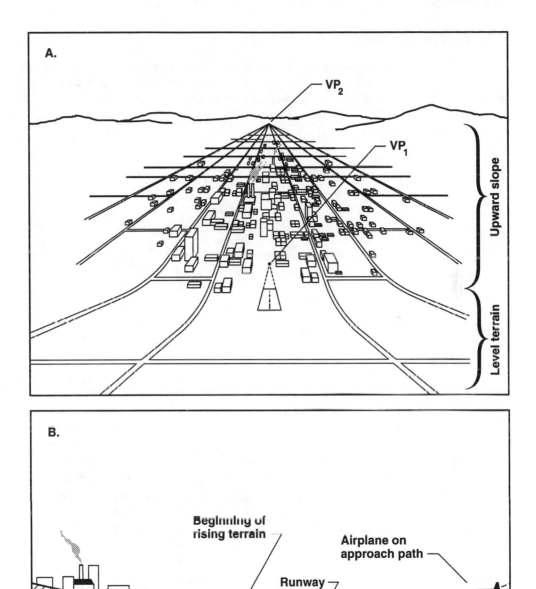

Fig. 4-35. *Upsloped lighted city illusion.*

Dynamic illusions

A dynamic visual illusion depends on retinal image movement to occur. They don't require the pilot to move his head or eyes but only that the image of an object moves across the retina of his eye during relatively stable visual fixation.

Many dynamic visual illusions can occur at night. Some of the more prominent ones are listed in TABLE 4-2.

Table 4-2.
Dynamic visual illusions at night.

Altered reference plane illusion
Autokinetic illusion
Black hole approach illusion
Dark terrain takeoff illusion
Linear acceleration-induced illusions
Angular acceleration-induced illusions
Relative movement illusions
Inversion illusion
Elevator illusion

Altered reference plane illusion. This illusion can occur during day or nighttime when one is flying toward a cloud or a line of mountains. One will often experience a strong feeling that he needs to gain altitude even though his clearance altitude is adequate. This illusion is partially a result of the well-known linear perspective effect, where parallel lines appear to converge toward one another with distance. The linear plane in which the pilot is travelling might be parallel with the earth's surface and also well above the mountains in the distance (or the cloud), but the visual separation distance will seem to be much less. The pilot might erroneously compensate by gaining altitude. This illusion is not as likely to occur during very dark conditions.

Autokinetic illusion. If one stares steadily at a single motionless point of light in an otherwise dark environment, it will seem to move around in various directions and at different speeds after a short period of time (typically from five to fifteen seconds), which is known as the autokinetic illusion (FIG. 4-36). Likewise, a motionless light on the ground at night might appear to move somewhat if there are no other fixed light sources visible at the same time. Because ground lights are seen through cockpit windows and because the airplane is continuously moving relative to the ground, the autokinetic illusion can have a number of potentially dangerous consequences. One of them is that the pilot might become confused into thinking that a stationary light on the ground is actually an airplane below his or her own airplane. Another is the opposite situation where a single visible star might be misidentified as a moving vehicle on the ground, which will give the impression of having a pitch attitude that is too low.

If the night pilot suspects that he or she is seeing the autokinetic illusion, it is wise to make certain that the light source is not really moving. This is accomplished by: (a)

Fig. 4-36. *Autokinetic illusion.*

stabilizing the airplane as much as possible, (b) noticing the angular distance between the light and some cockpit structure, and (c) looking at the cockpit structure for five to ten seconds to see if the light is moving. Use of peripheral vision will make this judgment more accurate than looking directly at the light.

In conclusion, the autokinetic illusion can lead to confusion and disorientation at night and, if detected, should be checked out.

Black hole approach illusion. What pilot has not heard of the infamous black hole approach? In general, it refers to night approach situations in which there are no ground lights or other visible detail short of the runway; however, there are really a variety of different black hole illusionary environments that the night pilot should know about. He or she should also know what to look for and what to do to cope with these slightly different, but potentially dangerous, illusions. These subjects are discussed here. Also, it should be emphasized that what the night pilot sees outside the cockpit should: (1) agree with his or her instrument readings at all times and (2) contribute to his or her correct assumptions about what is seen. An illusory condition might exist if either of these situations does not occur.

The most familiar (type 1) black hole approach situation is found when the approach end of the runway is built on the edge of a lake, an ocean, or unlighted gravitationally level terrain for example, and a town or city is seen stretching off into the distance beyond the runway, also on level terrain. Figure 4-37 illustrates this situation. The runway seems to float in a sea of darkness with only its own lights and other lights that are farther away available to define the ground plane. Many pilots will look for vertical guidance information in the angle that lies between the line of sight to the farthest visible light (dashed line) and the nearest light. The pilot might descend into the terrain long before reaching the runway.

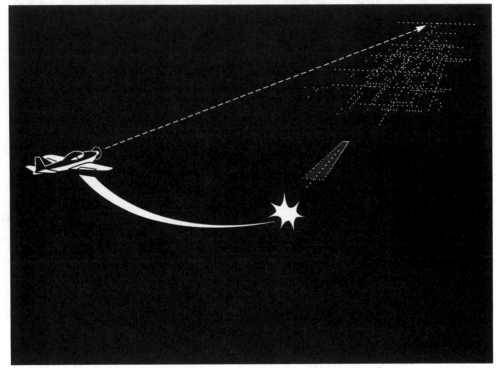

Fig. 4-37. *Type 1 black hole approach.*

The type 2 black hole approach situation consists of a grouping of lights located nearer the airplane and a pitch black area extending to a more distant lighted runway. The type 3 black hole approach is the same as a type 1 but the ground plane slopes up with increasing distance beyond the runway. The type 4 black hole approach situation is one where the runway is the only lighted detail on flat, level ground. No lights are seen in front of, behind, or beside it. The excellent pioneering research of Kraft and Elworth (1969) on these subjects is acknowledged.

What is the basis of this illusion? Three illustrations provide the background information needed to understand it. The first element in understanding the black hole approach illusion is diagrammed in FIG. 4-38 where the aircraft is maintaining a constant altitude. At some point, the visual angle at the pilot's eyes between the near and far end of the runway is, for instance, five degrees. As the aircraft nears the runway this visual angle will slowly increase. In short, the runway looks larger the nearer one gets to it.

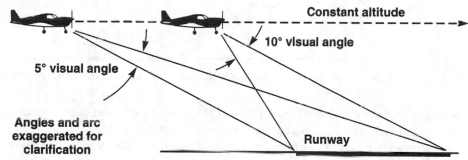

Fig. 4-38. *Element 1 of the black-hole approach illusion: constant altitude visual angle change.*

Next consider how the same visual angle would appear to change if the aircraft could descend only vertically. Figure 4-39 diagrams this second element. This visual angle would become smaller and smaller as altitude decreased.

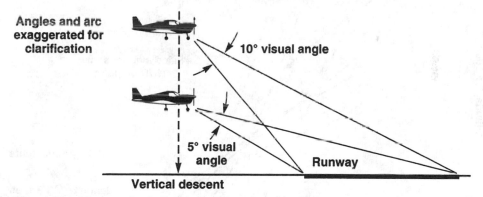

Fig. 4-39. *Element 2 of the black-hole approach illusion: vertical descent visual angle change.*

It should be apparent that if the pilot flies along a particular curved approach path that is the proper combination of horizontal and vertical displacement, this visual angle will not change or will change so slowly that it will not be noticed. This approach path is diagrammed in FIG. 4-40. There is good reason to believe that pilots will fly a much more rapid descent than they should in the absence of a perceptible change in this (or an equivalent) visual angle. In other words, pilots are likely to unwittingly maintain a constant visual angle all the way to the ground and, more

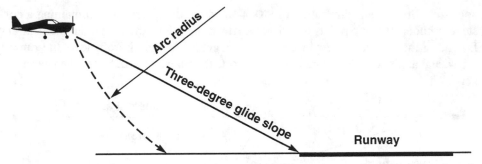

Fig. 4-40. *Element 3 of the black-hole approach illusion: arc of constant visual angle.*

importantly, this arc radius curve will intersect the ground well short of the runway. A point is reached, however, about two to three miles from the runway threshold (for a three degree glide path angle) where the error will finally become obvious because the visual system is now able to perceive the changing visual angle as is diagrammed in FIG. 4-41 and FIG. 4-42.

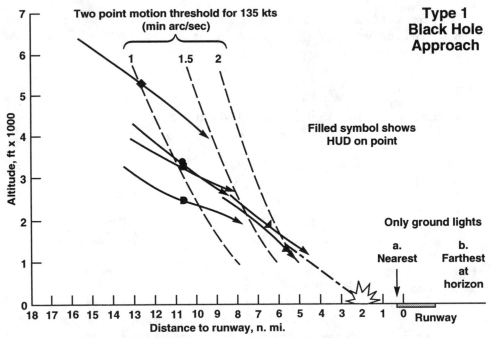

Fig. 4-41. *Experimental results for type 1 black-hole approaches made toward a lighted runway and a more distant group of ground lights.* Haines, Price, and Miller, 1980

The type 2 black-hole approach consists of a totally dark region on the ground within the pilot's field of view, except for the runway a long distance ahead, and a small, well-defined group of lights located on or near the flight path and much nearer

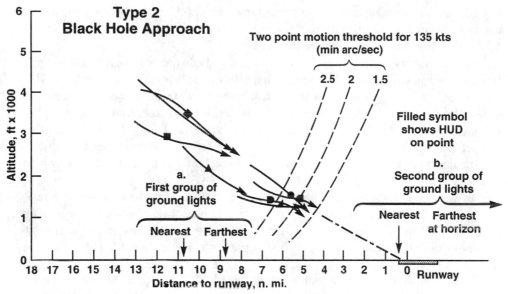

Fig. 4-42. *Experimental results for type type 2 black-hole approaches made toward a lighted runway and much closer group of ground lights with darkness in between.*

Haines, Price, and Miller, 1980

to the approaching aircraft. Once the pilot has passed over the foreground group of lights, he or she is then suddenly confronted with a totally black surface. Any vertical guidance information that was previously provided by the change in vertical angle between the two groups of lights is suddenly gone. If the pilot continues to depend on the external scene for this same information, an excessively large descent rate can build up without any obvious indication. Of course, the solution is to continually cross-check information from the altimeter, vertical rate, pitch attitude, and airspeed, and compare this information with the outside scene. If something doesn't look right trust the instruments.

The type 3 black hole approach situation is also particularly hazardous. Here the ground is totally dark, except for the runway lights and lights of a city beyond it, and both are situated on rising ground behind the runway. Here the pilot will try to detect the slowly changing vertical angle between the nearest light (usually located at the runway) and the farthest ground light. It is known that the human visual system is not capable of discriminating this changing angle unless it changes faster than one to two minutes arc per second. The typical pilot will try to maintain a constant angle and might descend into the ground well short of the runway (Kraft 1978).

One author with coworkers (Haines, Price, and Miller 1980) conducted a simulator study at NASA Ames of the effects of type 1 and 2 black hole approach visual conditions flying with and without a head-up display for vertical guidance information (Bray 1980). In this study, each of eight rated commercial B727 airline pilots flew 24 coupled instrument landing system (ILS) approaches (an autopilot locked onto the altitude and azimuth guidance from ground transmitters). They also flew manual visual approaches toward two different computer-generated ground light patterns representing the two black-hole type environments.

In the first (type 1) approach environment studied, the only lights visible were those at the runway threshold (group a.) and a second group at the horizon (group b.) with a totally dark gap between them. Calculations were then made to determine where the eye would have to be in altitude and distance from the runway for the vertical angle between the group a and the group b to change at 1, 1.5, 2, and 2.5 degrees arc per second. These three angle rate values were selected because they are close to the angular rates below which the human eye cannot perceive motion and above which it can. These curves are plotted on FIGS. 4-41 and 4-42.

In the second (type 2) black-hole approach environment studied, there was a relatively small but highly visible group of ground lights located between 8.8 to 10.8 miles short of the runway (group a.) and another group extending from the runway threshold to the horizon (group b.). It was pitch black for almost 9 miles between these two groups of lights.

The simulated airplane dynamics were modelled after a 140,000 pound (gross weight) swept-wing turbojet airplane. Reference airspeed was 135 knots with 30-degree flap setting and engine power set to 74 percent.

Each approach started with the autopilot on and the airplane at 7,500 feet altitude, about 27 miles from the runway. The autopilot was programmed to fly the aircraft along one of four randomly selected glide paths, only one of which intersected the ground at the correct touchdown point on the runway (-3 degrees). Two other glide slope angles (-3.5 and -3.25 degrees) intersected the ground well short of the runway and the -2.75 degree glide path intersected the ground well beyond the far end of the runway. This was done to determine: (1) at what point each pilot would recognize that he was flying toward the wrong aim point, (2) when they would turn the HUD on (if it was available), and (3) how they would control their vertical descent after turning the HUD on. Winds were calm and atmospheric visibility was clear on the computer-generated night visual scene generator.

The pilots' main task was to monitor the performance of the aircraft's autopilot and to take manual control if they thought it was necessary for any reason. This method permitted an assessment of the illusory strength of these two black hole visual approach conditions. For instance, if these pilots could not visually discriminate the fact that their aircraft was flying toward an erroneous aim point on the ground, it was reasoned that the first thing they would do is turn on the HUD (because it gave them vertical guidance information) and (later) disconnect the autopilot. This is just what happened.

The results for the type 1 black hole approach condition where all of the lights were at and beyond the runway are shown in FIG. 4-41. Distance to the runway is shown on the horizontal axis and altitude on the vertical axis. The three dashed curved lines (labelled two-point motion threshold) represent the locations in the air where the angle between a and b will change at the rates shown. Each curve is essentially the arc of constant visual angle portrayed in FIG. 4-40. Note that these pilots tended to turn the HUD on relatively far from the runway (as shown by the filled symbols), perhaps suggesting that the black hole condition made it more difficult to assess the aircraft's vertical descent rate. Also note that the HUD was turned on when the two-point motion threshold values were from one to two minutes arc per second as predicted by earlier laboratory research. Most importantly, when these descent profiles are projected down to the ground, they intersect the ground plane well short of the runway (dash-dot-dash line), a finding similar to that reported by Kraft and Elworth (1969).

Figure 4-42 presents the results for the type 2 black-hole approach condition trials. Here it was pitch dark between the nearest group of lights (labelled a.) and the lights at the runway (group b.). As before, the three curved dashed lines are calculated for three two-point motion thresholds for an airspeed of 135 knots. Their different direction than before is due to the different lighting geometry. Note that four of the pilots waited until they were only from five to six and one-half miles from the runway before turning the HUD on for vertical guidance information. These distances are well past the near grouping of lights. These HUD on distances correspond to a motion threshold of from 2 to 2.5 minutes of arc per second, which is very nearly the same as their motion sensitivity threshold. Apparently, the prominent visual cue for deciding when to turn the HUD on is when the angle between the nearest and farthest ground light is perceived as becoming smaller. Finally, note that the projection of these descent paths intersects the runway area fairly accurately, which suggests that they cross-checked their cockpit instruments for guidance information as they should have.

What should the night pilot do to avoid the black-hole approach illusion and its consequences?

- Become as knowledgeable about its contributory causes as possible.

- Don't fall into the trap of thinking that all the descent information that is needed is to be found outside the cockpit. The smooth, clear night approach toward these kinds of terrain features might lull some pilots into a false sense of self-sufficiency, even complacency; he or she might reason that because everything looks all right, everything is all right. The research has shown that this evaluation can be deadly wrong.

- Look back inside for instrument information regularly. The pilot should scan altitude, vertical rate, airspeed, and distance to go and then mentally compare this information against the outside scene. If something just doesn't look right, trust the instruments.

Dark terrain takeoff illusion. This illusion can occur while taking off from a lighted or an unlighted runway during a dark night with no visible horizon ahead of or to either side of the pilot during takeoff. Because he or she might look up from the instrument panel just after the wheels leave the ground but cannot see the horizon dropping away beneath the aircraft, the aircraft might be allowed to settle back down onto the runway or, worse, the terrain off the end of the runway. This illusion probably has different contributory causes than the black hole approach illusion. Most likely it results both from a false mental expectancy of how the horizon should be appearing to move, along with a false (or misinterpreted) cue produced by the forward acceleration of the aircraft. The best solution is to take a quick glance outside just at takeoff and then return to the instruments until reaching a height of at least 500 feet agl.

Linear acceleration-induced illusions. When the body is accelerated in the dark along a straight path with no visual cues available to help judge one's acceleration, one is less able to tell that one is accelerating; thus, visual cues enhance sensitivity to self-movement as has been found in several laboratory studies (Huang and Young 1981).

When the body is subjected to even very small accelerations, the middle ear where the balance organ is located, can send false information to the brain (or at least its perception can be wrong) (EN 4-2). We can believe that we are moving when we are not, or vice versa. There is even evidence that pressure sensors in the skin can produce much the same kind of false perceptions. In an interesting article written in 1946 that dealt with a history of aircraft accidents during night takeoffs, Collar (1946) had five highly experienced pilots fly various kinds of maneuvers with a blindfolded pilot trying to describe his motion sensations. TABLE 4-3 presents an abbreviated review of his interesting findings as well as those of McFarland (1953); these findings relate directly to the subject of body acceleration-induced illusions.

Table 4-3. Comparison of aircraft movements
and associated sensations reported by sightless pilots
(Partially adapted from Collar 1946; and McFarland 1953, Table 4.8).

Airplane Movements	Pilot Sensations
Normal takeoff with gradually increasing right-hand turn with nose dropping, followed by shallow dive (repeated 3 times).	Steady climb straight ahead. (A climbing turn was correctly perceived on only one of three repeated trials.)
Normal takeoff to 500 feet with gradually increasing right-hand turn but dropping the nose while keeping a steady backward pressure on the stick (repeated twice).	Steady climb followed by right-hand turn, nose dropping in a dive. The perception of the dive was very delayed almost to ground level when air speed was over 200 mph[1].
Normal takeoff and climb to 400 feet followed by a gentle dive.	Climbing turn to the left followed by a gentle straight dive that was perceived late.
Normal takeoff and straight climb to 300 feet followed by climbing right turn to 400 feet, gradually steepening the turn and changing to a diving turn through 180 degrees to ground level.	Straight climb followed by left climbing turn changing to a right-hand turn and level flight. Pilot had no idea of altitude loss nor sense of diving.

Table 4-3. *Continued*

Airplane Movements	Pilot Sensations
Normal takeoff followed by an early climbing left turn from 50 to 300 feet, followed by a diving left turn until down wind at ground level.	Straight climb followed by climbing right turn, with a right-hand diving turn following immediately. Observer felt he was still climbing when actually diving.
Normal climb to 200 feet followed by gradual right-hand diving turn through 180 degrees.	Climbing turn to the left.
Climb to 200 feet followed by a gradual left-hand climbing turn to 400 feet, moving into a left diving turn through 180 degrees down to an altitude of 50 feet.	Climb, followed by a climbing turn to the right. Observer never perceived any sense of diving or loss of height.
Level turn	Continuous straight flight[2]
Level turn	Ascent[3]
Skidding in a flat turn	Banking in the opposite direction[4]
Level flight at night approaching a row of ground lights at an angle (to direction of flight)	Tilting or banking[5]
Going into a slow bank	Level flight[6]
In level flight after a slow recovery from a sudden roll.	Continuing tilt and lean in the opposite direction (to compensate)[7]

[1] This is essentially the *graveyard spiral* where the coordinated turn has ceased stimulating the balance organ. The disoriented pilot will pull back on the controls, tightening the spiral and increasing the loss of altitude.
[2] The rate of change is not great enough to stimulate the semicircular canals of the balance organ.
[3] The forces acting on the otoliths of the middle ear are the same in each case, depending upon the turn rate and judged ascent rate.
[4] The resultant forces on the otoliths are equivalent in their physiological effect.
[5] Misinterpretation of the row of lights as being the true horizon dead ahead.
[6] Forces on the otolith organ are not great enough to stimulate them.
[7] The rate of change wasn't great enough to produce an awareness of the roll recovery.

Enough is known about how the vestibular apparatus of the middle ear works to understand each of the above false perceptions. A wide variety of illusory perceptions can be produced in blindfolded pilots during these flight maneuvers. The same thing can be said for the sighted pilot at night who does not scan the instrument panel for this vital information and cross-check it against what is seen outside. The unsuspecting pilot might be fooled into thinking his or her airplane is doing one thing when it is actually doing something quite different. It can't be said too often: "Don't trust your senses by themselves. Cross check, cross check, cross check." If you are in doubt about whether you face such an illusion, don't do anything immediately, until you are certain that your decision is based upon true information.

Another illusion that is related to simple forward acceleration is that of an apparent displacement of the vertical. Buley and Spelina (1970) state, "In the absence of visual pitch information, a pilot under longitudinal acceleration cannot distinguish between the true vertical and the resultant of the gravity and acceleration vectors. Thus, after takeoff an illusion of excessive pitch-up may occur and if, due to corrective pilot control input and/or flap retraction, the aircraft enters a shallow dive, the pilot may still experience a sensation of climb." This effect can be deadly and occurs more frequently over textureless terrain in darkness.

Accelerations of commercial type airplanes on takeoff would produce an apparent tilt of the vertical of between five and ten degrees arc.

Another illusion is known as the *leans*. Its effect is a perception of being in a banked turn when one is actually flying with wings level. It occurs after one has rolled the airplane so slowly and without deliberate input that the vestibular system has not detected the new roll attitude. Then, when the roll attitude is detected, he corrects the situation more rapidly; the pilot experiences an angular acceleration above his detection level, which leads to an illusion of rolling to wings level in the opposite direction.

Angular acceleration-induced illusions. While the pilot's entire body might be moving through the air inside of the cockpit, he can also move his head, torso, and limbs to some degree. The balance/acceleration sensing organs within the middle ear provides highly sensitive and useful information concerning angular (rotational) acceleration to our brain as does our visual system. There are many situations, however, in which we can be fooled. Sometimes we receive conflicting information from our eyes, balance/acceleration organs, skin, joints, and other organs. If not dealt with correctly, this array of conflicting information can kill the unsuspecting pilot.

Our balance/acceleration organs possess sensitivity thresholds. A threshold is another way of saying the dividing line that separates one kind of behavior from another. For example, an above-threshold acceleration would always be noticed while a below-threshold acceleration would never be noticed. Research has shown that man's threshold is seldom a single point. Indeed, there is a region of uncertainty that separates each type of threshold. With regard to the balance/acceleration organs in the head, there is an amount of head movement in terms of its displacement and vibration frequency that is so small that we cannot perceive it. Even though our head might be moving, we would not know it. As the distance through which the head moves increases per second, a point is reached where the pilot knows for certain that his head is being moved. It is usually somewhere between these two conditions that head movement-induced illusions occur.

If one voluntarily moves his head, neck muscles send very useful neural signals to the brain confirming this movement. We expect to see the world slide past our eyes when we turn our heads and thus we can disregard the blurred visual image that is produced. But what happens when we do not turn our head but still see the world move? The visual system will send one kind of information to the brain while the balance/acceleration organs will send no signal. Which is the correct situation? This situation occurs when one is flying in a bank while trying to hold one's head very still relative to the cockpit. Or consider another potentially conflicting situation.

What if one sits perfectly still in the cockpit during flight and no control inputs are made but one still sees the external environment move (if ground lights are visible)? What could cause this? After a short period of analysis, the experienced pilot will deduce that some outside wind force had produced the anomalous visual movement. The balance/acceleration organs might not signal the brain that they had detected any movement. If they don't, then a potential conflict situation will be set up. But what if nothing can be seen on the ground due to darkness? Then there will be an even greater potential for an illusion and an incorrect pilot control input.

If the pilot should be in a prolonged constant rate turn that has ceased sending neural signals to the brain that he or she is in a turn and then an abrupt head movement is made, it can lead to an illusory feeling of rotation or movement in an entirely different axis. This *coriolis illusion* (or *effect*) can not only disorient the night pilot, but can produce intense symptoms of nausea. The pilot might maneuver the airplane into a dangerous attitude just to try to stop the illusory rotation. The best way to prevent this illusion is not to make any sudden head movements during prolonged turns.

Relative movement illusions. This illusion refers to any situation in which, as occurs during formation flying, one sees motion of another airplane but interprets it as being his own airplane's motion. A danger of such situations is that the pilot will become confused and make the wrong control input which might lead to a midair collision.

Another illusion can occur when flying relatively near to the ground during an approach. If one is flying at a slow speed into an unexpectedly strong headwind, visual details on the ground might appear to be moving past too slowly. Pilots might misinterpret this as being too high, which might lead them to add power and descend too rapidly during their final approach. The solution is to perform the visual cross-check more frequently between inside and outside information.

Inversion illusion. Pilots have experienced an illusion of tumbling backwards soon after making an abrupt change from a climb to level flight. This is known as the inversion illusion. Some pilots might erroneously lower the nose of the aircraft as a result of this effect, which might intensify the illusion. It is always better to make a smooth vertical transition from climb to level flight.

Elevator illusion. This illusion is produced by a rapid vertically upward or downward acceleration as is caused by updrafts and downdrafts, respectively. Some pilots will push the aircraft into a nose down attitude soon after the updraft has occurred or into a nose up attitude after a downdraft. The best course of action to take immediately after one encounters an obvious updraft or downdraft, if there is sufficient altitude, is not to do anything but to cross-check airspeed, altitude, and vertical rate.

5
Vertigo
and disorientation

ANYONE CAN QUICKLY AND UNEXPECTEDLY SUFFER THE EFFECTS OF VERTIGO and disorientation. It is essential for the night pilot to understand something about these subjects and become fully prepared to cope with the malady.

TYPES OF DISORIENTATION

Vertigo is often defined as a state of temporary spatial confusion sometimes accompanied by an excessive and uncontrollable dizziness, loss of balance, nausea, buzzing in the ears, blurred vision, double vision, sweating, and some reduction in mental abilities. The most reasonable explanation of its cause is that it is produced when one is in an environment that produces conflicting sensory cues, for instance, when the balance organ in the middle ear doesn't match what one sees. This can occur particularly at night when the external scene cues are the stars and air turbulence leads to random body jostling. Most people find that vertigo leads to bodily disorientation. Experienced pilots have reported disorientation even though correct information is available from flight instruments.

A noted aeromedical examiner who writes for several popular pilot magazines has suggested that there are a number of different types of disorientation: postural, directional, temporal, and vestibular (Reinhart 1989). Consider them as they might apply to flying at night.

Postural disorientation is defined as a disturbed feeling relative to the force of gravity. This awareness comes mainly from our vision and *proprioception* (sense of touch). At night, when one has been sitting for long periods of time without moving, one can begin to lose track of where up is. Such distortions can lead to an inaccurate sense of our overall sense of orientation in the cabin.

Directional disorientation happens when we are lost, or when we ignore or overlook landmarks and checkpoints. When one suddenly realizes that he is no longer where he thought he was, a gripping form of disorientation takes place. Nighttime flying is particularly prone to this type of effect.

Temporal disorientation refers to when one senses that time has been compressed or expanded relative to one's normal perception of time. An example provided by Reinhart is the long and boring trip where the pilot is tired and the flight seems to take forever. Perhaps this is because one's sense of time is distorted.

Vestibular disorientation refers to the general feeling that one's flight path isn't correct in some way. By calling this effect vestibular, it emphasizes the role played by the middle ear's balance organ. Flying an uncoordinated turn produces this effect as does excessive head turning during a turn in flight. Vestibular disorientation is often subtle in its onset, yet it is the most disabling and dangerous of all disorientation.

Commenting on disorientation in aircraft, Leibowitz and Post (1979) remark, "When the ground is not visible through the windscreen, movement of the aircraft fails to result in simultaneous visual motion and the only reliable visual source of orientation information is the artificial horizon. Because spatial orientation is normally mediated by large portions of the visual field, the use of a relatively small, about 5 degrees of arc, artificial horizon in the aircraft represents an unnatural situation . . . . These unnatural abstract cues are most vulnerable to interference by stress and/or unusual environmental conditions and the pilot may not be able to override the discrepant information provided by misleading orientation stimuli."

In limited visibility conditions, the chances of maintaining normal aircraft attitude without instrument training are very low. One must learn to rely on the artificial horizon display for basic attitude information regardless of its relatively small angular size. Read the instruments. They are the best insurance you will ever have. If you are a recently licensed daytime VFR pilot and want to fly alone at night, don't do it, at least not until you have had plenty of instrument time.

In general, it is probably true to say that a pilot's tolerance to disorientation is reduced by fatigue, dim or dark cabin lighting, glare of instrument lights, and piloting different types of airplanes.

It is fair to say that two pilots in the same cockpit are not very likely to experience vertigo at the same time; therefore, the two-pilot flight crew becomes a good solution to this problem.

FLICKER VERTIGO

Flicker vertigo refers to an abrupt and uncontrollable sensation of disorientation that is produced by a flickering light. It is a condition that must be taken seriously by all night pilots because it can be highly incapacitating. And even if the pilot has flown many hundreds of hours at night and has never experienced flicker vertigo, that does not mean that he or she is immune. It is possible that the inducing conditions have not yet occurred. It can lead to many symptoms ranging from a loss of body balance and directional orientation to vomiting and double vision.

If flying in cloud, haze, or fog at night, turn off the strobe lights and any other repetitive outside lights that can reflect off the fog droplets into the eyes.

AVOIDING OR REDUCING VERTIGO

Vertigo can be reduced by avoiding the flight conditions that cause it; understand its causes and physiological effects; obtain instrument flight training; maintain instrument proficiency; rely on the accuracy of your instruments more than on your own senses, particularly when you are not certain which one is accurate; try taking an airsickness drug an hour or two prior to a night flight while there is a second pilot present and see if it helps; and accept the fact that vertigo can happen to anyone, even you. Experienced pilots have learned that even light to moderate air turbulence can lead to more than a mere unpleasant flight. Turbulence combined with excessive head movement can produce vertigo, particularly at night when there are few outside visual cues to provide a stable visual reference. Keep the head oriented in the same orientation in the cockpit without pitching up or down or yawing the head back and forth excessively, particularly in turbulent air.

Airsickness drugs taken internally or through a skin patch might be effective in reducing or eliminating the symptoms of vertigo for passengers. Pilots should consult with their FAA medical examiner before using such drags because various side effects are possible. Many pilots have found that reducing head motions is equally effective. Vertigo is a condition that includes disorientation as one of its symptoms. Numerous visual phenomena (illusions) can contribute to extreme disorientation that might contribute to vertigo. Many of these illusions are discussed in chapter 4.

6
Fatigue

IN THE MOST GENERAL SENSE, FATIGUE IS LIKE BEING TIRED ALL OVER. Every pilot who has flown after not getting enough sleep or who has taken off at sunset immediately after completing a long cross-country flight doesn't need to be told about fatigue. As common as fatigue is, it is not well understood. Many studies have been carried out to try to understand it better, for example Bartley and Chute (1947). Indeed, there are various kinds of fatigue.

VISUAL FATIGUE

Visual fatigue is a common experience among pilots with otherwise normal vision. It refers to an inability to maintain efficient visual function. As is shown in TABLE 6-1, a variety of symptoms are possible.

To find out if you are experiencing visual fatigue, close your eyes, then roll your eyes around and see if you feel a scratchiness. This is the eyeball test.

Because continuous visual monitoring of cockpit and external information is required of all pilots, visual fatigue must be taken seriously and when its symptoms appear, steps should be taken to alleviate them.

As is true concerning other factors affecting pilot performance at night, if visual fatigue occurs along with other events such as poor weather, multiple time zone dislocations, and the like, the result can add up to a situation that cannot be coped with effectively.

So what can be done to counteract visual fatigue? A number of possibilities are presented in TABLE 6-2.

Table 6-1. Prominent symptoms of visual fatigue.

Feelings of tiredness or burning in the eye region
Dry, scratchy feeling in the eye region
Heavy eyelids
Frontal area headache
Double vision
Temporary image blurring
Red eye (conjunctival inflammation)
Slowed visual focus (accommodation)
Excessive tearing
Frequent eye blinks
General bodily discomfort or tiredness

Table 6-2. Useful countermeasures for visual fatigue.

Scheduled visual rest periods
Make the viewing conditions best possible
If you wear eyeglasses, keep them scratch-free
Avoid self-imposed stressors such as tobacco, alcohol, various drugs, sleep loss
Change the eye focus distance periodically
Use eye drops
Adjust cockpit lighting for best vision
Avoid prolonged eye focus at short distances (8 inches or closer)

SKILL FATIGUE

Skill fatigue refers to the loss of one's ability to carry out certain flying skills for a number of different reasons. Consider nighttime visual eye scan. The night pilot must follow a precise outside cockpit eye scan in order to be able to visually detect an approaching airplane that might be just at the limit of visibility. Because this oculomotor skill involves knowing where to look in the darkness and how long to fixate (look at without moving the eyes) at given locations, if it isn't practiced very often, this skill can become significantly degraded. In essence, the skill has become fatigued to the point of being ineffective. So lack of opportunity to repeat the skilled action actually contributes to its fatigue.

An attitude of complacency can also contribute to skill fatigue when the pilot assumes that his or her proficiency level is going to be fully adequate to meet all in-flight challenges. Such an attitude can lead one across the threshold to an incident or an accident.

EFFECTS OF FATIGUE ON NIGHT FLYING ABILITY

Fatigue can reduce flight safety by reducing the night pilot's margin of safety. When one is in good physical condition and has planned thoroughly for the night flight, one has a valuable extra margin of time, confidence, physical strength, intellectual capacity, and equipment to use when flight conditions begin to deteriorate. If one is fatigued, it can reduce self-confidence, physical strength, and intellectual capacity.

Another concern has to do with flying at night occasionally versus all the time. For those pilots who must fly at night to make a living, it is important to understand that the continuing transition from daylight to nighttime flight, day after day, can lead to problems all their own. As one aviation airline official once said, "Each pilot has to find out what works best for a routine and then stick to it. It takes a lot of discipline, but if you don't stick to it you'll soon feel lousy." Indeed, some pilots will be able to adapt to the night routine cleanly while others will fight it continually. Those who plan or carry out night operations should understand the difference between an occasional night flight and repetitive night operations.

PART 2

Night flying:
Aids, equipment
and procedures

7
Preparation for night flight

IT HAS OFTEN BEEN SUGGESTED BY THE MOST SEASONED OF NIGHT AVIATORS that preparation is the most important variable contributing to the success of the night flight. In most cases, that belief is probably true. Stellar performance can only be accomplished after diligent preparation.

PILOT AND EQUIPMENT MINIMUMS

Certainly, all pilots are quite aware that an airplane's performance is not significantly altered by a transition from a light to a dark environment. Perhaps it is primarily that reasoning which prompts some pilots to launch into the night skies without first considering their own limitations or to assess the possible resulting utilitarian limitations of their aircraft. As discussed in chapters 2 through 6, a pilot's performance, unlike the machine he or she flies, is significantly altered by such a transition.

Current research and common sense dictate that the human factor cannot be overlooked. Indeed, because of human factors research findings, there is cause to overhaul the archaic preflight procedures of yesteryear. Night flying requires that pilots have a complete realization of their abilities and limitations and observe more caution than during day operations. Although careful planning of any flight is essential for maximum safety and efficiency, night flying demands more attention to all details of preflight preparation and planning.

When considering their limitations, some pilots, too frequently, do not consider their own minimums prior to every flight. Certainly, at the time of the most recent flight physical, every pilot who received a medical certificate was in generally adequate health. But, even though a pilot might possess a medical certificate, that pilot might not be medically qualified to fly at the time of the flight. It is the responsibility of every pilot to reevaluate his or her condition prior to every flight. Such minor medical complications as an infected tooth, an earache, or a simple cold can measurably alter a pilot's performance to such a degree as to seriously affect flight safety.

The personal evaluation referred to above should also include an honest appraisal of one's current psychological state as well. Increasing age and experience should endow the pilot with common sense and honesty about what type of person the pilot really is. But this is not always the case, particularly when certain personality variables (including, but not limited to, pride, stubbornness, anger, complacency, immaturity, and denial) take over. Fatigue and tiredness can bring any pilot's basic personality traits to the surface, traits that can contribute to poor piloting performance.

The inexperienced pilot is not uniquely obligated to ponder the questions pertinent to personal minimums. Consider, also, the professional pilot. Today's professional pilots cope with the physical and psychological demands placed upon them very well during the day and, generally, during the night. Today's generation of aircraft with supporting systems so technically advanced can push pilots beyond the limits of human physiology under certain conditions. A pilot might be able to fulfill his or her job functions adequately during daytime hours but might become incapable of operating the aircraft's sophisticated systems efficiently and correctly during periods of physical or mental fatigue at night.

It is not uncommon for a pilot of a sophisticated aircraft who masterfully pilots an aircraft during the day to fall victim to human frailty at night. It is entirely possible for a pilot performing the same daytime piloting procedures to encounter a decrease in situational awareness and/or an increased incidence of mental overload condition due to different types of fatigue encountered at night.

What is the answer? It then becomes necessary to raise personal minimums or to cancel a proposed night flight when a pilot is not totally fit to fly. Just as an instrument pilot is required to raise his or her instrument approach minimums when a local altimeter setting is not available or when an approach navigational aid is not in service; so too must a night pilot consider his or her own set of biological limitations. There is little to be gained for a pilot to be pushed to his or her envelope of physiological and psychological limits. (The pilot's workplace can become the most demanding office in the world at 4 a.m. while executing an instrument approach procedure at an airport where the visibility conditions are at or near minimums, while communicating with air traffic control, and when the pilot is barely able to keep one eye open.)

After considering the medical aspects of flight discussed in part I, it is necessary to review the proficiency aspects of flight. Because the environment is different from daylight operations, even the most proficient of pilots in daytime operations must reflect upon those ramifications brought on by a dark environment. Several basic concerns must be studied. Among them are:

- The amount of illumination that can be reasonably expected throughout the entire flight allowing for delays in departure and landing.
- The type and the quality of visual cues available.
- The type of navigational aids available.
- The total and recent night flight experience the pilot has and the resulting degree of proficiency and developed judgment of the pilot.
- The meteorological conditions that could be encountered during the flight.
- The type of aircraft flown and the equipment available to the pilot and the degree to which the aircraft and supporting equipment is suited for night flight.
- The complexity of the operations that the pilot could be required to perform.

Prior to each flight, when determining the equipment that is to be employed for the flight, pilots should consider additional factors such as:

- Are all of the aircraft systems and navigational aids functioning properly? If not, should the flight be canceled or the flight minimums raised?
- Is the type of aircraft suited for the proposed flight environment?
- Is there adequate system redundancy?
- Are the aircraft and its associated systems so complex or is the pilot so inexperienced that he or she might be unable to properly operate the aircraft and the supporting systems at any time during the flight should unexpected piloting demands arise?

Finally, to determine the correct pilot and equipment minimums, it is necessary to weigh and balance the biological and proficiency considerations with the type of equipment to be employed and the expected flight environment. Naturally, it is best for an inexperienced pilot to choose those situations that are the least challenging with regard to skill and judgment and pose little risk. Older, more experienced and proficient pilots often have another set of factors that become a higher priority as the aging process becomes more pronounced. Areas of concern relating to age like eyesight and fatigue become more significant factors in the pilot minimums equation.

The following are a few examples of how pilot and equipment minimums should be considered in the minimums equation with different flight environments:

- If a pilot is inexperienced, noninstrument rated and/or has limited instrument proficiency, he or she should choose those flight environments that provide the least challenge and afford the maximum visual cues. For example, a proposed flight on a full moon night, with clear skies and excellent visibility, numerous en route navigational aids, and profuse discernible cross-country visual aids would be appropriate if the aircraft would be landing at airports that are relatively easy to access with a minimum potential for confusion and that have an abundant variety of visual approach aids.

- If the flight environment provides a challenging set of meteorological conditions at the destination airport, an instrument pilot that is legally qualified for the flight but not very proficient may elect to not descend to published approach minimums but instead execute a missed approach procedure at an altitude higher than the published minimums and fly to an alternate airport where the flight environment is less challenging. (Too often, instrument pilots attempt to fly an airplane as low as the instrument approach procedure legally allows without considering what their personal minimums should allow.)

- If the anticipated flight environment would place a high demand on pilot skill during that period of time of the pilot's sleep-wake cycle where he or she is not likely to be in a high state of arousal, the pilot should consider flying with an appropriately trained copilot.

- If part of the aircraft's navigational equipment or part of the ground-based navigational equipment that would be used to assist in an approach to an airport is inoperative, or if any of the important elements of the approach lighting system that would be used to assist in an approach to an airport are inoperative, every pilot should assess the situation to determine if safety would be compromised during that phase of the flight.

- If a local altimeter setting is not available for an airport of intended landing, the pilot should consider available visual and electronic navigational aids that provide glide slope information, topographical features, and possible meteorological conditions, along with quality and quantity of visual cues and degree of moonlight illumination. After reviewing the conditions, a determination can be made as to the relative degree of safety that is provided in that flight environment and what changes, if any, should be incorporated into the proposed planned flight.

The previous examples are just a few of the countless different possible scenarios; each and every situation contains a unique chemistry of pilot, flight environment, and the aircraft with its supporting systems. Adequate preflight preparation requires the proper planning of the integration of the pilot, hardware, and flight environment.

METEOROLOGICAL CONSIDERATIONS

Meteorological conditions can change dramatically during the nighttime hours. Preparation for a night flight should include a thorough study of the available weather reports and forecasts, with particular attention given to temperature/dew point spread because of the possibility of formation of ground fog during the night flight. Restrictions to visibility during night flights are insidious in nature and have contributed to a very high percentage of accidents.

Emphasis should also be placed on awareness of wind direction and speed. Because there are fewer visual cues, drifting cannot be detected as readily at night as during the day. Each weather briefing must consider all possibilities of changes in wind direction and speed at different altitudes.

Flying during the winter months should be regarded with a supplemental set of guidelines. Such potential hazards as ice and frost formation are not uncommon when an airplane descends from a high altitude where the ambient air is cold to a lower altitude where the airplane encounters a warm, moist air environment. (Check the aircraft's heater and defroster prior to encountering these conditions.)

Any type of precipitation in a cold environment can create an emergency condition if the pilot is not experienced or not proficient enough to contend with the situation, or if the aircraft and supporting equipment is not suited for the situation. Freezing rain in a nearly totally dark environment, for example, can become a challenge for most pilots in most general aviation aircraft.

Once again, it is necessary to consider the balance of the pilot and the hardware with the meteorological conditions of the flight environment.

SPECIAL EQUIPMENT

Perhaps the first step in the adequate preparation for a night flight is to consider the human limitations aspect of the flight and determine how best to make up for those deficiencies encountered during periods of darkness by employing special equipment. As a result of those human limitations, certain aircraft inadequacies can be amplified. For example, the human eye functions differently during periods of darkness and is not as efficient. Consequently, any deficiencies in the lighting of the aircraft's cockpit or instrument panel can seriously add to the risk factor.

Lighting and vision aids

Following are some general suggestions regarding special interior lighting in an aircraft from a human factors point of view. Underlying all of these suggestions is the concept of maintaining a state of relative dark-adaptation of the eye, that is, doing anything necessary to maintain the eye's excellent sensitivity level it possesses once it has been in the dark for 20 minutes or more.

Two D-Cell flashlights are helpful in the cockpit. Two flashlights are definitely preferred over one. The reason? In the event one flashlight becomes inoperative in a totally dark cockpit, it would become very difficult and time-consuming to change batteries or a light bulb. Additionally, safety would be compromised when the pilot is distracted while determining why the flashlight is inoperative and subsequently changing a bulb or batteries. (Most commercially built airplanes have cockpit lights to provide general illumination for the night pilot. Some include spotlights for reading charts as well. But as night pilots get older, they require more light to read the same level of detail. For this reason, it is always a wise plan to carry extra flashlights with fresh batteries.) The selection of a flashlight without magnetic base mounts is essential because a magnetic compass can so easily be affected by the immediate presence of a magnet. Far too many aviators have become lost during periods of darkness when a magnetic compass rendered inaccurate readings after a flashlight with a magnetic base mount was placed near the magnetic compass.

The experienced night pilot might want to construct a special flashlight bracket to hold a D-Cell flashlight rigidly on the ceiling overhead and aimed downward and away from the eyes as is diagrammed in FIG. 7-1. Note that a light red gelatin filter can be added over the lens to help maintain a state of dark-adaptation, yet still permits one to read colored charts.

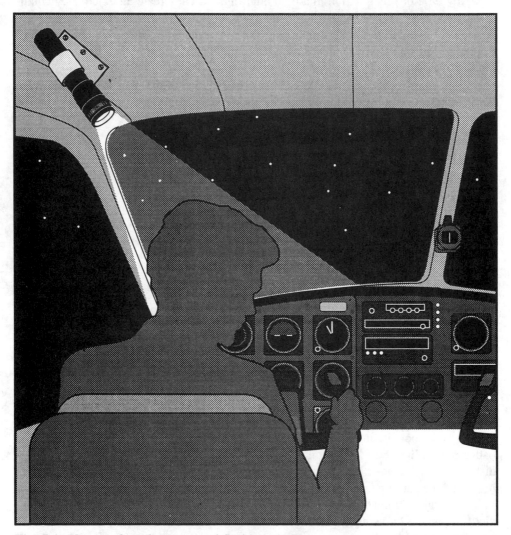

Fig. 7-1. *Homemade ceiling-mounted flashlight holder.*

Other appliances are available to assist the pilot in mounting penlights and other instruments in a variety of positions. Additionally, Velcro can be used to mount grease pencils, pencils, and pens in convenient locations around the cockpit. Figure 7-2 illustrates one such device known as a lamplifter.

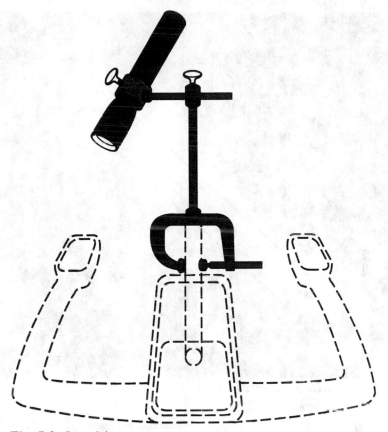

Fig. 7-2. *Lamplifter.* Based upon Wimer Enterprises device.

Chemical light sticks add an extra margin of safety. The light sticks can be a very valuable tool. Because their shelf life is considerable, they can sit in the bottom of a flight bag for years and when activated last for hours. Additional benefits of this type of cockpit lighting are that it comes in several different colors and can be beneficial in maintaining dark-adaptation because the light is a soft glow. This device is depicted in FIG. 7-3.

Small penlights are always handy to have in the pilot's pocket. They can also be held in a pilot's mouth, if necessary.

The standard white-and-red dual-bulb and dual lens flashlights are quite versatile because they can fulfill two entirely different lighting functions. During twilight, before the eyes have become fully dark-adapted, the white light can be used for illuminating cockpit details and after dark the pilot should switch to the red lens illumination. Figure 7-4 is a drawing of such a flashlight.

The flex-neck flashlight is a favorite of many pilots because it can be easily mounted in many different places with the aid of Velcro and then adjusted to any position desired. Figure 7-5 shows one design for this type of flashlight.

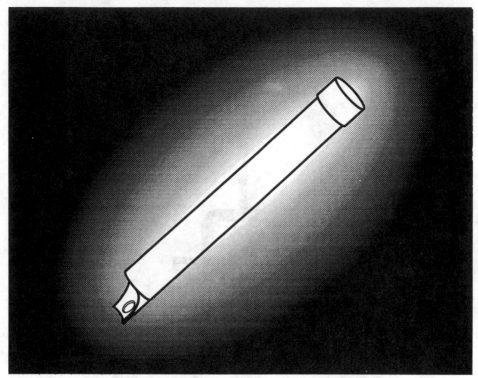

Fig. 7-3. *Cyalume chemical light stick.*

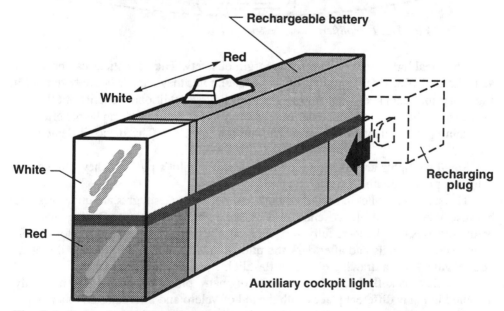

Fig. 7-4. *Red and white light flashlight.*

134

Fig. 7-5. *Flexible neck light.*

The miner's style of headlamp is also very useful during the preflight inspection, loading the airplane, while inside the cockpit prior to start-up, start-up, shutdown, unloading the airplane, and especially in the event of an emergency electrical failure. It is shown in FIG. 7-6.

A battery-operated portable fluorescent light when mounted to the cockpit ceiling slightly behind the pilot's head can be of use during emergencies providing gentle white cockpit illumination.

Figure 7-7 illustrates a cockpit zoom light. It can be plugged into a cigarette lighter, in some instances. The width of its beam can be adjusted for reading a map or flooding a cockpit with light.

Spare, long-life storage batteries are nice to have available during preflight or after shutdown, but should not be intended as replacement batteries during flight (FIG. 7-8).

Among miscellaneous items that would be beneficial is an illuminated magnifying glass with self-contained batteries that will enlarge an area two or three times over a

Fig. 7-6. *Miner's style head lamp.*

Fig. 7-7. *Zoom light.*

Fig. 7-8. *Code:Red emergency battery.*

region of about four (or more) inches. Short-length (typically 5 inches) low-wattage fluorescent tube lamps are also available that operate on four AA batteries. They can be temporarily attached to different surfaces in the cockpit using short Velcro pads.

Navigational aids and other special equipment

A number of useful navigational aids are available for the night pilot.

Moving map displays are a significant safety enhancement to navigation in areas of mountainous terrain and/or high density traffic areas. One such device is shown in FIG. 7-9. Typically, a symbol representing the pilot's own aircraft remains centered in the display and other navigation and complex airspace information appears in their correct relative locations elsewhere on the display. Incorporated with an existing

Fig. 7-9. *Argus 5000 Moving Map Display.*

Loran C or navigation management system, the device shown here can display a number of operating modes, one of which is an en route mode with a heading-up oriented display and compass rose (as shown). There is also an optional automatic direction finder (ADF) pointer, nondirectional beacon (NDB) digital bearing, and other features displayed on the illuminated (green) screen that can be very useful at night.

Another, similar loran-based flight management system developed for the general aviation aircraft is illustrated in FIG. 7-10. A green electroluminescent display screen shows the aircraft's flight path that is integrated with a navigation system and database. It includes a departure, en route, and approach mode and displays the airplane's exact realtime visual position relative to navigation aids and airports in addition to terminal control areas, airport radar service areas, military operation areas, and all other special use airspace. The system can be updated by means of a database card that is available by special order or subscription.

Various terrain avoidance systems are available to the general aviation community. As is true for many of the special equipment items described here, the types of usage as well as the price ranges vary. Figure 7-11 and 7-12 illustrate similar devices manufactured by different firms. Part A of FIG. 7-11 shows a digital panel display and part B shows an analog panel display device manufactured by the same firm.

A redundant navcom system that is independent of the aircraft's electrical system can be of great benefit if the unit has an adequately illuminated display for use at night. Figure 7-13 shows such a device.

The clock, stopwatch, and timer have numerous uses in the cockpit at night. All timepieces should have integral lighting capability. Because the quantity and quality of

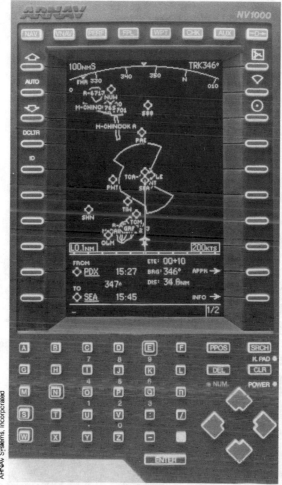

Fig. 7-10. *Loran based flight management system.*

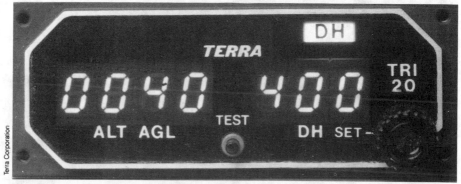

Fig. 7-11A. *Terra TRA 3500 radar altimeter.* Terra Corporation

Fig. 7-11B. *Analog panel display.*

Fig. 7-12. *Ground proximity advisory system.*

Fig. 7-13. *Icom IC-A20 navcom.*

ICOM America, Incorporated

visual cues at night is not comparable to that found during the daytime, a clock and a stopwatch are of increased importance in constantly determining aircraft positions. The clock should have a multiple preset alarm capability to allow the pilot to preselect times (hence locations) where and when critical functions should occur: switching fuel tanks, initiating predescent checklists, consuming midflight snacks, or completing arousal heightening exercises. Refer to FIG. 7-14.

Carbon monoxide detection at night remains an important concern. Of the two types of systems available, the electronic detectors are preferable because no visual

Fig. 7-14. *Davtron model 877 chronometer.*

inspection of the detector is necessary in the detection of carbon monoxide. Refer to FIG. 7-15 and FIG. 7-16.

Another available model of the above carbon monoxide detector plugs into the cigarette lighter and hangs on the instrument panel or a bulkhead. After a one minute warmup, the detector will buzz intermittently if a carbon monoxide concentration exceeds about 50 parts per million. As the concentration of carbon monoxide increases, the buzzer will sound more frequently.

An aircraft instrument training hood is a practical tool for multipilot crews when encountering electrical storms at night. While in the close proximity of lightning, one pilot can wear the hood to avoid both pilots becoming temporarily flash-blinded.

Additional navigational charts for adjacent areas should be available for the planned flight. (Additional discussion is in chapter 11.)

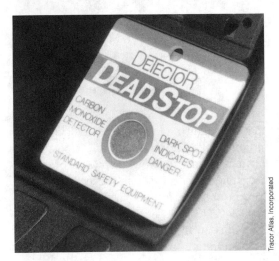

Fig. 7-15. *DeadStop carbon monoxide detector mounted in center console.*

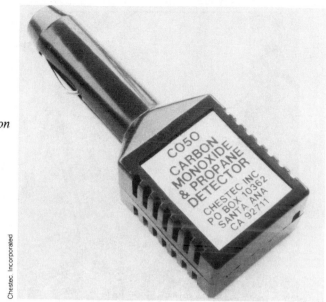

Fig. 7-16. *Electronic carbon monoxide detector.*

Chestec Incorporated

With the aid of a grease pencil, lighted plexiglass kneeboards equipped with rheostat switches can be used for copying clearances, jotting down weather notes, and making in-flight computations. They can also be used to view navigational charts when the charts are placed beneath the lighted plexiglass. Lighted yolk-mounted clipboards provide a similar function. One such device is diagrammed in FIG. 7-17.

When a fatigued pilot continuously receives erroneous information from an inoperative or malfunctioning flight instrument, the possibility of safety being compromised increases. An instrument cover then can further reduce mental fatigue by lessening the pilot's cognitive requirements of instrument interpretation and discrimination. Refer to FIG. 7-18.

The use of an antifog spray and a dry, lint-free cloth during certain meteorological conditions can be useful in maintaining a clear windshield.

Noise suppressors, earplugs, and other hearing protectors can reduce fatigue by eliminating noise; however, a lightweight, comfortable headset with boom microphone has additional benefits. The headset/microphone combination is not only convenient because it frees the pilot's hands, it also improves communications efficiency. There is less noise so the pilot has improved hearing and, as a result, the tendency of shouting into the microphone is reduced. This tool significantly reduces cockpit stressors.

Aircraft that are nonpressurized should all be equipped with portable oxygen systems that are of adequate size to afford abundant oxygen throughout the entire flight with a reasonable reserve in the event the flight is of a longer duration than initially anticipated. The night pilot should practice all aspects of its operation blindfolded. (See blindfold test in chapter 13.)

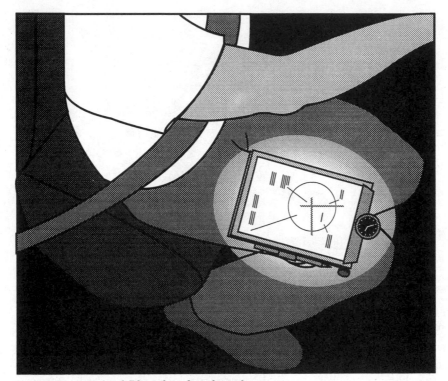

Fig. 7-17. *A lighted Plexiglass kneeboard.*

Shown in FIG. 7-19 is an equipment organizer that can be built in a home work-shop. It is strapped to an adjacent empty seat. As shown, it consists of a foam rubber base thick enough to firmly hold such items (within slots) as flashlights, pencils, drink dispensers, and sealed plastic boxes. In one of the boxes should be several cool damp cloths that may be used to wipe the forehead, neck, and wrists of the fatigued pilot. One or more plywood lids can hinge down to hold flight charts and other flat material. A fold-up, battery-powered lamp provides illumination.

These suggested items are a small selection of many different possible cockpit tools. It is important to remember that a common sense approach should be adopted in the determination of what tools should be used for each particular pilot, aircraft, and flight environment.

Of paramount importance to the pilot, in addition to having the special equipment available, is the placement of the equipment. If a piece of equipment is not easily accessible and the pilot decides, as a result, not to use the equipment, the equipment is of no value. Consequently, all equipment should be stored in areas that would promote easy usage. Once the place for a piece of equipment is located, the pilot should not unreasonably switch the location of the equipment from flight to flight. A pilot should be able to locate all of the special equipment in the cockpit blindfolded, just as he or she should be able to locate the instruments on the instrument panel blindfolded. (For

Fig. 7-18. *Instrument cover.*

additional information regarding the blindfold test, refer to chapter 13.) Intelligent cockpit management at night is much more important than during the day. For example, if an emergency develops en route that would necessitate a landing at the closest airport, a pilot has little time to fumble around in the cockpit to look for a sectional chart and then determine the next course of action.

Simple cockpit distractions can contribute to increased workload and lengthen the amount of time needed to carry out required tasks. They can also impair the pilot's eye-scanning behavior, possibly leading him or her to miss important information. These sources of distraction should be removed whenever possible. For example, if an aircraft has a radio with a hand microphone that rests within a cradle on the instrument panel, the pilot must take his or her eyes off the instrument panel or outside scene in order to locate the microphone. The eyes might then need to refocus and become light-adapted to some degree as the hand reaches for it. The pilot must also lean forward and grasp it correctly. Finally, he or she must press the activate switch while holding it up to the lips in the correct location.

Using a hand microphone appears to be an insignificant act; it is actually a long string of interrelated activities, each possessing sources of distraction for the pilot. During this time, the night pilot could become distracted by a totally different event

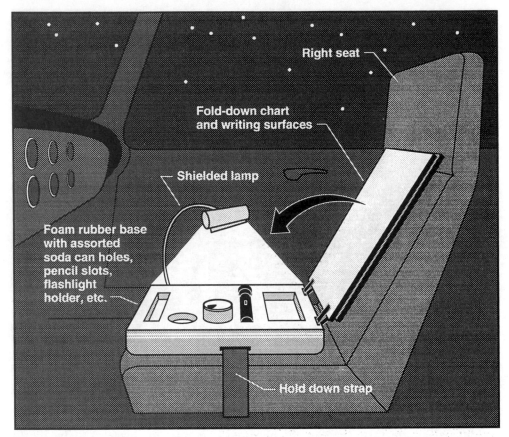

Fig. 7-19. *Night pilot's companion.*

that could, in turn, lead to some loss of attitude control, particularly in rough air. As mentioned earlier, the pilot should consider installing a push-to-talk button on the control wheel and buying a headset with an attached boom microphone. This hands-free approach will more than pay for itself in added pilot confidence, satisfaction, and safety.

PROPER PREFLIGHT PLANNING

Safety is the key ingredient in the preflight planning process. When compared to most other avocations and most other professions it can be said that flying at night is hazardous. Like the establishment of pilot and equipment minimums previously discussed, preflight planning must incorporate the basic principles of risk management.

Ideally, preflight planning for a night flight should utilize many of the same elements of those used for a flight in instrument meteorological conditions. The reason is simple; both night flight and flight into instrument meteorological conditions often lack horizon situational cues and both the night pilot and the instrument pilot can unexpectedly encounter adverse weather conditions.

Like the instrument pilot, the night pilot should plan for rejected landings for every airport of intended landing. Reviewing the terrain and proper procedures for a go-around is critical to safety.

Proper preflight planning for the night pilot must go beyond the regular regimen as exercised by the instrument pilot. Common sense must prevail during the course of planning for a night flight. Even though a pilot should check the *Airman's Information Manual* and all applicable different types of notams, seemingly simple tasks—calling a remote airport to verify that fuel will be available for a fuel stop during the night—are practical and necessary.

The following are some suggestions that pilots should incorporate into the planning of a night flight.

Fly as high as practical to increase glide path distance and visual range, as well as to increase electronic navigation and communications range. Navigational reception increases with altitude. The low en route altitude charts used by instrument pilots provide very useful information even for the VFR pilot regarding minimum obstruction clearance altitudes, minimum en route altitudes and minimum reception altitudes. By having this information, the night pilot is better able to plan appropriate flight altitudes. (This information is not found on sectional or world aeronautical charts.)

Always have several alternate courses of action if the flight cannot be completed as intended. Perhaps one of the best ways to not become an accident statistic is to always keep an option open. Countless accidents have occurred when pilots used up all of their options. Several different alternate airports should be located on the aeronautical charts. All appropriate flight information regarding each possible alternate airport should be logically organized in the event an alternate airport becomes a final destination. (The time to determine the direction of a traffic pattern is before takeoff and not when the airplane comes into contact with a mountain on the wrong side of the airport.)

Chart a course that is practical. Using loran at night is not always the safest way to navigate. Course lines that allow flight close to airports offer an extra margin of safety.

Study the topography and obstructions along the intended route of flight thoroughly. A pilot should decide prior to takeoff the general locations where off-airport landings are best made, not en route after the engine has stopped.

Organization is more important at night than during the day. For example, the use of radio navigation aids and communication facilities adds significantly to the safety and efficiency of the night flight and should not be overlooked in preflight planning. An organized systematic approach to itemizing frequencies of navigational facilities and communications facilities is essential. The safety factor is enhanced when the pilot has all necessary flight information at his or her fingertips. (It is always nice to know whom to call to turn on the runway lights.)

Always plan for the unexpected. Sooner or later it will happen.

With regard to aeronautical charts, the following are a few suggestions for making navigation and other flight operations easier during the nighttime hours:

Once the true course line is drawn on the map, short perpendicular lines should be marked at 10-mile intervals on the map. On one side of each mark, the distance traveled from the departure airport (or last checkpoint) can be noted and on the other side of the mark, the mileage remaining to the destination airport (or next checkpoint) can be noted.

At the conclusion of the flight planning process, approximate locations can be noted on the map as reminders to the pilot as to where it will soon become necessary to change fuel tanks.

Prominent checkpoints along the prepared course should be noted with mileages. Rotating beacons at airports, lighted obstructions, lights of cities or towns, and lights from major highway traffic all provide excellent visual checkpoints. Additionally, lakes, rivers, and streams provide good visual checkpoints on clear moonlit nights. Whenever a checkpoint is passed, the time should be noted next to each checkpoint. (This potential safety aid is especially helpful when a pilot becomes unsure of the aircraft's current position. It then becomes possible to determine the elapsed time from the last known checkpoint and when using the previously determined ground speed it is quite easy to determine the new probable position of the aircraft on the chart.)

The mileage should be noted on the map between prominent checkpoints in order to determine the ground speed periodically. More frequent ground speed calculations are necessary at night because there are fewer visual cues that would ordinarily alert a pilot to a significant drift or headwind condition.

Predetermined locations, where the in-flight workload should be lightest and a pilot or crewmember could consume food and/or a beverage, should be noted whenever necessary.

The predescent arousal heightening procedure location should be conspicuously marked on a chart in addition to any flight logs entries. (The arousal heightening procedure is discussed in detail in chapter 3.)

It is always helpful to mark the location on the course line at which a preplanned descent should be initiated. (After calculating descent distances, quite often pilots are surprised at the distance from the airport needed to initiate a gradual descent. This is one computation that is too frequently overlooked.)

Additional reminders can also be noted on aeronautical charts. For example, a geographical position at which the microphone should be keyed to activate a pilot-controlled lighting system should be noted on a sectional chart.

All charts should be folded in such a manner as to quickly facilitate transitioning from one chart to another.

All charts should be stowed in a readily accessible location and systematically arranged in an order that would promote convenient use and minimum cockpit confusion.

Course lines should be drawn in black or dark blue so as to be more distinguishable. Red or magenta lines should not be drawn on charts because red and magenta lines are absorbed by the red light environment.

All possible forced landing sites should be appropriately marked on the charts.

8
Safety at night

AMONG THE MAIN PRIORITIES THAT THE NIGHT PILOT SHOULD SET ARE those that enhance flight safety. All pilots, those with low levels of experience as well as those with high levels of experience, must exercise increased caution at night. Total time, the amount of recent experience, or the time in type do not allow any pilot to relax his or her vigilance. Complacency represents a far greater risk to the very experienced pilot than does limited aeronautical skill and knowledge to the fledgling aviator.

Any pilot will acknowledge that safety is an important priority. But just how important is it? Any other priority should be secondary. Perhaps no single topic is as important. Although many pilots acknowledge that safety is a high priority, they continually ignore some of its finer points. For example, almost everyone knows that even having a slight case of flu impairs thinking and slows reaction time but some pilots still fly anyway. During the day, most pilots "can get away with it," but nighttime flying often presents the highest of demands of a pilot's skill when a pilot is generally least able to meet those demands.

There must be increased emphasis placed on nighttime piloting activities. When the pilot views night flying first and foremost from the standpoint of safety and sets his or her priorities appropriately, then night flying will be far more enjoyable and rewarding and also safer.

INTERESTING AND SURPRISING STATISTICS

Approximately 16 percent of major aircraft accidents that occurred during the first eight years of commercial jet operations (before 1967) occurred during night approaches over unlighted terrain or water toward clearly visible cities or airports. In all of these accidents, the visibility was good so that flight crews could have referred to light patterns on the ground. Kraft (1969) reported that in 1967 the accident rate occurring under these same conditions rose to 17.5 percent. These statistics are surprising for two reasons: (1) this viewing situation should provide some of the best viewing conditions available for carrying out an approach and (2) highly trained professional pilots and flight crews, many of them senior captains, were involved in these accidents. Subsequent research on the *black-hole approach* illusion conducted by Drs. Conrad L. Kraft and Charles L. Elworth conclusively proved the described viewing conditions are definitely not optimal for nighttime visual approaches.

Although investigators at the time of the accidents concluded that most of them were as a result of pilot error, Drs. Kraft and Elworth discovered that human factors limitations were involved and that the nighttime black hole approach illusion was probably the main contributing factor in these accidents. Today, pilots are better trained to meet the challenges of the black hole approach thanks to these scientific investigations.

An aviation-related database that is managed by the Emil Buehler Center for Aviation Safety contains almost 15,000 reports from the National Transportation Safety Board (NTSB) of general aviation accidents that have occurred since 1982. A recent search of 7,274 accidents showed that 1,138 (16 percent) occurred at night. TABLE 8-1 breaks these particular accidents down into subcategories.

Table 8-1. Contributory causes to general aviation night accidents.

Contributory-Cause	Number	Percentage
Weather related	318	27.9
En route phase of flight	278	24.4
VFR flight into IMC weather	130	11.4
Instrument approaches	124	10.9
Fuel (starvation/exhaustion)	107	9.4
VFR descent into terrain/wires	36	3.1
Control loss in cruise flight	17	1.4
Others	128	11.5

Pilots should note that a significant percentage of these contributory causes of night accidents involve human factors in some form. Once night pilots realize the central importance of knowing about their own capabilities and limitations, they will become safer night pilots. This can only be accomplished through proper pilot education and training in overcoming these nighttime human factors limitations.

A small percentage of accidents, approximately 10 percent, is truely accidental; mechanical engine failure is one example. The remaining percentage of accidents is almost always related to the pilot's performance or lack of performance. What does this mean? Accidents, generally, are caused, they don't simply happen.

ALWAYS HAVE A WAY OUT—THE CARDINAL RULE

It is a reassuring feeling when a pilot has one or more backup plans in the "old bag of tricks." This little bit of pilot wisdom does not merely apply to having one or more alternate airports, but taken one more step, can apply to such areas as having a redundant aircraft electrical energy source, a spare microphone, and a second pair of easily accessible prescription glasses.

That extra margin of safety is so necessary when flying at night.

THE FLIGHT PLAN

Most pilots realize that they should file flight plans. But pilots often forget that if there is a deviation in a planned flight, the pilot should amend the flight plan to reflect those changes. There have been too many nighttime fatalities because flight plans were not filed, not followed, or not amended. The potential benefits, especially in regard to night flight, in taking the time to file a flight plan far outweigh any inconveniences. Filing a flight plan for a night flight can certainly become the deciding factor if a crash victim is located in a darkened environment in time to save his or her life. Accident statistics clearly reinforce this philosophy.

CHECKLISTS

During aviation's early years, checklists were not considered to be as important as they are today. Because those primitive aircraft had fewer systems, there were fewer items to remember; and, consequently, fewer items to forget. There weren't too many gear-up landings in 1915. Additionally, there were far fewer cockpit distractions to divert a pilot's attention from the task at hand. During the evolution of aircraft complexity and the resulting piloting activities and cockpit distractions, the requirements of piloting skills and better checklists also have increased.

Today, night flying for civil aviation is more common than during any other time in aviation history. With this increase in nocturnal flight activity comes an increased need for proper design and usage of checklists. Because the body's state of arousal is generally lowest during periods of darkness, checklists should be designed as precisely as possible to compensate for a pilot's decreased capability to see and understand them during nighttime hours.

Unfortunately, few checklists are specifically designed for nighttime operations. Any pilot who has ever tried to read the emergency section of an older checklist printed in red ink in a darkened cockpit using a red light source realizes this fact. Cockpit errors or omissions can be deadly. What pilots don't do can create more problems than many of their actions.

There is cause in some instances to redesign and reprint checklists for nighttime operations to account for possible human factor limitations and different nighttime flying procedures. Almost every pilot can find one or more items that should be added to an aircraft checklist that would enhance nighttime flight safety. Often the missing checklist items are not the fault of the manufacturer, but rather they relate to a particular type of piloting operation. For example, a checklist reminder to reset a pilot-controlled lighting system while flying on the downwind leg could save a pilot a few anxious seconds during an approach and landing by preventing the runway lights from shutting off prematurely.

While every pilot knows what a checklist is, it might not be as apparent that checklists play a number of important roles, particularly at night. They include providing an aid to the flight crew in remembering each and every physical procedure involved in configuring the airplane consistently; providing a logically sequential framework with which to achieve internal and external cockpit operational requirements; providing clear sequences of eye-hand coordination movements and patterns of visual fixation; providing means for ensuring that the airplane's configuration is correct despite possible reductions in the pilot's mental, physiological, and psychological condition related to circadian rhythm or other effects; providing for mutual supervision (cross-checking) among the flight crew members; providing clear guidance for which duties are to be carried out by which pilot to help reduce workload, help optimize crew coordination, and encourage all flight crew members to remain in the activity loop; and providing the flight crew with a greater sense of confidence that everything is configured as it should be.

Most of these roles become even more important at night due to the possibility that some checklist items may be left out or their execution excessively delayed because the pilot is engaged (or pilots are engaged) in other flight-related duties. From a human factors standpoint, the checklist is another interface between the pilot and the airplane and this interface must be clearly visible at night under all conditions of illumination.

Safety can be enhanced at night through the proper use of checklists. The night pilot flying alone faces the very real dilemma of needing the checklist at each phase of flight while also having to keep the aircraft under control while reaching for it, turning pages or knobs (as in the scrolling checklist), properly illuminating it, and reading it, at least when using older hardware and techniques. Stories abound of pilots who perform checklist items out of the proper order, leave critical items out, or who think that they can remember everything without any help. A review by Degani and Wiener (1990) that summarizes pilot interviews, NTSB cases, International Civil Aviation Organization (ICAO) reports, NASA Aviation Safety Reporting System databases, field observations, and industry literature stated that "distractions and interruptions can 'break' the checklist process and might result in a checklist error or omission. Conversely, the checklist process itself can be a distracter for other cockpit tasks and duties."

Checklists may be used several different ways. Each method has its own critics and proponents and there is ample controversy about which method is best. Perhaps the answer lies in the type and complexity of aircraft and supporting systems, the number of crewmembers, the style of piloting operation, and the flight environment. Three of the more common checklist procedures are "call-do-list" or "recipe-list" method, "do-then-check" method, and "challenge-response" method.

The "call-do-list" method is often used by the single pilot in that it leads and directs the pilot in configuring the aircraft's systems. This method is simply that checklist item 1 is located, read, and then carried out; checklist item 2 is located, read, and carried out; and so forth until the checklist is completed. Note that with this method the checklist is merely a memory aid that is used in a step-by-step manner. If an item is bypassed, there is the possibility that it will be left out or that an item might go unnoticed if the overall sequence is disrupted.

The "do-then-check" method is more often preferred by the experienced professionals than the "call-do-list" method. The "do-then-check" method essentially is to perform cockpit duties first from memory and then use the checklist to check if all of the duties have been performed correctly. The pilots who employ this method use the checklist to look for omissions and generally believe that the checklist should not be utilized as a do list.

The "challenge-response" method has been employed for decades by professional pilots and is quite different from the previously mentioned methods. This method assures accuracy and good communication when using different types of checklists ranging from routinely used checklists to emergency checklists. The challenge and response technique requires that pilot A initiates each checklist item by saying it out loud exactly as it is written on the checklist. Pilot B, responsible for performing the duty, repeats the challenge, looks at the item, touches it and then confirms with a verbal response that the checklist item has been completed as required. The manner in which the effectiveness of the "challenge-response" method is enhanced is by announcing a checklist item out loud, looking at the item and touching each item, thereby stimulating the senses of hearing, touch, and sight. Note that each item should be touched even if an item does not require any adjustment.

This method has been proven effective whether one pilot issues both the challenge and response or two pilots are involved in the challenge and response. When one pilot accomplishes a checklist, that pilot issues a challenge, and then looks and touches the item prior to responding.

Single-pilot checklist

Safety must be paramount in the mind of the night pilot with regard to how checklists are designed and used. Remember that not only do printed checklists possess weaknesses, pilots also possess weaknesses. Here are several recommendations for the single pilot with regard to printed checklists that must be read after dark.

Take all printed checklists home and after dark try reading each one in very dim illumination such as will be found at night in the cockpit. You may also experiment with additional light sources as suggested in chapter 9. If any single word or line of print cannot be easily read because the letters, numbers, or symbols are not large enough (or are printed in red or magenta if your aircraft is equipped with red cockpit lighting) have a new checklist printed and laminated, if necessary. Most local print shops are capable of providing the printing and lamination service. Perhaps you have access to a computer and laser printer to produce a customized checklist with readable type; have someone else proofread it to ensure nothing was inadvertently omitted.

For younger pilots (under 30 years of age) the (print) type used should be no smaller than $1/8''$ high with high contrast, black letters on a white background. For added versatility, the printer should use extra-heavyweight paper or lightweight white cardboard for the base.

For intermediate age pilots (30-45), the size and width of all characters should be increased. No letter or number should be less than $3/16''$ high. A highly legible font should be used such as helvetica bold, futura heavy, memphis bold, gill sans, or other such san serif style in heavy or bold weight.

For middle-age and older pilots (over 45), the height of all letters and numbers should be no less than $1/4''$ and printed in a bold font. The spacing between each line should also be increased (to $1/8''$) over normal daylight viewing spacing. The same fonts previously mentioned should be used.

The checklist for different phases of flight should each be visually distinctive from all others in two or more ways when read in the dark. For example, the preflight checklist might have thick, dark check marks printed across the top and bottom $1/4''$ of each page while the approach and landing checklist has black arrowheads pointing downward (to the ground) along the top and bottom of each page, and the like.

Mount all checklists in a three-ring binder that permits easy page turning and that holds each page down flat, even in a light airstream. This binder should be capable of being held directly in front of the pilot rather than to one side, which would require an excessive amount of head rotation. Single page checklists can be laminated in clear heavy plastic but the plastic should have a matte finish rather than a glossy finish.

If a checklist for each flight phase will not fit on a single page (so that the page must be turned to complete it), make sure that the item just before and after the page-turning break are not linked in time or flight criticality.

When carrying out the items on a checklist, do so in the correct order that is listed, unless flight conditions exist that the pilot knows will permit an out-of-sequence operation.

A hand-held checklist may be indexed item by item using a grease pencil to mark each item after it has been completed. This approach is better than merely holding a thumbnail on an item because: (a) if the checklist is interrupted for a long period of time, the marked position might change, even though the checklist itself must be held the entire time; (b) a two-column checklist might make it more difficult to mark the right-hand column item with the thumbnail; and (c) the thumb might cast shadows onto the printed page.

Do not conduct the checklist operations by memory only. The human memory is subject to temporary disruption via distractions, microsleep, fatigue, tiredness, and other stressors, especially during nighttime hours.

Future cockpits will probably include more and more computer-based electronic hardware including an advanced design checklist display. These human factored displays will involve such features as automatically-controlled display contrast that will be optimized for all cockpit lighting conditions, auditory annunciation of checklist items, visual attention-getting features that will be activated only when needed, and artificial intelligence capabilities that will analyze how an individual pilot controls an airplane under different conditions of flight to make automatic adjustments.

One currently available device is the Heads-up Checklist (HUC), which is a relatively small, light-weight talking checklist device shown in FIG. 8-1. It has many features that are well human factored including a GO button that advances to the next check-list item; the button can be remotely located on the control wheel. Use of a clearly audible voice annunciation of checklist items is another step in reducing pilot workload and unnecessary distraction.

Fig. 8-1. *Heads-up checklist.*

Some types of aircraft, especially corporate, have dozens of check items in the preflight inspection. Items on the checklist have been overlooked merely because the pilot had to look back and forth from airplane to checklist. A hand-held device is now available that permits this walk-around to be done efficiently and without undue pilot distraction. Figure 8-2 shows a microprocessor-based talking checklist device (EN 8-1) that includes a printer as well as a light emitting diode (LED) information display and an audible voice that announces each item. A data cartridge can store up to 500 checklist items.

COMMON ERRORS AT NIGHT

In addition to improper (or lack of) checklist usage, the following points recognize a few of the more common nighttime pilot errors:

One of the biggest errors that pilots make at night is launching off into the darkness when they should remain on the ground. The reasons for not going are all very

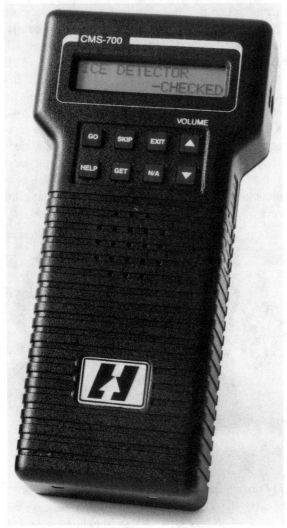

Fig. 8-2. *Preflight checklist device.*

individual, but invariably all reasons relate to one or more of the conditions of the nighttime triangle. The integration of the pilot, the flight environment and/or the aircraft, and the associated equipment is not suitable for the proposed flight.

Another very common error is that of treating a night flight as though it were almost like a day VFR flight. It certainly is true that the aircraft performs as well, if not better in some instances, during the hours of darkness, but that is just about where the basic similarities end. Although most pilots are aware of the basic differences between daytime and nighttime flying, it is sometimes difficult to switch one's mental gears. It is so easy to forget the differences that demand that a pilot reflect upon the new set of parameters required for night flight. For example, a pilot might forget that he or she might not be feeling as refreshed at 2 a.m. as at 9 p.m. Generally, this problem gradually disappears with greater levels of experience and currency.

Inadequate preflight planning and preflight of the aircraft have been contributing factors in a significant number of accidents. Because more extensive preflight planning and preflighting of the aircraft are required for night flight, some pilots might be prone to skip or abbreviate some of the more time-consuming steps like obtaining a more thorough weather briefing to determine possible excessive headwinds, potential instrument meteorological conditions between two VFR airports or weather conditions at potential alternate airports; or determining if an airport will be attended in the middle of the night for refueling; or checking the condition of the aircraft battery prior to taxi; or checking all of the cockpit and instrument lighting; or visually checking the fuel supply.

Fuel mismanagement continues to plague general aviation flight. Many aircraft crash due to fuel starvation when there is still a tank full of fuel.

Cockpit distractions are an ongoing contributor to pilot error. Continuity of thought is often lost because of distractions in the cockpit. Operational distractions like ATC traffic alerts frequently become a causal factor in excursions from the desired flight path; nonoperational distractions like unnecessary cockpit conversations could cause a pilot to not change frequencies in a navigational receiver at the appropriate time, for example. To better manage this type of distraction, many pilots have their own special rule that forbids unnecessary conversation during crucial phases of flight.

Pilots have found themselves in trouble simply because they have not accepted the reality of potentially dangerous situations. Too often pilots suffer from the "it can't happen to me" or "I can make it" syndromes.

When the weather conditions appear to be rapidly deteriorating at the destination airport, for example, if the pilot is legally qualified but not competent to meet the challenges that the situation requires, or if the aircraft and equipment is not suitable to meet the increased requirements of the mission, logic would dictate that a change in the flight plan be executed. It is sometimes best to swallow your pride and turn around or divert to an alternate airport, rather than try to beat out or slip in under the weather. Another dangerous situation that can and has developed is when a pilot encounters unexpected high headwinds in flight and decides to take a chance and tries to make it to the destination airport without taking on additional fuel, when landing and refueling at a different airport would be a logical course of action. Countless stories have been told about pilots who pushed it too far and ended their journeys by paying a terrible price. Exercising a little common sense and accepting the reality of a potentially dangerous situation can keep a pilot out of a lot of trouble.

SEE AND BE SEEN

The basic concept of see and be seen remains the basis of all private flying in the United States today. This principal emphasizes that it is the responsibility of all aviators to not only see other airplanes and hazards in the sky around them, but also take precautions to maximize the visibility (conspicuity) of their own airplane to other pilots flying nearby.

The following are some useful rules to follow in order to enhance your visibility to other aircraft nearby and also to detect other aircraft sooner at night:

Look outside the cabin at least twice as long as you look at the instrument panel. If you are flying in high density air space, increase this ratio to three or four times.

Use a repetitive eye scan as subsequently described. It will significantly improve your chances of picking up another airplane seen against a darker background.

Finally, when it comes to detecting the presence of another aircraft, it is a truism that four eyes in the cockpit are better than two when a disciplined eye scan pattern is employed by each person. This is yet another justification for having a two-pilot flight crew at night. A number of research studies have proven the utility of having everyone in the cockpit visually search for other traffic as long as each viewer assumes the task of searching a particular region of the sky. The pilot in command, of course, still has the full responsibility for seeing and avoiding other aircraft.

If you have passengers with you, have them also look outside in different directions. The pilot in command can delegate some of this important duty (but not final responsibility) in a systematic way that divides the visible part of the sky into as many regions as there are passengers. It is very important to completely brief willing and able passengers about this on the ground prior to departure.

Use the communications equipment as needed to let others know your position.

Because most pattern accidents occur on final approach, always visually check the area ahead extending out from the runway's centerline for other traffic before turning from base to final.

Always assume that the closer the aircraft is to the airport, the higher the probability will be that there are more airplanes in the vicinity of one's aircraft.

Turn the landing lights on when approaching terminal areas several miles before entering the traffic pattern or in areas of reduced visibility. It is also a sound practice to activate landing lights in locations where there could be a large concentration of birds.

When visual contact of another aircraft has been made, the pilot should momentarily activate the aircraft's landing lights alerting the other pilot of visual recognition.

Because a large portion of midair collisions involve a faster airplane overtaking and striking a slower one, greater visual emphasis should be given to exploring the regions almost directly ahead of and behind the airplane, if possible.

Conspicuity at night

Light source intensity, contrast, and visual angle of an oncoming airplane at night are the three most important factors affecting whether or not a pilot will see another aircraft sooner or later. If it is pitch dark, even the angular size of the oncoming airplane becomes an irrelevant factor. Use of an anticollision strobe light is not only required, but makes good sense.

Another important factor is where one looks because when the eyes are dark adapted, one is effectively blind in the central region of the retina (the cone region corresponding with the line of sight) to dim light sources. Because of this fact, it is always better to look from five to ten degrees arc off-axis from where one believes there might be another oncoming airplane. Five degrees of arc is roughly equivalent to looking at the width of a baseball held at arm's length from the face. Ten degrees of arc is about equivalent to the angular size of a grapefruit held at arm's length. By not looking directly at a very dim light, one will place the light's image on a more sensitive part of the retina (of the dark-adapted eye).

An easy way to enhance the pilot's ability to detect outside obstacles is to dim interior cockpit lighting.

Improved night scanning

Remember that the part of the retina that possesses the sharpest resolution for seeing small detail is the same area that is very insensitive to light in the dark. Visual resolution varies from very fine (directly on the line of sight) to very poor (at the edge of the visual field). A useful rule of thumb is that looking only five degrees arc from some point reduces one's visual resolution by a factor of over four times. This means that a distant object will need to increase in angular size from one minute of arc to about four minutes of arc in order to be correctly discriminated. If a small airplane at a distance of seven miles away is just visible when looked at directly, it might not be perceived until it is only four miles away if looked at even five degrees arc from the line of sight (the fovea) (Halnes 1975; Tolc et al. 1982).

It is always best to adopt a systematic visual scan that will cover most of the outside scene that is visible. A pattern like that shown in FIG. 8-3 is suggested for night flying because it will cause the sometimes dim lights of another airplane to strike the more sensitive areas of the retina more of the time and from a far wider range of possible outside locations than if one performs only a circular visual scan of constant radius about the flight path. Like an instrument panel scan, always begin at the same spot (For example, position P1). Move horizontally to the left about 20 degrees of arc and then pause for about 3/4 second or so at point P2. Continue scanning smoothly to the left another 20 degrees and pause again at P3. Continue this scan-pause-scan activity following the direction of these dashed lines until reaching point P17 after which go back to the starting point. This sequential pattern will eventually become second nature.

A practical definition of night

As the sun falls farther and farther below the local horizon, the sky darkens with ever greater speed. To the observer, this period of twilight seems quite gradual, even unnoticeable. If it is overcast, the twilight period that separates day from night will shorten quite significantly.

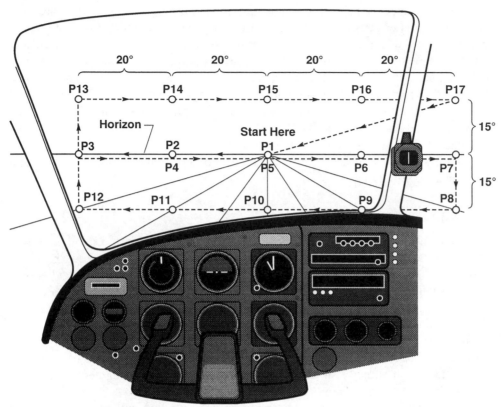

Fig. 8-3. *Recommended night scan pattern.*

Night has different definitions. The legal definition according to FAR Part 1 is "the time between the end of evening civil twilight and the beginning of morning civil twilight, as published in the *American Air Almanac*, converted to local time."

For practical purposes in this book, night will be defined as any part of the 24-hour period when one cannot read a normal size (such as you are reading now) printed page under ambient skylight. In clear air, this works out to be near the end of the twilight period. Of course, most of the night period is much darker than this. The full moon on a clear night will not produce sufficient illumination to permit one to read normal size print on a white paper either.

MOTIVATION

Motivation is a major factor in safety. All nocturnal airmen should be aware that not only does a good attitude play a significant role in motivation, but a pilot's physical state also is a very key ingredient in the motivation equation. When a pilot is very fatigued, his or her degree of motivation is likely to diminish quickly. Consider the pilot who after a hard day's work is on final approach after midnight local time.

Ordinarily, this pilot would be motivated to use the checklist, but instead, he or she decides not to because he or she is tired and, as a result, has a gear-up landing. This exact scenario happens too frequently. Consequently, not only must a pilot possess a safe attitude, but he or she must be physically able to maintain a high degree of motivation. The human factor cannot be overlooked in regard to safety at night.

The night pilot should take every precaution necessary to ensure as safe a flight as possible. Suggestions given in this chapter and elsewhere in this book should be followed to achieve a very high level of safety.

9
Aeronautical lighting

MANY AIRPORT LIGHTING AIDS ARE IN USE IN AMERICA TODAY. THIS CHAPTER presents a description of lighting aids along with diagrams and photographs showing their appearance. Also, a portion of this chapter describes interior and exterior aircraft lights.

AIRPORT LIGHTING AIDS

Approach lighting systems (ALS)

Approach lighting systems provide the basic means to transition from instrument flight to visual flight for landing. Operational requirements dictate the sophistication and configuration of the approach light system for a particular runway. Approach light systems are a configuration of signal lights starting at the landing threshold and extending into the approach area a distance of 2,400 to 3,000 feet for precision instrument runways and 1,400 to 1,500 feet for nonprecision instrument runways.

Some systems include sequenced flashing lights that appear to the pilot as a ball of light traveling toward the runway at high speed (twice a second). Of course, the runway might or might not be visible due to atmospheric conditions. Sometimes known as the *rabbit*, these flashing approach lights can disorient some night pilots through an effect that is thought to be similar to flicker vertigo. This is particularly true in haze and ground fog conditions where each high intensity strobe light seemingly blooms into a much larger source of light, filling the entire windshield area. It is permissible to ask the tower to turn them off if they pose a problem.

The upper portion of FIG. 9-1 shows three configurations of approach lights referred to as *precision instrument configurations* because they are based on careful scientific analyses of what vertical and lateral guidance information is needed during night approaches in varying visibility conditions. Part A shows the approach light system with sequenced flashing lights (ALSF1) configuration and part B shows the

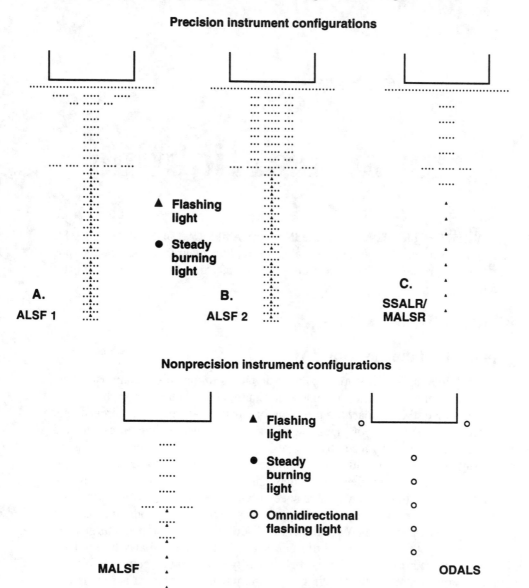

Note: Civil ALSF-2 may be operated as SSALR during favorable weather conditions

Fig. 9-1. *Precision instrument approach light configurations.*

ALSF2 configuration. Part C shows the simplified short approach light system with runway alignment indicator lights (SSALR)/medium intensity approach lighting system (MALSR) configuration whose sequenced strobe lights do not reach all the way to the threshold.

The lower portion of FIG. 9-1 shows two other nonprecision instrument configurations referred to as the MALSF and the omnidirectional flashing approach light system (ODALS).

Figure 9-2 shows the ALSF1 precision instrument configuration of approach lights portrayed on a modern computer-generated flight training simulator. Notice the high degree of detail that is possible.

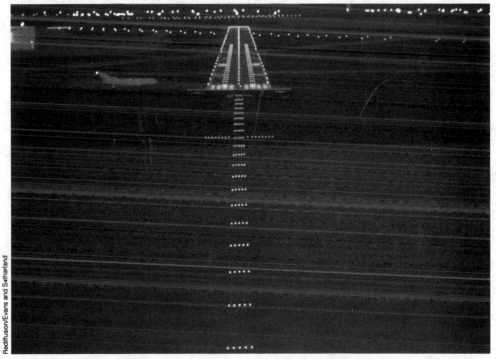

Fig. 9-2. *Simulated approach scene showing the ALSF1 approach lighting configuration.*

Visual glideslope indicators

Different systems have been developed and installed over the years to help the night pilot align the aircraft with the centerline of the runway and descend along a given flight path to a given spot (*flight path intercept point*). These lighting systems are called visual glide slope indicators.

Visual approach slope indicator (VASI). The VASI is a system of lights arranged to provide visual descent guidance information during the approach to a runway. These lights are visible from 3 to 5 miles during the day and up to 20 miles or more at night. The visual glide path of the VASI provides safe obstruction clearance within plus or minus 10 degrees of the extended runway centerline and to 4 nautical miles from the runway threshold. Descent, using the VASI, should not be initiated until the aircraft is visually aligned with the runway. Lateral course guidance is provided by the runway or the runway lights. VASI installations might consist of 2, 4, 6, 12, or 16 light units arranged in bars referred to as near, middle, and far bars. Most VASI installations consist of 2 bars, near and far, and might consist of 2, 4, or 12 light units. Some VASIs consist of three bars (near, middle, and far) that provide an additional visual glide path to accommodate aircraft with an elevated cockpit. This installation might consist of either 6 or 16 light units. VASI installations consisting of 2, 4, or 6 light units are located on one side of the runway, usually the left. Where the installation consists of 12 or 16 light units, the units are located on both sides of the runway. Figure 9-3 is an illustration of the two-bar and three-bar VASI units.

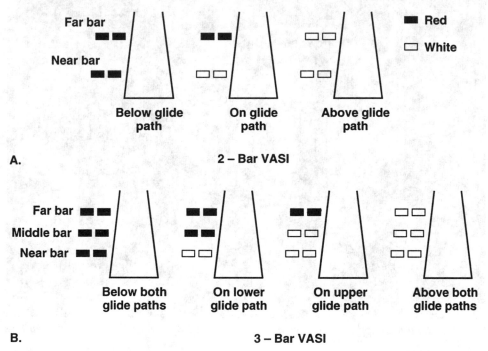

Fig. 9-3. *Two- and three-bar visual approach slope indicators.*

Two-bar VASI installations provide one visual glide path that is normally set at 3 degrees. Three-bar VASI installations provide two visual glide paths. The lower glide path is provided by the near and middle bars and is normally set 3 degrees while the upper glide path, provided by the middle and far bars, is normally 1/4 degree higher. This higher glide path is intended for use only by aircraft with an elevated cockpit to provide a sufficient threshold crossing height. Although normal glide path angles are three degrees, angles at some locations might be as high as 4.5 degrees to give proper obstacle clearance. Pilots of high performance aircraft are cautioned that use of VASI angles in excess of 3.5 degrees might cause an increase in runway length required for landing and roll out.

The basic principle of the VASI is color differentiation between red and white. Each light unit projects a beam of light having a white segment in the upper part of the beam and red segment in the lower part of the beam. The light units are arranged so that the pilot using the VASIs during an approach will see the combination of lights shown in FIG. 9-4.

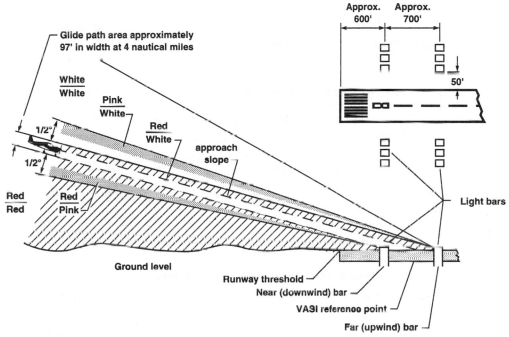

Fig. 9-4. *Typical visual approach slope indicator colors.*

Precision approach path indicator (PAPI). The Precision approach path indicator (PAPI) uses light units similar to the VASI, but are installed in a single row of either two or four light units. These systems have an effective visual range of about 5 miles during the day and up to 20 miles at night. The row of light units is normally installed on the left side of the runway and the glide path indications are as depicted (FIG. 9-5).

Tri-color systems. Tri-color visual approach slope indicators normally consist of a single light unit projecting a three-color visual approach path into the final approach area of the runway. The below glide path indication is red, the above glide path indication is amber, and the on glide path indication is green as is shown in FIG. 9-6. These types of indicators have a useful range of approximately one-half to one mile during the day and up to five miles at night depending upon the visibility conditions.

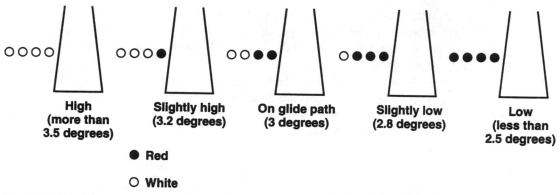

Red

White

Fig. 9-5. *Precision approach path indicator.*

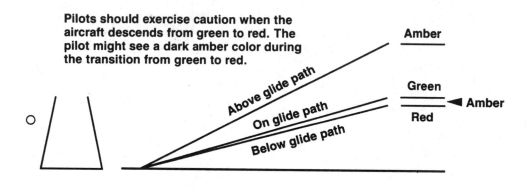

Pilots should exercise caution when the aircraft descends from green to red. The pilot might see a dark amber color during the transition from green to red.

Tri-color visual approach slope indicator

Fig. 9-6. *Tri-color approach slope indicator.*

Pulsating systems. Pulsating visual approach slope indicators normally consist of a single light unit projecting a two-color visual approach path into the final approach area of the runway upon which the indicator is installed. The below glide path indication is normally pulsating red and the above glide path indication is normally pulsating white. The on glide path indication is a steady white light. Figure 9-7 shows this system. The useful range of this system is about four miles during the day and up to 10 miles at night.

Alignment of elements systems. Alignment of elements systems might be installed at smaller general aviation airports. This is a low-cost system consisting of painted plywood panels, normally black and white or fluorescent orange. Some of these systems are lighted for night use. Figure 9-8 shows the above, on, and below glide path appearances of the three panels. The useful range is approximately three-quarters of a mile. To use the system, the pilot positions his aircraft so the elements are in alignment.

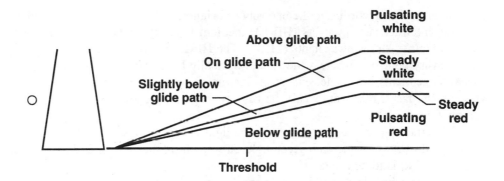

Pulsating visual approach slope indicator

Caution: When viewing the pulsating visual approach slope indicators in the pulsating white or pulsating red sectors, it is possible to mistake this lighting aid for another aircraft or a ground vehicle. Pilots should exercise caution when using this type of system.

Fig. 9-7. *Pulsating visual approach slope indicator.*

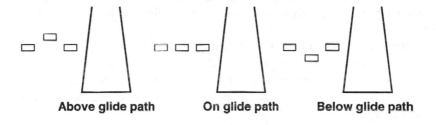

Alignment of elements

Fig. 9-8. *Alignment of elements visual approach slope indicator.*

Runway end identifier lights (REIL)

REILs are installed at many airfields to provide rapid and positive identification of the approach end of a particular runway. The system consists of a pair of synchronized flashing lights located laterally on each side of the runway threshold. REILs might be either omnidirectional or unidirectional facing the approach area. They are effective for:

- Identification of a runway surrounded by a preponderance of other lighting.
- Identification of a runway that lacks contrast with surrounding terrain.
- Identification of a runway during reduced visibility.

Runway edge light systems. Runway edge lights are used to outline the edges of runways during periods of darkness or restricted visibility conditions. These light systems are classified according to the intensity or brightness they are capable of producing: high intensity runway lights (HIRL), medium intensity runway lights (MIRL), and the low intensity runway lights (LIRL). The HIRL and MIRL systems have variable intensity controls, whereas the LIRLs normally have one intensity setting. The runway edge lights are white, except on instrument runways when amber replaces white on the last 2,000 feet or half the runway length, whichever is less, to form a caution zone for landings.

Lights marking the runway ends emit red light inward toward the runway to indicate the end of runway and emit green light outward from the runway end to indicate the threshold to landing aircraft.

In-runway lighting. Touchdown zone lights and runway centerline lights are installed on some precision approach runways to facilitate landing under adverse visibility conditions. Taxiway turnoff lights might be added to expedite movement of aircraft from the runway.

Touchdown zone lighting (TDZL). Two rows of transverse light bars are arranged symmetrically about the runway centerline in the runway touchdown zone. The system starts 100 feet from the landing threshold and extends to 3000 feet from the threshold or the midpoint of the runway, whichever is the lesser.

Runway centerline lighting (RCLS). Flush centerline lights are spaced at 50-foot intervals beginning 75 feet from the landing threshold and extending to within 75 feet of the opposite end of the runway.

Runway remaining lighting. Centerline lighting systems are in the final 3,000 feet as viewed from the takeoff or approach position. Alternate red and white lights are seen from the 3,000-foot point to the 1,000-foot points, and all red lights are seen for the last 1,000 feet of the runway. From the opposite direction, these lights are seen as white lights.

Taxiway turnoff lights. Flush lights are spaced at 50-foot intervals defining the curved path of aircraft travel from the runway centerline to a point on the taxiway. These lights are steady burning and emit green light.

Control of lighting systems. Operation of approach light systems and runway lighting is controlled from the air traffic control tower (ATCT). At some locations, the FSS might control the lights where there is no control tower in operation. Pilots may request that lights be turned on or off. Runway edge lights, in-pavement lights, and approach lights also have intensity controls that may be varied to meet the pilot's request. Sequenced flashing lights (SFL) may be turned on and off. Some sequenced flashing light systems also have intensity control.

Pilot control of airport lighting. Radio control of lighting is available at selected airports to provide airborne control of lights by keying the aircraft's microphone. Control of lighting systems is often available at locations without specified hours for lighting and where there is no control tower or FSS or when the tower or FSS is closed (locations with a part-time tower or FSS) or specified hours. All lighting systems that are radio controlled at an airport, whether on a single runway or multiple runways, operate on the same radio frequency. (Refer to TABLES 9-1 and 9-2.)

Table 9-1. Runways with approach lights.

Lighting system	No. of int. steps	Status during nonuse period	Intensity step selected per no. of mike clicks		
			3 clicks	5 clicks	7 clicks
Approach lights (med. int.)	2	Off	Low	Low	High
Approach lights (med. int.)	3	Off	Low	Med.	High
MIRL	3	Off or low	♣	♣	♣
HIRL	5	Off or low	♣	♣	♣
VASI	2	Off	◆	◆	◆

Notes:

♣   Predetermined intensity step

◆   Low intensity for night use. High intensity for day use as determined by photocell control

171

Table 9-2. Runways without approach lights.

Lighting system	No. of int. steps	Status during nonuse period	Intensity step selected per no. of mike clicks		
			3 clicks	5 clicks	7 clicks
MIRL	3	Off or low	Low	Med.	High
HIRL	5	Off or low	Step 1 or 2	Step 3	Step 5
LIRL	1	Off	On	On	On
VASI♥	2	Off	♦	♦	♦
REIL♥	1	Off	Off	On/Off	On
REIL♥	3	Off	Low	Med.	High

Notes:

♥ The control of VASI and/or REIL may be independent of other lighting systems

♦ Low intensity for night use. High intensity for day use as determined by photocell control

172

With FAA-approved systems, various combinations of medium intensity approach lights, runway lights, taxiway lights, VASI and/or REIL may by activated by radio control. On runways with approach lighting and runway lighting systems (runway edge lights, taxiway lights, and the like), the approach lighting system takes precedence for air-to-ground radio control over the runway lighting system that is set at a predetermined intensity step, based on expected visibility conditions. Runways without approach lighting might provide radio controlled intensity adjustments of runway edge lights. Other lighting systems, including VASI, REIL, and taxiway lights might be either controlled with the runway edge lights or controlled independently of the runway edge lights. The control system consists of a 3-step control responsive to 7, 5, and/or 3 microphone clicks. This 3-step control will turn on lighting facilities capable of either 3-step, 2-step or 1-step operation. The 3-step and 2-step lighting facilities can be altered in intensity, while the 1-step cannot. All lighting is illuminated for a period of 15 minutes from the most recent time of activation and cannot be extinguished prior to the end of the 15-minute period (except for 1-step and 2-step REILs that may be turned off when desired by keying the mike 5 or 3 times, respectively).

Suggested use is to always initially key the mike 7 times; this assures that all controlled lights are turned on to the maximum available intensity. If desired, adjustment can then be made, where the capability is provided, to a lower intensity (or the REIL turned off) by keying 5 and/or 3 times. Due to the close proximity of airports using the same frequency, radio controlled lighting receivers may be set at a low sensitivity requiring the aircraft to be relatively close to activate the system. Consequently, even when lights are on, always key mike as directed when overflying an airport of intended landing or just prior to entering the final segment of an approach. This will assure the aircraft is close enough to activate the system and a full 15 minutes lighting duration is available. Approved lighting systems may be activated by keying the mike (within 5 seconds) (TABLE 9-3).

Table 9-3. Runway light system radio activation.

Key Mike	Function
7 times within 5 seconds	Highest intensity available
5 times within 5 seconds	Medium or lower intensity (Lower REIL or REIL-off)
3 times within 5 seconds	Lowest intensity available (Lower REIL or REIL-off)

For all public-use airports with FAA standard systems, the *Airport/Facility Directory* contains the types of lighting, runway, and the frequency that is used to activate the system. Airports with instrument approach procedures (IAPs) include data on the approach chart identifying the light system, the runway on which they are installed, and the frequency that is used to activate the system. Where the airport is not served by an IAP, it might have either the standard FAA approved control system or an independent type system of different specification installed by the airport sponsor. The *Airport/Facility Directory* contains descriptions of pilot controlled lighting systems for each airport having other than FAA approved systems, and explains the type lights, method of control, and operating frequency in clear text.

Airport rotating beacons. The airport beacon has a vertical light distribution to make it most effective from one to 10 degrees above the horizon; however, it can be seen well above and below this peak spread. The beacon might be an omnidirectional capacitor-discharge device, or it might rotate at a constant speed that produces the visual effect of flashes at regular intervals. Flashes might be one or two colors alternately. The total number of flashes are:

- 12 to 30 per minute for beacons marking airports, landmarks, and points on Federal airways.
- 30 to 60 per minute for beacons marking heliports.

The colors and color combinations of beacons are (EN 9-1):

- White and green, lighted land airport
- *Green alone, lighted land airport
- White and yellow, lighted water airport
- *Yellow alone, lighted water airport
- Green and yellow and white, lighted heliport

Military airport beacons flash alternately white and green, but are differentiated from civil beacons by dual-peaked (two quick) white flashes between the green flashes. In control zones, operation of the airport beacon during the hours of daylight often indicates that the ground visibility is less than 3 miles and/or the ceiling is less than 1,000 feet. ATC clearance in accordance with FAR 91 is required for landing, takeoff, and flight in the traffic pattern. Pilots should not rely solely on the operation of the airport beacon to indicate if weather conditions are IFR or VFR. At some locations with operating control towers, ATC personnel turn the beacon on or off when controls are available in the tower. At many airports, the airport beacon is turned on by a photoelectric cell or time clocks and ATC personnel cannot control them. There is no regulatory requirement for daylight operation and it is the pilot's responsibility to comply with proper preflight planning as required by a Federal Aviation Regulation.

Taxiway lights. Even a familiar airport might appear strangely different at night during the taxiing operations. If the pilot gets lost or is unsure which way to turn ask for immediate assistance from ground control, if it is available. If it is unavailable, go slower and try to visualize the correct pathway directions in your mind, then see if they actually appear that way when approaching them. It is always better to go too slow or to stop than to taxi onto an active runway inadvertently.

Taxiway edge lights. Taxiway edge lights are used to outline the edges of taxiways during periods of darkness or restricted visibility conditions. These fixtures emit blue light that is not particularly conspicuous from the air.

Taxiway centerline lights. Taxiway centerline lights are used to facilitate the movement of ground traffic under low visibility conditions. They are located along the taxiway centerline in a straight line on straight portions, on the centerline on curved portions, and along designated taxiing paths in portions of runways, ramp, and apron areas. Taxiway centerline lights are steady burning and emit green light.

AIR NAVIGATION AND OBSTRUCTION LIGHTING

Aeronautical light beacons. An aeronautical light beacon is a visual navigation aid (NAVAID) displaying flashes of white and/or colored light to indicate the location of an airport, a heliport, a landmark, a certain point of a Federal airway in mountainous terrain, or an obstruction. The light used might be a rotating beacon or one or more flashing lights. The flashing lights might be supplemented by steady burning lights of lesser intensity. The color or color combination displayed by a particular beacon and/or its auxiliary lights tell whether the beacon is indicating a landing place, landmark, point of the federal airways (EN 9-2), or an obstruction. Coded flashes of the auxiliary lights, if employed, further identify the beacon site.

All dangerous obstructions to flight located near an airport must be marked with red obstruction beacons.

Code beacons and course lights. The code beacon, which can be seen from all directions, is used to identify airports and landmarks and to mark obstructions:

- Green coded flashes not exceeding 40 flashes or character elements per minute, or constant flashes 12 to 15 per minute, for identifying land airports.
- Yellow coded flashes not exceeding 40 flashes or character elements per minute, or constant flashes 12 to 15 per minute, for identifying water airports.
- Red flashes, constant rate, 12 to 40 flashes per minute for marking hazards.

Course lights. The course light, which can be seen clearly from only one direction, is used only with rotating beacons of the federal airway system: two course lights, back to back, direct coded flashing beams of light in either direction along the course of the airway.

Obstruction lighting. Obstructions are marked and lighted to warn airmen day and night. They might be marked and lighted in any of the following combinations:

- Aviation red obstruction lights. Flashing aviation red beacons and steady burning aviation red lights during nighttime operation. Aviation orange and white paint is used for daytime marking.
- High intensity white obstruction lights. Flashing high intensity white lights during daytime with reduced intensity for twilight and nighttime operation.

When this type system is used, the marking of structures with red obstruction lights and aviation orange and white paint might be omitted.

- Dual lighting. A combination of flashing aviation red beacons and steady burning aviation red lights for nighttime operation and flashing high intensity white lights for daytime operation. Aviation orange and white paint might be omitted. High intensity flashing white lights are being used to identify some supporting structures of overhead transmission lines located across rivers, chasms, gorges, and the like. These lights flash in a middle, top, and lower light sequence at approximately 60 flashes per minute. The top light is normally installed near the top of the supporting structure, while the lower light indicates the approximate lower portion of the wire span. The lights are aimed toward the companion structure and identify the area of the wire span. High intensity, flashing white lights are also employed to identify tall structures, such as stacks and towers, as obstructions to air navigation. The lights provide a 360 degree coverage about the structure at 40 flashes per minute and consist of from one to seven levels of lights depending upon the height of the structure. Where more than one level is used, the vertical banks flash simultaneously.

AIRCRAFT LIGHTING

FAR 91 requires that all airplanes operating on the ground or in the air between sunset and sunrise must display lighted position (navigation) lights. Almost all airplanes possess many other inside and outside lights to aid the pilot in seeing and being seen.

Interior lights

Aircraft interior lighting is and has been nonstandardized. Cockpit and instrument lighting has been one of the most overlooked and neglected areas in aviation research and design, especially among general aviation aircraft manufacturers. Consequently, the area of cockpit illumination is one of the major areas of aircraft design deficiency. And because of this deficiency pilots are prone to more frequent problematic mishaps in the cockpit, sometimes leading to accidents.

The complete answer is not entirely simple. Additional cockpit lighting is beneficial, especially to the older aircraft like DC-3s and Beech 18s that are still used extensively today. Pilots should remember that when many of these aircraft were designed, less emphasis was placed on nighttime utility in comparison to today's belief in nighttime as well as daytime utility. Airplane owners should seriously consider adding additional light sources to those cockpit areas that are poorly illuminated: fuel tank switch or lever, alternate air source control, emergency gear extension handle, fuse or circuit breaker panel. Many stories relate the common occurrence of the night pilot who became severely disoriented after looking down first for a flashlight that had rolled onto the floor and subsequently at the floorboards next to the seat for the exact orientation of the fuel tank switch.

Types of interior lighting are varied and include but are not limited to the following: flood, post, integral, eyebrow, map, dome, and independent beam lighting. Experienced night pilots often supplement these with additional light sources to meet special needs. These additional light sources are discussed in chapter 7: flashlights, penlight flashlight(s), cyalume chemical light stick(s), head-mounted miner's lamp, and internally illuminated kneepad writing surface.

As the night pilot gets older, he requires more light to read the same level of detail, particularly small letters and other markings. As suggested in chapter 8, it is always a good idea to take the actual flight charts, checklists, and other printed materials home prior to a night flight and, while sitting in a darkened room in a chair, experiment with these additional light sources to see (1) what problems are encountered in positioning them correctly, (2) whether or not all of the fine print and colors can be seen clearly, and (3) whether the light sources will remain stable enough during rough air and body movements. This simple preflight exercise can prove to be very enlightening indeed.

Cockpit lighting also should be carefully preplanned to provide the best possible balance between internal and external visibility. This will usually take the form of a continuously adjustable rheostat-type control of lamp intensity within all displays. The airframe manufacturer (most likely) will provide this capability, but the pilot needs to know how to make pre- and in-flight intensity adjustments at night. Here are a few general guidelines to do this. While sitting in the cockpit in total darkness:

1. Turn all interior lights down to minimum setting and look at a spot on the instrument panel that is located in the center of the instrument gauges, preferably where there is no lighted gauge.

2. Turn up the intensity of all panel lights slowly and note which instrument panel gauges, displays, and labels appear first, and which appear later. Do not look over at the individual gauges as they appear in the darkness. All of the primary flight information (altitude, airspeed, pitch-roll attitude, vertical rate, fuel level, and the like) should appear at the same time and should be equally visible. If some information appears brighter than other information, a voltage adjustment should be made to equalize them all.

3. Maintain the lighting of all panel gauges, displays, and labels level determined in step 2, slowly increase the intensity of all cockpit flood lights to maximum setting. Look at each glass-covered gauge in turn to see whether there are reflections of light from the ambient cockpit light sources. If any gauges are hard to see due to this reflected glare, reorient the direction of the ambient spotlights and floodlights so that the glare disappears.

4. Finally, look carefully through all windows with the lights kept at the above settings. Are there light reflections on the window surfaces that impair visibility through any parts of the windows? If so, take appropriate actions to shield the offending light source(s). Recall that interior aircraft lights can influence how well the pilot can see outside. Indeed, the windows will

reflect a certain portion of this interior light back into the pilot's eyes, which might cause reduced visual contrast and possible confusion. Are the lights inside or outside the airplane's cockpit? Experiment with every cockpit light control at night on the ramp or in the hangar to determine which lights reflect into the eyes from the windows. These window reflections will also make it more difficult to see lights located on the ground and in the air because the visual contrast will be reduced.

Because light is the single most powerful stimulus to staying alert at night, some human factors experts recommend increasing cockpit illumination levels as high as possible to help stay awake. In high traffic density areas where the see and be seen principle is essential, cockpit lighting should not be increased over the level needed to read instruments and find cockpit equipment. It might be more feasible to increase cockpit illumination at high altitude for aircraft that are under positive radar control.

Now that radio and other forms of electronic navigation are commonplace, today's nocturnal aviator relies less on specific ground referenced visual cues during cross-country flight. This trend has made it possible to increase the level of cockpit illumination to some degree and permits use of white floodlights and map lights to read colored aviation charts. Remember that red ink becomes virtually invisible under red lighting (EN 9-3). If the pilot needs to check a chart under intense white light, he should close one eye (during viewing) to keep its sensitivity to darkness at an acceptable level.

Because the visual system takes many minutes to achieve an adequate level of sensitivity to a darkened environment, red cockpit illumination was used in military aircraft during World War II to permit basic visual discriminations of form and motion to be made while preserving dark sensitivity and also to make it more difficult for the lighted cockpits to be seen by enemy aircraft. Before many of these aviators entered their aircraft, their eyes were already dark adapted by adjusting their eyes in a naturally darkened environment, by wearing red lens goggles, and/or by subjecting their eyes to a red light environment. These principles are still valid and can still be practiced today. Rod receptors, which populate much of the retina, are significantly less sensitive to red wavelengths. Because civilian flight operations do not require this level of dark sensitivity, commercial and private aircraft cabins typically possess white light sources that emit a large proportion of long wavelengths (such as red light). Some cabin floodlights also have red filters that the pilot can insert when necessary.

White cockpit illumination is preferred over red because it: (1) increases the visual contrast of printed labels, dials, and other displays making them easier to read; (2) makes it possible to use all colors on charts and maps, including red; (3) makes it possible to use red colored flags and reflective red warning messages; (4) generally reduces visual fatigue, probably because of the enhanced contrast; (5) reduces the visual problems experienced by the aging aviator when a near visual focus cannot be achieved without special optical correction and also hyperopia (far sightedness); (6) preserves somewhat better vision in a thunderstorm after a bolt of lightning has partially dazzled the eyes, that is, vision is restored somewhat sooner after the flash-blindness has occurred; and (7) tends to contribute to increased mental alertness over prolonged periods of time in an otherwise dark environment. (For these reasons, pilots should carry two flashlights capable of emitting white light.)

Exterior lights

Airplanes have a number of different external light sources that serve different purposes, all of which are to increase their conspicuity to other pilots flying in the area.

Position lights. Every aircraft must have position lights, also called *navigation lights*, that are to be located on the wing tips (approved aviation red on the left wing tip; approved aviation green on the right wing tip). Each wing tip light shines forward, upward, downward, and outward, but not behind the aircraft. A continuous aviation white light must be located in the tail, aimed directly backward from the direction of travel, and must be visible within at least a hemisphere of viewing positions. Figure 9-9 illustrates the location of these lights. These lights must be left on at all times after dark (flying or taxiing). They must also be on if the airplane is parked or moved to a location in close proximity to an area of the airport that is used for night operations, if the area isn't well lighted.

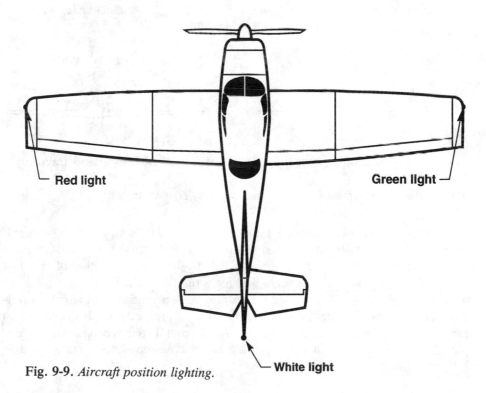

Fig. 9-9. *Aircraft position lighting.*

Consider the airplane's navigation (position) lights on the wing tips, which duplicate light location on ships at sea. The lights help other sea and air pilots determine relative position to each other and to the viewer. Figure 9-10 illustrates the appearance of the position lights on a small aircraft seen from six different vantage points.

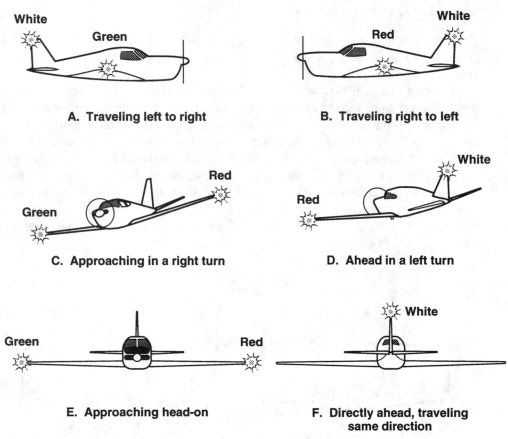

Fig. 9-10. *Small aircraft position lights seen from different vantages.*

If the pilot sees another airplane with a green or a red light and white light simultaneously, how can the pilot tell its direction of travel? Parts A B, or D give the answer. This figure should be memorized. Part C shows the direction of travel of another aircraft approaching in a slight banking turn. The white light in the tail is not visible from this vantage. Parts E and F illustrate the appearance of an aircraft travelling directly toward and away from the viewer's aircraft, respectively. In the case of an approaching airplane, remember the mariner's useful old saying "red, right, approaching" although not necessarily on a direct collision course, but at least in one's general direction.

Anti-collision lights. Although there are several different types of anti-collision lighting and a variety of ways to mount them on aircraft, their purpose is the same, to alert pilots of other aircraft approaching the aircraft equipped with the anti-collision lighting. The strobe anti-collision lighting system is much more effective in achieving its purpose in comparison to the older type of rotating beacon or flashing incandescent light anti-collision systems. Strobe flashes can be seen at significantly greater distances than position lights. Additionally, the flashes of the strobe are much more apparent at closer distances than are other types of anti-collision lighting.

Anti-collision lighting systems are usually mounted on the aircraft's midline on the top and/or bottom of the fuselage. All airplanes flying after dark must now have a red rotating beacon or white anti-collision light. Commercial airplanes might have red or white rotating or flashing strobe lights of very high intensity, often a million candlepower or more. Private airplanes might have a lower intensity rotating red or white strobe light. Pilots are advised to turn the anti-collision light(s) on during daylight hours when visibility is reduced. Maximum attention-getting value is obtained in two-strobe installations when the flash rates of both are the same, one per second, but one is offset in time from the other by about 0.4 second.

Anti-collision lighting is not without its limitations. During periods when an aircraft is flying in haze, fog or clouds, anti-collision lighting should not be used. Recall from chapter 5 that a pilot can experience flicker vertigo from the repetitive and intense light pulses that are seen in the surrounding atmosphere. Aircraft cockpits are not placarded with anti-collision lighting limitations.

Landing lights. Like the anti-collision lighting systems, landing lights come in different sizes, aircraft locations, candle power, and numbers. Also, like the anti-collision lighting systems, landing lights are a necessity. The name can be misleading, in some instances, because some lights are intended for multiple purposes: taxi, takeoff, and landing. Other lighting systems are intended to be used only during takeoff and landing. For example, one position of the landing light selector switch would afford the pilot optimum illumination during the landing or takeoff phases of flight while another position would turn on only the taxi light to relieve the battery and electrical system of a heavy prolonged load. Usage of the taxi lights alone minimizes the amount of potential glare to other pilots nearby.

All night pilots should be aware that a very high percentage of lamps are rated for relatively short lives. This is, in part, due to the fact that their filaments must be operated at very high current values that also makes them extremely hot to touch. Additionally, overheating of the landing light bulbs could become a problem because of inadequate airflow to carry away the excessive heat generated; therefore, pilots should restrict the usage of landing and taxiing lights to those periods when they are really needed. Of course, landing lights will significantly increase the conspicuity of an airplane, for instance while entering a traffic pattern, to other pilots flying nearby. It is wise to use the landing lights at night in the vicinity of an airport for this reason. If the airplane is operated for hire, it must have at least one electric landing light.

Exterior lights and pilot vision

Because the human visual system adapts to light faster than darkness, it is important to prevent bright light from entering the eyes from any light source at night. If the eyes are exposed to bright light, it will take a relatively long time to regain their earlier level of dark vision sensitivity; thus, if an airplane has intense anti-collision strobe lights they should not reflect back into the eyes, that is, reflect off airplane structure. And, if the airplane should fly into clouds, heavy rain, snow, or thick haze, the intense flashing strobe light(s) might reflect back into the pilot's eyes causing a dazzling glare effect, vertigo, and related disorientation symptoms. Naturally, upon entering such conditions, any strobe lighting should be turned off. Once in visual meteorological conditions again, be sure to turn the anti-collision light back on.

It is also wise to keep the transparent covers and domes that surround these external lights as clean as possible. A fractional loss in optical transmission can mean a large reduction in visual detection range. Underlying all of the above suggestions and facts concerning aircraft lights is the idea of maintaining a state of relative dark adaptation of the eye. The night pilot should take whatever action is necessary to maintain the eye's enhanced sensitivity it possesses in the dark and to supplement existing aircraft lighting systems with others that will optimize his or her vision inside and outside the cockpit.

10
Terminal procedures

ADAPTATIONS OF TERMINAL PROCEDURES ARE NECESSARY WHEN OPERATING an aircraft at night: preflight inspection, engine start-up and run-up, taxi operations, aborted takeoffs and rejected landings, takeoff, climbout, approaching and descending into the traffic pattern, final approach variations, landings, and shutdown procedures.

PREFLIGHT INSPECTION

The nocturnal aviator should make a more extensive preflight inspection of the aircraft than would be made during the day. A thorough preflight check of the airplane, and a review of its systems and emergency procedures, is of particular importance for night operations. Because each airplane has its own checklist, it is not intended in this chapter to cover all the specific points; however, selected areas, in addition to those involved on all flights, should be included on the night preflight check.

Prior to each flight, every pilot should consider whether it would be advantageous to preflight the aircraft in a daylight environment. Depending upon such factors as the complexity of the aircraft, overall condition of the aircraft, and meteorological conditions expected during the planned flight, the advantages of such a preflight inspection in many instances outweigh any disadvantages. The risk factor can be reduced significantly, especially if an aircraft would ordinarily be preflighted in a dimly lit setting. Pilots should be cautioned that a daylight preflight inspection should not be a substitute for an additional inspection prior to a night flight because an airplane's state of airworthiness can be altered in just a few minutes.

All personal equipment along with the additional special equipment discussed in chapter 7 should be checked prior to flight to ensure proper functioning. It is very disconcerting to find, at the time of need, that a flashlight, for example, doesn't work, or the oxygen system doesn't have adequate oxygen for the planned trip.

All airplane lights should be turned on momentarily and checked for operation. Position lights can be checked for loose connections by tapping the light fixture while the light is on. If the lights blink while being tapped, further investigation to determine the cause should be initiated. Each interior light should be checked, and if controlled by a rheostat, should be checked at all levels of light intensity.

The parking ramp should be examined prior to entering the airplane. During the day, it is quite easy to see stepladders, chuck holes, stray chocks, and other obstructions, but at night it is more difficult, and a check of the area can prevent taxiing mishaps.

After the pilot is seated in the cockpit and prior to starting the engine, all personal items and special equipment to be used on the flight should be arranged in such a manner that they will be readily available and convenient to use. The night pilot's companion illustrated in chapter 7 will help achieve this goal. Additionally, the pilot should preset as many communications and navigation frequencies as appropriate before takeoff, which will help reduce the workload in flight.

START-UP

The airplane manufacturer's recommended engine starting procedures should always be followed; however, extra caution should be taken at night to assure that the propeller area is clear. Turning on the rotating beacon or flashing other airplane lights will serve to alert any person nearby to remain clear of the propeller. To avoid excessive drain of electrical current from the battery, it is recommended that unnecessary electrical equipment remain off until after the engine has been started.

TAXI OPERATIONS

Before attempting to taxi an airplane, a pilot should let his or her eyes adapt to the dark environment. Needless accidents occur during periods of darkness during taxiing operations when pilots have not allowed their eyes sufficient time to become fully adjusted to the dark environment. Because the aircraft comes closest to other objects during taxi, the eyes especially need to be as completely adapted as possible to the nighttime environment.

Before starting the engine, aircraft position lights should be turned on and checked for operation. The check can be made by observing the lights' glow on the ground under the wingtips and the tail. After starting and before taxiing, the taxi or landing light should be turned on. It is generally recommended that landing lights be used only intermittently while taxiing, but sufficiently to assure that the taxi area is clear. While using the lights during taxiing, consideration should be given to other airplanes so as to not blind the pilots with the landing lights. Taxi slowly, particularly in congested areas, and if taxi lines are painted on the ramp or taxiway, these lines should be followed to ensure a proper path along the route.

Taxiing at night is an important phase of airplane operations that can, under certain circumstances, lead to significant loss of visual sensitivity. It is important that all night pilots take precautions against any circumstances that can lead to a loss of visual sensitivity.

Recall from chapter 4 that how well the pilot deals with light adaptation, glare sources, and loss of light sensitivity is determined by how much light is permitted to enter the eyes. As light energy falls on the retina, the remaining visual sensitivity is proportionally reduced. Conversely, the longer one is in the dark, the more light sensitive the visual system becomes. Figure 4-15 illustrates the general temporal course of this process.

It is generally accepted that increasing both the intensity and duration of a light flash will increase the time required to readapt to the same level of dark sensitivity.

During taxi operations, it is important that the night pilot not look directly into any bright light sources, such as intense landing and taxi lights of other airplanes. Because older pilots generally need more light in order to see, they might be tempted to look directly at an oncoming airplane to try to determine its distance, direction, and closure rate on the ground at night. It is always better to close one eye during such glances. If possible, it is also wise to not look at it directly but to look just to one side of the bright light. Open the closed eye immediately after looking away from the light source. In addition, keep the instrument panel lighting as low as is possible. If it is necessary to look directly at a bright light, then turn up the instrument panel lights to an intermediate level so that they will remain visible after looking at that light.

While taxiing to the runway, the magnetic compass and the gyro-driven instruments should be checked for proper operation. Usually a malfunctioning instrument can be detected. For example, if the attitude indicator's horizon takes a prolonged time to stabilize, or if the heading indicator or the turn coordinator fail to indicate a turn while the airplane is turning during taxi operations, an instrument shop should inspect the possible faulty condition. Every pilot should study the appropriate documentation regarding instrument inspection and operation to diagnose faulty operation during taxi.

ENGINE RUN-UP

The pretakeoff run-up should be performed using the airplane's checklist. Each item should be checked carefully; proper functioning of any component must never be taken for granted. During the day, unintended forward movement of the airplane can be detected quite easily, but at night the airplane could creep forward without being noticed unless the pilot is especially alert for this possibility; therefore, it is important to lock the brakes during the run-up and that attention be given to any unintentional forward movement.

ABORTED TAKEOFFS AND REJECTED LANDINGS

The pilot must first consider carefully the dangers involved in night takeoffs and landings and then be mentally prepared to carry out the safest course of action.

Inherent takeoff dangers

A complacent mental attitude is a natural danger. Safe flying dictates that a pilot be prepared to take immediate action, ready to abort every takeoff or reject every landing at the first indication of trouble.

Surprisingly, the more experienced a pilot, the more likely he or she is to fall prey to the pilot expectancy syndrome, expecting to land or take off successfully every time. Hundreds, sometimes thousands, or even tens of thousands of hours of flying time reinforce this expectancy.

When a pilot is confronted with the unexpected during a takeoff or landing, there are generally just a few seconds to determine and execute an alternate course of action. During these few seconds a pilot's proficiency and mental preparedness can make the difference between an accident or incident and a safely performed procedure.

Instrument pilots rehearse numerous variations of missed approach procedures during their practice and training. Every instrument approach begins with thinking about the possibility of executing a missed approach. Multiengine pilots practice aborted takeoffs and rejected landings with plans to cope with a possible engine failure. Accordingly, the night pilot must have a similar plan of action.

Unfortunately, many pilots flying at night do not have the same state of mental preparedness or plan of action as the proficient multiengine pilot or instrument pilot. Current statistics demonstrate that a significant percentage of accidents occurring at night resulted from pilots unable to execute an aborted takeoff or a rejected landing. Each of these maneuvers is critical to pilot and passenger safety at night.

Complacency is a major contributor to departure accidents. Because takeoffs are a relatively easy procedure, pilots expect little difficulty with them. This false anticipation is dangerous. Too often, pilots are lulled into expectancy, which promotes complacency.

Studies show that pilots typically do not take immediate corrective actions during a night takeoff when encountering a problem because they have not been mentally prepared to abort the takeoff. It is only natural for a pilot to anticipate that he or she is going to make a normal takeoff and departure; however, every pilot should be equally mentally prepared to abort the takeoff if the maneuver is necessary.

There are many signs of a complacent pilot during the typical takeoff. First, the pilot expects to make a problem-free takeoff. Second, by not being mentally prepared, the decision-making process is sluggish, taking far too long in time and valuable runway. Third, maximum pilot performance requires an immediate, total power reduction, which is not common to the complacent pilot. Fourth is poor braking technique and failure to transfer the aircraft weight to the main wheels.

Preparation for an aborted takeoff begins prior to taxiing onto the runway. It requires that a pilot adopt a proper mental set. Every pilot should review the typical and esoteric problems that can cause an aborted takeoff. Some of the countless examples are a malfunctioning airspeed indicator, engine roughness, any unusual noise or smell, directional control difficulties, strange vibration, not having the normal amount of acceleration, or any other unusual occurrence. Any of these symptoms warrants an immediate aborted takeoff. Of primary concern to the pilot is that he or she remain ever vigilant during the night takeoff and, if necessary, take immediate action while there is adequate time to do so safely. All pilots should understand that preflight ends when flight (lift-off) begins.

An aborted takeoff can be managed with five steps:

1. Be mentally prepared to abort the takeoff at any time. After completing the takeoff checklist, a pilot should double-check to be certain that he or she is mentally prepared to abort the takeoff immediately if anything goes wrong. Accidents occur frequently after pilots initiate the proper actions, but only after it is too late to do so safely.

2. Retard the throttle completely and immediately. Any delay in closing the throttle might eat up valuable runway that can't be spared.

3. Simultaneously apply maximum brakes and retard the throttle. Many pilots wait until the throttle is closed before applying the brakes; however, this consumes excessive runway distance.

4. Retract the flaps. By retracting the flaps and reducing the amount of lift being generated by the wings, more weight is displaced to the wheels, which increases braking effectiveness. All pilots should use care not to raise the landing gear lever in place of the flap lever.

5. Apply back pressure on the control yoke to nearly the full aft position while simultaneously retarding the throttle, applying the brakes and retracting the flaps. The application of back pressure provides three main benefits. First, weight is taken off the nosewheel, transferring the weight to the main tires and increasing braking effectiveness. Second, the increased download on the tail adds additional weight to the main wheels that, in turn, further increases braking effectiveness. Third, the probability of wheelbarrowing or loss of directional control is reduced.

When considering a night takeoff, a good general rule to follow is computing the accelerate-stop distance. Basically, the determination of the accelerate-stop distance allows the pilot to judge whether the runway is adequate to accelerate to rotation speed and then abort the takeoff. Although the accelerate-stop distance calculations are primarily used by multi-engine pilots, single-engine pilots also can find these calculations especially beneficial for night flight.

The accelerate-stop distance for a multiengine aircraft is simply the sum of the distance required to accelerate the aircraft from a standing start to the speed V_1, and assuming the critical engine to fail at V_1, the distance required to bring the airplane to a full stop from the point corresponding to V_1 (EN 10-1). To determine a similar accelerate-stop distance for a single-engine aircraft, simply add the normal takeoff distance to the anticipated landing distance under such existing conditions as takeoff weight, wind velocity, density altitude and condition and slope of runway: wet, ice, snow, grass. Any aborted takeoff should be able to be executed easily within this computed distance.

Accidents happen almost every night as a result of pilots who were not prepared to reject unsatisfactory approaches even when there was adequate time, speed, and altitude. The most common error encountered during rejected landings is not applying maximum allowable power. Most aircraft on final approach are in high-drag, low-airspeed configurations and will continue to settle at a very high rate unless the pilot initiates immediate and unrestricted corrective measures.

Rejected landings

There is a solution for unsatisfactory rejected landings:

1. Be mentally prepared to reject the landing at any time.
2. Rotate the nose while simultaneously applying maximum allowable power.
3. Retract the flaps to the initial go-around setting.
4. Retract landing gear after a positive rate of climb has been achieved.
5. Retract the remaining flaps after a safe altitude has been reached and a safe airspeed is read from the airspeed indicator.

Pilots must be especially aware of obtaining adequate go-around aircraft performance at high density altitude airports. Because every airplane has a critical density altitude at which a positive climb rate cannot be established in the landing configuration, it is critically important for pilots conducting flight operations to and from high density altitude airports to know the airplane's limitations before encountering a situation requiring extraordinary aircraft performance.

Determining an airplane's go-around performance at altitude is perhaps better than relying on book performance figures:

1. Climb to a density altitude equal to the density altitude of a high elevation airport.
2. Establish the aircraft for an approach in the landing configuration with appropriate approach speed and rate of descent.
3. Initiate a simulated go-around without retracting the gear or flaps and note the airplane's climb capability. Many pilots are amazed at the lack of climb performance.
4. Retract the landing gear and retract the appropriate amount of flaps and, once again, ascertain the airplane's performance.

Experienced mountain pilots often conduct a similar test before committing to landing at a high density altitude airport. While flying in the downwind leg of the pattern, with the mixture adjusted for that altitude, with the airplane in the landing configuration and at normal approach speed, apply full power and attempt to climb. If the simulated go-around in the pattern is marginal or impossible, then the pilot should consider approaching with less than full flaps and not extend full flaps until after the pilot is sure of completing a safe landing and prepared to make a final commitment to land. It is much safer to execute a high density altitude go-around if the flaps are not in a fully extended position.

TAKEOFFS

Night flying, naturally, does demand more attention of the pilot than comparable daytime VFR flying activities. The most impressive difference is the limited availability of outside visual references; therefore, the flight instruments should be used to a greater degree in controlling the airplane. This is particularly true on night takeoffs and departure climbs. The cockpit lights should be adjusted to a minimum brightness that will allow the pilot to read the instruments and view the switches and yet not hinder the pilot's outside vision. This also will eliminate light reflections on the windshield and windows.

Several choices are often available to the pilot regarding runway directions and lengths. It seems that there are also as many rules of thumb and theories regarding night flying as there are pilots; however, there is one bit of pilot wisdom that remains irrefutable: "Use all of the runway. The runway behind you does no good."

Before taxiing onto an active runway for takeoff, the pilot should exercise extreme caution to prevent conflict with other aircraft. Even at controlled airports where the control tower issues the clearance for takeoff, it is recommended that the pilot check the final approach course for approaching aircraft. At uncontrolled airports, it is recommended that a slow 360-degree turn be made in the same direction as the flow of air traffic while closely searching for other aircraft in the vicinity.

After ensuring that the final approach and runway are clear of other air traffic, the airplane should be lined up with the centerline of the runway. If the runway has no painted centerline, the pilot can use the runway lighting and align the airplane midway between and parallel to the two rows of runway edge lights. After the airplane is aligned, the heading indicator should be noted or set to correspond to the known runway direction. To begin the takeoff, the brakes should be released and the throttle smoothly advanced to takeoff power. As the airplane accelerates, it should be kept moving between and parallel to the runway edge lights. This can best be done by looking at the more distant runway lights rather than those close in and to the side.

Even though the control movements for night takeoffs are the same as those for daytime takeoffs, the technique for night takeoffs is different with respect to the quantity, quality and interpretation of visual cues. The flight instruments should be monitored more closely. As the airspeed reaches the normal lift-off speed, the pitch attitude should be adjusted to that which will establish a normal climb by referring to both outside visual references such as lights, and to the attitude indicator. The airplane should not be forcibly pulled off the ground; it is best to let it fly off in the lift-off attitude while cross-checking the attitude indicator against any outside visual references that might be available.

A number of potentially dangerous situations are present during night takeoffs: forward acceleration-induced pitch control error (explained in chapter 4), dark-terrain takeoff illusion, incorrect centerline alignment, and increased difficulty reading the panel instruments.

The dark-terrain takeoff refers to the situation where it is totally dark beyond the takeoff end of the runway. This includes any visual environment at night where the pilot has no visual contact with the ground: cloud, rain, haze. There is as much chance of there being no visible horizon as there is of a false horizon during takeoff.

Almost as soon as the wheels leave the ground, many pilots look outside during daylight hours; however, nothing is visible outside at night, no attitude reference information at all, unless it is a clear moonlit night. In this dangerous situation (dark terrain takeoff illusion explained in chapter 4), the pilot might inadvertently place the airplane in a bank or shallow descent and contact the ground. A takeoff stall also can occur if the pilot depends on a pitch attitude reference that is entirely based upon the outside scene. Launching into a dark-terrain environment should be approached as if the pilot were flying into instrument meteorological conditions. The pilot should immediately look back at the instruments for attitude control information, cross-checking altitude, bank angle, airspeed, and climb rate. In summary, stay on instruments during takeoff at least until the airplane is 500 feet above the ground, the wheels are retracted, and airspeed is well above marginal limits.

Incorrect runway centerline alignment is possible at night due to reduced or non-existent illumination and consequent reduction of peripheral visual cues. In this situation, keep the line of sight directed at the far end of the runway on centerline. The low eye height of a pilot in a small airplane during takeoff roll (FIG. 10-1) makes it more difficult to see where the airplane is located on taxiways and the runway. The night pilot should always verify that the airplane is aligned on the centerline.

It is generally more difficult to read cockpit instruments at night. Research has shown that most pilots have to look at each instrument a fraction of a second longer (or more) at night than during daylight hours. When this time is accumulated over all of the different instruments in a single scan, it can add up to an appreciable increase in eye scan time. If instrument panel lights are not set to the proper brightness, the pilot might misread them, for instance increasing pitch after takeoff at the wrong indicated airspeed.

CLIMB-OUT

After becoming airborne, the darkness of night often makes it difficult to note whether the airplane is getting closer to or farther from the surface. It is extremely important, then, to ensure that the airplane continues in a positive climb and does not settle back to the runway. This can be accomplished by ensuring that there is a positive

Fig. 10-1. *Simulation view on the runway centerline during takeoff.*

climb rate showing on the vertical velocity indicator and a gradual but continual increase in the altimeter indication (FIG. 10-2). It is also important to note that the airspeed is well above the stall speed and that it continues to accelerate.

Necessary pitch adjustments to establish a stabilized climb should be made with reference to the attitude indicator. At the same time, the wings should be checked for a level attitude using the attitude indicator and the heading indicator. It is recommended that no turn be made until reaching a safe maneuvering altitude of a minimum of 400 or 500 feet above ground level.

In addition to the necessary pitch adjustments, heading adjustments must be instituted for the appropriate wind correction angle. Because there are fewer visual cues at night, especially at a remote airport during an overcast night, it is easy to let wind drift go unnoticed. Consequently, it is prudent to ascertain the amount of possible wind correction angle that will be necessary prior to the takeoff roll.

Although the use of the landing lights provides help during the takeoff roll, they become ineffective after the airplane has climbed to an altitude where the light beam no longer extends to the surface. The light can also be deceptive when it is reflected by haze, smoke, or fog that might exist in the takeoff climb; therefore, if the landing light is used for the takeoff roll, it may be turned off after the climb is well established.

The climb-out phase of flight at night can lead to several pilot control input errors that can prove disastrous. One of these conditions has to do with various illusions caused by acceleration effects upon the body (*see* chapter 4). Another condition is that of not staying on instruments. Once the wheels have left the ground at night, a pilot is

Fig. 10-2. *Establishment of a positive climb.*

very nearly in the equivalent of instrument conditions; one must instinctively turn to the instrument panel and not the outside world for guidance information. The unsettling transition from visual to almost blind conditions during a climb-out is enhanced by even light air turbulence, quick changes in weather (especially visibility), the surrounding darkness, loss of the feeling of solid contact with the runway, and that great dark void ahead of you . . . out there.

DESCENT

The descent portion of a night flight need not result in a high task load if it is properly preplanned. It is not uncommon for a pilot to forget to look at the chart, kneeboard, stopwatch, or navigational aid that serves as a reminder to start down at the appropriate place. The result, too often, is one of a high rate of descent coupled with an increased workload that, in turn, can contribute to information overload and other distractions, which leads to stress, which leads to bad decisions, which leads to accidents. Accidents generally happen as a result of a chain of poorly planned events.

Many of the problems associated with nighttime descents are insidious in nature and happen when a pilot's state of arousal is very low. Problems surface when the aircraft is in a state of transition and the pilot is not mentally or physically up to the task at hand. Preparation for descent should start while the aircraft is still at en route altitude, well before the actual descent begins. In keeping with the general principle of staying ahead of the aircraft, the night pilot should increase his or her mental alertness level, particularly if the pilot is very tired and sore from a long-duration en route flight segment. (Activities for increasing pilot arousal are discussed in chapter 11.)

The main consideration is that the pilot's body be at an increased state of arousal to carry out all of the required descent tasks. Additionally, the use of a timer/alarm timepiece can be of paramount importance. If the alarm is set to sound and/or flash at the approximate time when an aircraft is approaching the descent point, the pilot will have the opportunity to exercise those options available to increase his or her state of arousal. The importance of this procedure should not be underestimated.

Once the pilot has had adequate time to properly prepare for the descent, if topographical and meteorological conditions permit, a gradual descent should be established far enough away from the airport to reduce the workload. Because distractions can create problems it is important to spread the workload out over a longer period of time, if possible.

During the descent, the pilot should consider the following tasks in addition to any other tasks prescribed in the checklists:

1. Look outside for other aircraft and obstructions; a passenger in the front seat should also look outside. The pilot should assign regions of the airspace for each passenger to scan as recommended in chapter 8. It is still the pilot's responsibility to see and avoid all other air traffic.
2. Review notes and charts for topographic obstructions.
3. Check the local conditions at the airport of intended landing, such as the following (but not necessarily limited to): type of lighting system used, active runway, inbound and local traffic, any new notams, and meteorological conditions including, but not limited to, wind speed, reports of wind shear, visibility and obstructions to vision, and the temperature-dew point spread.
4. Reset the altimeter.
5. Reset the heading indicator to compass heading.
6. Calculate the possible crosswind component for the amount of surface wind. (*See* chapter 13.)
7. Review preflight notes and navigational charts for such information as airport elevation, and other terrain characteristics and obstruction features.
8. Determine if a safe landing can be executed with the known conditions regarding the pilot, the aircraft, and the flight environment.
9. Review the descent checklist.
10. Set frequencies in the communications and navigation equipment appropriate for the type of anticipated and piloting procedures. (If the aircraft is equipped with equipment that would facilitate the setting of additional frequencies for

communications and navigation backup in the event of a go-around, the pilot should set the appropriate frequencies in the communications and navigational equipment.)

11. Prepare for the unexpected go-around. Study initial heading and altitude requirements. Mentally prepare for an alternate course of action including diverting to an alternate airport.

APPROACHING THE AIRPORT

The probability of a midair collision is increased as an aircraft approaches an airport or navigational facility. Although aircraft become highly visible at night with the use of strobe lighting, midair collisions can and do occur at night even when the visibility is unrestricted. Consider, for example, the eye's blind spot as discussed in chapter 4 and the need for a repetitive and consistent eye scan. Other contributing factors to nighttime midair accidents include cockpit distractions, lack of situational awareness, fatigue, low state of arousal, and information overload, to just name a few.

Aircraft flying at lower altitudes over cities or areas that are well illuminated with a variety of different kinds of lights are sometimes very difficult to distinguish from the ground lighting. If the pilot falls into the trap of expecting to see only moving lights below him or her, a hovering helicopter might be ignored. An extra degree of vigilance must be maintained during this set of visual conditions.

If the visibility conditions are such that it would be advantageous to the pilot to have the amount of illumination of the runway lighting system increased in intensity or the approach lighting system activated, the pilot should make the request in ample time for his or her eyes to become adapted to the new lighting conditions. A period of from 10 to 15 seconds is required to achieve this new level of photochemical adaptation within the retina. The pilot should not request that these lights be changed when the aircraft is closely approaching or already flying over the lighting system.

In the case of pilot-controlled lighting systems, pilots should activate the systems at distances away from the airports that permit the aircraft to land with an adequate margin of time before the lighting system shuts off.

When approaching a region where there are several airports contained within a sea of lights, the pilot should have already determined several unique identifying features that allow rapid recognition of the desired airport of landing. Recall from chapter 7 that during the preflight planning process the pilot should study the location and (expected) appearance of all obstructions and other airport identifying features in such publications as the *Airport/Facility Directory* or appropriate navigational charts. These identifying features should not necessarily be limited to visual recognition. For instance, electronic approach navigational aids like the MLS, ILS, VOR, NDB, or ground-based radar should be employed whenever possible.

Prior to entering the traffic pattern, the prelanding checklist should have been completed.

TRAFFIC PATTERN

When arriving at the airport to enter the traffic pattern and land, it is important that the runway lights and other airport lighting be identified as early as possible. If the airport layout is unfamiliar to the pilot, sighting of the runway might be difficult until within close proximity to the airport due to the maze of lights observed in the area. Figure 10-3 illustrates this effect. The pilot should fly toward the airport beacon light (unless he or she is navigating by electronic navigation systems) until the lights outlining the runway are distinguishable. To fly a traffic pattern of the proper size and direction when there is little to see but a group of lights, the runway threshold and runway edge lights must be positively identified. Once seen, the approach threshold lights should be kept in sight throughout the airport traffic pattern and approach.

Fig. 10-3. *Simulated cockpit view of airport and runway lights in surrounding city lights during an approach.*

Generally, the safest procedure while approaching an airport for landing is to enter the published traffic pattern. Not only has the traffic pattern been carefully planned to take into account local topographic and other obstructions, but the fact that other pilots will also tend to follow it imposes greater regularity in the locations of the approaching aircraft.

By flying the traffic pattern that is located within close proximity to the airport, a pilot is effectively minimizing the probability of flying the aircraft into an invisible hillside, tower, or other obstruction. Many nighttime accidents could have been avoided if pilots had only flown a tight traffic pattern.

An aspect of night flying that is often overlooked is that it generally takes more time to interpret the visual cues and initiate the correct piloting action, when compared to daytime visual piloting. For this reason, shortly before entering the traffic pattern, it is convenient to complete some of those tasks that would normally be accomplished only after entering the traffic pattern in the daytime. For example, if a pilot is flying a retractable gear aircraft at night, already having the speed reduced and the gear in a down and locked position is advantageous in certain situations. Additionally, if approaching a tower-controlled airport located near a city with an abundance of bright lights, it certainly is convenient to have the tower personnel increase or decrease the intensity of part of the runway lighting system to suit the specific visibility conditions present.

How can the night pilot determine whether it is a right- or a left-hand pattern at an uncontrolled and unfamiliar airport? Several things can be done. First, the pilot should have read (while flight planning the flight) about the destination airport in the *Airport/Facility Directory* where traffic direction will be indicated. Second, the pilot can telephone the airport or nearest flight service station before taking off, or by radio en route. Third, he or she can look for a segmented circle system that is located near the approach end of the runway and is illuminated at night. This circular pattern has landing strip indicators located outside the circumference of the circle at 90 degree compass positions that point left or right relative to the center of the circle. The direction each points is the traffic pattern direction. The center of the circle has an illuminated wind cone as well as a landing direction indicator in the form of a T or tetrahedron with its long leg aligned with the runway.

APPROACH TO LANDING

Distance might be deceptive at night due to limited or misleading lighting conditions, lack of intervening references on the ground, and the inability of the pilot to compare the size and location of different ground objects. This also applies to the estimation of altitude and speed. Consequently, more dependence must be placed on flight instruments, particularly the altimeter and the airspeed indicator.

Inexperienced pilots often have a tendency to make approaches and landings at night with excessive airspeed. Every effort should be made to execute the approach and landing in the same manner as during the day. A low, shallow, approach is definitely inappropriate during a night operation. The altimeter and the vertical velocity indicator should be constantly cross-checked against the airplane's position along the base leg and final approach.

After turning onto the final approach and aligning the airplane midway between the two rows of runway edge lights, the pilot should note and correct for any wind drift. Throughout the final approach, power should be used with coordinated pitch changes to provide positive control of the airplane, enabling the pilot to accurately adjust airspeed and descent angle. A VASI is also very helpful in maintaining the proper approach angle.

When a pilot is executing a straight-in approach, the safety factor is enhanced considerably if some type of electronic or visual glide slope is used during the approach procedure.

Usually, when approximately halfway along the final approach, the landing light should be turned on. Earlier use of the landing light might be ineffective because the light's beam will usually not reach the ground from higher altitudes, and might be reflected back into the pilot's eyes by any existing haze, smoke, or fog. This disadvantage might be overshadowed by the safety advantage provided by using the "operation lights on" procedure in the terminal area.

Perhaps the single aspect of night flight that has been researched the most is landings. From aviation's earliest days to today, night landings have been on the minds of a wide segment of the aviation community, from pilots to design engineers. The reason for the interest in night landings is a disproportionately high accident rate. Even though the landing phase accounts for less than two percent of total flight time, a very high percentage of accidents occur during this phase.

For the last several decades, night landing accidents have been prevalent not only in general aviation but also commercial aviation. One of the major contributing factors to the high number of night landing accidents in past years is the aviation community's lack of education in factors involved in the process of night landings.

Most pilots have heard that it is very difficult to execute a good landing without a good final approach. This statement is certainly true for the daytime landing and it is even more accurate for the nighttime landing because there are fewer visual cues at night. A stabilized, straight-line glide path approach is of paramount importance. With the aircraft in a constant airspeed, vertical speed and pitch angle profile, the pilot has more time to evaluate what visual cues are available, monitor the altimeter, airspeed, and vertical rate, evaluate the correctness of the approach and to initiate any small flight path corrections that are needed.

Many pilots who have had the misfortune of premature terrain contact believed that their aircraft were on normal approach paths; however, accident statistics have conclusively documented that pilot perception of the approach path is often seriously in error. The error can be caused by such factors as a lack of visual cues, lack of understanding and interpretation of visual cues, visual illusions or a combination of these factors.

Here is one pilot's experience, "Flying into Carroll County on a May evening, nearby Baltimore weather was reported as 7,000 overcast with two and a half miles visibility. Why, then, I thought, was my airplane still inside clouds at 3,000 feet? Simple. I wasn't directly over Baltimore; only the weather at your present position counts. My base airport has rather low-intensity runway lights, but we do have runway end identifier strobes. Still, I thought, this could definitely be a missed approach and a trip to Baltimore, even though I had been counting on a 7,000-foot ceiling. Out of 3,000 feet on the VOR approach, I caught sight of the ground. There was some low scud, but not much. The rotating beacon and the lights in the vicinity of the airport were visible, and I clicked the mike to fire the runway end strobes. For some reason the strobes at the other end of the runway were more visible than those on the approach end, but I finally got that sorted out and had the airplane set up on the VASI. When about 300 feet above the ground, the airplane passed through a tiny piece of scud. It was only good for startle value, passing almost instantly, but it was a good reminder that night visual approaches had best be done with the missed approach procedure cocked and ready to go." (Collins 1989)

In this brief account of a rather typical night approach are found a wide variety of visual events that can cause the inexperienced pilot either to panic or make incorrect conclusions and airplane control responses. Reread this account and make note of everything that was specifically visual in nature and think about what you would have done under these circumstances. Thinking through hypothetical situations is a healthy activity for the night pilot. Such mental rehearsal has saved many lives.

Before the subject of visual cues involved in a night landing is considered, it is important to realize that almost 50 percent of air carrier, business, and personal flying accidents occur during approach and landing and that this phase of flight typically occupies a very small portion of the total flight time. Many of the nighttime jet air carrier accidents occurred over unlighted terrain or over water toward well-lighted cities and/or airports. Obviously, it is very important to have a good understanding of what the visual light cues from the ground mean and how they can sometimes appear different from what they actually represent.

The following brief discussion concerns visual cues that are involved in accomplishing a night landing to lighted and unlighted runways. The flight dynamics of a night landing (approximately the last 50 feet of altitude through the roll-out) are the same as for a daytime landing. Indeed, light level does not influence atmospheric dynamics or aircraft handling qualities. But night conditions can definitely influence the pilot who controls the airplane. These influences are of primary interest.

Statistical research has found that night air carrier approach accidents are from three to four times more prevalent than daytime approach accidents; however, this statistic is misleading: How many accidents were involved and what kinds of accidents were they? If landing is included in the approach phase, then this statistic makes more sense. Yet even if the accident rate is this high, one must ask why. The answer might lie in the nature of the visual information facing the night pilot during landing. Indeed, pilots who have survived accidents in VFR conditions said that they had the runway in sight and felt that their airplane was on a normal, safe approach path. Nevertheless, the airplane still struck the ground or water (typically) well short of the runway. It is clear that the flight crew's judgments of all available information played a significant part in this situation.

It is important to note that at night when the outside view is beautiful and compelling, there is a tendency to keep looking outside too long, even neglecting vitally important instrument information altogether. The night pilot must adopt a regular visual scan pattern that integrates both inside as well as outside cues. The worse the outside visibility is, the longer the pilot should keep his eyes inside the cabin on instruments at night.

Straight-in approach to a lighted runway

Among the different approaches to landing to be discussed, the straight-in approach to a lighted runway is perhaps the best in terms of providing many different useful visual cues.

Consider the following brief review of some useful geometrical facts that can be applied to straight-in approaches at night. Figure 10-4 shows a runway where W is the runway width and the shaded region partway down the runway represents fog or other visual occlusion. If both edges of the runway were extended, they would appear to meet at point H (horizon), although the pilot knows that the runway ends well before this distant point.

Corner angles L (left) and R (right), if visible, provide the night pilot with information about his alignment with the centerline of the runway. If R is larger than L, the pilot knows that the aircraft is right of the centerline. If angle L appears as large as angle R the aircraft is on or very nearly on the correct centerline. Unfortunately, this angle is not always readily visible at night. In the remainder of this discussion, situations are presented that can be solved by knowing either one of at least two visual variables or factors.

If the pilot is located on the runway's centerline where L and R are determined completely by runway width and eye height above the ground, then he or she can estimate his altitude by estimating the angular size of L and R. The apparent size of W is determined by runway width and the slant range between the pilot's eyes and the threshold. Vertical angle D is determined by the angular distance of the runway's threshold beneath the horizon; the pilot can use the apparent size of W to estimate his distance to the threshold; however, if he or she cannot see the far end of the runway, then W' is determined by the apparent runway width and the slant range from the eye to the obscuration (R). So, if the pilot knows W he or she can use W' to estimate the distance to the region of obscuration.

During an actual approach in a fixed-wing airplane, these visual angles and distances are constantly changing. What happens to this dynamic visual information? It is clear that lights seen ahead of the airplane will all appear to spread out radially from a common point on the ground, known as the *flight path intercept point* (FPIP). This point is the only spot on the ground that will not seem to expand. Likewise, the angular width of the runway W will expand continuously until it disappears from sight behind the cockpit structure. Nonetheless, its apparent angular expansion will not become apparent at great distances from the runway, certainly not beyond several miles, unless the pilot can look for extended periods of time and integrate the constantly changing perception of this angle.

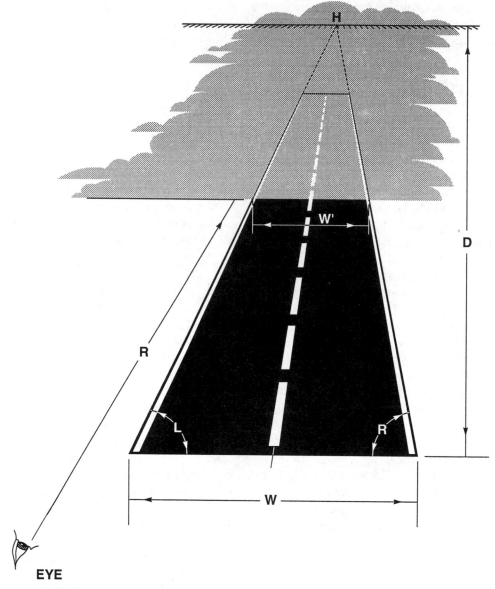

Fig. 10-4. *Geometrical relationships for the straight-in approach.*

If the pilot knows the runway width and also knows the distance to the threshold, he or she can use the rate of angular change of W to estimate approach velocity. And in the same way, angles L and R will get progressively smaller during an approach. These angles are determined by W and the airplane's altitude and rate of descent; therefore, if the pilot knows W and has earlier estimated the altitude (from corner angles L and R), an experienced pilot will be able to estimate rate of descent.

Finally, the angular rate at which the lights along the runway edge appear to sweep past the pilot just before touchdown is determined by W and forward speed. Forward speed can be estimated if the pilot knows W. Clearly, runway width plays a central role in many approach-related visual judgments. Pilots should take time to think through each of the above geometric facts in order to be able to extract as much information from the visual scene as possible.

For runways whose edges are outlined by white lights, the perspective view (the apparent convergence) of the edge lights that extend toward the dimly defined or invisible horizon provides valuable information about the *approach slope angle* (ASA) (FIG. 10-5). Here it is seen that there are at least three major angles that can play a role in judging one's ASA at night.

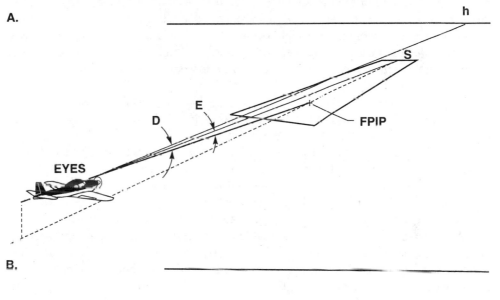

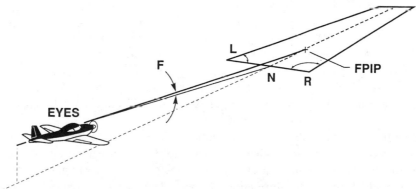

Fig. 10-5. *Perspective view of a runway showing various vertical angle cues to judge approach slope angle.*

Referring to the top part of this figure, Angle D is an angle between a line connecting the eyes with the horizon (h) and another line connecting the eyes with the flight path intercept point (FPIP). As one progresses along the descending flight path, this angle decreases to some small, fairly constant value. If this angle appears to get bigger one is flying too high (or at least above the glide path). Because the horizon isn't always visible, the pilot may also discriminate another angle (E), which is the angle between a line connecting the eyes with the far end of the runway (S) and another line connecting the eyes with the runway touchdown point.

In the bottom part of this figure, there are two other angles that are either consciously or unconsciously judged during an approach. Angle F is an angle between a line connecting the eyes and the FPIP and a second line connecting the eyes and the near (approach) end of the runway (N). Of course this angle becomes progressively larger during a nominal approach. By experience, one will come to develop a sense for what angular rate of change should occur when flying along the correct approach slope. The angles at each front corner of the runway, (R) and (L), also change slightly during an approach, but contribute more to one's forward velocity perception than to one's vertical position or velocity.

Laboratory research at NASA (Haines and Kiefel 1988) has found that the human eye is organized such that perception of angular change is better at the fovea (at and near one's line of sight) than it is in the periphery. This means that angles D, E, and F are seen as changing most effectively when the pilot is fixating the FPIP, which should correspond with the intended touchdown point on the runway. In addition, those angles that are becoming larger are perceived about as accurately as those that are decreasing in size. This finding suggests that these same three angles, whether increasing or decreasing, are about equally valuable cues during an approach.

Another set of angular cues is available to the alert pilot during an approach to landing at night. These cues are sometimes referred to as parafoveal streamers. The parafovea is that part of the retina that allows peripheral vision. *Streamers* are the paths that each light source on the ground seem to follow across the visual field over time. The effect is similar to that of a photographic time exposure of a moving object. Each moving light is blurred across the film plane. The approximate appearance of the parafoveal streamers for a straight-in approach on runway centerline that is too steep is shown in FIG. 10-6. All of the streamers will point back to a common location, which is the FPIP. By tracing each ray, it is discovered that the FPIP is about at the runway's threshold so the pilot should raise the nose of the aircraft slightly. Of course, as altitude and range decrease during the approach, these lights will appear to stream by faster and faster.

These streamers are difficult to perceive without looking in one spot for many seconds, which is difficult and somewhat dangerous to do because the normal eye scan is disrupted; thus, the parafoveal streamer cues should not be relied upon to provide clear and ready flight path information. Experts feel that experienced pilots develop an unconscious sense of the shape, apparent velocity, and FPIP origin of the streamers.

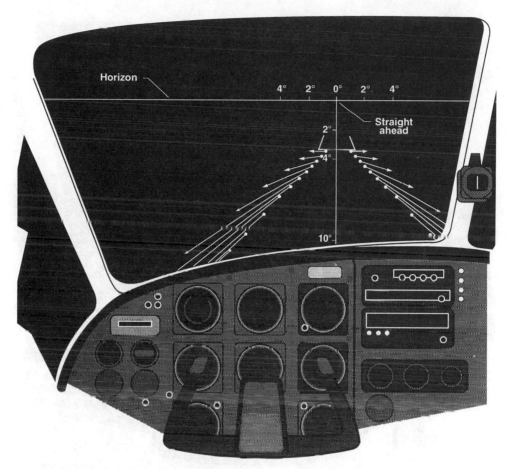

Fig. 10-6. *Parafoveal streamer paths for straight-in approach.*

Now consider the appearance of parafoveal streamers for a slightly banked and crabbed approach offset to the right of the runway. Figure 10-7 illustrates this situation. Notice that because the aircraft is flying straight ahead (not on a curved path), the streamers will all be straight lines. Each will point back to a common point, here about 2.75 degrees glide path angle and straight ahead of the aircraft.

If the airplane should approach the FPIP (labelled X in part A of FIG. 10-8) along a straight-line three-degree flight path, there will be a uniform apparent expansion of the runway's outline. The individual runway lights that outline the runway surface will produce the parafoveal streamer effect. For example, the right front corner light on the runway a will stream to b, to c, to d, and so on, during the approach. The two vertical arrows show that the apparent vertical height of the runway (from the front end to the rear end) will increase by a regularly increasing proportion as the airplane continues this approach.

Fig. 10-7. *Parafoveal streamer paths for a straight-in approach with crosswind correction and slight bank angle.*

If the airplane approaches the FPIP along a curved flight path (part B of FIG. 10-8) the runway outline's width will increase faster than its vertical angle will decrease. The eye is not particularly sensitive in discriminating small or slowly changing angles that make a curved approach (in the vertical plane) more difficult to discriminate. The pilot should compare the visual changes seen outside the cockpit with altitude, vertical rate, and airspeed information from the instrument panel. If there are any discrepancies, the pilot should rely on the instrument information until he or she is sure the outside scene is providing reliable guidance information.

The last straight-in night approach considered here is one flown parallel to but laterally offset to the right of the runway. Figure 10-9 illustrates the appearance of the parafoveal streamers from two rows of ground lights. Note that each streamer is a straight line (because the flight path is straight) and also that each points to the FPIP

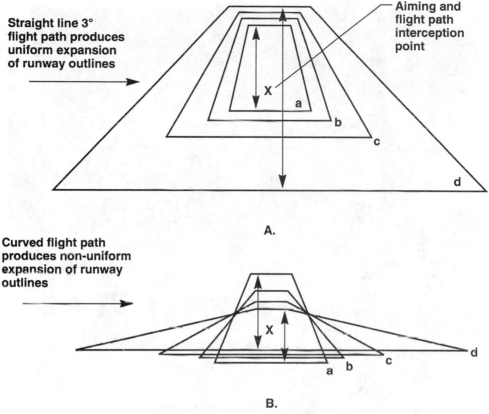

Straight line 3° flight path produces uniform expansion of runway outlines

Aiming and flight path interception point

X
a
b
c
d

A.

Curved flight path produces non-uniform expansion of runway outlines

X
a
b
c
d

B.

Fig. 10-8. *Symmetrical and asymmetrical apparent runway outline expansion pattern for a straight-in and curved approach path.*

located some distance to the right side of the runway and about 2.5 degrees below the horizon.

If above or below the glide path, the runway will appear to get progressively longer or shorter, respectively.

A technique that has been used by many pilots at night to fly a relatively consistent glide path is known as the gun-sight technique. Here, the pilot must sit with his or her head fixed in one location relative to the seat and glare shield and must be able to see the FPIP on the runway. The airplane is flown so that the FPIP is seen at a given spot on the windshield, which shall be called the windshield aim point. This is akin to the concept used in the head-up display. Experienced pilots use this technique almost unconsciously; a (windshield aim point) spot on the windshield located some angular distance above the glare shield serves as the (front) gun-sight. Crosswind correction can even be added if necessary by allowing a constant lateral offset of the FPIP from the windshield aim point. The night pilot should be aware of several difficulties and even dangerous situations than can arise using the gun-sight technique.

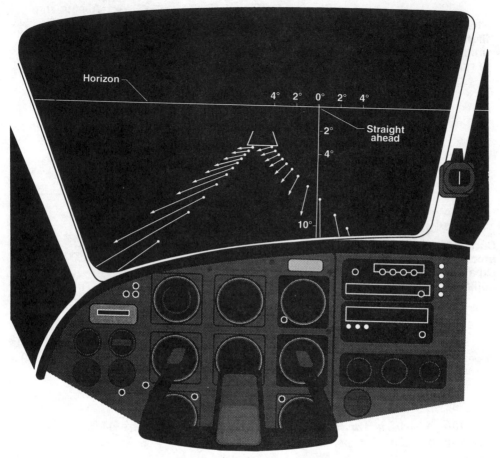

Fig. 10-9. *Parafoveal streamer paths for a straight-in approach laterally offset from the runway.*

The gun-sight technique is reliable only when: (1) the pitch attitude of the airplane remains constant, (2) the pilot's vertical eye position remains constant relative to the windshield aim point, (3) a spot near the FPIP remains visible on the runway, and (4) the air is smooth. When any of these conditions change, as they often do, the gun-sight technique will take you to a different FPIP than intended. And at night it is more difficult than ever to tell when any of these conditions have changed. Because the distance from the eye to windshield is so much smaller than the distance from the windshield to runway, even a tiny vertical movement of the head and eyes can cause a huge longitudinal shift of the apparent FPIP on the ground. And in turbulent conditions, the head is often bouncing up and down. When encountering turbulent air it is definitely the time to ignore the gun-sight technique and go back to the basics of a disciplined instrument scan combined with outside surveillance.

Another effect to be aware of is an illusion where very bright runway lights will tend to make the runway seem closer than it really is. The same kind of effect is observed in very clear air conditions as well.

The following account illustrates several interesting visual effects that occurred due to fog at night. The pilot could not see the runway but only the sequenced runway centerline strobe lights that exploded repetitively into view through the fog. Here is part of his story.

"Our approach was to ILS-equipped Runway 27. I was first officer and had an excellent view of the entire spectacle. The ceiling was reported as about 100 feet with visibility at one-half mile. From my vantage point, it became obvious that visibility from the ground was very different than it was from the cockpit. The truth was, there was no ceiling. The clear night sky spread over our plane like a broad canopy. The ground fog below us spread over the ground in a thin, cotton-like layer. It reached from what seemed about 200 feet altitude down to the ground. As we approached the airport we passed over numerous lights on the ground and they were all perfectly visible below us. But when I looked farther ahead more horizontally, the flashing rabbit swept through the fog like a laser. Each white light exploded into view, each appearing much larger than it really was. We started down the glide path and it became clear that we wouldn't reach the top of the fog layer until we also reached our decision height. Finally we got there. What I saw was a huge area of intense white light from all of the runway centerline, edge, and approach lights blending together. I had difficulty sorting them all out."

Instead of visual conditions improving by decision height, in this case visibility deteriorated. This situation is represented in part (A) of FIG. 10-10, which portrays three different kinds of fog and the drastically different visual range each produces. This same approach would have been relatively easier if it had happened during the daylight hours because the pilot's eyes would have been light-adapted. This would have reduced the intense glare and flash-blindness that can occur in nighttime fog conditions. This pilot's account continued.

"This particular runway had no VASI and we had to quickly alternate our visual reference from the cross-hairs and vertical rate to the somewhat confusing array of bright lights streaming toward us. I was able to make out the green threshold lights and some of the white edge lights that ran off into the misty distance. The captain followed his glide slope down until the intense strobes were behind us. At 50 feet we got our course guidance and roll attitude from the runway lights. The flare and roll-out was normal even though we never did see the far end of the runway. Apparently, the fog became much thicker at that end."

The following words constitute wise advice from an experienced professional pilot about how to cope with a nighttime low visibility approach. In short, don't do anything abruptly, get the airplane in trim and properly set up at or before the outer marker (EN 10-2), if there is one. Set up means that the descent rate, angle of attack, roll attitude, and airspeed should be correct and holding constant. If the runway is not clearly defined visually, or the pilot is uncertain about centerline alignment by the

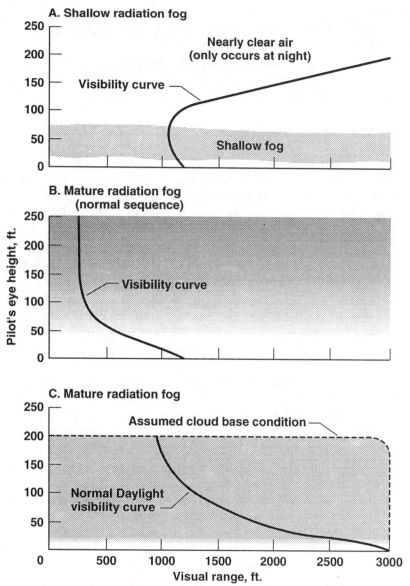

A. Shallow radiation fog

Nearly clear air
(only occurs at night)

Visibility curve

Shallow fog

**B. Mature radiation fog
(normal sequence)**

Visibility curve

C. Mature radiation fog

Assumed cloud base condition

Normal Daylight
visibility curve

Pilot's eye height, ft.

Visual range, ft.

Fig. 10-10. *Visual range at different eye heights above the ground for three types of fog.*

time decision height is reached, he or she should execute an immediate missed approach procedure. Nighttime visual effects can distort perception in strange ways. The pilot should never continue any approach beyond the point where he or she does not understand what is being seen.

Simulator research has shown that one must look at an outside scene for at least two or three seconds before it makes enough sense to provide useful guidance and control information and that this decision time lengthens by at least one second at night over daytime low visibility approaches (Haines 1980).

Slant range visibility is the distance one can see ahead, from the cabin to the ground, and this distance is far more important than *runway visual range* (RVR), which is the horizontal atmospheric transmission at the ground near the touchdown point on the runway. At night, ground fog can produce almost zero horizontal visibility yet provide a reassuring view of runway lights while on final approach. Nevertheless, even slant range visibility can change rapidly. Part B of FIG. 10-10 illustrates a mature radiation fog condition in which slant range will remain at a low value until breaking out of the fog near the ground. Part C illustrates a different condition where visual slant range opens up progressively as the pilot descends.

For these and other reasons, instrument rated pilots operating under FAR Part 91 after having received a clearance to execute an instrument approach procedure have the privilege of continuing an instrument approach, regardless of future visibility reports; thus, the pilot's own evaluation of visibility is the last and best source of guidance for decisions regarding whether he or she should continue an approach or not. Yet the pilot shouldn't become complacent about this privilege due to the sometimes unusual and unexpected visual effects that fog and rain can have on visibility of ground lights. The more the night pilot knows about these visual effects, the better able he or she will be to cope with them.

If the runway lights begin to appear fuzzy or indistinct during the final approach, the pilot should exercise extreme caution. He or she might be seeing the effects of ground fog that can lead to a very rapid reduction in visibility as the aircraft nears the runway. Fog can form in minutes and can obscure part or all of the runway environment.

As a general rule, snow, smoke, haze, patches of fog, and rain on the windshield along with restricted runway visibility can make one think that he is higher than he really is. This can cause the pilot to pitch the airplane down a few degrees and contact the ground short of the runway. Likewise, if the end of the runway can't be seen, it might cause the pilot to imagine that the horizon is lower than it really is with the same result as above. When in doubt about the glide path angle, always cross-check the outside scene with information from the attitude indicator, altimeter, and vertical velocity indicator.

To summarize much of the previous discussion concerning the appearance of the FPIP when on the proper glide path, the following statements should be considered.

- The FPIP will appear to remain in the same position in the windshield's outline (it won't move up or down unless pitch attitude of the aircraft is changed).
- All ground lights and other visible detail will appear to move radially away from the FPIP. Lights located nearer to the aircraft than the FPIP will move down the windshield while lights located farther than the FPIP will appear to move up the windshield.
- The runway's shape will remain the same but will appear to become larger and larger relative to the windshield outline.

If the aircraft is rising above the proper glide path:

- The FPIP will appear to move toward the aircraft.
- The runway will appear to lengthen.

If the aircraft is descending below the proper glide path:

- The FPIP will appear to move away from the aircraft.
- The runway will appear to shorten.

Straight-in approach to unlighted runway

This situation is similar to the infamous black hole approach situation discussed in chapter 4 except that the runway's surface is also just a big black hole that might be surrounded by other lights on the ground. It ranks high on the list of the most difficult approaches to fly successfully because of the relatively small number of external visual cues available with which to judge altitude, vertical rate, roll attitude, and runway alignment and its capacity for generating the illusion of being higher than one actually is. A good plan is to refer to your instruments most of the time until you are certain that you can see the texture of the runway in the reflected light of the landing lights. (Any type of approach to an unlighted runway is potentially very dangerous and is definitely not recommended.)

Curved approach to lighted runway

Curved and descending approaches made at night are more difficult to execute accurately than during daylight hours because of the relative lack of ground plane information with which to judge both horizontal and vertical angles, rates, and rate changes. What is meant by horizontal angles? Figure 10-11 shows a computer-simulated nighttime view of a runway when seen from a lateral offset location relative to the runway's centerline.

A curved approach flight path is illustrated in FIG. 10-12 where it is seen that both vertical and horizontal visual angles of fixed points on the runway are changing continually because one's position in altitude and centerline offset is also changing continually. This situation can complicate one's guidance and control tasks at night because a smooth combination of bank angle, yaw angle, vertical speed, and forward speed are required to bring the airplane to the final intercept point situated on the glide path. A continual visual assessment is required about where one is and whether one is going to intercept, overshoot, or undershoot the straight-in glide path line correctly. During a curved approach not only does the runway outline appear to enlarge (very slowly) but its two long edges point more and more toward the pilot.

What do parafoveal streamers look like during a curved approach at night? Figure 10-13 portrays this with the aircraft approximately located at point D, E or F of FIG. 10-12. The principles presented here can be applied as well to other ground light patterns. It can be seen that each light on the ground will appear to travel along curved

Fig. 10-11. *Simulated cockpit view of runway on final approach with lateral displacement.*

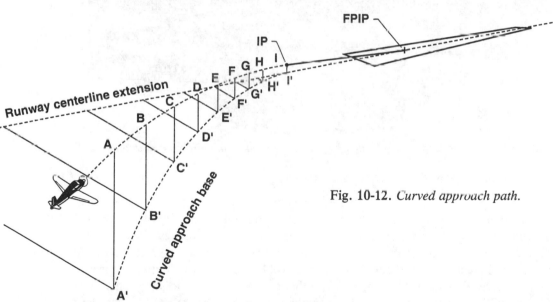

Fig. 10-12. *Curved approach path.*

paths away from a single projection point that is straight ahead of the airplane and at a depression angle equivalent to the current glide path angle (typically 3 degrees). The pilot should continue looking at or near the intended FPIP throughout the early stages of the night approach and gradually he or she will become aware of how these ground plane lights appear to "slew" across the field of vision.

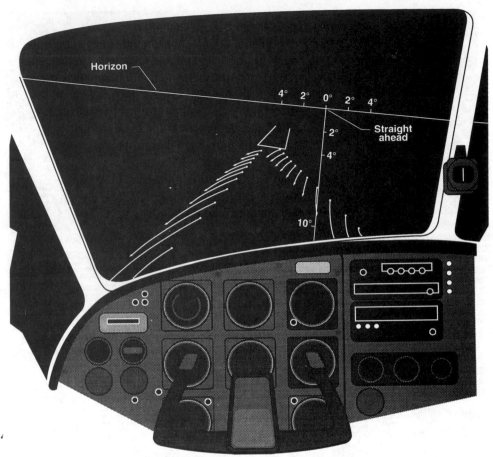

Fig. 10-13. *Parafoveal streamer paths for curved approach and slight bank angle.*

Curved approach to unlighted runway

This type of approach is perhaps the most difficult of all because outside visual information is almost totally absent with which to judge the accuracy of intersecting the runway's centerline, height above the ground, descent rate, and even whether the runway is level or not. If the pilot cannot avoid such an approach, several possible alternatives should be considered. First, if possible, make a low altitude approach over the runway without landing, but with the landing lights on, to study all visible features of the runway's surface and surrounding obstacles. Continue to fly a standard traffic pattern and be prepared to execute a missed approach at any instant if something doesn't seem right. Second, it is best to fly the curved portion of the approach as far away from the runway as possible to allow maximal time to make necessary small adjustments in runway alignment, cross-wind correction, airplane trim, airspeed, descent rate, and the other flight control inputs that might be involved during the straight approach path portion of the flight. This is illustrated in FIG. 10-14. At least 10

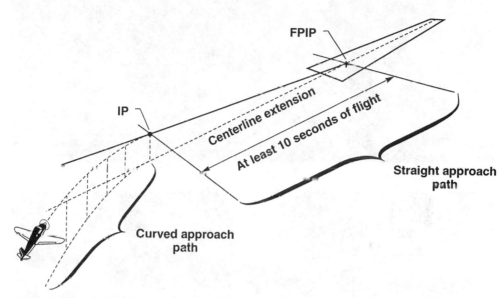

Fig. 10-14. *Extended centerline intercept approach.*

seconds of flight distance on runway centerline is recommended. Of course, this technique will also give the pilot more time to correctly sort out the sometimes ambiguous and confusing visual information that might be seen ahead.

The black hole approach

The black hole approach illusion as previously discussed represents an insidious threat to every uninformed nocturnal aviator. The answer is quite simple. When flying in a black hole approach environment, the pilot should fly in the traffic pattern if not using a visual or electronic glide slope.

ROUNDOUT AND TOUCHDOWN

The roundout (sometimes referred to as *flare*) and touchdown should be made in the same manner as in day landings; however, judgment of height, speed, and sink rate is impaired by the scarcity of observable objects in the landing area. The inexperienced pilot might have a tendency to roundout too high until attaining familiarity with the apparent height for the correct roundout position. Figure 10-15 illustrates the general appearance of a lighted runway during four points on final night approach to the runway. To aid in determining the proper roundout point, it might be well to continue a constant approach descent until the landing light reflects on the runway, and tire

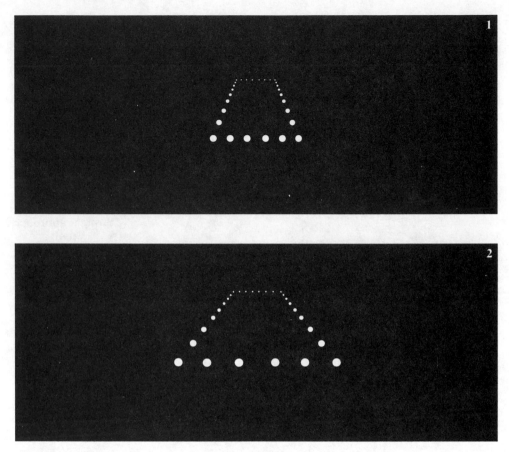

Fig. 10-15. *Roundout when tire marks become visible.*

marks on the runway, or runway expansion joints, can be seen clearly, as in the third panel of this figure. At that point, the roundout for touchdown should be started smoothly and the throttle gradually reduced to idle as the airplane is touching down.

A word is in order concerning use of landing lights at night. Landing lights in small aircraft are generally aimed so that the runway surface becomes illuminated at a wheel altitude of about 10 feet or so, which is supposed to assist in making the nose-up roundout maneuver. This light also illuminates only a hundred feet or so of the runway ahead. Some small aircraft pilots who have had to land at night without their landing light actually found their roundout and touchdown to be smoother than when they landed with the landing lights on. Upon reflection they noticed that during such final approaches they had looked much farther down the runway (on centerline) without the landing light and it is likely that they were better able to judge their roll and

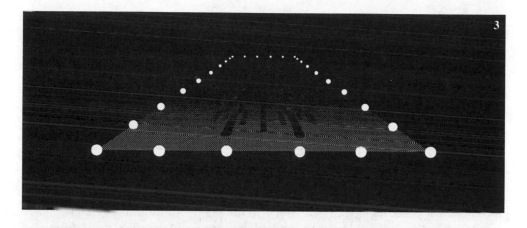

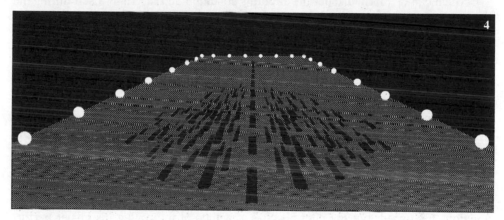

Fig. 10-15. *Continued*

pitch attitude near the runway surface because of their greater reliance on peripheral vision, which is more sensitive to motion than is the central visual field.

Every pilot should practice making landings both with and without the landing light to be able to cope with the times when the landing light does not operate. Every pilot should also make night landings while looking farther down the runway than just the area that is illuminated by the landing light.

During landings without the use of landing lights, or where marks on the runway are not discernible, the roundout may be started when the runway lights at the far end of the runway first appear to be rising higher than the airplane. This, of course, demands a smooth and very timely roundout, and requires, in effect, that the pilot "feel" for the runway surface, using power and pitch changes as necessary for the airplane to settle softly on the runway.

A second type of landing procedure when landing lights are not used is to set the aircraft in a landing attitude when approaching the runway surface and adjust the power for a very low rate of descent. The tires ideally will then touch the surface very smoothly. This second type of "lights-out" landing procedure is not recommended for short runways because this technique requires more runway than the standard type of landing procedure.

SHUTDOWN

One of the most overlooked phases of nighttime flying is shutdown. The reasons vary from fatigue and lack of motivation, to carelessness, or ignorance; however, whatever the reason for a lack of diligence, the shutdown phase does require as much attention as any other phase of flight. The degree of the precision demonstrated during the shutdown phase can greatly contribute to the safety of future night flights.

Much can be learned about the aircraft's condition and the flight itself during the shutdown. For example, even if the aircraft's heater and/or defroster were not used on the flight, by checking them to determine if they are operating properly prior to shutdown a pilot can possibly prevent an aggravating experience during the following flight. Instruments that function with the aid of a gyro also give indications of condition during the shutdown phase. Additionally, in many instances, navigational or other electrical equipment that seemed to be functioning properly prior to the flight might not have functioned to the degree of desired accuracy once the equipment warmed-up. In these instances, it is often best to try to isolate the problem while the aircraft is on the ground and prior to turning the systems off.

As previously discussed, there is a higher probability for short-term memory loss during nighttime hours; therefore, documentation of the flight immediately after the flight can be of great benefit to the pilot. Not only can aircraft and equipment malfunctions be logged, but the pilot also has a method of improving his or her performance on future flights as well. A reminder such as marking a new visual reference point on the map that would be a suitable visual reference for switching navigational aid frequencies often improves the ease of piloting during the night. Additionally, just a note in a diary as a reminder to get that extra rest before the next night flight can cause a pilot to remember the fatigue that was experienced during the last leg of the flight.

11
Cross-country flight

CROSS-COUNTRY FLYING AT NIGHT CAN BE A RELAXING AND A PERSONALLY satisfying experience, particularly when the pilot knows that everything possible has been done to ensure maximum safety. This chapter reviews flight considerations that are of special importance to the nocturnal aviator.

SUMMING IT UP

Richard Gless of the Air Safety Foundation staff has rightly suggested, "Night cross-country should be conducted under instrument flight rules. If this is impractical, a VFR flight plan should be filed and radar flight following requested." (1990)

EN ROUTE VISUAL RECOGNITION

During night cross-country flights, one will be able to see anywhere from very great distances in clear air conditions, down to almost nothing at all in IMC conditions. If one can see the ground at all, it is a good idea to look for as many visual ground cues as possible.

Light patterns

Medium- and large-size towns will quite often have lines of streetlights that form squares. Because they are all of the same type of light bulb, they will also appear the same color and brightness and will tend to stand out from lights around them. It is likely that these lines of lights will be oriented along north-south and east-west lines.

If possible, a pilot can fly parallel with one of them and cross-check the magnetic compass heading. Be forewarned that some towns are not laid out on such a geocoordinate basis. A prominent example is the San Francisco peninsula where the main thoroughfares run approximately northwest-southeast.

Anyone who has flown at night knows that a familiar daylight site can become totally foreign in darkness. When the eyes see only points of light, there might be little spatial correspondence with the ground's topography or man's improvements, such as buildings, farms, and roads. One example of this potentially dangerous effect is when a professional pilot flew the same air route many times a month during daylight hours only. His route took him over a series of many small lakes. He almost memorized their shapes and locations relative to towns nearby them. Then he had to fly the same route at night. When flying over the same lake region, he could not find the lakes. He became spatially disoriented. He had no idea about his whereabouts. Fortunately, he reached his destination safely that night. Only later did he discover that fishermen were using lights to attract fish during a night fishing derby on several lakes. Again, don't take anything for granted at night. Cross-check everything.

Colored lights

Most cities have installed same-color streetlights that stand out visually from other lights around them. Low-pressure sodium streetlights have a characteristic yellow color; high pressure sodium lights are definitely whiter. Many other colored lights are visible, but not necessarily as predominate as the sodium lighting.

Flashing lights

Approaching an airport, the first flashing light that is usually observed is the alternating white and green beacon that can be seen from almost any position. It will flash from twelve to thirty flashes per minute. Next in conspicuity is likely to be the intense white strobe lights of the runway approach lights called "rabbits" because they seem to jump repeatedly toward the runway. Next, one might see yellow flashing lights on utility vehicles or red flashing lights on emergency (fire and rescue) vehicles.

All tall buildings and other obstructions such as water towers located near an airfield are required to have flashing light beacons to signal their presence to pilots. Sectional and other aviation charts have them prominently marked. If one can clearly identify these beacons they can serve as an aid to navigation. For example, high intensity (one million candle power or more) strobes are often attached to the sides of very tall radio towers that would otherwise be impossible to see; one will be able to pinpoint one's location relative to the towers.

There are also many different kinds of flashing lights on highways (signs, construction warnings, traffic signals, ambulances, tow trucks, and fire fighting vehicles, for example), all of which indicate that a highway is below.

Moonlight

There is a noticeably significant difference flying at night in clear air with and without the moon present. It is important for the night pilot to understand some basic facts about the moon and the illumination it produces. The moon produces no light of its own but reflects sunlight that strikes approximately one-half of its surface. Moonlight is approximately 650,000 times less intense than sunlight (Rudaux and De Vaucouleurs 1959, 125). Because the moon can be seen from a range of viewing angles as it rotates about the earth it changes the proportion of illuminated to unilluminated area seen from the earth. A *lunation period* is defined as the period between successive new moons and is equal to 29 days, 12 hours, 44 minutes, and 3 seconds. TABLE 11-1 gives the relative percentage of the moon's illuminance (compared to 100 percent for full moon) for each of twelve equally spaced phases during the lunation period. The phases during the last half of the lunation period show somewhat less illuminance than their first-half counterparts. This is due to sunlight scattering off darker topographical features on the lunar surface.

*Table 11-1. Lunar phases
and percentage of
the moon's illuminance.*

Moon Phase	Percentage
1. New moon	0
2.	0.5
3.	3
4. First quarter	8.5
5.	22
6.	47
7. Full moon	100
8.	less than 47
9.	less than 22
10. Last quarter	less than 8.5
11.	less than 3
12.	less than 0.5

The full moon (maximum brightness) produces approximately 0.034 foot candles (0.34 lux) of illumination at the earth's surface on a clear night which is enough to make clouds and snow easily visible from the air but it isn't enough illumination to read by. The apparent half-moon (first quarter) yields under ten times less illumination than the full moon and the crescent moon yields approximately ten times less illumination than the first quarter moon. Illumination level remains fairly constant after the moon has reached an angle of approximately forty degrees arc or more above the horizon but drops faster and faster as it approaches the level of the horizon, assuming a completely clear atmosphere.

There is reason to believe that fewer night-landing accidents occur during lunar phases ranging from the full moon to 1st and 3rd quarters. Presumably this is due to the availability of more visible landing cues from the ground that are illuminated by moonlight.

Moonlight should be used to good advantage in at least these ways:

- If the flight passes over rivers or lakes the pilot should look for these bodies of water that will reflect the light of the moon.
- If clouds are clearly visible one should navigate around rather than through them at night when there is a choice.
- Moonlight might provide enough illumination to discriminate flat fields from hills and mountainous areas; such discriminations can provide valuable aid in navigation and obstacle avoidance.

TOPOGRAPHICAL CONSIDERATIONS

As discussed in earlier chapters visual cues are different at night and the night sky is filled with visual illusions, some of which we all view unassumingly. Everyone has noticed how the moon seems to be so big when it first appears on the horizon and then shrinks as it rises in the night sky. Some people assume that the moon is just moving farther away from the earth. However, that is definitely not the case. It is, in fact, just another visual illusion.

En route nighttime piloting requires a special understanding of not only the factors that can lead to visual illusions but also the understanding of the new set of visual parameters that accompany nighttime cross-country flights.

Snow

When the ground is covered with a blanket of snow on a clear night, visual navigation can be a delightful experience. Roads are easy to distinguish due to the contrasting dark bands left by vehicle tires against the white landscape, even when there is little moonlight. Similarly, runways that have buried landing lights and runways at unlighted airports can still be distinguished as dark stripes against the white snow. Pilots should look for other nighttime visual cues of contrasting areas where there is any type of traffic or the contrasting terrain provided by white shorelines next to bodies of water.

Mountain flying

Pilots should be aware that on moonless nights mountains are very difficult to see due to the scarcity of visual cues and, if an aircraft is not at an altitude that is higher than the mountain tops, flight toward a mountain might not allow adequate time to initiate effective evasive action measures. Mountain flying is not recommended at night under any of the following circumstances:

- If there is any chance of encountering precipitation or areas of reduced visibility.

- If there is a widespread overcast condition in a remote region that has few illuminated ground visual cues.
- If an aircraft has extremely limited high altitude performance capability. Only turbocharged single-engine, high performance multiengine, or jet aircraft should be used for nocturnal mountain flight.
- If you are an inexperienced night pilot, an aircraft engine apparently encounters "automatic rough" as soon as the aircraft approaches the mountain range. Such a flight that experiences this imaginary effect can prove to be quite traumatic.
- If oxygen equipment is not available.

Crossing mountainous terrain at night is only for the experienced night pilot that is flying an aircraft equipped with systems suitable for high altitude flight in meteorological conditions that promote a safe flight.

THREE MAJOR CONSIDERATIONS

During nighttime hours, pilots must be more cognizant of the aircraft's position, time constraints, and usable fuel. During daylight hours, relatively little intentional concentration by an experienced pilot is required to determine aircraft position and, as a result, it is much easier for the pilot to continually mentally recompute the position/time/fuel relationship. Flying in the dark with fewer visual cues, the brain might not produce these answers as quickly or as precisely. Consequently, the following nighttime procedures are suggested:

1. Continually mark the aircraft's position on a map and note the time passing each checkpoint. Ideally, use a lighted kneeboard.
2. Note if the flight is on schedule. If it is not, determine the amount of loss or gain in minutes. Then recompute the remaining flight time.
3. Recompute the amount of fuel remaining in minutes at each checkpoint.
4. Subtract the answer determined in step 3 from the answer found in step 2 to determine the safety margin in minutes.

The previous suggestions might seem sophomoric in nature and most experienced pilots would not employ them during daylight hours, but they are a sure way to enhance the pilot's state of situational awareness during nighttime hours.

Especially during nighttime hours, pilots need to think of usable fuel as time in flight, rather than just gallons per hour. It is essential to constantly redetermine the fuel remaining, in the event of a developing emergency that would cause the pilot to alter the flight plan. When an emergency surprises a pilot, he or she has enough to do and does not necessarily always have an opportunity to accurately calculate fuel remaining times. Remember, if a pilot possesses a high degree of situational awareness before an emergency happens, the overall degree of risk is lowered.

CHECKPOINTS

Most pilots have become lost or temporarily disoriented at one time or another. It can happen to anyone at any level of experience. (Ever hear the one about the private pilot who landed his airplane on the runway of an air force base or, the senior airline captain who landed on the wrong runway, at the wrong airport?) It does happen and can happen to you if you are not careful. Experience and proficiency cannot replace pilot motivation. Complacency can affect a pilot's ability to navigate as easily as it can affect performance in so many other areas.

Knowing the position of the aircraft at night should not be a difficult chore, but to do so correctly takes some practice. Most pilots have their own ways of determining aircraft position, unfortunately, sometimes those methods prove to be inadequate.

Rule of five

One approach that seems to work very well is the rule of five method, which employs the use of pilotage, dead reckoning, and electronic navigation. The number five is significant because this method requires the pilot to determine aircraft position in five ways:

- According to time-distance calculations the aircraft appears to be on time for this scheduled checkpoint.
- The VOR receiver or another electronic navigational aid indicates that the aircraft is on course.
- The previous checkpoint is still in sight and the aircraft appears to be located in the appropriate position relative to the last checkpoint.
- It appears that the next checkpoint is in sight at the approximate distance and location as depicted on the navigational chart.
- One very significant night visual cue that is unique for a certain checkpoint is identified and is located in a position that is consistent with the other checks.

The inherent value of this method is that the pilot is not allowed to become complacent and rely only on one type of navigation, but must utilize three types. Any combination of the three is satisfactory. For example, a pilot that is unable to locate the next checkpoint may look for another unique visual cue or establish an NDB cross-fix with the aircraft's ADF receiver.

POTENTIAL OPERATIONAL PROBLEMS

Microsleep

Recall from chapter 2 that a microsleep refers to a short period of sleep lasting from under a second to several seconds. Microsleep periods are particularly insidious because the pilot does not realize that he or she has fallen asleep and also because there can be short-term memory impairment during these brief periods. If, for example, the pilot should fall asleep flying at an en route altitude and just prior to radio communications of weather or approach data, there is the possibility that this information might not be remembered as efficiently. Similarly, the pilot might experience short term memory loss during virtually any other activity, often en route when the pilot is not at peak workload. The fact that a pilot can unknowingly experience periods of microsleep is good cause for adequate rest before a night cross-country flight.

Memory loss

A pilot's memory at times during the night might seem to play tricks. Human factors research has demonstrated that memory and performance efficiency vary on a 24-hour cycle. Understandably, the low point in this efficiency cycle occurs in the early morning hours and the high point of the cycle generally occurs during the midafternoon.

When such factors as stress, hurried flight operations, fatigue, interruptions, other distractions, or complacency are added to the negative aspects of this cycle, the pilot is very vulnerable to lapses of memory and reduced performance capability. Inexperienced pilots are not alone in encountering these potential problems; even after years of accident- and incident-free performance of routine tasks, a pilot's memory can be unreliable at times.

Fatigue

Yet another concern for the en route phase of night flight is pilot fatigue. Like microsleep, fatigue is insidious because it might lead some pilots to see and hear things inaccurately. The more experience a pilot has, it is more likely that a mental model or expectancy of what will occur in flight will develop. These expectancies range from phrases that the air traffic controller says to perceived glide slope instrument indications. The overly fatigued and experienced pilot might fill in expected words even though different words were spoken. An illustration is presented in FIG. 11-1; read the phrase quickly and then again more slowly.

STAYING ALERT AND EXERCISING

It should go without saying that pilots who plan to fly at night must remain alert throughout the entire flight. Indeed, a pilot will be more prone to fall asleep between the hours of midnight and 5 a.m. local time than other hours. Circumstances that diminish sensory, intellectual, or physical alertness must be anticipated. TABLE 11-2 presents a list of such circumstances.

When faced with any circumstances that diminish alertness at night, the pilot should take appropriate action to reduce or eliminate those circumstances.

One suggested way of staying more alert during long night flights is to carry an insulated container holding several very cold damp washcloths or hand towels and occasionally wipe your face, neck, and wrists (consider placing a few wet washcloths

Fig. 11-1. *Mental expectancy.*

Table 11-2.
Circumstances and events that can reduce alertness.

1. Lack of sleep/poor quality of sleep
2. Repetitive or randomly occurring cockpit distractions
3. Mental overload
4. Monotonous conditions
5. Too many simple operations required
6. A few very complex operations required
7. Drinking alcohol
8. Prolonged body vibration or other sensory overload
9. Natural circadian rhythm effects (chapter 3)

or towels in a freezer several hours prior to departure for a truly frosty awakening). Other suggestions are to eat an apple or one of the other snacks listed in TABLES 2-5 and 11-3, or consume a beverage containing caffeine to keep the body functioning in an alert mode. Another technique is to turn up the cabin lights to full intensity for 10-20 seconds (while keeping one eye closed, of course).

Another way to stay more alert during long night flights is to perform some sim-

*Table 11-3. Acceptable and
unacceptable snack foods for night flying.*

Acceptable	Unacceptable
Apples	High sugar content
Pears	Gaseous producing foods
Grapes	Gaseous producing liquids
Cheese slices	
String cheese	
Bagels and cream cheese	
Crackers	
Sourdough chips	
Hot coffee or tea	

ple stretching, twisting, and muscle-joint exercises in the cabin, at half-hour intervals. Of course, they should not be a distraction from specific cockpit duties or interfere with flight controls. Nine simple exercises are illustrated; you do not have to do each exercise during every exercise period, select three or four to perform in sequence. These exercises begin at the neck and generally work down to the legs. For example, select one from the first three, one from the middle three, and one from the last three.

A neck flexion exercise is depicted in FIG. 11-2. Part A shows the pilot in a relaxed

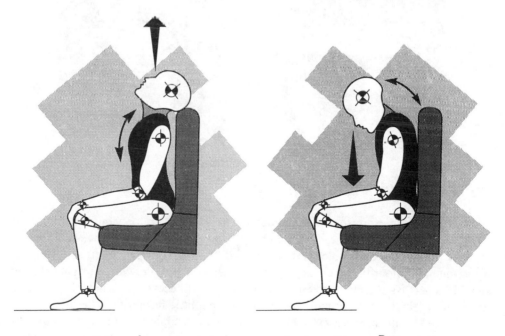

A.   B.

Fig. 11-2. *Neck flexion exercise.*

225

sitting posture with at least one arm resting on a leg. Slowly and deliberately lift the chin and extend the chest to look upward at the ceiling and then swing the entire head forward until the chin rests on the chest and the spine is curved (part B). Do this no more than twice and then continue the ongoing cockpit flying duties. This exercise should only be conducted when the aircraft is flying straight and level to avoid vertigo and disorientation.

Part A of FIG. 11-3 shows the first half of a shoulder rotation exercise. The head should be held erect during this exercise. Keep looking forward out of the window or at the instrument panel. While keeping one or both arms on the top of the legs, rotate the shoulders of both arms at the same time in the same direction. As is shown in part B, the shoulders are then rotated in the opposite direction. This should be done for four or five rotations per direction. If the left elbow should strike the arm rest, then lean to the right far enough to avoid it during this exercise.

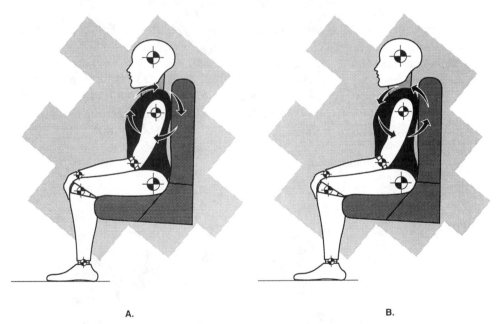

A.   B.

Fig. 11-3. *Shoulder rotation exercise.*

A floor reach exercise is diagrammed in FIG. 11-4. The pilot should sit erect with the head vertical. First, let the left arm hang vertically downward, if possible, beside the seat; if this is not possible, reach forward of the seat. Lower the left shoulder and try to touch the floor of the cockpit (part A), then do the same with the right arm and shoulder (part B). Again, reach in front of the seat, if necessary. Repeat this exercise two or three times, each time extending the reach a little farther than before.

Figure 11-5 illustrates an isometric exercise for the upper body. Part A shows how the pilot should raise the arms and elbows and lock both hands together while keeping the arms close to the chest. Then try to pull them apart without unlocking the hands.

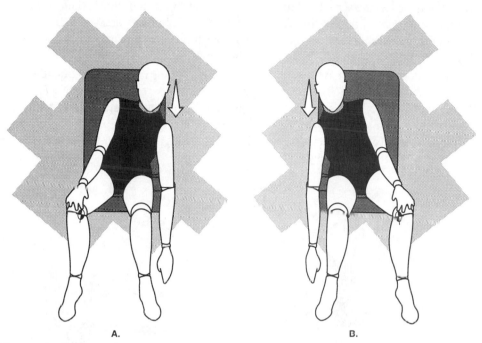

A.   B.

Fig. 11-4. *Floor reach exercise.*

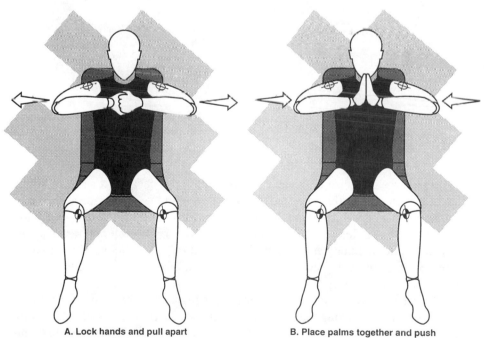

A. Lock hands and pull apart   B. Place palms together and push

Fig. 11-5. *Upper body isometric exercise.*

Keep the hands at the same level as the chin. Pull for a count of three, then relax. Part B shows the second part of this exercise where the palms are pressed together for a count of three. Repeat each exercise three or four times. Immediately after completing these exercises, try to totally relax all of the arm muscles.

The stomach stretch exercise illustrated in FIG. 11-6 is designed to strengthen and relax the abdominal muscles through repeated inhaling (part A) and exhaling (part B). While keeping the head erect, first take a deep breath by constricting the stomach while rolling both shoulders forward slightly. The inhale stage of part B is performed by inhaling deeply while extending the chest and arching the lower back forward. Do each part three times in a row and then relax.

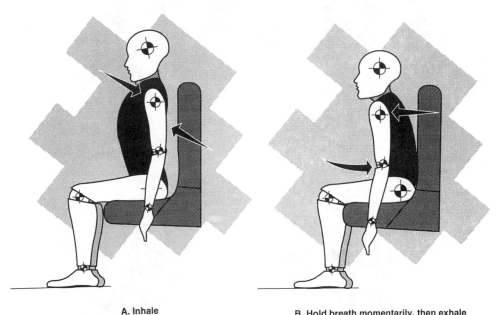

A. Inhale

B. Hold breath momentarily, then exhale

Fig. 11-6. *Stomach stretch exercise.*

A torso twist exercise is valuable for the night pilot because it involves so many different muscles. It is illustrated in FIG. 11-7. Part A shows that the pilot should hold the arms in front of the chest and then rotate the entire torso from the waist up to the right and then to the left as far as possible (part B). Try to keep both arms approximately in front of the body as the torso is twisted. Also, keep looking forward to keep the horizon in sight during each body twist. Repeat this exercise three times in each direction, and then relax.

The next exercise is suggested for long night flights to help the pilot stay relaxed, yet alert (FIG. 11-8). During this leg muscle exercise, the pilot sits erect and continues to look forward. The arms may hang vertically or be placed in the lap. First, place both feet flat on the floor of the cockpit near the front of the seat; lift the left leg sev-

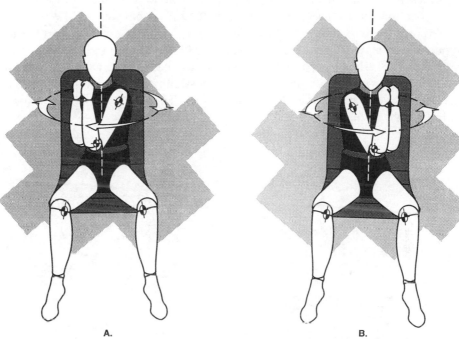

Fig. 11-7. *Torso twist exercise.*

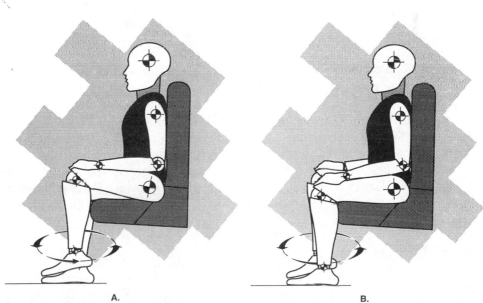

Fig. 11-8. *Leg muscle exercise.*

eral inches off the floor and rotate the foot in a small circle six or more times (part A); put the foot down and repeat the exercise with the right foot (part B).

The next exercise, shown in FIG. 11-9, is a neck side-flex exercise. Part A shows the pilot's starting posture where the head is tilted forward until the chin rests on the chest. Then, as is shown in part B, the head is flexed side to side. Do not do this exercise more than twice to each side. Reduce the possibility of inducing vertigo and disorientation by closing your eyes during the exercise. The aircraft should be in straight and level flight in calm air.

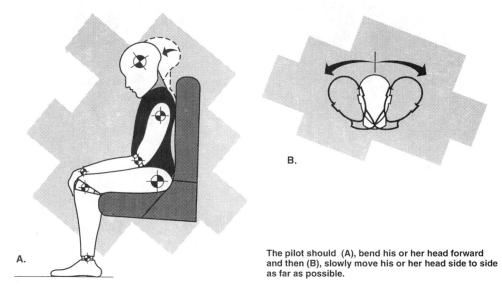

B.

A.

The pilot should (A), bend his or her head forward and then (B), slowly move his or her head side to side as far as possible.

Fig. 11-9. *Neck side flex exercise.*

The body lift exercise is diagrammed in FIG. 11-10. Place both hands on the top of the seat as far back on the seat cushion as necessary to balance the body during the lift. Push down on the seat to lift the entire body, including legs and feet, off the seat and floor of the cockpit. Keep the head erect and lean forward only as far as necessary. Repeat this lift exercise three times and then relax. It might be necessary to place the right hand on the edge of the adjacent seat for support.

Perhaps the best way of staying alert, in addition to being well rested, is talking to another person, ideally a second pilot, when the opportunity arises. The psychological value of periodic conversation cannot be ignored; however, realize that flying the airplane comes first.

EN ROUTE SAFETY

What can a pilot do on a long, lonely, late night cross-country flight when the whole world seems to be asleep? Stay alert and stay safe. In addition to trying to stay alert with icy cold wet towels and in-flight exercises, the mind requires constant intel-

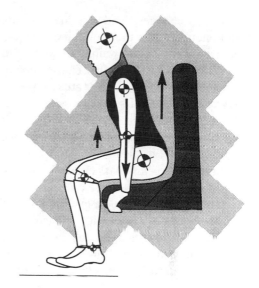

Fig. 11-10. *Body lift exercise. (Note: Because the seat belt must be loosened to perform the exercise, this exercise is only recommended when there is a two-pilot crew.)*

Elevation of the entire body
using only the arms.

lectual exercising in the wee hours of morning. Because the mind and the body usually want to go to sleep when the sun goes down, extra effort is required to remain at a high mental and physical state of arousal:

- Carry out normal cockpit duties with regularity. Don't become complacent.
- Constantly monitor all instruments looking for potential problems. Maintain a scan. Don't fixate.
- Look for other aircraft and obstructions.
- Be on the lookout for possible forced landing sites. Refer to the appropriate navigational chart for the route of flight. Note the potential forced landing sites, ideally airports, that were noted on the map during the preflight planning process.

DIVERSION TO AN ALTERNATE AIRPORT

As many experienced pilots can attest, the need to divert to an alternate airport might be a very traumatic experience at night. Suddenly, the pilot is confronted with a deluge of new thoughts, plans, emotions, and increased stress. Fear is often felt and there is a growing sense that everything is not all right. The reasoning might be "because something happened to force me to fly to the alternate landing field, something else will probably occur along the way as well." This illogical behavior must be brought under control immediately. A logical and disciplined mind is perhaps the best way of displacing anxiety, fear, and superstition from the mind at night. The pilot must think through each new procedure: course and wind correction, descent profile, radio frequency changes, landmark identification, and traffic pattern details. If all of this isn't enough to get the wandering mind off fear of imagined consequences, visualize that cup of hot coffee waiting for you on the ground at the new destination.

Additional navigational charts should be available for the planned flight. It is important to carry charts for areas adjacent to the planned route of flight if it is necessary to fly to one of several possible alternate airports or to circumnavigate weather. During periods of good visibility it is possible to see the lights of cities and airports at surprisingly great distances; therefore, it frequently becomes necessary to examine charts adjacent to planned routes. Without these adjacent charts, it is easy to become confused when landmarks and visually prominent light sources found on adjacent charts can't be identified.

If the pilot has done a good job of preflight course planning and in-flight navigation, he or she will have little difficulty locating the alternate airport.

Sectional charts are usually accurate enough to show the general illuminated outline of a city or town at night so that it can be recognized from the air. These charts should be carefully studied before takeoff for this reason. It is also wise to study them from different approach directions on each side of the planned direction of approach. Freeways, brilliantly lighted outdoor sports stadiums, and commercial radio/television towers with flashing strobe lights are also often visible for very great distances in clear air. Another visual cue that can be useful is the outline of a lake and a river that is visible because of reflected moonlight. Airports also will be more conspicuous because of other airplanes taking off and landing from the runway. Some pilots think that the place to look for the airport is the darkest ground area because usually much of the land is left undeveloped around the runways. This is only partially true; local topography and meteorological conditions can produce false impressions of dark areas. Sectional and approach charts should be studied carefully before they are needed to commit these details to memory.

EN ROUTE COMMUNICATIONS

There are several reasons for carrying out en route communications. Weather trends and notams can be updated along the route of flight. Pilots can monitor en route navigational aids for transcribed weather broadcasts (TWEB), automatic terminal information service (ATIS) for terminal information, and en route flight advisory service (EFAS) for en route weather. Because there are fewer meteorological visual cues during darkened conditions, it is wise to constantly monitor for weather trends. Weather conditions can change quickly during nighttime hours, so pilots must be especially alert for possible deteriorating atmospheric conditions. If negative trends are detected early enough, a flight can be safely diverted to an alternate airport. Remember, instrument meteorological conditions often occur between two airports that are reporting VFR conditions.

VFR pilots on flight plans should make position reports; pilots flying on instrument flight plans must make required reports. Traffic information and directional guidance can be obtained from air traffic control, if the controller's workload permits.

It is all too easy for a pilot to become complacent with the nighttime cockpit duties and choose not to use the communications equipment. Some pilots might find the communications chatter annoying and might elect to reduce the volume of the receiver. Pilots should be cautioned that such feelings, if not overcome, can lead the pilot into a state of subtle incapacitation. Nocturnal aviators should maintain a cockpit discipline that promotes timely execution of cockpit communications duties.

Air-to-ground communications that are not directly related to the flight are not recommended. A NASA study cited unnecessary communications as a leading cause of incidents resulting from cockpit distraction. Such distractions usually contribute to deviations from the desired flight path. Furthermore, pilots should not attempt to engage in casual conversation in the aircraft during critical phases of flight.

12
Emergencies

IN-FLIGHT EMERGENCIES OCCUR EVERY NIGHT. OFTEN THEY BEGIN IN VERY innocuous but insidious ways and can rapidly blossom into terrifying experiences and even death. This chapter deals with many of the more commonplace hardware and system failures that can occur in flight. It is largely the pilot's psychological, mental, and physical preparation for an emergency, before it happens, that can make the crucial difference between an incident and accident, between life and death. Setting personal priorities during a developing emergency is as crucial to optimal coping as realistically assessing one's current capabilities.

FLYING PRIORITIES

Prior to encountering an emergency situation, all pilots should be prepared to face that emergency. Even though emergencies differ in type and severity, basic priorities remain the same: aviate, navigate, and if necessary, communicate.

PSYCHOLOGICAL CONSIDERATIONS

Denial

Some pilots might be reluctant to admit to themselves that there could be an emergency situation. Of course, no one wants to look for trouble and it is less stressful to simply ignore the possibility of an aviation incident or accident. But the wise pilot will face the facts and think ahead of each phase of his flight.

Perhaps it is like the situation in the old adage "If the light isn't shining on it, it probably isn't really there." Of course, denial of reality is as old as mankind. Yet the night pilot is literally engulfed in the psychological counterpart of physical darkness so that when he or she looks at a developing emergency situation, it might not seem as obvious or as dangerous as it really is.

Many other deep-seated psychological predispositions are probably within some pilots that prevent them from thinking about "what could happen" during their night flight. A large number of trouble-free flight hours can lead some pilots into a false sense of security, complacency, or denial (chapter 3).

A pilot whose mind is allowed to become paralyzed at the thought that because of an emergency the aircraft will be on the ground in a short time, regardless of what is done, is severely handicapped in the handling of the emergency. An unconscious desire to delay this dreaded moment might lead to such errors as failure to lower the nose to maintain flying speed, delay in the selection of the most suitable touchdown area within reach, and overall indecision.

Desire to save the aircraft

A pilot who has been conditioned to expect to find a relatively safe landing area whenever the instructor closed the throttle for a simulated forced landing might ignore all basic rules of airmanship to avoid a touchdown in terrain where aircraft damage is unavoidable. The desire to save the aircraft, regardless of the risks involved, might be influenced by the pilot's financial stake in the aircraft and the certainty that an undamaged aircraft implies no bodily harm. There are times when a pilot should be more interested in sacrificing the aircraft so that all occupants can safely walk away from it.

Undue concern about getting hurt

Fear is a vital part of the self-preservation mechanism. When fear leads to panic, we invite what we most want to avoid. The survival records favor pilots that maintain their composure and know how to apply the general concepts and techniques that have been developed throughout the years.

CONSTRUCTIVE ASSESSMENT

Mental attitude

Keep a positive attitude because it's not all over until it's all over; never give up. This old saying holds a lot of truth for the night pilot facing an emergency situation. Before a constructive assessment can be made, a pilot must possess a positive attitude or, in some situations, it will be over. It makes good sense to maintain a positive attitude because such an attitude really helps to keep the available options open in the face of depression, when the more natural tendency might be to give up. Several factors can contribute to maintaining a positive attitude:

- Prior experience in successfully coping with simulated and/or actual in-flight emergencies contributes to confidence that greatly adds to maintaining a positive attitude. Pilot proficiency has no substitute.
- Possess a thorough knowledge and understanding of the aircraft and all of its systems. It is much easier to cope with the known than the unknown.
- Preflight planning is so very essential in coping with an emergency. If a pilot knows all of the potential landing sites, suitable for a night landing along the route of flight before takeoff, part of the emergency landing equation is already solved when confronted with the emergency. Remember, part of the preflight planning process is to always leave yourself an out.
- Be mentally prepared for the emergency because it helps prevent panic. Panic can interfere with a pilot's ability to correctly perceive the true nature of the emergency situation and can hinder or completely prevent a pilot from reacting in a timely and appropriate manner. Keep cool but don't freeze.

The degree of success in surviving a forced landing is not only dependent upon pilot skill, but also upon keeping a positive attitude. For without the proper mind set, skill is of very limited value.

Situational analysis

In a very high percentage of situations, the proper analysis of the emergencies by a calm and collected pilot has saved the night. It is not always necessary for the pilot to have the emergency analyzed immediately. Altitude above the ground translates into time to think, to ameliorate the problem, and implement emergency procedures. Proper analysis of certain emergencies can take time. Some accidents that could have been prevented resulted because the pilot or pilots did not take the necessary time to solve the problem, but chose to plan for an emergency landing instead. Engine failure due to fuel mismanagement is an ideal example of pilot inattentiveness; maintaining control of the aircraft, switching to another fuel tank, and restarting the engine is less stressful than immediately implementing all forced landing procedures (selected landing procedures may be implemented in case the engine does not restart).

TYPES OF EMERGENCIES

Not every possible type of nighttime emergency can be discussed within one book. The discussion that follows covers the primary areas of concern to all pilots flying at night.

Electrical failure

An electrical failure emergency is not uncommon, but the causes and cures vary. Advance warnings usually signal the onset of electrical failure. The warnings are often very subtle in nature and it takes a pilot in a high state of arousal to detect them. If the potential electrical problem is discovered soon enough, it might be ameliorated because most problems can be corrected in flight. Part of the immediate solution, as soon as signs of an impending electrical failure are detected, is to shut down all electronic equipment and electrical systems that aren't absolutely essential to the safety of the flight and utilize appropriate emergency equipment as discussed in chapter 7.

Once again, proper preparation for the emergency before the aircraft is airborne is the best insurance for safety. Proper pilot training and knowledge of the aircraft's handbook can avert a threatening emergency; however, it still might be necessary to fly directly to the nearest airport and land rather than risk the far more serious consequences of an emergency landing without electrical power.

Engine failure

Engine failures are extremely dangerous anytime they occur and call for self-control and a carefully planned set of procedures.

The most important priority that a pilot has anytime is to fly the airplane. Pilots sometimes become so preoccupied with the emergency situation that they actually forget to fly the airplane. A controlled forced landing is always preferable to an uncontrolled crash. If possible, the pilot must control the airplane until stopped.

Implement energy management measures. Extra airspeed should not be wasted. The aircraft should not be allowed to descend until the best glide speed has been attained. The extra altitude that is conserved or the extra distance that the aircraft is able to glide can make a big difference.

Try to determine the cause of the failure and correct it. Pilots should be aware that a high percentage of nighttime engine failures are pilot induced. A pilot should recall his or her actions during the previous few minutes. When a pilot reaches for anything close to the panel, in a darkened cockpit it is possible to turn off the mag switches. Trouble-shoot the problem mentally and then think through previously memorized emergency procedures. Take one positive action at a time and verify what happens. Don't panic and try to do everything at once. With the exceptions of engine failures during takeoffs and landings, seldom are these emergencies so crucial that there isn't time to apply each and every remedial procedure available. If time permits, review the emergency checklist.

The airplane should be turned away from congested areas and toward an airport or other suitable landing area. Orientation into the wind direction should be maintained, if possible, to avoid a downwind landing. Prior to touchdown, the wings should be kept as level as possible.

Weather

Flight into instrument meteorological conditions continues to be one of the major contributors to nighttime aviation accidents. This is one time when a pilot can be caught in foul weather. When encountering such conditions, executing a 180-degree turn is generally the best remedy. (In the event that icing is encountered, the pilot should use a high-powered flashlight to visually inspect the amount of ice buildup and determine the rate of ice accumulation. When using the flashlight, the pilot should always keep one eye closed.) Proficiency in flying by reference to instruments certainly offers the biggest payoff in this situation. Because weather conditions can change so radically at night, the pilot should contact the nearest flight service station to check weather conditions along a possible route of flight. (Contact the FSS only after it is safe to do so.) After assessing all the weather conditions, the logical decision is often to land as soon as practical rather than trying to continue to the original destination by circumventing the weather.

Lost procedures

It is certainly easy to become disoriented in a darkened flight environment. It is not unheard of for a pilot to become lost over the home airport when the stars are shining and the visibility conditions are excellent. Most pilots become lost at night due to a combination of factors, rather than just one. If a pilot understands some of the reasons why other pilots become lost, he or she is better equipped to avoid an anxious situation in a blackened sky:

- Flight into instrument conditions.
- Gradual loss of visual cues. This can happen when flying over a desolate area with an overcast sky or in an area of reduced forward visibility.
- Cockpit distraction.
- Complacency.

When the best efforts fall short and you become lost, it is possible to cope with the situation:

- Attempt to obtain a "fix" of the aircraft's position using the aircraft electronic navigation systems. VOR triangulation or loran work well. In the event a pilot is unable to receive a usable navigation signal, he or she should consider a climb to a higher altitude where reception is improved.
- Attempt to determine the aircraft's location by contacting ATC for a radar fix or contacting a flight service station specialist for a DF steer.
- Attempt to determine the aircraft's position on a navigational chart working from the last known position using time and distance relationships.
- Constantly look for new visual clues. Because the pilot's visual perspective is constantly changing, new clues as to the aircraft's location will constantly appear if flight visibility is adequate. Pilots should remember that a city or a town will have a different visual perspective at different altitudes and under different meteorological conditions. In this case, there is often no substitute for experience.

EMERGENCY LANDINGS

There are primarily two nighttime emergency landings: precautionary and forced.

The precautionary landing is a premeditated landing that can be on or off an airport. This type of landing becomes necessary when it is not advisable to continue, although it might be possible.

The precautionary landing has less risk of injury and damage than a forced landing. The nocturnal aviator is allowed more time to select a suitable landing site, more and better landing site selection, and adequate time to plan the approach. The precautionary landing is one option that should not be overlooked. Many fatalities have resulted because this option was consciously dismissed. It is always best to make a precautionary landing rather than to allow a situation to develop into an immediate forced landing. No pilot wants to make a precautionary landing at night but it certainly beats the alternative of a forced landing in a dark flight environment.

Unfortunately, precautionary landings are not as common as they should be, probably because most pilots are not mentally prepared for such a piloting procedure. Consider a pilot's basic pilot training. Most pilots are conditioned to land at airports unless, of course, the powerplant fails. Under these circumstances it is easy to understand why so many pilots give up their life-saving option of the precautionary landing.

If a pilot is totally aware of the precautionary landing option, the probability of exercising that option increases if a future situation should make a precautionary landing necessary. Every pilot must weigh all of the variables and then exercise sound judgment. It is generally a superior decision to risk a precautionary landing than to continue to the point where one's options rapidly diminish and the remaining few options are quite unsavory.

One or several of the following situations might warrant a precautionary landing:

- Adverse weather
- Inadequate fuel
- Loss of fuel pressure
- An apparent serious loss of oil such as a visible oil leak
- Partial loss of engine power
- Gradual loss of electrical power
- Significant vibrations of the airframe and/or powerplant
- Any instrument indications of low oil pressure, or excessive cylinder head or oil temperatures
- Excessive pilot fatigue or any other ailment that could lead to pilot incapacitation
- When the pilot is lost, the aircraft is low on fuel, and assistance is not available
- Unexpectedly strong headwinds when the fuel supply is inadequate
- Any other condition or set of conditions that could worsen if the flight were to continue

The forced landing does not provide the degree of choice of the precautionary landing. The forced landing is as immediate as the aircraft's gliding time to touchdown when the aircraft cannot continue further flight. Forced landings occur generally as a result of, but are not limited to, engine failure.

Preparation before the emergency

The best time to prepare for an emergency landing is before an emergency occurs. There is a reason for constantly checking weather even on a clear night when there is a full moon and when a pilot has unrestricted visibility and can see "forever." As previously discussed, the reason for checking weather frequently for the general area (and at many of the local airports close to the route of flight) is to check for weather trends. Weather trends not only include the temperature-dew point spread, en-route altitude winds and obstructions to vision, for example, but also include surface winds. The more a pilot knows, the safer he or she will be.

A low touchdown speed is one of the most critical elements in the emergency landing process. Naturally, a final approach into the wind is the best option, if safely possible.

The preflight planning process is generally recognized as being one of the most important elements in the safety aspect of night flight. This is certainly true when considering the aspect of human factors limitations. When the pilot decides which possible landing sites should be marked on the navigational chart, human factors limitations should become a prime consideration. For example, selection of possible landing sites should be restricted to sites that are relatively flat. Because the amount of ambient and aircraft lighting might not provide adequate visual cues for discrimination of sloping terrain, necessary aircraft control movements to compensate for the sloping terrain might not be executed in an efficient and timely manner.

Preparation for landing

Recall the importance of considering a multitude of possible different landing sites during preflight planning when a pilot has more time to study the topography along the route of flight.

A pilot might have to make an off-airport landing despite considerable thought that went into plotting out a special nighttime course close to more airports at the expense of a few more miles and more time. The choices of optional landing sites are numerous and should all be carefully considered. The final decision often depends on the existing conditions at the time of the emergency and play a part in selection: nature of the emergency, available moonlight, meteorological conditions, aircraft altitude and lateral location with respect to possible landing sites, dimension and slope of the potential landing sites, possible obstructions, and the amount of excess airspeed that can be translated into glide distance or additional altitude (if any).

All of the aforementioned factors are very rarely compatible and a pilot will generally have to quickly evaluate each factor's possible effect on the outcome of the landing. Compromises must be made. Consequently, the best combination of the factors, hopefully, will permit some allowance for errors in technique and/or perception. The most logical example would be a pilot overestimating the aircraft's gliding range and attempting to glide over obstacles in the approach path. The laws of physics have demonstrated countless times that colliding with an obstacle at the conclusion of a ground roll is far better than colliding with an obstacle while in flight before reaching the ground. In such cases, it is best to plan an approach over an unlighted unobstructed area, for example, than a lighted obstructed area. It is for this reason that all night pilots, as discussed in chapter 7, should thoroughly study the topography and obstructions along the intended route of flight.

Finally, knowing exactly where the aircraft is positioned is of importance in allowing the pilot to accurately and quickly determine the best choice of landing site location.

Body restraints

One consideration that is too often overlooked in the forced landing equation is that of occupant restraint. The appropriate use of seat belts and shoulder harnesses is too often dismissed. But these appliances can significantly reduce the chances of severe bodily injury. Forceful bodily contact with the interior of the aircraft's structure is dependent upon the seat and body security; seats must be securely fastened to the floor and the occupants securely fastened to a seat.

It is important that the aircraft occupants decelerate at the same rate as the aircraft cabin. If they do not, they will not benefit from the relative immobility provided by the restraining devices and will encounter a violent stop in the form of a second collision. If a seat belt is slack upon impact, the deceleration forces that the body will experience will actually be greater than those forces affecting the aircraft structure. The body will continue to move (after the aircraft has come to rest) until no slack in the seat belt remains. The improperly adjusted seat belt will cause the body to encounter more force than a properly adjusted seat belt; therefore, it is best to fasten all body restraints as tightly as possible. If an occupant has a choice of using a seat belt, shoulder harness, or both, he or she should, naturally, employ both restraints.

Aircraft configuration

There is no general hard-and-fast rule regarding the landing gear position at touchdown. Recommendations may be found in the aircraft operating handbook. Forced landings in tricycle gear aircraft have a lower probability of resulting in injuries or fatalities with the landing gear locked in the down position. This fact must be weighed against other considerations for the particular aircraft being flown. For example, if the gear collapsed, could it rupture a fuel tank? Every pilot of a low-wing aircraft should consider the possible rupturing of wing fuel tanks and subsequent post-impact fire.

Flaps reduce the aircraft stall speed and improve maneuverability at slow speeds but the timing in the use of flaps and the degree to which they are extended at night is critical. When time and circumstances permit, the use of flaps can be of great advantage to the conclusion of a safe forced landing. A night pilot must not forget that the use of flaps will also increase the drag and decrease the aircraft gliding distance. Premature use of flaps and the resulting loss of altitude can contribute to a serious accident.

If an airplane with a dead engine has a controllable-pitch propeller, the propeller should be set to the high-pitch, low-speed position for less drag. Another consideration for a very experienced and proficient pilot, after the determination has been made that the engine cannot be restarted, is to stop the propeller from windmilling by reducing the airspeed until the propeller stops. A windmilling propeller creates unnecessary drag, wasting valuable kinetic energy, which could be converted into additional gliding time and distance. Caution should be exercised because the required reduction in airspeed would probably place most aircraft very close to the stalling speed. The procedure should not be attempted by all pilots and then only if ambient lighting and altitude conditions allow such a procedure; the pilot must be certain that the extra altitude and/or distance gained is worth the risk.

The aircraft should be trimmed for the glide speed that is appropriate for the configuration of the aircraft. Proper application of trim can be quite beneficial in reducing the pilot's workload in a forced landing situation.

Pilot vision

When the pilot has completed troubleshooting procedures, communications procedures, and initial navigation procedures, it is then wise to reduce the amount of cockpit illumination as much as reasonably possible to allow the eyes to further adapt to the outside lighting. This procedure is consistent with one basic fact; the lower the level of illumination inside the aircraft, the better will be detail detection and recognition outside the aircraft. If the aircraft is unpressurized and is at an altitude of 5,000 feet above sea level or higher, the use of oxygen can greatly enhance the pilot's vision. Additionally, even if the aircraft is below 5,000 feet, the pilot might still benefit from the use of oxygen. Caution should be exercised in the use of oxygen in the event the pilot is hyperventilating as a result of the emergency.

Landing lights should be turned on in sufficient time to illuminate the terrain or obstacles along the flight path. If electrical energy conservation is an integral factor in the emergency landing procedure, it is best to save the battery's stored energy until the aircraft is, perhaps, within 200 feet of the terrain. Once the landing lights are activated, the pilot must make a rapid assessment of the landing site and maneuver around the larger, solid obstructions. It is important that the pilot not become visually fixated on one area, but should scan the frontal field of view.

Shutdown procedures

It is best to know the aircraft owner's manuals recommended procedures for a forced landing shutdown. Generally, the aircraft's electrical system and fuel system should be completely shutdown after a final determination that the aircraft cannot sustain flight and the shutdown is not premature. Remember, the lowering of flaps and the extension of landing gear cannot be overlooked. By deactivating the electrical system and restricting fuel flow, the pilot is lowering the probability of a post-crash fire. Certain pilots also have one of the aircraft doors cracked open to ensure a possible exit.

If time permits, the aircraft checklist should always be used during the shutdown procedure.

Approach to a forced landing

The approach to a forced landing is often the final contributing factor to success or failure of the landing. Although very difficult during some nighttime emergencies, the aircraft's attitude, airspeed, and sink rate should be carefully monitored.

An excessive nose-low pitch attitude can lead to the aircraft nose impacting the ground first, causing severe deceleration. Ideally, the aircraft should be in horizontal alignment with the ground at touchdown to effectively absorb the impact of the landing. The vertical velocity component should be almost zero. Conversely, as all pilots know, an extreme nose-up attitude can cause a stall/spin accident. Steep bank angles should also be avoided because they increase the stalling speed and probability of a wingtip strike.

A flat pancake landing at a high rate of descent can cause injury without causing damage to the cabin structure, especially with gear-up landings in low wing airplanes. Because such a landing is not cushioned by structural deformation and the fact that the human body has limited tolerance to vertical g loading, pancake landings have led to serious spinal injuries and even death. When the aircraft is close to the ground, the pilot should transition to minimum sink speed so that the deceleration that occurs is in the forward direction.

Two of the most critical variables in the severity of the deceleration process are ground speed and stopping distance. Pilots should note that the relationship of speed and energy is not linear. If, for example, the speed is doubled, the destructive kinetic energy is quadrupled. Even a seemingly small change in ground speed at touchdown can seriously affect the outcome of the forced landing. Now it should be easier to understand why downwind landings can be deadly. The touchdown during a forced landing should be made at the lowest possible controllable speed and a pilot should employ the flaps, if possible.

Most pilots faced with a forced landing will look for the largest available landing area. This strategy is especially wise considering the lack of visual cues during periods of darkness; however, most pilots are surprised upon discovering just how little stopping distance is required when the speed is dissipated uniformly.

TABLE 12-1 presents calculated time (seconds) and distance (feet) to stop for three different g levels and four ground speeds (mph). It should be noted that these values are based on an ideal deceleration where the deceleration forces are displaced evenly over the stopping distance. From TABLE 12-1, it can be determined that the stopping distance for an aircraft decelerating at 9 g's with a ground speed at 120 miles per hour

Table 12-1. Deceleration computations.

| Ground Speed (MPH) | Deceleration (g's) | | | | | |
| | 3 g's | | 6 g's | | 9 g's | |
	Time to stop (Seconds)	Distance to stop (Feet)	Time to stop (Seconds)	Distance to stop (Feet)	Time to stop (Seconds)	Distance to stop (Feet)
60	.92	40.33	.46	20.17	.31	13.44
80	1.22	71.70	.61	35.85	.41	23.90
100	1.53	112.04	.76	56.02	.51	37.35
120	1.83	161.33	.92	80.67	.61	53.78

is fewer than 54 feet. The same aircraft decelerating at 3 g's would stop in approximately 161 feet. Naturally, most general aviation aircraft will touch down at speeds fewer than 120 miles per hour and consequently require a much shorter stopping distance. Pilots should be aware of the relationship between ground speed and stopping distance; doubling the ground speed quadruples the stopping distance. Proper piloting technique cannot be overemphasized in the forced landing procedure. Precise execution of control movements is essential to the best possible outcome of a forced landing.

The average general aviation aircraft cabin is able to withstand at least nine times the acceleration of gravity (9 g's) in the forward direction.

Energy dissipation

The main goal of any pilot when executing a forced landing is for all occupants of the aircraft to be able to walk away without injuries, which happens in a large percentage of all cases. If luck holds out, the landing site will be long, smooth and free of any obstructions; however, there is another scenario where the landing site is not smooth terrain and might be full of potholes and covered with brush, rocks, and trees. Aviation accident investigation has shown that the amount of crushable structure between the aircraft occupants and the principal point of impact reflects directly on the magnitude of the transmitted crash forces and, as a result, occupant survivability.

When a pilot is faced with making a forced landing on inhospitable terrain where extensive aircraft damage is a possibility, the pilot must try to keep the cockpit and cabin area intact by sacrificing dispensable aircraft structure to absorb the impact forces upon terrain contact. During darkened conditions it would be very difficult to point the aircraft between two trees and let the two wings be torn away during the ground roll, although this procedure would be an ideal way to dissipate energy in many instances. But, if the aircraft's landing gear and flaps are able to be lowered, the flaps and gear will absorb a significant amount of energy.

Crushing metal is not the only means to absorb energy. Cultivated fields, dense crops, small trees, and brush are extremely effective in quickly decelerating an aircraft to a full stop with the aircraft often only sustaining minor damage. If a pilot can choose the off-airport terrain for a landing, the cultivated field with dense crops should be considered.

OTHER POSSIBLE EMERGENCIES

Communicate with the ground, giving them as much of the mayday message on the first transmission as possible. The search and rescue phase of assistance will be much better planned if location, altitude, and direction are given.

Climb, if possible, for improved communications, and better radar and direction finding detection.

The wise night pilot will develop a mind set that something is going to go wrong and preparations should be made for the worst. Plan ahead.

13
Flight and ground instruction

THIS CHAPTER EXAMINES INSTRUCTIONAL TECHNIQUES REGARDING NIGHT flight and ground instruction, including simulators, and how the ubiquitous human factor is related to each particular issue. This is particularly important because certain areas related to flying at night are commonly overlooked during the training stage; also, how a pilot is instructed can determine how safely that pilot flies for the rest of his or her flying career; and, a pilot's skills must be sharper for night flight.

GROUND INSTRUCTION

From the longer perspective of a pilot's entire nocturnal aviation career, ground instruction is just as important, if not more important, than learning the mechanics of aileron, elevator, rudder, and throttle manipulation in flight. Yet ground instruction is often considered a necessary evil that should be "gotten out of the way" before climbing into the cockpit. This mind-set is extremely dangerous. Factors relating to night flying should be learned first on the ground and only then in the air. The consummate night pilot possesses a thorough knowledge of the physiological and psychological considerations that have been presented throughout this book.

Too often, pilots launch their airplanes off into the black night sky unaware of many of their personal limitations and the resulting danger due to their lack of knowledge. There is good cause for all pilots to receive thorough ground instruction relating to night flight. It is only natural for an individual to assume that certain basic procedures can be accomplished in the same manner during the night as during the day. Unfortunately, this belief is incorrect. Student and private pilots are not the only pilots that fall prey to these incorrect assumptions. A significant percentage of very experienced pilots are not totally aware of their nighttime limitations and as a result should take the time to receive additional ground training pertaining to the latest in nighttime human factors research as it applies to them.

Learning when not to go

Perhaps, one of the most overlooked considerations in the nighttime instructional process is that of teaching a pilot when not to attempt a flight at night. For decades, the aviation community has talked about safety; however, frequently even the most basic approach in the instructional process centers on the achievement of a singular goal, flying from point A to point B. Of course, every pilot needs to know the mechanics of how to get there, but more instructional emphasis should be placed on limitations, thereby reducing night accident statistics.

The preflight personal night flight checklist presented in chapter 3 should be completed prior to every night flight regardless of whether or not a flight plan is filed. This checklist should help alert the night pilot to a number of personal symptoms to look for that could disqualify him or her from making a safe flight.

A flight instructor should verify the accuracy of each student's personal night flight checklist responses prior to an anticipated night flight by the pilot. If the instructor notices that a checklist item has uncovered a potential problem (lapse of attention, excessive anger or self-confidence, distractibility) in the student pilot, the instructor should point it out immediately so the student can exercise the best judgment possible and perhaps reschedule the flight. The student can then develop from this experience in a positive manner and exercise sound judgment in the future by electing not to fly when conditions are unsafe.

Blindfold test (cockpit familiarization)

Every nocturnal aviator should master the blindfold test. When all of the special equipment has been stowed in the cockpit and other appropriate places, the nocturnal aviator should then study the layout of the cockpit again. A blindfold should then be donned. By practicing the blindfold test the pilot is assured of knowing the location of every appropriate item in the cockpit. An instructor or another qualified pilot should call out each appropriate instrument panel gauge and other cockpit knobs, switches, levers, circuit breakers, fuse holders, fuel control levers, manual gear extension assemblies, and special equipment such as fire extinguishers, and oxygen systems. The pilot should be able to quickly and consistently locate every item.

Experienced pilots have been surprised when challenged by this test. Consequently, the blindfold test is not only for the student, but it is for every pilot who flies during periods of darkness. To be able to master this test requires really knowing the aircraft, its support systems, and its special equipment. This training not only prepares the pilot for an emergency situation, but also increases basic proficiency because it is more difficult to see controls, switches, levers and knobs at night.

Aircraft electrical system

An intricate part of the regimen of the ground instruction in preparing a pilot for night flying is teaching the pilot the nuances of the aircraft electrical system. Because night flight lacks the abundance of daytime visual cues, more emphasis must naturally be placed on internal cockpit navigational and aircraft lighting sources making the aircraft electrical system even more important.

All pilots should take the necessary time to learn the aircraft electrical system thoroughly. Spending an evening in the easy chair studying the documentation of the electrical system is good insurance for the proper operation of the aircraft electrical system. It can save a pilot a nightmare of a flying experience by preventing, for example, overloading the airplane electrical system. Also, just spending part of an easy Saturday afternoon with your favorite mechanic can be an enlightening experience regarding a checkout of the aircraft electrical system or contending with a potential electrical system emergency.

During the course of the ground instruction curriculum, all pilots should learn, as a minimum, the following about their particular aircraft electrical system:

- Potential causes of electrical failure at night: voltage regulator, ammeter, overvoltage, excessive charging, fuses, and circuit breakers.

- Early signs of impending failure. Discuss the gauge readings of instruments such as the ammeter.

- Growing symptoms of failure. Discuss such clues to system malfunction as dimming of navigation, cockpit, and landing lighting; intermittent VOR signal reception (off-flag, poor or no voice transmissions).

- How to best prepare for an impending electrical failure. Discuss the use of a portable self-contained navcom and how to reduce the amount of electrical load.

- What to do in the event of electrical failure. Discuss conserving power, turning off every nonessential source of electrical load, resetting circuit breakers, replacing fuses, and which pieces of equipment place the highest loads on the electrical system.

- In the event of a failure of the electrical system where the only remaining source of electrical energy is the battery, every pilot should know exactly how much power (in minutes) remains for the load produced when all of the airplane equipment is turned on and how much power remains for the load produced when the airplane's minimum equipment is turned on.

- The amount of electrical load placed on the system during low-rpm taxi operations.

- Any other electrical system peculiarities particular to their aircraft.

FLIGHT SIMULATORS

While there are a variety of flight training aids available to provide the new pilot with the intellectual background needed to understand flight procedures and events, the flight training simulator can provide the sight and feel of many flight characteristics. It has been the modern flight simulator that has perhaps had the greatest impact of any training device on improving flight safety partly because it has been designed to present specific aircraft information processing, decision- making, flight control, and skill development tasks, and permits the instructor to properly evaluate the pilot's skills and judgment.

Equipped with special highly realistic outside scene generation and other high-fidelity sensory stimulation capabilities (sounds of rain and hail, thunder with lightning flashes, turbulence and violent wind effects), the modern flight training simulator provides a safe, relatively low-cost alternative to actual flight; however, nighttime flight is far more than simple darkness. Its effects on human behavior are vast and subtle.

Although there is good justification for motion-based flight simulators for a wide array of uses (instrument flying, aircraft checkouts, crew coordination), it can become extremely beneficial in the instruction of night flight procedures and maneuvers; however, there is one caveat that must be considered: Flight simulators have disadvantages as well as advantages. Additionally, motion simulators must be employed in a manner that best simulates and is consistent with the expected mission of the pilot.

The proper simulator is a remarkable training tool. Benefits are numerous and modern simulators permit seemingly unlimited possibilities for training:

- A student can be allowed to fly in his or her worst physiological condition without affecting safety.

- Practice of very difficult or low-probability-of-occurrence events such as wind shear can be conducted safely and the entire event may be replayed over and over to permit a systematic analysis of what went wrong and what was done correctly.

- The simulator may be scheduled for almost 24 hours a day, regardless of weather.

- When equipped with the proper subsystems, the simulator can be used for part- and full-task training, such as operation of a radio navigation system apart from flight versus flying a cross-country mission.

Potential disadvantages and limitations of flight training simulators should be noted:

- The simulator is not capable of simulating different cabin altitudes and thereby creating an environment where a pilot's mental and physical processes are degraded. This is an especially noteworthy consideration because the human eye, as discussed in chapter 4, is the first tissue of the body to experience very pronounced decrements in efficiency due to lack of oxygen.

- Many simulators are not well designed in terms of motion transport delays so that what the trainee feels in the seat of the pants might not correspond with what is seen out the windows or correspond with what would be experienced in the actual airplane.

- Due to the high cost of the simulated visual presentations, some simulators do not have the visual simulation feature. Flight training in such simulators is limited to IFR conditions and precludes the final approach and landing phases where the pilot must look outside the cockpit for ground cues.

- In some instances a generic simulator is programmed to fly like a particular aircraft model even though the controls and displays are different. Negative transfer of training might occur when the pilot finally flies the actual aircraft. It is possible that skills that have been well-learned in the simulator may be completely carried over to the aircraft. This can lead to distraction, confusion, and even disorientation at night as the pilot tries to sort out why things seem different.

Another issue that must be emphasized is that flying during daylight hours or nighttime hours is no different in terms of aileron, elevator and rudder movement, throttle control or fuel management. Night flying is significantly different in regard to the myriad of human factors involved. Simply climbing into a flight training simulator at noon, turning off all of the lights, and turning on the night scene generator, if there is one, will not adequately prepare the enthusiastic pilot to fly with optimum proficiency at night. It will at best introduce him or her to flying a darkened night simulator during the daytime when the body's physiological capabilities are at their best. It can't produce such effects as body fatigue and sensory tiredness experienced late at night; it can't fully re-create the sometimes heavy workload that has preceded reaching the point of no return during an actual night flight. Ground and flight instruction should be carefully reconsidered from the standpoint of the pilot's physiological, psychological, and mental state as it exists when the full effects of the day have taken their toll.

Special considerations must be followed if optimum results are to be obtained through the use of a flight training simulator:

- The simulator must be used during those periods of time when a pilot would be piloting his or her aircraft at night and not just when it is convenient to do so during daylight hours. This enables the pilot to experience some of the psychological and physiological complications that can be encountered during a late night or early morning flight.

- The simulator training sessions should be lengthy enough for the student to become aware of physical and mental impairment that is common during a prolonged flight.

- The student should train in a simulator late at night or very early in the morning for several hours without resting before the session. Conversely, the student should also train following adequate rest prior to the session. This allows the student to better understand how rest can play such a crucial role in refreshing the pilot's mental, psychological, and physiological systems. A pilot is better able to develop safe judgment regarding go-no-go decision making.

- The simulator instructor must be adequately rested and regularly refreshed at all times. It is necessary that the instructor's senses are sharp and that his or her state of arousal and motivation are high. The quality of the instruction is largely dependent upon the instructor's physical and mental capabilities during the simulator session and after the session during the review and evaluation. It is imperative that the instructor is fit for his assignment so the student can be properly briefed as to the subtleties of the simulator session. The student can't gain maximum benefit if he or she has not been apprised of all of the performance deficiencies that were encountered, why they were encountered, and how to improve future performance. Pilot judgment can only be improved through a variety of realistic experiences and resulting correct interpretations of those experiences.

- The implementation of the usual stressors encountered at night should be regularly and constantly employed during the simulator session. Training during different times of the 24-hour period (late night versus early morning) not only provides the pilot with valuable practice of nighttime procedures, but also allows the pilot the opportunity of experiencing marked changes in his or her aeronautical performance in a variety of different physical conditions like fatigue and tiredness, flash blindness, disorientation and vertigo, muscular cramping, and others.

- Ideally, the instructor should have the background necessary to fully relate the consequences of fatigue based upon personal experience, which increases the awareness of the student.

- Worst case scenarios can be added at the conclusion of each simulator session when the student is fatigued and is feeling the greatest stress. For example, moderate to severe wind shear could be presented when least expected during a takeoff or landing; turbulence could be induced shortly after takeoff during a turn to induce vertigo.

FLIGHT INSTRUCTION

If there was ever a reason for obtaining an instrument rating and flying an instrument equipped aircraft, even if you never intend to fly in instrument conditions, night flying is that reason. During certain lunar and VFR conditions where a pilot is flying over mountainous areas, sparsely populated areas, open desert areas, or vast bodies of water, a VFR pilot essentially is flying without an outside horizon visual reference. Also, when a pilot flies off an airport that is located in an area with no lighting, such as a desert, that pilot is launching into a flight environment that requires instrument proficiency.

Remember that it is also so very easy to fly into clouds and weather at night completely unaware until the aircraft is actually within the clouds or weather conditions. The proficiency required for an instrument rating serves to heighten a pilot's awareness of flight conditions when there are fewer external visual cues.

The necessary flight instruction to prepare a pilot for night flight, ideally, incorporates most of the principles, procedures and maneuvers contained in the instrument rating curriculum; however, night flight instruction should not end with a student acquiring the skill and knowledge of a competent instrument pilot. Indeed, having an instrument rating doesn't guarantee safety at night. Additional information relative to such areas as how to cope most effectively with nighttime drowsiness, how to correctly visually scan the nighttime skies for other aircraft, how to cope with disorienting visual illusions and in-flight emergencies, and other subjects must be learned and committed to memory whenever possible.

Pilots anxious to try their wings during hours of darkness seem to have many of the same basic problems as students in other phases of flight training. The problems so often encountered involve the fundamentals of flying. Straight and level flight, climbs, turns, and descents all need to be mastered with a reasonable degree of precision before any pilot can fly with any degree of proficiency. A pilot might have the basics developed adequately for daytime flying but can have difficulty at night if not properly trained. The key to this problem is integrated flight instruction. That is, integrating the outside visual references with the inside instrument indications for the pilot to execute the proper control responses.

Some instructors take their students out during the daylight hours in preparation for their first hour of nighttime flight instruction. The reason is simple and quite logical. It is much easier and more effective for a student to observe the outside visual references with the exact corresponding instrument indications during daylight conditions and make mental or written notes. He or she is then better equipped to relate to the nighttime flight environment during the first nighttime instructional flight. Consider how many daytime VFR pilots rotate the aircraft to a takeoff/climb attitude or initiate a standard descent without being totally cognizant of the exact corresponding indications on the cockpit instruments.

It is certainly much easier for the night pilot to initiate a departure climb, for example, if he or she knows the exact amount of pitch attitude that should be displayed in the attitude indicator while establishing the aircraft pitch attitude rather than hunting for the correct pitch attitude. The application of proper power, pitch, and trim relationships are all very important to night flying procedures. This extra margin of awareness that instrument proficiency provides cannot be underestimated.

Nighttime flying is a fusion of mental agility, skill and judgment. In order for any airplane to maintain the proper flight path, a series of control corrections must be constantly initiated. As night flying proficiency improves, more frequent but smaller control movements will be made; the pilot will be able to rapidly receive and correctly interpret a large amount of flight information soon enough to initiate the desired control deflections in a timely manner.

This proficiency is not generally difficult to acquire. At night, the pilot must relearn to coordinate outside visual cues with instrument information and recognize how and when to change the balance between the two in the time allocated to viewing and interpreting outside visual references and cockpit instrument indications.

Because a high percentage of nighttime descents, such as an instrument approach procedure descent, seem to be an approximate 3-degree descent angle, and because nighttime visual approaches allow pilots to experience a myriad of visual illusions, it is most helpful for the new nocturnal aviator to know the appropriate aircraft configuration and required rate of descent to achieve a proper descent. This is another good reason for obtaining an instrument rating. The correct procedure is to maintain a constant pitch attitude and constant airspeed to achieve a stabilized rate of descent. A handy rule of thumb determines the approximate rate of descent to maintain a 3-degree approach slope angle: five times the ground speed (in knots) equals the approximate rate of descent (in feet per minute). A ground speed of 105 knots would require an approximate rate of descent of 525 feet per minute ($5 \times 105 = 525$). TABLE 13-1 indicates that this formula will provide an answer that is reasonably close to the exact rate of descent.

Table 13-1. Rate of descent table (ft. per min.).

Angle of descent (Degrees and tenths)	Ground speed (Knots)								
	30	45	60	75	90	105	120	135	150
2.5	130	200	265	330	395	465	530	595	665
3.0	160	240	320	395	480	555	635	715	795
3.5	185	280	370	465	555	650	740	835	925
4.0	210	315	425	530	635	740	845	955	1060
4.5	240	355	475	595	715	835	955	1075	1190

Precise execution of the basics is of paramount importance in precise nighttime piloting. Airspeed control is the single most important element in executing a superior landing. But precise airspeed control begins with a stabilized approach. And a stabilized approach requires a constant rate of descent, which is dependent on maintaining constant pitch attitude and airspeed. In short, the basics are interrelated.

One of the chronic problems that pilots often encounter at night is excessive airspeed during the approach and landing phases of flight. Airspeed control is so critical to landing safely at night because the landing roll-out distance ratio increases by the square of the ratio of the actual touchdown speed divided by the normal touchdown speed, assuming all other factors remain constant. The following example demonstrates this relationship:

D = landing roll-out distance
V_t = actual touchdown speed
V_n = normal touchdown speed

$D = (V_t/V_n)(V_t/V_n)$
70 knots = actual touchdown speed
60 knots = normal touchdown speed
$D = (70/60)(70/60) = 1.36$

Notice that if all other factors regarding the landing remain constant, the landing distance will increase by 36 percent. Such an increase in landing distance sometimes warrants the execution of a go-around.

Wind drift correction

Another problem that pilots often experience is wind drift. Fewer visual cues at night make it more difficult to judge the amount of wind drift and the corresponding amount of required wind drift correction (*crab angle*). It is almost instinctive for an experienced pilot to automatically institute the amount of drift correction during the day due to the abundance of visual cues available; however, this is not the case while flying in a dark flight environment and can become a particularly difficult situation while on final approach in a black hole environment or during a dark terrain takeoff.

What is the answer? Two simple steps involve memorization of some numbers and simple multiplication.

Step 1. Determine the crosswind correction component. The pilot must be aware of the crosswind component and be able to determine the size of crosswind correction needed to compensate for its effect (TABLE 13-2). After memorizing only five (sine) numbers, in the light areas of the table, a pilot can quickly determine a crosswind component by simply multiplying the sine of the appropriate crosswind angle times the wind speed. The sines for the angles in the shaded areas need not be memo-

Table 13-2. Crosswind component correction table.

Angle	0°	10°	20°	30°	40°
Sine	.0000	.1736	.3420	.5000	.6428

Angle	50°	60°	70°	80°	90°
Sine	.7660	.8660	.9397	.9848	1.000

rized because the sine of 10 degrees, for example, is approximately 0; sines for angles greater than 60 degrees are approximately 1. It is best to round off the sine of 20 degrees to 0.342, or approximately 1/3. Correspondingly, the sine of 50 degrees is 0.766 or approximately 3/4.

Here is an example to illustrate step 1: Runway 32 is in use, wind is from 350 degrees at 28 knots, crosswind angle is 30 degrees:

$$350 - 320 = 30$$

From the chart, note that the sine of 30 degrees is 0.5. The crosswind component of 14 knots is obtained by multiplying the sine (0.5) times the wind speed (28).

Step 2. Determine the crosswind correction angle. When the crosswind component is derived, a pilot can determine if the aircraft maximum crosswind component would be exceeded and, if it is not exceeded, he or she can also determine how much crosswind correction angle should be initiated.

Only one additional step is required to determine the amount of crosswind correction angle. The pilot should commit to memory the six crosswind component wind speeds (knots) and corresponding crosswind component angles shown in Table 13-3. But only one horizontal row of numbers need be memorized, namely the row corresponding to the approach speed (knots) for the aircraft that you fly. This process might seem a little complicated at first; however, when a pilot has memorized these values, he or she can make a reasonable estimate of the crosswind correction angle.

Recall that the crosswind component in step 1 is 14 knots and the aircraft approach speed is 80 knots; a pilot can estimate that the crosswind crab angle should be approximately 10 degrees, slightly less than the 11 degrees shown in TABLE 13-3. Is this too much mental work? Probably not, especially when a pilot has little or no visual information available as to the amount of wind drift, but is able to mathematically determine the approximate amount of crab angle necessary to maintain the proper track over the featureless, dark ground. This simple two-step process makes the pilot's job much easier and the safety factor is enhanced. Remember that these calculations may be applied to takeoffs (if there is sufficient time to make the mental calculation), as well as during landings.

Table 13-3. Crosswind correction angle table.

Approach speed (Knots)	Crosswind component (Knots)					
	7	10	15	20	25	30
40	10°	14°	22°	30°	39°	49°
50	8°	12°	17°	24°	30°	37°
60	7°	10°	14°	19°	25°	30°
70	6°	8°	12°	17°	21°	25°
80	5°	7°	11°	14°	18°	22°
90	4°	6°	10°	13°	16°	19°
100	4°	6°	9°	12°	14°	17°
110	4°	5°	8°	10°	13°	16°
120	3°	5°	7°	10°	12°	14°
130	3°	4°	7°	9°	11°	13°

Even if the pilot does not memorize the exact crosswind correction angle for each crosswind component, he or she should be aware of the range of crosswind correction angles for the range of crosswind components displayed in the table for the aircraft approach speed; hence, his or her extent of judgment concerning crab angle estimation is broadened.

Cockpit management procedures

Not only must the pilot become proficient with all applicable night flight maneuvers, but also become very familiar with the appropriate cockpit management procedures for the particular aircraft being flown. Efficient cockpit management at night is much more important than during the day. If an emergency, such as poor weather or partial engine power loss, develops during the en route phase of a cross-country flight (land at the closest airport), the pilot has no extra time to fumble around in the cockpit to look for a sectional map to determine the next course of action.

Because many aircraft that are still flown regularly are decades old, the complicated but important chore of cockpit management becomes more complex. The bridge between pilot and an old aircraft is considerably lengthened at night because the aircraft was designed and built when even the best engineers were unaware of human factors. Consequently, it is the incumbent duty of every pilot to determine which procedures best suit the pilot, the intended flight and the type of aircraft being flown.

Cockpits are rarely similar; the cockpit standard for the industry has become one of nonstandardization. Significant thought should be placed on the development of cockpit management procedures that allow for the inadequacies of the cockpit and pilot limitations as much as possible (EN 13-1).

PROCEDURES AND MANEUVERS

Beyond basic maneuvers required for the instrument rating checkride, additional maneuvers should be practiced (EN 13-2):

- Takeoffs and landings at night with and without the aid of aircraft landing lights.

- Landing at night with and without flaps.

- Takeoffs and landings at night with the aircraft at the lowest possible weight and at full gross weight.

- Takeoffs and landings at night with the use of several different approach lighting aids at several approach lighting intensities (include pilot-controlled lighting systems).

- Practicing as many variations of the black hole approach as possible.

- Practicing the black environment takeoff procedure with special emphasis on scanning the cockpit instrument panel upon leaving the ground until an altitude of 400 feet (or higher) is attained.

- Flying under a variety of nighttime illumination and meteorological conditions: full moon, partial moon, and no moon; ground fog, clear and clouded skies; precipitation.

- Emergency landing gear extension procedures with and without cockpit lighting.

- Engine failure procedures (discussed in chapter 12).

- Setting up drift corrections during the landing and takeoff phases of flight.

- Practicing in turbulent conditions because turbulence can contribute to vertigo in a darkened flight environment.

- Fly the aircraft and practice normal cockpit duties such as writing on a kneeboard and using the communications equipment without using any of the standard cockpit or instrument lighting, supplemented only by a flashlight and other standby lighting aids as the only source of cockpit illumination.

- Replacing fuses and resetting circuit breakers without the aid of the normal cockpit lighting.

- Practice maximum glide speed and transition to the slowest speed with full flap extension that yields the slowest sink rate in anticipation of a forced landing.

- Practice DF steer approaches for various airports under a variety of lighting conditions.

- Practice crosswind takeoffs and landings.

- Proper application of instrument and cockpit lighting during typical operations and conditions: takeoff, landing, electrical storms, and en route flight.

- Practice any other relevant nighttime emergency procedure applicable to the type of aircraft being flown. Proper habit patterns developed during training often make the difference during an actual emergency situation.

- It might be necessary to practice additional maneuvers and procedures due to the particular type of piloting activity anticipated and/or aircraft being flown.

Flight practice builds valuable piloting skills so that flying becomes almost second nature. It is this second nature that allows the night pilot to keep the remaining 80 percent or so of skill level in reserve for when it is needed. The inexperienced pilot might tend to develop a myopic fixation on one instrument at night, staring at the heading indicator or vertical velocity indicator while neglecting the other information obtained from the other flight and aircraft system instruments. Proper training leads eventually to broadened situational awareness, reduced information overload, and an increased capability to handle more cockpit tasks and in-flight emergencies.

HUMAN FACTORS RECONSIDERED

Recall from part I that the human body has become primarily adapted for daytime activity and as a result the pilot is not as well equipped for flying during the night as during the day. Consequently, preparing a pilot for night flight is not as quickly accomplished as many would initially assume.

The following human factor considerations are some of the general areas that must be reviewed carefully prior to nighttime flight instruction.

Night vision

Neither the quantity nor the quality of visual cues at night can compare to those found during the day. Also as previously discussed, without sufficient rest, the body's performance is markedly different during the night. Naturally, the first step in the transition from daytime flight to nighttime flight is the reestablishment of pilot and aircraft and outside visual relationships. As simple as it might seem, in the essential promotion of safety, it becomes necessary for every pilot to become reacquainted with outside visual cues that, in many instances, can appear quite different during periods of darkness in a variety of different meteorological conditions. Additionally, a new set of visual cues must also be acquired to enhance piloting performance.

Head movement

With or without the eyes open, the night pilot can become dizzy and disoriented by certain kinds of head motions. This is particularly true if the aircraft is in a turn where side forces are acting on the middle ear's balance organ. Pilots should not turn their heads quickly or repeatedly and, especially, should not roll their heads from side to side (onto the shoulders) more than once or twice at a time. Exercises like neck muscle stretching should be done only during straight and level flight with the airplane under stabilized control.

Circadian rhythms

Remember that the human body possesses an internal clock that regulates many physiological systems; this clock can be desynchronized by crossing time zones rapidly, nonnatural shift in the light-dark cycle in the visual environment or air temperature, and by other influences. It is vitally important to adopt a regular sleep-wake cycle and to get enough sleep each day.

Arousal and alertness

Humans are more mentally and physically alert during certain hours of the day than during others. Each pilot should find out when he or she is most (and least) alert and also what is effective in maintaining arousal level. Also, human performance will tend to be lower at very low and very high levels of arousal and higher at moderate levels of arousal; however, arousal does not necessarily change slowly or continuously, but can jump from an almost lethargic semisleep state to near panic during the early stages of an in-flight emergency. The associated pilot performance can go from bad to worse as well.

Stress and stressors

Stressors produce stress in the body and a low to moderate amount of stress is to be desired because it helps keep the pilot awake and also motivate him or her to some degree. Overt and covert stressors are present when flying at night and the wise pilot will try to discover what they are. Likewise, the wise pilot will want to discover his or her own stress responses under different situations. This is an excellent use of high fidelity training simulators that present very real flying conditions. Performance tends

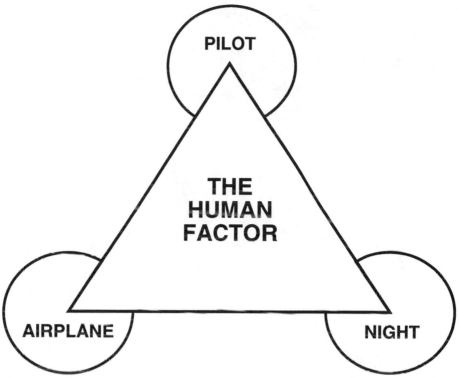

Fig. 13-1. *Connecting pilot, aircraft and night environment.*

to degrade during periods of very low and very high stress and workload; performance tends to improve at moderate levels of stress.

Future generations of aircraft will incorporate the latest in human factors research to aid the pilot for night flying. Until then, all pilots must be educated adequately to bridge the gap between their own human limitations and their aircraft limitations to meet the challenges of the nighttime flight environment.

It is necessary at this point to return to the three elements of FIG. 1-1 that are integrated by the ubiquitous human factor. Many of the complex physiological, psychological, and intellectual factors in this book form the basis for human performance and prove that they are clearly linked to each other (FIG. 13-1). Better awareness of and proper application of the many intricate dimensions of the human factor make the links possible.

Appendix

Federal Aviation Regulations

THE FOLLOWING FEDERAL AVIATION REGULATIONS (FARS) ARE SIGNIFICANT to the night aviator. Most of the selected regulations are important to the general aviation pilot flying fixed-wing aircraft and operating under Part 91; other regulations concern all pilots. Not all regulations applicable to night flight are included in this appendix; for example, flight operations relating to Part 135 and 141 have been omitted.

Certain regulations have been edited for the purpose of concisely identifying sections of those regulations that apply to nighttime operations.

Pilots should refer to a complete and current set of FARs when necessary due to the periodic regulatory changes and because selected night flight operations are different for general aviation than air carrier operations.

PART 1 DEFINITIONS AND ABBREVIATIONS

1.1 General definitions

"Night" means the time between the end of evening civil twilight and the beginning of morning civil twilight, as published in the American Air Almanac, converted to local time.

PART 61 CERTIFICATION: PILOTS AND FLIGHT INSTRUCTORS
SUBPART A—GENERAL

61.57 Recent flight experience: Pilot in command

(d) Night Experience. No person may act as pilot in command of an aircraft carrying passengers during the period beginning 1 hour after sunset and ending 1 hour before sunrise (as published in the American Air Almanac) unless, within the preceding 90 days, he has made at least three takeoffs and three landings to a full stop during that period in the category and class of aircraft to be used. This paragraph does not apply to operations requiring an airline transport pilot certificate.

61.89 General limitations

(a) A student pilot may not act as pilot in command of an aircraft—

(1) That is carrying a passenger;

(2) That is carrying property for compensation or hire;

(3) For compensation or hire;

(4) In furtherance of a business;

(5) On an international flight, except that a student pilot may make solo training flights from Haines, Gustavus, or Juneau, Alaska, to White Horse, Yukon, Canada, and return, over the province of British Columbia;

(6) With a flight or surface visibility of less than 3 statute miles during daylight hours or 5 statute miles at night;

(7) When the flight cannot be made with visual reference to the surface; or

(8) In a manner contrary to any limitations placed in the pilot's logbook by the instructor.

61.93 Cross-country flight requirements (for student and recreational pilots seeking private pilot certification)

(c) Flight training. A student pilot, in addition to the presolo flight training maneuvers and procedures required by paragraph 61.87(c), must have received and logged instruction from an authorized flight instructor in the appropriate pilot maneuvers and procedures of this section. Additionally, a student pilot must have demonstrated an acceptable standard of performance, as judged by the authorized flight instructor certificated under this part, who endorses the student's pilot certificate in the appropriate pilot maneuvers and procedures of this section.

(1) For all aircraft—

(i) The use of aeronautical charts for VFR navigation using pilotage and dead reckoning with the aid of a magnetic compass;

(ii) Aircraft cross-country performance, and procurement and analysis of aeronautical weather reports and forecasts, including recognition of critical weather situations and estimating visibility while in flight;

(iii) Cross-country emergency conditions including lost procedures, adverse weather conditions, and simulated precautionary off-airport approaches and landing procedures;

(iv) Traffic pattern procedures, including normal area arrival and departure, collision avoidance, and wake turbulence precautions;

(v) Recognition of operational problems associated with the different terrain features in the geographical area in which the cross-country flight is to be flown; and

(vi) Proper operation of the instruments and equipment installed in the aircraft to be flown.

(2) For airplanes, in addition to paragraph (c)(1) of this section—

(i) Short and soft field takeoff, approach, and landing procedures, including cross-wind takeoffs and landings;

(ii) Takeoffs at best angle and rate of climb;

(iii) Control and maneuvering solely by reference to flight instruments including straight and level flight, turns, descents, climbs, and the use of radio aids and radar directives;

(iv) The use of radios for VFR navigation and for two-way communication; and

(v) For those student pilots seeking night flying privileges, night flying procedures including takeoffs, landings, go-arounds, and VFR navigation.

61.101 Recreational pilot privileges and limitations

(b) Except as provided in paragraphs (f) and (g) of this section, a recreational pilot may not act as pilot-in-command of an aircraft—

(1) That is certificated—

(i) For more than four occupants;

(ii) With more than one power plant;

(iii) With a power plant of more than 180 horsepower; or

(iv) With retractable landing gear.

(2) That is classified as a glider, airship, or balloon;

(3) That is carrying a passenger or property for compensation or hire;

(4) For compensation or hire;

(5) In furtherance of a business;

(6) Between sunset and sunrise;

(7) In airspace in which communication with air traffic control is required;

(8) At an altitude of more than 10,000 feet MSL or 2,000 feet AGL, whichever is higher;

(f) For the purpose of obtaining additional certificates or ratings, while under the supervision of an authorized flight instructor, a recreational pilot may fly as sole occupant of an aircraft—

(1) For which the pilot does not hold an appropriate category or class rating;

(2) Within airspace that requires communication with air traffic control; or

(3) Between sunset and sunrise, provided the flight or surface visibility is at least 5 statute miles.

SUBPART D - PRIVATE PILOTS

61.107 Flight proficiency

The applicant for a private pilot certificate must have logged instruction from an authorized flight instructor in at least the following pilot operations. In addition, his logbook must contain an endorsement by an authorized flight instructor who has found him competent to perform each of those operations safely as a private pilot.

(a) In Airplanes.

(1) Preflight operations, including weight and balance determination, line inspection, and airplane servicing;

(2) Airport and traffic pattern operations, including operations at controlled airports, radio communications, and collision avoidance precautions;

(3) Flight maneuvering by reference to ground objects;

(4) Flight at slow airspeeds with realistic distractions, and the recognition of and recovery from stalls entered from straight flight and from turns;

(5) Normal and crosswind takeoffs and landings;

(6) Control and maneuvering an airplane solely by reference to instruments, including descents and climbs using radio aids or radar directives;

(7) Cross-country flying, using pilotage, dead reckoning, and radio aids, including one 2-hour flight;

(8) Maximum performance takeoffs and landings;

(9) Night flying, including takeoffs, landings, and VFR navigation; and

(10) Emergency operations, including simulated aircraft and equipment malfunctions.

61.109 Airplane rating: Aeronautical experience

An applicant for a private pilot certificate with an airplane rating must have had at least a total of 40 hours of flight instruction and solo flight time which must include the following:

(a) Twenty hours of flight instruction from an authorized flight instructor, including at least—

(1) Three hours of cross country;

(2) Three hours at night, including 10 takeoffs and landings for applicants seeking night flying privileges; and

(3) Three hours in airplanes in preparation for the private pilot flight test within 60 days prior to that test. An applicant who does not meet the night flying requirement in paragraph (a)(2) of this section is issued a private pilot certificate bearing the limitation "Night flying prohibited." This limitation may be removed if the holder of the certificate shows that he has met the requirements of paragraph (a)(2) of this section.

(b) Twenty hours of solo flight time, including at least—

(1) Ten hours in airplanes;

(2) Ten hours of cross-country flights, each flight with a landing at a point more than 50 nautical miles from the original departure point. One flight must be at least 300 nautical miles with landings at a minimum of three points, one of which is at least 100 nautical miles from the original departure point; and

(3) Three solo takeoffs and landings to a full stop at an airport with an operating control tower.

SUBPART E— COMMERCIAL PILOTS

61.129 Airplane rating: Aeronautical experience

(a) General. An applicant for a commercial pilot certificate with an airplane rating must hold a private pilot certificate with an airplane rating. If he does not hold that certificate and rating he must meet the flight experience requirements for a private pilot certificate and airplane rating and pass the applicable written and practical test prescribed in Subpart D of this Part. In addition, the applicant must hold an instrument rating (airplane), or the commercial pilot certificate that is issued is endorsed with a limitation prohibiting the carriage of passengers for hire in airplanes on cross-country flights of more than 50 nautical miles, or at night.

(b) Flight Time as Pilot. An applicant for a commercial pilot certificate with an airplane rating must have a total of at least 250 hours of flight time as pilot, which may include not more than 50 hours of instruction from an authorized instructor in a ground trainer acceptable to the Administrator. The total flight time as pilot must include—

(1) 100 hours in a powered aircraft, including at least—

(i) 50 hours in airplanes, and

(ii) 10 hours of flight instruction and practice given by an authorized flight instructor in an airplane having a retractable landing gear, flaps, and a controllable pitch propeller; and

(2) 50 hours of flight instruction given by an authorized flight instructor, including—

(i) 10 hours of instrument instruction, of which at least 5 hours must be in flight in airplanes, and

(ii) 10 hours of instruction in preparation for the commercial pilot flight test; and

(3) 100 hours of pilot in command time, including at least—

(i) 50 hours in airplanes;

(ii) 50 hours of cross-country flights, each flight with a landing at a point more than 50 nautical miles from the original departure point. One flight must have landings at a minimum of three points, one of which is at least 150 nautical miles from the original departure point if the flight is conducted in Hawaii, or at least 250 nautical miles from the original departure point if it is conducted elsewhere; and

(iii) 5 hours of night flying including at least 10 takeoffs and landings as sole manipulator of the controls.

SUBPART F—AIRLINE TRANSPORT PILOTS

61.153 Airplane rating: Aeronautical knowledge

An applicant for an airline transport pilot certificate with an airplane rating must, after meeting the requirements of paragraph 61.151 (except paragraph (a) thereof) and 61.155, pass a written test on—

(a) The sections of this Part relating to airline transport pilots and Part 121, Subpart C of Part 65, and paragraph 91.1 through 91.13 and Subpart B of Part 91 of this chapter, and so much of Parts 21 and 25 of this chapter as relate to the operations of air carrier aircraft;

(b) The fundamentals of air navigation and use of formulas, instruments, and other navigational aids, both in aircraft and on the ground, that are necessary for navigating aircraft by instruments;

(c) The general system of weather collection and dissemination;

(d) Weather maps, weather forecasting, and weather sequence abbreviations, symbols, and nomenclature;

(e) Elementary meteorology, including knowledge of cyclones as associated with fronts;

(f) Cloud forms;

(g) National Weather Service Federal Meteorology Handbook No. 1, as amended;

(h) Weather conditions, including icing conditions and upper-air winds, that affect aeronautical activities;

(i) Air navigation facilities used on Federal airways, including rotating beacons, course lights, radio ranges, and radio marker beacons;

(j) Information from airplane weather observations and meteorological data reported from observations made by pilots on air carrier flights;

(k) The influence of terrain on meteorological conditions and developments, and their relation to air carrier flight operations;

(l) Radio communication procedure in aircraft operations; and

(m) Basic principles of loading and weight distribution and their effect on flight characteristics.

61.155 Airplane rating: Aeronautical experience

(a) An applicant for an airline transport pilot certificate with an airplane rating must hold a commercial pilot certificate or a foreign airline transport pilot or commercial pilot license without limitations, issued by a member state of ICAO, or he must be a pilot in an Armed Force of the United States whose military experience qualifies him for a commercial pilot certificate under paragraph 61.73 of this Part.

(b) An applicant must have had—

(1) At least 250 hours of flight time as pilot in command of an airplane, or as copilot of an airplane performing the duties and functions of a pilot in command under the supervision of a pilot in command, or any combination thereof, at least 100 hours of which were cross-country time and 25 hours of which were night flight time; and

(2) At least 1,500 hours of flight time as a pilot, including at least—

(i) 500 hours of cross—country flight time;

(ii) 100 hours of night flight time; and

(iii) 75 hours of actual or simulated instrument time, at least 50 hours of which were in actual flight. Flight time used to meet the requirements of subparagraph

(1) of this paragraph may also be used to meet the requirements of subparagraph (2) of this paragraph. Also, an applicant who has made at least 20 night takeoffs and land-

ings to a full stop may substitute one additional night takeoff and landing to a full stop for each hour of night flight time required by subparagraph (2)(ii) of this paragraph. However, not more than 25 hours of night flight time may be credited in this manner.

(c) If an applicant with less than 150 hours of pilot-in-command time otherwise meets the requirements of paragraph (b)(1) of this section, his certificate will be endorsed "Holder does not meet the pilot-in-command flight experience requirements of ICAO," as prescribed by *Article 39 of the "Convention on International Civil Aviation." Whenever he presents satisfactory written evidence that he has accumulated the 150 hours of pilot-in-command time, he is entitled to a new certificate without the endorsement.

(d) A commercial pilot may credit the following flight time toward the 1,500 hours total flight time requirement of paragraph (b)(2) of this section:

(1) All second-in-command time acquired in airplanes required to have more than one pilot by their approved Aircraft Flight Manuals or airworthiness certificates; and

(2) Flight engineer time acquired in airplanes required to have a flight engineer by their approved Aircraft Flight Manuals, while participating at the same time in an approved pilot training program approved under Part 121 of this chapter. However, the applicant may not credit under subparagraph (2) of this paragraph more than 1 hour for each 3 hours of flight engineer flight time so acquired, nor more than a total of 500 hours.

(e) If an applicant who credits second-in-command or flight engineer time under paragraph (d) of this section toward the 1,500 hours total flight time requirement of subparagraph (b)(2) of this section—

(1) Does not have at least 1,200 hours of flight time as a pilot including no more than 50 percent of his second-in-command time and none of his flight engineer time; but

(2) Otherwise meets the requirements of subparagraph

(b)(2) of this section, his certificate will be endorsed "Holder does not meet the pilot flight experience requirements of ICAO," as prescribed by *Article 39 of the "Convention on International Civil Aviation." [*Not in this text.] Whenever he presents satisfactory evidence that he has accumulated 1,200 hours of flight time as a pilot including no more than 50 percent of his second-in-command time and none of his flight engineer time, he is entitled to a new certificate without the endorsement.

(f) Reserved.

PART 91 GENERAL OPERATING AND FLIGHT RULES
SUBPART A—GENERAL
91.3 Responsibility and authority of the pilot in command

(a) The pilot in command of an aircraft is directly responsible for, and is the final authority as to, the operation of that aircraft.

(b) In an in-flight emergency requiring immediate action, the pilot in command may deviate from any rule of this part to the extent required to meet that emergency.

(c) Each pilot in command who deviates from a rule under paragraph (b) of this section shall, upon the request of the Administrator, send a written report of that deviation to the Administrator.

91.7 Civil aircraft airworthiness

(a) No person may operate a civil aircraft unless it is in an airworthy condition.

(b) The pilot in command of a civil aircraft is responsible for determining whether that aircraft is in condition for safe flight. The pilot in command shall discontinue the flight when unairworthy mechanical, electrical, or structural conditions occur.

SUBPART B—FLIGHT RULES GENERAL

91.103 Preflight action

Each pilot in command shall, before beginning a flight, become familiar with all available information concerning that flight. This information must include—

(a) For a flight under IFR or a flight not in the vicinity of an airport, weather reports and forecasts, fuel requirements, alternatives available if the planned flight cannot be completed, and any known traffic delays of which the pilot in command has been advised by ATC;

(b) For any flight, runway lengths at airports of intended use, and the following takeoff and landing distance information:

(1) For civil aircraft for which an approved airplane or Rotorcraft Flight Manual containing takeoff and landing distance data is required, the takeoff and landing distance data contained therein; and

(2) For civil aircraft other than those specified in paragraph (b)(1) of this section, other reliable information appropriate to the aircraft, relating to aircraft performance under expected values of airport elevation relating to aircraft performance under expected values of airport elevation and runway slope, aircraft gross weight, and wind and temperature.

SUBPART B—FLIGHT RULES

VISUAL FLIGHT RULES

91.151 Fuel requirements for flight in VFR conditions

(a) No person may begin a flight in an airplane under VFR conditions unless (considering wind and forecast weather conditions) there is enough fuel to fly to the first point of intended landing and, assuming normal cruising speed—

(1) During the day, to fly after that for at least 30 minutes; or

(2) At night, to fly after that for at least 45 minutes.

(b) No person may begin a flight in a rotorcraft under VFR conditions unless (considering wind and forecast weather conditions) there is enough fuel to fly to the first point of intended landing and, assuming normal cruising speed, to fly after that for at least 20 minutes.

91.155 Basic VFR weather minimums

(a) Except as provided in paragraph 91.155 (b) and 91.157, no person may operate an aircraft under VFR when the flight visibility is less, or at a distance from clouds that is less, than that prescribed for the corresponding altitude in the following table:

(b) Inapplicability. Notwithstanding the provisions of paragraph

(a) of this section, the following operations may be conducted outside of controlled airspace below 1,200 feet above the surface:

(1) Helicopter. When the visibility is less than 1 mile during day hours or less than 3 miles during night hours, a helicopter may be operated clear of clouds if operated at a speed that allows the pilot adequate opportunity to see any air traffic or obstruction in time to avoid a collision.

(2) Airplane. When the visibility is less than 3 miles but not less than 1 mile during night hours, an airplane may be operated clear of clouds if operated in an airport traffic pattern within one-half mile of the runway.

(c) Except as provided in paragraph 91.157, no person may operate an aircraft, under VFR, within a control zone beneath the ceiling when the ceiling is less than 1,000 feet.

(d) Except as provided in paragraph 91.157, no person may take off or land an aircraft, or enter the traffic pattern of an airport, under VFR within a control zone—

(1) Unless ground visibility at that airport is at least 3 statute miles; or

(2) If ground visibility is not reported at that airport, unless flight visibility during landing or takeoff, or while operating in the traffic pattern, is at least 3 statute miles.

(e) For the purposes of this section, an aircraft operating at the base altitude of a transition area or control area is considered to be within the airspace directly below that area.

91.157 Special VFR Weather minimums

(a) Except as provided in paragraph 93.113 of this chapter, when a person has received an appropriate ATC clearance, the special weather minimums of this section instead of those contained in paragraph 91.155 apply to the operation of an aircraft by that person in a control zone under VFR.

(b) No person may operate an aircraft in a control zone under VFR except clear of clouds.

(c) No person may operate an aircraft (other than a helicopter) in a control zone under VFR unless flight visibility is at least 1 statute mile.

(d) No person may take off or land an aircraft (other than a helicopter) at any airport in a control zone under VFR—

(1) Unless ground visibility at that airport is at least 1 statute mile; or

(2) If ground visibility is not reported at that airport, unless flight visibility during landing or takeoff is at least 1 statute mile.

(e) No person may operate an aircraft (other than a helicopter) in a control zone under the special weather minimums of this section, between sunset and sunrise (or in Alaska, when the sun is more than 6 degrees below the horizon) unless:

(1) That person meets the applicable requirements for instrument flight under Part 61 of this chapter; and

(2) The aircraft is equipped as required in paragraph 91.205(d).

SUBPART B—FLIGHT RULES
INSTRUMENT FLIGHT RULES

91.171 VOR Equipment check for IFR operations

(a) No person may operate a civil aircraft under IFR using the VOR system of radio navigation unless the VOR equipment of that aircraft—

(1) Is maintained, checked, and inspected under an approved procedure: or

(2) Has been operationally checked within the preceding 30 days, and was found to be within the limits of the permissible indicated bearing error set forth in paragraph (b) or (c) of this section.

(b) Except as provided in paragraph (c) of this section, each person conducting a VOR check under paragraph (a)(2) of this section shall—

(1) Use, at the airport of intended departure, an FAA-operated or approved test signal or a test signal radiated by a certificated and appropriately rated radio repair station or, outside the United States, a test signal operated or approved by an appropriate authority to check the VOR equipment (the maximum permissible indicated bearing error is plus or minus 4 degrees); or

(2) Use, at the airport of intended departure, a point on the airport surface designated as a VOR system checkpoint by the Administrator, or, outside the United States, by an appropriate authority (the maximum permissible bearing error is plus or minus 4 degrees);

(3) If neither a test signal nor a designated checkpoint on the surface is available, use an airborne checkpoint designated by the Administrator or, outside the United States, by an appropriate authority (the maximum permissible bearing error is plus or minus 6 degrees); or

(4) If no check signal or point is available, while in flight—

(i) Select a VOR radial that lies along the centerline of an established VOR airway;

(ii) Select a prominent ground point along the selected radial preferably more than 20 nautical miles from the VOR ground facility and maneuver the aircraft directly over the point at a reasonably low altitude; and

(iii) Note the VOR bearing indicated by the receiver when over the ground point (the maximum permissible variation between the published radial and the indicated bearing is 6 degrees).

(c) If dual system VOR (units independent of each other except for the antenna) is installed in the aircraft, the person checking the equipment may check one system against the other in place of the check procedures specified in paragraph (b) of this section. Both systems shall be tuned to the same VOR ground facility and note the indicated bearings to that station. The maximum permissible variation between the two indicated bearings is 4 degrees.

(d) Each person making the VOR operational check, as specified in paragraph (b) or (c) of this section, shall enter the date, place, bearing error, and sign the aircraft log or other record. In addition, if a test signal radiated by a repair station, as specified in paragraph (b)(1) of this section, is used, an entry must be made in the aircraft log or other record by the repair station certificate holder or the certificate holder's representative certifying to the bearing transmitted by the repair station for the check and the date of transmission.

91.177 Minimum altitudes for IFR operations

(a) Operation of aircraft at minimum altitudes. Except when necessary for takeoff or landing, no person may operate an aircraft under IFR below—

(1) The applicable minimum altitudes prescribed in parts 95 and 97 of this chapter; or

(2) If no applicable minimum altitude is prescribed in those parts—

(i) In the case of operations over an area designated as a mountainous area in part 95, an altitude of 2,000 feet above the highest obstacle within a horizontal distance of 4 nautical miles from the course to be flown; or

(ii) In any other case, an altitude of 1,000 feet above the highest obstacle within a horizontal distance of 4 nautical miles from the course to be flown. However, if both a MEA and a MOCA are prescribed for a particular route or route segment, a person may operate an aircraft below the MEA down to, but not below, the MOCA, when within 22 nautical miles of the VOR concerned (based on the pilot's reasonable estimate of that distance).

(b) Climb. Climb to a higher minimum IFR altitude shall begin immediately after passing the point beyond which that minimum altitude applies, except that when ground obstructions intervene, the point beyond which that higher minimum altitude applies shall be crossed at or above the applicable MCA.

SUBPART C—EQUIPMENT, INSTRUMENT, AND CERTIFICATE REQUIREMENTS

91.205 Powered civil aircraft with standard category U.S. airworthiness certificates: Instrument and equipment requirements

(a) General. Except as provided in paragraphs (c)(3) and (e) of this section, no person may operate a powered civil aircraft with a standard category U.S. airworthiness certificate in any operation described in paragraphs (b) through (f) of this section unless that aircraft contains the instruments and equipment specified in those paragraphs (or

FAA-approved equivalents) for that type of operation, and those instruments and items of equipment are in operable condition.

(b) Visual flight rules (day). For VFR flight during the day, the following instruments and equipment are required:

(1) Airspeed indicator.

(2) Altimeter.

(3) Magnetic direction indicator.

(4) Tachometer for each engine.

(5) Oil pressure gauge for each engine using pressure system.

(6) Temperature gauge for each liquid-cooled engine.

(7) Oil temperature gauge for each air-cooled engine.

(8) Manifold pressure gauge for each altitude engine.

(9) Fuel gauge indicating the quantity of fuel in each tank.

(10) Landing gear position indicator, if the aircraft has a retractable landing gear.

(11) If the aircraft is operated for hire over water and beyond power-off gliding distance from shore, approved flotation gear readily available to each occupant, and at least one pyrotechnic signalling device. As used in this section "shore" means that area of the land adjacent to the water which is above the high water mark and excludes land areas which are intermittently under water.

(12) Except as to airships, an approved safety belt with an approved metal-to-metal latching device for each occupant 2 years of age or older.

(13) For small civil airplanes manufactured after July 18, 1978, an approved shoulder harness for each front seat. The shoulder harness must be designed to protect the occupant from serious head injury when the occupant experiences the ultimate inertia forces specified in paragraph 23.561(b)(2) of this chapter. Each shoulder harness installed at a flight crewmember station must permit the crewmember, when seated and with the safety belt and shoulder harness fastened, to perform all functions necessary for flight operations. For purposes of this paragraph—

(i) The date of manufacture of an airplane is the date the inspection acceptance records reflect that the airplane is complete and meets the FAA-approved type design data; and

(ii) A front seat is a seat located at a flight crewmember station or any seat located alongside such a seat.

(14) An emergency locator transmitter, if required by paragraph 91.207.

(15) For normal, utility, and acrobatic category airplanes with a seating configuration, excluding pilot seats, of 9 or less, manufactured after December 12, 1986, a shoulder harness for—

(i) Each front seat that meets the requirements of paragraph 23.785(g) and (h) of this chapter in effect on December 12, 1985;

(ii) Each additional seat that meets the requirements of paragraph 23.785(g) of this chapter in effect on December 12, 1985.

(c) Visual flight rules (night). For VFR flight at night, the following instruments and equipment are required:

(1) Instruments and equipment specified in paragraph (b) of this section.

(2) Approved position lights.

(3) An approved aviation red or aviation white anticollision light system on all U.S.-registered civil aircraft. Anticollision light systems initially installed after August 11, 1971, on aircraft for which a type certificate was issued or applied for before August 11, 1971, must at least meet the anticollision light standards of part *23, *25, *27, or *29, as applicable, that were in effect on August 10, 1971; except that the color may be either aviation red or aviation white. [*Not in this text.] In the event of failure of any light of the anticollision light system, operations with the aircraft may be continued to a stop where repairs or replacement can be made.

(4) If the aircraft is operated for hire, one electric landing light.

(5) An adequate source of electrical energy for all installed electrical and radio equipment.

(6) One spare set of fuses, or three spare fuses of each kind required, that are accessible to the pilot in flight.

(d) Instrument flight rules. For IFR flight, the following instruments and equipment are required:

(1) Instruments and equipment specified in paragraph (b) of this section, and, for night flight, instruments and equipment specified in paragraph (c) of this section.

(2) Two-way radio communications system and navigational equipment appropriate to the ground facilities to be used.

91.209 Aircraft lights

No person may, during the period from sunset to sunrise (or, in Alaska, during the period a prominent unlighted object cannot be seen from a distance of 3 statute miles or the sun is more than 6 degrees below the horizon)—

(a) Operate an aircraft unless it has lighted position lights;

(b) Park or move an aircraft in, or in dangerous proximity to, a night flight operations area of an airport unless the aircraft—

(1) Is clearly illuminated;

(2) Has lighted position lights; or

(3) Is in an area which is marked by obstruction lights.

(c) Anchor an aircraft unless the aircraft—

(1) Has lighted anchor lights; or

(2) Is in an area where anchor lights are not required on vessels; or

(d) Operate an aircraft, required by paragraph 91.205(c)(3) to be equipped with an anticollision light system, unless it has approved and lighted aviation red or aviation white anticollision lights. However, the anticollision lights need not be lighted when the pilot in command determines that, because of operating conditions, it would be in the interest of safety to turn the lights off.

Endnotes

Chapter 2

1. Available from Gate 4 Productions, 5942 Edinger Street, Suite 113, Huntington Beach, CA 92649.

2. A calorie (c) is a unit of heat. One calorie will raise the temperature of one kilogram (2.2 pounds) of water one degree centigrade.

Chapter 3

1. A small number of individuals exhibit a trait-array that is known as *psychoticism*, which differentiates between normal and psychotic individuals. Because this condition is quite rare, it will not be dealt with further.

2. This test is the Eysenck Personality Inventory. Pilots who might be interested in taking this test should contact the nearest psychological testing service, found in most major metropolitan areas. A local telephone directory often advertises such services.

3. An FAA Advisory Circular entitled "Cockpit Resource Management Training" (AC 120), defines cockpit resource management (CRM) as the effective use of equipment, crewmembers, and technical skills to achieve safe and efficient flight operations. It also states that ". . . between 60 and 80 percent of air carrier incidents and accidents have been caused, at least in part, by a failure of the flight crew to make use of readily available resources." Most of the

problems encountered by flight crews have very little to do with the more technical aspects of operating a multicrewmember airplane but tend to be associated with poor group decision making, ineffective communication, inadequate leadership, and generally poor management. These cockpit problems can be less visible in the dark cockpit and are, therefore, even more insidious than they might be otherwise.

4. The concerned pilot should seek professional assistance through an employee assistance program with counselors that can provide helpful stress-reduction activities and valuable follow-up. If the pilot does not have access to such assistance, counselling psychologists are advertised in most telephone books. An aeromedical examiner may be consulted for possible referrals, as well.

5. These carefully planned, eight-week meetings teach how to restructure old beliefs and fears about flying. Exercises are employed involving breathing control, progressive relaxation, and experiencing the reality of flight without fear. Accurate information is provided along with professional counseling and therapy; group participation and individual techniques help change behavior and thinking. Contact Fear of Flying Clinic, 1777 Borel Place, No. 307, San Mateo, CA 94402, for a list of support groups in various parts of America.

Chapter 4

1. This represents a range of more than 11 log units of ambient illumination or a change of one part in 10 with 9 zeros following it. This dynamic photochemical adjustment takes place relatively fast, generally within $1/2$ to $3/4$ hour after entering a dark environment. This process helps to optimize vision in dark environments.

2. The semicircular canals within the middle ear signal angular acceleration while another organ located near-by called the *otolith organ* senses linear acceleration. Detailed information on these organs is found in medical textbooks, flying handbooks, basic psychology texts, and physiology texts.

Chapter 8

1. This device is a CMS-700 available from Heads Up Technologies, 2611 Westgrove, Suite 110, Carrollton, TX 75006.

Chapter 9

1. Green alone or amber alone is used only in connection with a white and green or white and amber beacon display, respectively.

2. Airway beacons are remnants of the lighted airways that antedated the present electronically equipped federal airways system. Only a few of these beacons

exist today to mark airway segments in remote mountain areas. Flashes in Morse code identify the beacon site.

3. The reader might be interested in the text *Human Factors in the Design and Evaluation of Aviation Maps* by V.D. Hopkins and R.M. Taylor, Neuilly-sur-Seine Publ., 1979.

Chapter 10

1. V_1 is the initial engine failure speed for multiengine aircraft. If engine failure occurs prior to attaining this speed, the aircraft must be stopped.

2. The outer marker is a radio navigation device located on the ground and aimed vertically upward as a narrow cone of radiation. It is generally located on an extension of the runway's centerline and provides the pilot with a cockpit indication of passage over it.

Chapter 13

1. It is becoming increasingly common for a corporate pilot to fly different models of a single type of aircraft according to NASA's Aviation Safety Reporting System (ASRS) publication *Callback* (Issue #133; June, 1990). After analyzing 150 ASRS reports involving fleet inconsistencies, W.P. Monan, an ASRS aviation safety research consultant found that nonstandardized cockpit configurations were causally related to 110 altitude busts, 15 course deviations, and 25 less common but equally hazardous types of events. Stated contributing factors included the pilot's own expertise and long familiarity with the standard cockpit configuration and layout. One responding pilot wrote, "One tends to do things from habit patterns instead of actually noticing details which may differ from the norm." In the darkened cockpit these differences can become almost invisible. At best, these differences will be harder to discriminate than during daylight hours.

2. The reader might be interested in the text, Flatau, Courtney L., and Jerome Mitchell. 1980. *The Instrument Pilot Handbook: A Reference Manual and Exam Guide*. New York: Van Nostrand Reinhold Company.

Abbreviations

AAAS—American Association for the Advancement of Science
ADF—automatic direction finder
AGARD—Advisory Group for Aerospace Research and Development (NATO organization)
AGL—above ground level
ALS—approach light system
ALSF1—approach light system with sequenced flashing lights (in ILS Category I configuration)
ALSF2—approach light system with sequenced flashing lights in ILS Category II configuration)
AOPA—Aircraft Owners and Pilots Association
ARSA—airport radar service area
ASA—approach slope angle
ASRS—Aviation Safety Reporting System
ATC—air traffic control
ATCT—air traffic control tower
ATIS—automatic terminal information service
CCW—counterclockwise
CGI—computer generated image
CO—carbon monoxide
CRM—cockpit resource management
CRT—cathode ray tube
DEP—design eye point
DF—direction finder
EFAS—En Route Flight Advisory Service
FAA—Federal Aviation Administration
FAR—Federal Aviation Regulation
FPIP—flight path intercept point
FSS—flight service station
g—gravitational field strength
HIRL—high intensity runway light(s)
HUC—heads up checklist
HUD—head up display

Hz—hertz
IAP—instrument approach procedure
ICAO—International Civil Aviation Organization
IFR—instrument flight rules
ILS—instrument landing system
IMC—instrument meteorological conditions
IP—intercept point
LED—light emitting diode
LIRL—low intensity runway light(s)
LOS—line of sight
MALSF—medium intensity approach lighting with sequenced flashing lights
MALSR—medium intensity approach lighting system with runway alignment indicator lights
MIRL—medium intensity runway light(s)
MLS—microwave landing system
MOA—military operations area
NASA—National Aeronautics and Space Administration
NAVAID—navigational aid
NAVCOM—navigation receiver integrated with communications transceiver
NDB—nondirectional beacon
NREM—nonrapid eye movement
NTSB—National Transportation Safety Board
ODALS—omnidirectional flashing approach light system
OI—obvious incapacitation
PAPI—precision approach path indicator
RCLS—runway centerline light system
REIL—runway end identifier light
REM—rapid eye movement
REP—reference eye position
RT—reaction time
RVR—runway visual range
SFL—sequenced flashing lights
SI—subtle incapacitation
SSALR—simplified short approach light system with runway alignment indicator lights
TCA—terminal control area
TCAS—traffic alert and collision avoidance system
TDZL—touchdown zone light(s)
TWEB—transcribed weather broadcast
V_1—takeoff decision speed
VASI—visual approach slope indicator
VFR—visual flight rules
VOR—very high frequency omnidirectional range station

Bibliography

Anon. 1987. *Work, Aging and Vision*. National Research Council. Washington, D.C.: National Academy Press.

————. 1988. ATP-IR:TT8260; IT963; file no. AAB-87/10-1534, *Aviation Monthly*. July.

Bartley, S.H., and E. Chute. 1947. *Fatigue and Impairment in Man*. New York: McGraw-Hill.

Beard, R.R., and N. Grandstaff. 1970. *Carbon monoxide exposure and cerebral function*. Annals of the New York Academy of Science. Vol. 174, Pp. 385-395.

Beebe-Center, J.G., L. Carmichael, and L.C. Mead. 1944. *Daylight training of pilots for night flying. Aeronautical Engineering Review*. Vol. 3, Pp. 1-10.

Birren, J.E., and N.W. Shock. 1950. *Age changes in rate and level of dark adaptation. Journal of Applied Physiology*. Vol. 2, Pp. 407-411.

Bray, R.S. 1980. *A head-up display format for application to transport aircraft approach and landing*. Washington D.C.: National Aeronautics and Space Administration, Technical Memo 81199.

Buley, L.E. and J. Spelina. 1970. *Physiological and psychological factors in "The Dark Night Takeoff Accident." Aerospace Medicine*. Vol. 41. Pp. 553-556.

Calvert, E.S. 1954. *Visual judgments in motion. Institute of Navigation Journal*. Vol. 7. Pp. 233-251.

Collar, A.R. 1946. *On an aspect of the accident history of aircraft taking off at night.* Aeronautical Research Council, London: Technical Report 2277.

Collins, R.L. 1989. *Precision is its own reward. AOPA Pilot.* July, Pg. 82.

Degani, A., and E.L. Wiener. 1990. *Human factors of flight-deck checklists: The normal checklist.* Contract NCC2-377. Washington, D.C.: National Aeronautics and Space Administration, Contractor Report 177549.

Duncan, C.E., M.G. Sanders, and K.A. Kimball. 1980. *Evaluation of Army aviator human factors (fatigue) in a high threat environment.* U.S. Army Aeromedical Research Laboratory, Fort Rucker, AL, Report No. 80-8.

Eysenck, H.J., and S. Rachman. 1965. *The causes and cures of neurosis: An Introduction to Modern Behavior Therapy Based on Learning Theory and the Principle of Conditioning.* EDITS.

Gillingham, K.K. and J.W. Wolfe. 1986. *Spatial orientation in flight.* Brooks AFB.: USAF School of Aerospace Medicine. Technical Report 85-31.

Gless, R.D. 1990. *Night Flying, Flight Instructors Safety Report.* AOPA Air Safety Foundation. Vol. 16. Pp. 1-9.

Golbey, S.B. 1988a. *Pilot fatigue. AOPA Pilot.* March. Pg. 125.
_____. 1988b. *Wynken, Blynken, and Nod. AOPA Pilot.* August. Pg. 98.

Griffin, J. 1981. *Instrument Flying.* Blue Ridge Summit, Pa.: TAB Books.

Haines, R.F. 1975. *A review of peripheral vision capabilities for display layout designers.* Proceedings of the Society for Information Display. Vol. 16. Pp. 238-249.
_____. 1977. *A layout designer's data projection reticle. Human Factors.* Vol. 19. Pp. 567-569.
_____. 1980. *Head-up transition behavior of pilots during simulated low-visibility approaches.* Washington, D.C.: National Aeronautics and Space Administration, Technical Paper 1618.
_____, T.A. Price, and D. Miller. 1980. *A simulator study of flight path control toward black hole visual environments with and without head-up display.* Joint FAA/NASA Head-up Display Evaluation Program, Report 13, NASA-Ames Research Center, Moffett Field, Calif.
_____, and S.M. Kiefel. 1988. *Vertical displacement threshold sensitivity along the horizontal meridian as a function of stimulus rate, duration, and length. Aviation, Space, and Environmental Medicine.* Vol. 59. Pp. 321-329.

Harris, Sr., J.L. 1977. *What makes a visual approach nonvisual. Airline Pilot.* May. Pp. 14-18.

Huang, J. and L.R. Young. 1981. *Sensation of rotation about a vertical axis with a fixed visual field in different illuminations and in the dark. Experimental Brain Research.* Vol. 41. Pp. 172-183.

Iavecchia, J.H., H.P. Iavecchia, and S.N. Roscoe. 1988. *Eye accommodation to head-up virtual images. Human Factors.* Vol. 30. Pp. 689-702.

Johnson, L.C., and W.L. McLeod. 1973. *Sleep and awake behavior during gradual sleep reduction. Perception, Motor Skills.* Vol. 36. Pp. 87-97.

Klein, K.E., H.M. Wegmann, G. Athenassenas, H. Hohlweck, and P. Kuklinski. 1976. *Air operations and circadian performance rhythms. Aviation, Space and Environmental Medicine.* Vol. 47. Pp. 221-230.

Kraft, C.L. 1969. *Measurement of height and distance information provided pilots by the extra-cockpit visual scene,* Visual Factors in Transportation Systems. Proceedings of the Spring Meeting, NAS-NRC Committee on Vision. Pp. 84 101. Washington, D.C.

———. 1978. *A psychophysical contribution to air safety: Simulator studies in visual illusions in night visual approaches.* In Pick, Jr., H.L. H.W. Leibowitz, and J.E. Singer. (Eds.). Psychology—From Research to Practice. New York. Plenum Press. Pp. 363-385.

———, and C.L. Elworth. 1969. *Flight deck work load and night visual approach performance.* AGARD CP No. 56, Advisory Group for Aerospace Research and Development of the North American Treaty Organization.

Lauber, J.K. 1989. *Address before the International Society of Air Safety Investigators. ISASI Forum.* August.

———, and P.J. Kayten. 1988. *Sleepiness, circadian dysrhythmia, and fatigue in transportation system accidents. Sleep.* Vol. 11. Pp. 503-512.

Leibowitz, H.W. and R.B. Post. 1979. *The two modes of processing concept and some implications.* Proceedings of Vision Seminar. Italy.

Lipschutz, L., T. Roehrs, A. Spielman, H. Zwyghuizen, J. Lamphere, and T. Roth. 1988. *Caffeine's alerting effects in sleepy normals.* In Chase, M.H., D.J. McGinty, and C. O'Connor (Eds.). Sleep Research. Brain Information Service/Brain Research Institute. University of California, Los Angeles.

Lyman, E.G., and H.W. Orlady. 1981. *Fatigue and associated performance decrements in air transport operations.* Washington, D.C.: National Aeronautics and Space Administration. Contractors Report 166167. Ames Research Center, Moffett Field, Calif.

McAdams, F. 1978. *Human error in air carrier accidents.* Washington, D.C.: National Transportation Safety Board. Notation 2297, Special Study.

McFarland, R.A. 1953. *Human Factors in Air Transportation.* 1st. edition. New York. McGraw-Hill.

_____, and J.N. Evans. 1939. *Alterations in dark adaptation under reduced oxygen tensions. American Journal of Physiology*. Vol. 127, Pg. 37.

Mertens, H.W. and M.F. Lewis. 1982. *Effect of different runway sizes on pilot performance during simulated night landing approaches. Aviation, Space and Environmental Medicine*. Vol. 54. Pp. 500-506.

Nicholson, A.N., and B.M. Stone. 1987. *Sleep and wakefulness: Handbook for flight medical officers*. 2nd. ed., Seine, France: Advisory Group for Aerospace Research and Development.

Pitts, D.G. 1969. *Visual illusions in aircraft accidents*. Proceedings of the Spring Meeting, NAS-NRC Committee on Vision. Washington, D.C.: National Research Council.

Price, B., and D.C. Holly. 1982. *Sleep loss and the crash of flight 182. Journal of Human Ergonomics*. Vol. 11. Supplement. Pp. 291-301.

Reinhart, R.O. 1989. *The Mid-morning blahs. Business & Commercial Aviation*. November. Pg. 112.

Roffwarg, H.P., J.N. Muzio, and W.C. Dement. 1966. *Ontogenetic development of the human sleep dream cycle. Science*. Vol. 152. Pp. 604-619.

Rudaux, L. and G. De Vaucouleurs. 1959. Larousse *Encyclopedia of Astronomy*. New York: Prometheus Press.

Schmedtje, J.F., C.M. Oman, R. Letz, and E.L. Baker. 1988. *Effects of scopolamine and dextroamphetamine on human performance. Aviation, Space and Environmental Medicine*. Vol. 59. Pp. 407-410.

Simonelli, N.M. 1983. *The dark focus of the human eye and its relationship to age and visual defect. Human Factors*. Vol. 25. Pp. 85-92.

Thomas, M. 1990. *Managing Pilot Stress*. New York. Macmillan Publ. Co.

Tole, J.R., A.T. Stephens, R.L. Harris, and A.R. Ephrath. 1982. *Visual scanning behavior and mental workload in aircraft pilots. Aviation, Space and Environmental Medicine*. Vol. 53. Pp. 54-61.

Weintraub, D.J., R.F. Haines, and R.J. Randle. 1985. *Head up display (HUD) utility II: Runway to HUD transitions monitoring eye focus and decision times*. Proceedings of the Human Factors Society, Annual Meeting, Pp. 615-619.

Weitzman, E.D., D.F. Kripke, D. Goldmacher, et al., 1970. *Acute reversal of the sleep waking cycle of man. Archives of Neurology*. Vol. 22. Pp. 483-489.

Yerkes, R.M. and J.D. Dodson. 1908. *The relation of strength of stimulus to rapidity of habit formation. Journal of Comparative Neurological Psychology*. Vol. 18. Pp. 459-482.

Index

Other Bestsellers of Related Interest

THE AVIATOR'S GUIDE TO FLIGHT PLANNING—Donald J. Clausing

Encompassing all types of fixed-wing, general aviation flying, this book will show you how to develop a complete flight plan—not just fill out an FAA Flight Plan form. Topics covered include adverse versus unsafe weather conditions, weather briefing analysis, VFR and IFR flight logs, high-altitude flying, groundspeed calculations, preflight and enroute fuel planning, field performance, and much more. 272 pages, 73 illustrations. Book No. 2438, $17.95 paperback only

AVOIDING COMMON PILOT ERRORS: An Air Traffic Controller's View—John Stewart

This essential reference—written from the controller's perspective—interprets the mistakes pilots often make when operating in controlled airspace. It cites situations frequently encountered by controllers that show how improper training, lack of preflight preparation, poor communication skills, and confusing regulations can lead to pilot mistakes. 240 pages, 32 illustrations. Book No. 2434, $17.95 paperback only

GENERAL AVIATION LAW—Jerry A. Eichenberger

Although the regulatory burden that is part of flying sometimes seems overwhelming, it need not take the pleasure out of your flight time. Eichenberger provides an up-to-date survey of many aviation regulations, and gives you a solid understanding of FAA procedures and functions, airman ratings and maintenance certificates, the implications of aircraft ownership, and more. This book allows you to recognize legal problems before they result in FAA investigations and the potentially serious consequences. 240 pages. Book No. 3431, $16.95 paperback, $25.95 hardcover

EMERGENCY!: Crisis in the Cockpit—Stanley Stewart

Experience the most terrifying incidents in aviation history! In this book, dozens of actual airline incidents and near-misses are recounted in vivid detail by those who experienced them firsthand. You'll feel the heart-stopping suspense of being in the cockpit—where raw nerves are all that stand between life and death—as crew members prevent emergency situations from becoming fatal accidents. 272 pages, 51 illustrations. Book No. 3499, $16.95 paperback, $24.95 hardcover

UNDERSTANDING AERONAUTICAL CHARTS—Terry T. Lankford

Filled with practical applications for beginning and veteran pilots, this book will show you how to plan your flights quickly, easily, and accurately. It covers all the charts you'll need for flight planning, including those for VFR, IFR, SID, STAR, Loran, and helicopter flights. As you examine the criteria, purpose, and limitations of each chart, you'll learn the author's proven system for interpreting and using charts. 320 pages, 183 illustrations. Book No. 3844, $17.95 paperback, $27.95 hardcover

STANDARD AIRCRAFT HANDBOOK—5th Edition—Edited by Larry Reithmaier, originally compiled and edited by Stuart Leavell and Stanley Bungay

Now updated to cover the latest in aircraft parts, equipment, and construction techniques, this classic reference provides practical information on FAA-approved metal airplane hardware. Techniques are presented in step-by-step fashion and explained in shop terms without unnecessary theory and background. All data on materials and procedures is derived from current reports by the nation's largest aircraft manufacturers. 240 pages, 213 illustrations. Book No. 3634, $11.95 Vinyl only

THE ILLUSTRATED GUIDE TO AERODYNAMICS—2nd Edition—H. C. "Skip" Smith

Avoiding technical jargon and scientific explanations, this guide demonstrates how aerodynamic principles affect every aircraft in terms of lift, thrust, drag, in-air performance, stability, and control. It includes new material on airfoil development and design, accelerated climb performance, takeoff velocities, rules, laminar flow airfoils, planform shapes, computer-aided design, and high-performance lightplanes. 352 pages, 269 illustrations. Book No. 3786, $18.95 paperback, $28.95 hardcover

THE PILOT'S HANDBOOK OF AERONAUTICAL KNOWLEDGE: Revised and Expanded Edition
—Paul E. Illman

All the technical and operational information you'll need to prepare for private and commercial pilot certification is contained in this easy-to-read book. Based on official government documents—and updated for the 1990s with the latest technical data, flying tips, and general aviation guidance—it reviews everything from navigation technologies and flight planning through radio communications and air traffic control. 416 pages, 226 illustrations. Book No. 3517, $19.95 paperback only

ABCs OF SAFE FLYING—3rd Edition
—David Frazier

This book gives you a wealth of flight safety information in a fun to read, easily digestible format. The author's anecdotal episodes as well as NTSB accident reports lend both humor and sobering reality to the text. Detailed photographs, maps, and illustrations ensure that you'll understand key concepts and techniques. If you want to make sure you have the right skills each time you fly, this book is your one-stop source. 192 pages, Illustrated. Book No. 3757, $14.95 paperback, $22.95 hardcover

Prices Subject to Change Without Notice.

Look for These and Other TAB Books at Your Local Bookstore

To Order Call Toll Free 1-800-822-8158

or write to TAB Books, Blue Ridge Summit, PA 17294-0840.

Title	Product No.	Quantity	Price

☐ Check or money order made payable to TAB Books

Charge my ☐ VISA ☐ MasterCard ☐ American Express

Acct. No. _____ Exp. _____

Signature: _____

Name: _____

Address: _____

City: _____

State: _____ Zip: _____

Subtotal $ _____

Postage and Handling
($3.00 in U.S., $5.00 outside U.S.) $ _____

Add applicable state and local
sales tax $ _____

TOTAL $ _____

TAB Books catalog free with purchase; otherwise send $1.00 in check or money order and receive $1.00 credit on your next purchase.

Orders outside U.S. must pay with international money in U.S. dollars

TAB Guarantee: If for any reason you are not satisfied with the book(s) you order, simply return it (them) within 15 days and receive a full refund. **BC**